# RIVER OF
# DARKNESS

# RIVER OF DARKNESS

## JAMES GRADY

**WARNER BOOKS**

A Time Warner Company

Warner Books, Inc., 666 Fifth Avenue, New York, NY 10103

A Time Warner Company

Printed in the United States of America
First printing: October 1991
10  9  8  7  6  5  4  3  2

**Library of Congress Cataloging-in-Publication Data**

Grady, James, 1949–
    River of darkness / James Grady.
      p.   cm.
    ISBN 0-446-51554-X
    I. Title.
    PS3557.R122R58  1991
    813'.54—dc20               91-7948
                                 CIP

*Book design by Giorgetta Bell McRee*

To Luke,
*De Oppresso Liber*

Every ship of state sails on a river of darkness.

**—Gen. William Cochran**
Deputy Director, CIA

# RIVER OF DARKNESS

# WANDERER

At seven minutes to midnight on an L.A. winter Sunday, Jud Stuart looked into the bar mirror and realized that the skinny guy in the plaid sports coat had been sent to kill him.

*It's about time,* thought Jud.

Perched on a stool by the front door, the skinny guy snapped a kitchen match to light a Camel. Nine stools away, Jud smelled sulfur over the tavern's dried urine and stale beer. In the flicker of the match, Jud studied the killer's face and was sure they'd never met.

Jud's shaking hands knocked over the empty shot glass as he raised his beer schooner like a chalice. He drained the cup of its tangy brew, and along with fear and anger, a cold sense of relief flowed through him. After a thousand aimless and drunken days, he was on familiar ground. The assassin made sense.

The bartender was beefy and lied about having played college football. He sidled down to Jud, bobbed the toothpick in his mouth toward the coins by Jud's empty glasses.

"Ain't enough there for another round," he told Jud.

"Then I better go straight," muttered Jud. He was a big man on a barstool, barrel-chested with a truck-tire gut. Short reddish-brown hair. His arms were thick as most men's calves. Once his face had been boyishly handsome, now it was slack, pale. Except for the flat blue of his bloodshot eyes.

Deception was the only way he could think of to escape. He closed his eyes, deliberately fell backward off the barstool, his arms wide to secretly use a judo breakfall.

But the alcohol in his blood ruined his timing, and he crashed honestly to the tile, smacking his head and blacking out.

"Looks like a walrus," said the bartender.

The drunks at the bar didn't look and didn't laugh. The man in the plaid sports jacket had paid more for his clothes than anyone else in the bar; he was cleaner. He watched the bartender sweep Jud's change into his own pocket as he walked around the bar.

"Get up!" yelled the bartender. "Get up or it's the bull pen."

The bartender kicked Jud's blue-jean-clad shin. Unconscious, Jud's stillness was true.

"Shit!" The bartender grabbed Jud's ankles. "I don't get paid to haul shit." He jerked: Jud's body scooted an inch.

"Hell," said the bartender, "he must weigh a ton!"

"I'll help you," volunteered Plaid Jacket.

The bartender handed him one of Jud's feet. Jud wore cheap black high-top sneakers and no socks. The bartender jerked his head toward the back door, counted, "One, two, three!"

They pulled Jud across the floor. His chopped-sleeve sweatshirt slid up over his massive belly and hairless chest.

The bartender said, "You're stronger than you look."

"Yes," answered Plaid Jacket.

Jud felt his head bounce as they dragged him out the back door. He kept his eyes closed, his weight lifeless. The men dragging him rested on the porch landing.

"The bull pen," said the bartender, nodding down to the wood-fenced, packed-dirt yard. "'Course these guys are steers."

Their laughter echoed in the cool night. The bartender squinted down the shadowed staircase.

"Ain't nobody else sleepin' it off down there," he said. "Let's see if he can do it hi'self."

Jud let them muscle him to his feet. His head hung low on his chest, so he risked opening his eyes a slit. Saw a hand belonging to a plaid sleeve holding his right arm.

"Hey! Buddy!" The bartender shouted in Jud's left ear. "You all right? You can make it, right?"

To Plaid Jacket, the bartender said, "He can make it."

The bartender shoved Jud down the steps. Whirling, bouncing off the brick wall and the railing, Jud crashed to the ground. After a few seconds, he rolled on his side.

"See?" said the bartender. "Drunks, you can't hurt 'em."

He led Plaid Jacket inside for a beer on the house.

*Get up,* Jud told himself as he lay gasping in the dirt. *Only got until Plaid Jacket establishes his cover.*

He found the wall and used it to brace himself. Sitting. Standing. Leaning against the bricks. Not falling down.

From inside the bar, Jud heard laughter. Willie Nelson singing about *federales* and finks. Jud was surprised the bar had a jukebox. The only person inside who'd waste pocket change on music would be Plaid Jacket. Not a waste for him, realized Jud: cover.

A seven-foot wood fence surrounded the bull pen in the California night. The falls had knocked some of the liquor from his system. Jud shuffled to the fence, to the gate.

Locked. He caressed the lock's smooth face. If he had tools, thirty seconds. If his hands didn't shake. He gripped the top of the fence—couldn't lift his bulk off his toes.

In the bar, another record started, a woman singing sweet and clear. Jud loved women who could sing sweet and clear and loud enough to cover whatever Plaid Jacket had planned.

Last good chance. Jud retreated until he was under the porch. Three deep breaths: he charged, resisting the urge to yell as he careened through the darkness like a human cannonball.

Smacked into the wooden gate.

Sprang back like a beach ball, sprawling on the ground as the fence shook and the gate held.

Jud lay on his back, his shoulder swelling, eyes open to the night where smog hid the stars. He could surrender, fade into blackness. He imagined Plaid Jacket laughing on his barstool.

*They could have at least sent someone with more class.*

He got up.

Inside, the woman stopped singing. Glasses clinked. In his mind, Jud saw Plaid Jacket slide off his stool, fish in his pocket for a quarter, feed the jukebox, and turn. Motion established. Cover.

Jud staggered up the stairs. Found no loose boards, no bricks or pipes, no jagged piece of glass. He stared at his trembling hands. The skills of a dozen teachers had been soaked out of that flesh. Tonight, there wasn't a drunk in the bar who couldn't beat him. And it wasn't a drunk who'd try.

Dion's "The Wanderer," which had been a hit when Jud raged through adolescence, spilled out into the night.

Iron bars covered a window in the wall behind the half-open door. A drainpipe ran beside the window to the roof.

"Hey!" came the bartender's yell from inside the Oasis. "Where you going?"

Jud slid behind the door, stepped on the windowsill, and grabbed the bars. He teetered but made it, back against the bricks, clinging to the drainpipe and heels on the window's ledge.

Then he did his best to let go inside, to relax, to not-think. *One chance, one play.*

A form interrupted the light filtering through the open door. From his perch, Jud could see the top of a man's balding head and the shoulders of his plaid jacket.

"Somebody has to make sure he's okay!" the man yelled. He stepped onto the porch, intent on the darkness of the yard. While his eyes scanned the stairs inches from his shoes, his hand reached behind him, pushed the door shut.

Jud loosed his grip and fell off the windowsill, his arms wide as he surrendered to gravity and the night.

He slammed into Plaid Jacket like a walrus plopping on a leopard seal. The two men crashed down the wooden stairs, thudding onto the packed dirt. Jud landed on top.

The man beneath him was bony and still, his head at an awkward angle. Jud probed the man's neck; found *no pulse.*

Next thing Jud realized he was leaning against the fence. Vomiting. His head swam and bile burned his throat each time he gasped. Tears stung his eyes and he blinked them away.

*It was the fall,* Jud agreed. *If I hadn't been drunk, I'd be dead, too. He was supposed to be stunned so I could run. He wasn't supposed to die. Not him, too.*

Jud silenced his conscience, bent to search the corpse.

A dime-store notepad and pen in the plaid jacket. A pack of Camels and a box of kitchen matches. From the pants came two hundred dollars in bills and loose change. Fingernail clipper. A handkerchief. A set of car keys, house keys. A wallet. Half a dozen credit cards matched the California driver's license, which matched the face well enough. No work ID of any kind. First-rate paper cover. Innocent. He found no gun, but a good field man wouldn't need one. Jud strapped the man's digital watch to his own bare wrist, filled his pockets with the dead man's things, looked down. Swallowed hard.

Walked up the stairs, eyes forward.

No one else who didn't belong had come into the bar. Plaid Jacket's backup might be waiting outside.

*Fuck it,* thought Jud. *Don't back down.*

The bartender had his rear to the room, watering a rummy's shot. He glanced in the mirror as Jud walked by.

"Hey!" called the bartender, turning. "What about you?"

"Keep the change," Jud muttered.

Jud stepped outside beneath the red neon OASIS sign, silently screaming as he waited for the bullet to cut him down.

Nothing.

A dozen parked cars, all empty. No one in the doorways. No one crouched on the skid-row fire escapes. A police siren wailed down distant boulevards, wrong direction and too soon to be for Jud. He didn't have the time to match the dead man's keys to a parked car. Jud had no car. His $17-a-night hotel was four blocks away, easy to stumble home to after a hard night at the Oasis. Or to crawl. But he wouldn't risk going there. He had next to nothing in his room. Suitcases of worn clothes. A couple snapshots. Keys to a Mercedes he gave to Lorri when she left. His wallet held his driver's license and empty slots for credit cards.

And the men from yesterday finally wanted him dead.

What the hell, he thought. Make 'em work for it.

The least important difference between California and the East Coast is that the sun rises three hours earlier over the Atlantic. On that last Monday in February 1990, dawn broke in Washington, D.C., at 7:21, EST, filling Nick Kelley's suburban Maryland bedroom with gray light. Nick slept quietly beside his wife, her black hair spread on her pillow like a Japanese fan.

The telephone rang.

Which spooked their rottweiler, who barked and woke the baby in the next room; Saul cried. The phone rang again before Nick could grab the receiver. Beside him, Sylvia stirred.

"'Lo?" whispered Nick into the phone.

"This is the A T and T operator. Will you accept a collect call from, ah, Wolf?"

Nick closed his eyes, sighed. Opened his mouth to say no, then shook his head and said, "Yes."

"Who is it?" mumbled Sylvia, sitting up, brushing her hair off her forehead. She wore a long, white nightgown.

"Jud," whispered her husband as he sat on the edge of the bed.

"Shit," she said. Nick half-hoped her curse hadn't carried over the phone line, half-hoped it had. Sylvia flipped the covers back, padded from the room to care for their son.

"It's me," Jud said on the other end of the line.

"I guessed," replied Nick. Partly for his wife, he said, "Do you know what time it is?"

At a corner pay phone in Los Angeles, Jud checked the dead man's watch.

"Zero four-thirty, my time," he told Nick.

"You woke the baby."

"Oh. Sorry. How is he? Saul, right?"

"He's fine." Nick sighed. He ran his hand through his steel-flecked black hair—prematurely gray, he noted. *And this is how it got that way.* "He was due to wake up anyway."

"Look, I just called to tell you, if you don't hear from me for a while—"

"I haven't heard from you for a while."

"—I've got to go under."

"Again?" said Nick flatly. He yawned. Nick was a wiry man, almost too lean for his just under six-foot height.

"This time is different." Jud's calm tone held none of his practiced drama.

"Is something wrong?"

"No shit."

Nick licked his lips; Sylvia was still out of the room. "Does it have anything to do with us?"

"With you?" said Jud, understanding. "Doubt it."

*What if you're wrong?* thought Nick.

"We had us some times, didn't we, partner?" said Jud.

"Yeah."

"You know I love you like a brother."

Nick's face burned. Sylvia walked back in the bedroom, their sixteen-month-old son in her arms. The sleepy baby burrowed his face into Mommy's chest.

"Uh, yeah." Nick avoided Sylvia's glare. "Me, too."

"In case I don't get to, tell Saul about me."

"Tell him what?"

"The truth."

"What's that? Where do I start?"

"With good-bye," said Jud. A pair of headlights rolled toward him. He hung up.

On the East Coast, Nick heard the phone click, waited, then hung up, too, and knew that *finally*, this had been the call.

In Los Angeles, the headlights flowed past Jud. He rested his throbbing forehead on the pay phone, closed his eyes.

Jud had caught a bus seven blocks from the Oasis. He played the forgettable wino for the bored black bus driver, five laughing Hispanic women dressed in janitor's uniforms, three stoic Korean men, and a sleeping black woman, a bowling-ball bag on the seat beside her. In the green light of the bus's interior, Jud made a convincing wino.

When he went to work for Angel Hardware & Lock six months earlier, Jud mastered the alarm system and cut himself a set of store keys. Inside the store, he turned on the coffeemaker and started a can of tomato soup on the hot plate. He went to his time card. He was owed for eleven shifts, plus overtime.

One shelf held dusty gym bags. Jud ripped the tags off two and cruised the aisles. Swiss army knives. A nylon jacket. Four pairs of work socks; a soldier could always use socks. Jud blushed when he realized he wasn't wearing any. Leather work gloves and cotton gardening gloves. A flashlight. From the workroom, he took lockpicks and tension bars, master keys, compact screwdriver and wrench kits, a ball peen hammer, a jimmy, and a plastic shimmy.

The tomato soup was bubbling. He ate the whole can, drank strong coffee. He put socks on under his sneakers. In the bathroom, he found a bottle of aspirin and a safety razor. He took four aspirin, put the bottle and razor in his bag.

Jud let himself into the owner's office and snapped on the snake-necked desk light. Musty papers, ledgers, lock parts, and tools covered the desk. Jud took $131 from a cashbox. He sat in the desk's squeaky chair, thought about the fat, cigar-smoking owner who drove a Caddy and hated and feared the world. Taped to the bottom of the middle drawer, Jud found an envelope with pictures of hard-looking women naked except for black boots and whips. The envelope also held three $100 bills. Jud put the money in his pocket, the pictures back in the envelope, retaped it to the drawer. The owner would tell no one of that loss. Clipped inside the right-hand drawer, Jud found a dusty snub-nose .38 revolver.

The gun was loaded. Jud cleaned and oiled the weapon. He wedged the gun between his belt and his right kidney, hoped the nylon jacket would cover it, hoped he could still do the cop draw.

He scrawled *We're even* across his time card and dropped it on the office desk.

Bags in hand, he walked six blocks to a pay phone. He leaned against a light pole and tried to clear his brain before he called Nick. After they talked, he rested his forehead on the phone. The Dodgers were using his head for batting practice. When he breathed, he tasted tomato soup, cheap whiskey, and bile. The gun dug into his back.

*Don't need bullets,* he thought, *I'll just blow on 'em.*

He picked up the receiver, reconsidered: *Do that last.*

On a sleeping residential street four blocks away he found a Chevy without a locking gas cap. Jud wore the cotton gloves. He slid the plastic shimmy along the passenger window, sprang the door lock, popped off the ignition cover, spliced the wires into a switch stolen from his old shop. The engine purred. He put his two bags on the front floor, eased the Chevy into gear, and coasted down the block with the lights out.

He drove back to the pay phone, parked so the receiver was a fast step away from the open car door. Stared at the phone until it became nothing. Punched in a toll-free number.

On the other side of the continent, where it was now 8:26 A.M., five men in conservative shirts and ties sat in a windowless room, enjoying croissants and coffee at their computer-laden desks. Clocks on the wall showed the time in every U.S. zone, Greenwich, London, Paris, Rome, Berlin, Moscow, Beijing, Hong Kong, and Tokyo. The men laughed about a woman they barely knew.

A blue phone rang on the second desk from the left. The desk's computer screen automatically split. The man at the desk looked like a Yale professor, an image he'd cultivated since graduating from the University of Wyoming five years before. He adjusted his earphone and mike headset, held up his hand for silence, then flipped a switch to answer the call.

"Hello?" he said, his eyes on his computer screen.

"Why don't you answer 'Security Force' anymore?" said Jud.

"Hello?" repeated the man, frowning.

"This is Malice."

The man typed MALICE onto the screen, pushed the enter key. Within seconds, a six-word column appeared on the screen's left side. The man chose the first word.

"Is that *M* as in *mother?*" he asked.

"*M* as in *malign.*"

"*E* as in . . . "

"*Enigma,*" said Jud. "Lame, don't waste time running the list. You know who I am."

The right side of the screen lit up.

"Yes," said the man who'd answered the call as he read the computer's instructions. "I think I know who this is."

The man's coworkers looked over his shoulder. One whispered, "Malice—I had him twice."

"Shame on you guys," said Jud. "Shame on you."

"What?" said the man who'd answered his call.

"That was no way to say good-bye," Jud told them.

"I'm not sure what you mean."

"Ask around the Oasis Bar, Lame. You'll figure it out. If you're cleared high enough."

"What can I do for you?" asked the man Jud had called.

Suddenly, in L.A., the dead man's watch began to beep. Jud poked buttons on the watch dial. The beeps didn't stop.

"Do you hear a beeping noise?" asked the man in front of the computer screen.

Jud banged the watch on his wrist against the pay phone's glass wall. The glass cracked, but the watch kept beeping.

"Are you there?" said the smooth voice in Jud's ear.

Jud curled his arm outside the phone cubicle so the beeping watch was on the other side of the glass.

"Can I help you?" tried the would-be Yalie one last time.

"You tell 'em I said hello, huh? Not good-bye, Lame. Not like that. You tell 'em all I said *hello.*"

Across the bottom of the right-hand screen the computer printed the number of Jud's pay phone.

"Tell who?" asked the man. He kept his voice calm.

"Yeah," said Jud. "Yeah."

He hung up.

The watch quit beeping.

"God, I don't need this," muttered Jud. He fastened the dead man's watch around the telephone receiver. Left that high-tech prankster for *them*. Drove away in the stolen Chevy. To the west waited the ocean. South was Mexico and bad karma. East was where he'd been. Jud headed north, the direction a mouse took in search of the wren he loved in the only happy story Jud remembered from his childhood.

# THE CHOSEN ONE

**M**ajor Wesley Chandler, United States Marine Corps, drove past two sheriff's deputies parked at the mouth of a suburban Virginia cul-de-sac, their windows cracked so they wouldn't suffocate, their engine chugging so they wouldn't freeze in the March night. He nodded to them; they noted his uniform and nodded back, comrades-in-arms against the barbarians.

Cars lined the residential street, middle-class mobility machines. He saw no limousines. And no parking spaces.

A man with an unbuttoned overcoat stood in the porch light's glow at the rambling Tudor home that matched the address on Wes's notepad. A second man wrapped in Washington's ubiquitous Burberry trench coat lounged against a blue sedan with three antennae on its trunk. The Burberry was unfastened. A plastic tube ran from the coat to the man's left ear. The two men's eyes rode with Wes as he cruised past the house.

He drove back to the mouth of the cul-de-sac. The parking space he found was too close to the corner for the law, but the deputies didn't seem to care.

Wes shut off his engine. The night chill reached through the car to stroke him. He checked his watch and remembered the two phone calls that had summoned him here.

The first phone call had come to his office at the Naval Investigative Service headquarters on Thursday. Yesterday. He'd been staring at the computer screen in his gray-walled cubicle a mile from the Capitol building, trying to convince himself that the memo he was writing really mattered. That first call had been from a woman.

"Is this Major Chandler from New Mexico?" she'd said.

"That's where I was born."

"I'm Mary Patterson. Way back when, I was Congressman Denton's secretary. We met when the Academy bused the cadets up from Annapolis to meet the members who appointed them."

"That was twenty-five years ago," said Wes.

"Now I'm working with the boss at his new shop."

"Congratulations."

"That's why I'm calling you," she said. "Mr. Denton wants to honor the people from his days on the Hill—like his staffers and you fine men who did him proud at the service academies. Just an informal cocktail party after work."

"When?"

"Tomorrow," she said. "Can I tell him you'll be there?"

"I'll try," said Wes.

"Oh." Her voice chilled. "Well, do try. Please."

The second phone call had come at nine-thirty A.M. Friday.

"Major Chandler," said a man's gravel voice, "my name is Noah Hall. Exec assistant to Director Denton. We've never met."

The gray walls of Wes's office drew closer.

"You will go to his reception tonight, right?"

"Since you put it that way," answered Wes.

Noah Hall chuckled. Agreed Wes should wear his uniform.

"You bringin' a date?" asked Hall.

"No, should I?" *And who should I get?* Wes wanted to add.

"Come alone." Noah Hall told Wes when to be there.

Wes's heels clicked on the sidewalk as he walked into the cul-de-sac. He exhaled silver clouds that vanished in the night. These houses were elegant barns. Sculpted hedges, chiseled trees, lawns trimmed even in their seasonal death. The rainbow flicker of television shone through the window of one home.

Laughter floated to Wes from his destination. The man by the door watched him approach, while the eyes of the man at the curb swept the street. In the dark yard behind the house, Wes spotted the pinpoint orange flare of a cigarette cupped in an over-confident hand. ·

"Cold for this, isn't it?" Wes told the man at the door who unwisely had his hands deep in his overcoat pockets.

"Don't we know it?" replied the man, with a smile, grateful for the professional recognition. "Go on in."

Wes opened the door.

Warmth rolled over him like a wave. A smoky fireplace burned somewhere amidst the babble of voices. A woman screeched in delight: late thirties, cigarette in one hand, white wine in the other. She wore wedding rings, but her male companion with graying sandy hair, tweed suit, and bow tie looked not of the marriage persuasion. A Latin maid bustled past Wes, a tray of Swedish meatballs and bite-sized crab cakes clutched in her hands. She'd fled El Salvador after the right-wing death squad La Mano Blanca gang-raped her. On the interior stair landing stood another man with a suit and a tube running from under his jacket to his ear. The carpet beneath Wes's feet was thick, the air rich in perfumes: rose and lilac and musk.

"You must be Major Chandler!" A woman in her fifties stepped from the crowd. "You're our only Marine. I'm Mary Patterson."

As she shook his hand, Wes felt her eyes soak him up.

In a roomful of quality men, Wes might not be the first man you'd notice, but he was the man you'd remember, even if he wasn't wearing his Marine uniform. He was six three and well muscled. He gave an impression of strength rather than size, of energy contained rather than exuded. He was handsome, though nothing about his face was magazine-ad pretty. His brown hair was cut military short and brushed flat, but with style beyond any Marine barber. His nose was big, but not prominent, his mouth wide with even teeth and full lips. Time had etched a furrow across his brow, in the corners of his mouth, and shrapnel had nicked a scar on his chin. His eyes were black, wide, and large, but so deep set they looked like hooded slits.

Mary led him into a crowded living room. Wes spotted a Navy commander, wife on his arm, laughing with a man who Wes didn't know was a counsel for the Senate Appropriations Committee. A glassy-eyed Army captain with routine ribbons on his chest and broken veins on his nose grinned anxiously at the silver star on the shoulder of a fellow Army officer. The general caught Wes's gaze, nodded, then returned to his discussion with a man in a three-piece blue suit who headed a downtown firm of only ninety-three lawyers and the lean, bearded carpenter husband of the former secretary whose screech first attracted Wes's attention.

"Have you met Mrs. Denton?" asked Mary Patterson.

"I've never had the chance," replied Wes.

Across the room, a woman whose beauty had matured into elegance shook the hand of a Washington editor for a Florida newspaper chain. His wife, who'd gone from congressional aide to solid waste management specialist at the Environmental Protection Agency, nervously made the introductions.

"I'm so glad you were able to make it," Mary Patterson told Wes as they waited for journalist and bureaucrat to move on.

"Lucky, wasn't it?"

"Mrs. Denton," said Mary, and the elegant woman beamed at Wes.

Behind her, Wes saw a beefy man leaning against the fireplace mantel, a glass of amber liquor swirling in one fist. The man's horseshoe-bald head glistened, and his knotted tie dangled below an open white shirt collar, but he stayed by the flames. And kept his beady hazel eyes on Wes.

Mary said, "This is Major Chandler."

"So very nice to meet you," intoned Mrs. Denton.

"Thank you for inviting me," said Wes.

"Why, dear, we couldn't have had the party without you."

"Mrs. Denton!" A man grasped Mrs. Denton's reflexively offered hand. "Do you remember me? I was assistant press aide for the congressman in his second term. Bill. Bill Acker."

"Of course, Bill! Who could forget you?"

"I'm working with N double-A RE now, at the Association's HQ downtown. Pretty broad-based stuff, not like the usual special interest lobbying, and I'm . . ."

Mary steered Wes away, told him: "She's so sweet."

Mrs. Denton embraced a young woman, pulled her in front of the unforgettable Bill Acker.

The fat man with beady eyes shifted his position down the mantel, his gaze locked on Wes.

"We should find the boss," said Mary.

Laughter drew their eyes to the far side of the room.

Ralph Denton looked better than his newspaper photos. He carried too many pounds, but he was tall and his legs were strong. Green eyes twinkled beneath his thin gray hair.

"Sir!" Mary called out. A glance acknowledged her. He shook a half dozen hands, then swung to Mary and Wes.

The beady-eyed man had moved from the mantel to the bar, where he could watch Wes meet Ralph Denton.

"Director Denton," said Mary, "remember Wesley Chandler from Taos? Burke Chandler's son. Burke died after you left the Hill. You appointed Wesley to Annapolis in—1964, wasn't it?"

"Yes," said Wes as he shook his host's hand. The older man had a dry and strong grip.

"Okay if I call you Wes?" asked Denton.

Wes nodded.

"Looks like you've done fine," said the director, eyeing the ribbons on Wes's chest.

"I've had some luck."

"Haven't we all, son," said Denton. He spotted an elderly couple handing their coats to the maid. "Amazing times, huh?"

"Yes sir."

"Would you excuse me?" He squeezed Wes's shoulder and bustled toward the couple.

"Well, Major," said Mary. "Lovely to see you. Stick around. Enjoy yourself. There's quite a buffet. Have a drink."

She melted into the crowd.

The man with beady eyes had moved from the bar to a bookcase. He chatted with a heavily made-up woman ten years of fervent self-denial past her prime and pretended not to watch Wes.

Wes joined an Air Force colonel at the bar. The senior officer smiled and they exchanged names. Wes pointed to the ice chest of beers, waved away the bartender's offer of a glass. Wes turned back to the crowd: he couldn't find the beady-eyed man.

"Good to see Mr. Denton back in town," said the Air Force officer. "I wish he'd never lost that election way back when. He'd be Speaker of the House now. Or a ranking senator."

"He's done fine," said Wes.

"No shit. You get back to New Mexico much?"

"No. You?"

"Nah." The officer wore pilot's wings. He swallowed Scotch. "Shame about Sawyer. Takes the top job at CIA, gets us through invading Panama, then two weeks ago his heart goes *boom*. Kind of surprised to see Denton replace him."

"Why?" asked Wes.

"Us blue suits expected Billy Cochran to get it. He has the stars, library between his ears, clean hands. Was a whiz at running NSA."

Wes sipped his beer. Where was beady eyes?

The fly-boy nodded toward Wes's ribbons.

"I flew '15s there," he said. "When were you in country?"

"A long time ago," said Wes.

"Amen." The ex-pilot raised his glass to Wes. He looked from side to side. "Your guys hear anything about the budget cuts?"

"I don't know anything about that," said Wes.

"You mean anything good," said the ex-pilot. He shook his head, wandered away.

A waiter took Wes's empty beer can. Amidst the sweat and smoke, Wes smelled steaming meat. Whatever the buffet offered, it'd be better than a dinner he could burn for himself.

Watermelon balls, kiwi fruit, a half dozen shrimp, carrot slices, raw cauliflower, Swedish meatballs on sticks dripping thin gravy onto Wes's paper plate. Beady eyes waited until Wes finished, then ambled to the corner where Wes stood alone.

"Good eats, uh?" said beady eyes.

"Yes," answered Wes. He put down his plate.

"I'm Noah Hall. We talked."

"I came."

"Damned if you didn't." Noah had a face like a bulldog. He used Wes's napkin to mop his shiny dome. "New Mexicans, eh? Friendly folks."

"Where you from, Noah?"

"Which campaign?"

They chuckled.

"They do it right," said Noah, "they'll bury me in Chicago. Or Boston. They're smart, they'll burn me where I lay."

"That can be arranged," said Wes.

"You're a regular pistol, ain't you, Major?"

"I'm qualified."

"Good. Because the Director would take it as a personal favor if you stuck around after this to-do, had a chat with him."

"What about?"

"What do you care? He's a big enough boy you ought to be happy to make him happy."

"I'm happy to accommodate Mr. Denton in any way I can."

"Let's accommodate him out of down here," said Noah. "We'll just mosey upstairs, two guys looking for the gents'."

"Are there any gents here?"

Noah laughed himself into a smoker's hack. He clapped Wes on the back and steered him through the crowd.

"Couple decades ago," Noah said as he led Wes up the stairs, "when we were younger and full of more 'n' piss 'n' vinegar, party like this, we'd be sneakin' up here to get laid."

"You're not my type," said Wes as they reached the third floor. A man in a suit rose from the folding chair pulled up outside one of the closed doors. He nodded to Noah.

Noah smiled as he led Wes to the sentry, opened the door.

"What is your type, Wes?" Noah nodded him inside.

Thick curtains blocked the windows; behind them, Wes would have seen newly installed glass containing micro-thin wires that turned the windows into bulletproof panes of electric static. On the desk sat stacks of correspondence, newspaper clips, a locked briefcase, and three phones: one black, one blue, one red. The blue and red phones were fitted with scramblers. Three padded, high-back chairs sat empty on the carpet. Floor lamps lit the room.

"That's a gents'," Noah said, pointing to a door. "The cabinet's got hard stuff. You want another beer, don't you?"

"Okay," said Wes, following Noah's push.

"Bring our buddy a few brews from downstairs," Noah said to the sentry. "I'll keep an eye on the door."

"My post is security," answered the man. "Not service."

"My post is Executive Assistant to the Director. Nice duty around here. I'd hate like hell to have it suddenly shifted to site intelligence, scrounging subway schedules in Mongolia."

The guard blinked.

"It's okay," said Noah. "I got the Marines with me."

The man grimaced, but hustled downstairs.

"Gotta be sure everybody knows his place." Noah nodded after the guard. "He'll write a memo 'bout this to cover his ass, so if any of the data around here ends up compromised, it'll be our heinies on the line."

"Sure," said Wes.

"What would you do if that boy were under your command?"

"Ship him to Mongolia."

"They got subways there?" Noah laughed.

The President of the United States had effusively inscribed the color photograph of himself and Denton hanging above the cold fireplace. History caught the two men with their jackets off, ties loosened, on the edge of their seats in the Oval Office.

"Better one at the office," said Noah. "This town, you want the office, you gotta have pictures for the wall."

Noah nodded to the presidential photograph.

"Raised a shitload of money for him, yes he did. And someday, it'll be Ralph Denton that signs photos like that."

The sentry returned with four beers. He jerked open a cooler door and slammed the cans down on a rack, stood in the hall.

"Make yourself at home," said Noah. He left Wes alone.

For seventy-one minutes Wes waited in the closed room. He skimmed the book titles, the rows of video cassettes, let his eyes flick over documents on the desk, the locked briefcase, the three phones. He went to the bathroom, didn't open the cooler. The dead green eye of a wall-mounted television watched his every move. He picked the chair that afforded the best view of the door and offered the narrowest profile to the windows, settled into the cushions, and remembered squatting in the steamy bush west of Da Nang. At least there were no leeches here.

At the click of the turning knob, Wes stood. Ralph Denton entered, Noah lumbering in his shadow. Noah shut the door.

"Sit down, Wes, please," said Denton, waving his hand.

Wes complied. Noah leaned his back against the door.

"Sorry to be so long," said Denton. He sank into the chair on Wes's right. Yawned. "You want a drink?"

"He's got some beers in the fridge," said Noah.

"Enough for me to share?" asked Denton.

"Noah knows," said Wes. "They're yours."

Noah fetched them each an unopened brew, then poured himself a Scotch while Denton and his guest popped the cans.

"*Semper fi,*" said Denton, who'd been seventeen years old in Marine boot camp on VJ Day. Wes joined him in the toast. The beer was cold and tangy. Noah slumped in the empty chair.

"What do you know about my job?" Denton asked Wes.

"You're the new Director of the Central Intelligence Agency," answered Wes. "And as such, the Director of Central Intelligence, overseeing the rest of the Intelligence community."

"That's good," said Denton. "Most people only realize one of my four jobs. You named two. I'm also the President's chief confidant on intelligence matters. But we're here about you.

"A Marine major," said Denton. "A lawyer. Never married. Why'd you go to the Naval Academy?"

"You appointed me."

The three of them laughed.

"I haven't forgotten. You were a midlist graduate."

"My passions ran less to math than I'd thought."

"What do they run to?" said Noah.

"I'm more human oriented," Wes told Denton.

"Why'd you opt for the jarheads instead of sailor white?" asked Noah.

Wes smiled at him, slow and cold. "That seemed like where the action was in 1968."

"Do you enjoy being where the action is?" asked Denton.

"I enjoy doing a job worth doing well."

"Yes," said the DCI. "Vietnam, platoon leader, volunteered to Force Recon, which meant an extended tour. Two Bronze Stars, a Purple Heart. One negative evaluation."

"File says you weren't good at delegating authority," interjected Noah.

"Recon Command didn't like captains going out on long-range patrols," said Wes. "I didn't like sending men where I wasn't willing to go."

Denton said, "That attitude cost you a promotion."

Wes shrugged.

"You took the Excess Leave Program," said Denton. "Went to law school—which slowed you on the ladder even more. You're currently assigned to the Naval Investigative Service."

"A gumshoe," interjected Noah.

"Leaving aside the Laird Commission for the moment, you've never had any intelligence assignments—correct?"

"NIS handles counterintelligence, but I've been working criminal issues. Recon was tactical. Practical."

"Ah," said the political czar of America's spies. "Practical. Do you have anything against intelligence work?"

Wes took a long pull on his beer before he answered.

"I like knowing things," he said. "I prefer doing things. Intelligence work, the technical stuff, ELINT, satellites, SIGINT—it's passive. Analysis is fascinating, but takes years to get good at, years that deepen you, but narrow you. HUMINT, spooking, well, that's not something Marines do much of."

"Didn't you deal with intelligence when you worked for the Laird Commission in 1986?" asked Denton.

"My assignment with the Commission was to find out what went wrong with Marine security procedures at the Moscow embassy and in our Leningrad consulate, and examine whether the Corps had systemic problems that helped the KGB recruit and operate Sergeant Lonetree. I didn't concern myself with intelligence issues."

"But you rubbed elbows with spooks there, didn't you?" said Noah.

"Soviets or ours?" asked Wes.

"Either," said Noah.

"Both," answered Wes. "I stayed at the American embassy compound in Moscow. The third day, when I went for my morning run, the KGB uniformed guard at the gate greeted me in English, 'Good morning, Major Wesley Burke Chandler from New Mexico. How are things in the Marine Corps today?' Our spooks were the ones who left the room whenever I came in."

"But you never worked with them?" said Noah.

"No one but Marines and Commission members."

"The records reflect you did a fine job," said Denton. "Wes, do you have any friends in the Intelligence community?"

"Should I count either of you?"

They all laughed.

"Let me rephrase that," said the former congressman. "Do you have anyone in this business who you owe?"

"Should I count either of you?"

"You damn well better, son." Denton smiled.

"I pay my debts," said Wes. "I know FBI and NIS spy catchers, some Navy Intelligence. More Marine Intelligence. A few men over at the Joint Special Operations Agency—CIA uses them, you tell me if they count. Guys I met in jump school who kept changing their uniforms. I don't *owe* any of them."

"Who do you owe?" asked Noah.

"I owe rent, the monthly balance on my credit cards. A hardware salesman who was a good lance corporal. Several women I was less than gracious to. My folks are dead."

"We don't expect you to be a virgin," said Noah. "Hell, better if you're not. We don't need details we don't want to know. But we gotta be sure you ain't *infected.*"

"You know who I am."

"Wes," said Denton, "we're not targeting you, we're doing what you would do in our shoes. We're doing our job."

"What you say in this room stays in this room," said Noah. "What you hear stays in here, too."

"I might not get to heaven," said Wes, "but my tombstone will be clean."

"Heaven isn't where I have in mind to send you," said Denton.

"What do you have in mind?" asked Wes; added, "Sir."

"My fourth job," said DCI Ralph Denton. "Working for me in my fourth job.

"I'm the lightning rod for everything that goes wrong in intelligence," said Denton. "That's the job, and I accept it. But that doesn't mean being stupid. That doesn't mean working blind.

"Something's happened."

Three days earlier, Tuesday, at eleven A.M., Ralph Denton opened the door from his new office on the seventh floor of the "old" building at Langley and led Noah Hall and Mary Patterson into the carpeted corridor. Ralph crossed to the unmarked conference room door, winked at his longtime aides, then turned the handle.

"Good morning," he called out to the people milling around the conference table.

From the crowd stepped William Cochran, Deputy Director of Central Intelligence. *Number two on the charts, but number one in their hearts,* thought Denton. His deputy was the only man Denton ever met who could carry the name Billy with dignity. On a day like today, when he wasn't wearing his three-star Air Force general's uniform, Billy could walk through a crowd of strangers and they'd never remember his trim build or average height. He wore thick glasses with black metal frames.

"Sir," said Billy, "should I make the introductions?"

"Sure," said Ralph, letting Billy play it big.

The Executive Director. Five Deputy Directors. The only one Ralph knew was August Reed III, Deputy Director of Operations, who'd cut his teeth on the 1953 CIA plot that created the Shah of Iran and signaled the independence of the CIA from British intelligence. Reed had a waiver to stay on past retirement age.

Denton abruptly realized that he and Reed were the only

people in the room who'd been adults during World War II—if Denton's teenage days in the Marines counted as adulthood. In the 1960's, Ralph's oldest boy harassed the father he never dared confront by walking around the house singing "the times, they are a'changin'." Ralph remembered the song that morning as he saw faces unlined by the days that shaped his vision.

"You remember the Comptroller, the Inspector General and the General Counsel," said Billy, ticking off their names.

The house eunuchs, Noah had called them, in charge of keeping the Agency honest. The Comptroller was the only black in this pool of white faces. The only two women were the flack from Public Affairs and the Director of Science and Technology.

"This is the Chief of the Covert Action Staff," said Billy. Denton wanted his own man in charge of covert operations, so it was just a question of how quickly this current chief of dirty tricks could be eased out.

"Good to be working with you," said Denton.

"Hope you don't mind," said August Reed III, "I dragged along Timothy Jones. Tim runs our Counter-Intelligence Center."

Denton beamed as he shook Jones's clammy hand. Denton and Noah had carefully drawn up the meeting list. Jones hadn't been on it.

"Glad you're here," said Denton. He caught Noah's eye, then focused on the CIA's number two: "Aren't we, Billy?"

"Of course, Mr. Director," said Billy.

"This is General Prentice, from the National Intelligence Council," said Billy. The NIC was composed of representatives from the rest of the Intelligence community—the National Security Agency, the military intelligence groups, agencies that were sometimes larger in size and clout than the CIA.

"Prentice will be the eyes and ears for the big boys," Denton told Noah. "Make sure he sees and hears what we want."

Denton shook more hands. At Noah's suggestion, Denton had invited the heads of Finance and Security.

"Guns and money," Noah had argued. "Can never have enough and you can't ever tell."

A handsome man in his thirties shook Ralph's hand. "Legislative Liaison. I handle the White House, too."

"That makes two of us, son," said Denton. He grinned so the men standing nearby knew it was just a joke. They laughed.

Billy asked, "Do you have a preference for seating, sir?"

The room was a windowless box. A lectern stood at one end of the table. Ralph strolled through the crowd toward the other end. "Hell, Billy, doesn't really matter today."

Ralph kept the enjoyment off his face as the high and mighty jockeyed for chairs, mindful of the mysteries of rank. Only Billy seemed unruffled. He sat at the middle of the table. Noah and Mary sat along the wall. Ralph glanced at his watch.

"Sixty-three minutes ago," said Ralph, "the President helicoptered back to the White House."

In his mind, he heard the chopping beat of the two Presidential helicopters, one for the official Ralph was beginning to worry he would never be, plus a decoy for the terrorists Ralph hoped would keep quiet during his reign as America's chief spy.

"He left me sworn in as DCI," continued Ralph. All CIA personnel whose clearance and duties allowed them to had attended the ceremony in the "bubble" amphitheater. "I scheduled you senior executives here today to ask for your help in making my tenure as smooth as possible.

"Maintenance is moving my desk so that instead of facing the forest out my window, my chair looks in, to where you will be sitting. You'll be facing out to the world, and I'll ask you to tell me about it. That's the way I intend to run this agency.

"That also means, Billy, that you're now truly my right-hand man." The Deputy Director's office lay that direction from Ralph's new office arrangement.

"I'll do my best," said Billy.

*I'll bet,* thought Ralph. He continued:

"Let's start straight: crucial issues will not be hidden from me in a forest of daily problems. You are to tell me what I need to know and what I want to know. The burden of that task is on your shoulders. If I don't want to know for security or deniability reasons, fine. But don't protect me against what I will read on the front page of the *New York Times.*"

Denton's swearing in speech had been warm, open.

"I look around these halls and I see good people, worried that any moment history and Congress are going to come along and break their rice bowls."

Only Billy smiled.

"Well, I didn't take this chair to watch it get whittled down because some people wonder how valuable intelligence agencies are now that the Berlin Wall is rubble."

"Hear, hear," chimed in Gus Reed.

"Before I even got this chair, our friends on Capitol Hill and in the press warmed it up for me. The next time we spend a million dollars to buy a tinhorn Panamanian dictator like General Noriega, I want a warranty that makes sure he stays bought."

Chuckles warmed the room. But was that a flick of a gaze from August Reed to the twerp he'd dragged along? wondered Ralph. He looked at Billy: the general's glasses were impenetrable.

"We've got to trust each other," continued Ralph. "Work with each other. But I'm the man in charge. I walk in my own shoes—not Andy Sawyer's, God rest his soul. Not anybody else's."

The room was silent.

"The only thing left on my agenda today is a question," said Denton. "Not counting routine matters, is there anything that I should be aware of? Any issue or problem that because of the transition between Sawyer and me fell through the cracks?"

A perfect out for them, thought Ralph, if there's anything. But none of them should rise to the bait, being fully aware that this was a time and place of his choosing.

"Ah, well . . ." The timid voice from the end of the table.

The twerp, thought Denton. Timothy something. Counter-Intelligence something. Whose voice spoke through his mouth?

"Yes, Tim?" Ralph smiled.

"Something's happened," said Jones. He sighed as the weight of the words left him.

Ralph was watching Billy, not Timothy Jones. Slowly, Billy's Coke-bottle-bottomed glasses turned toward the nonentity who had dared to speak.

"It's not *really* my territory," babbled Jones. "I suppose this is more up Mike's alley"—Jones nodded to the head of Security—"but it's a CIC oversee, too, so—"

"Timothy." Denton spoke like an ice ax. "What happened?"

"We got a phone call," said Jones. "Yesterday morning. The Watch Office. On the Agent-In-Distress number."

"Who called?" said Denton.

"An ex-contract type, I guess. He, ah . . . He was drunk, probably nothing, you know, but . . . Weird."

"And?" asked the Director of Central Intelligence.

"And . . . you asked if anything unusual happened. I mean, we get hot calls from time to time, plus wrong numbers and cranks, so this might not really be unusual."

"What's been done?" said Denton.

Jones swallowed. "That really is Mike's department. *I* was given no indication that this guy could be another Lee Howard."

In 1985, Lee Howard, a former CIA analyst with a history of alcohol and drug problems, first sold secrets he knew and then escaped to the Soviet Union while under surveillance by the FBI.

Denton turned not to Mike Kramer, head of Security, but to both Jones's and Kramer's boss: August Reed III.

"What about all this, Gus?"

"Naturally," said Gus, "we're keeping a close eye on the situation."

"What is *the situation?*" pressed the new DCI.

"Just the rattling of odd, old ghosts," said Gus, who'd been a Skull and Bones man. "Drunken ghosts, I might add. Nothing important. Certainly no business."

Denton returned the smile and as his eyes swung from August Reed III, said, "What do you think, Billy?"

"For now," said Billy evenly, "I think we should leave troubled ghosts alone."

Denton let his eyes float from Billy's clouded glasses to Noah's impassive face. The second hand of a clock on the wall swept full circle.

"Anything else?" asked Denton. No one spoke. The new CIA Director smiled at this troops. "Meeting adjourned."

In Denton's study, Noah looked from Wes to Denton.

"It was Billy's grenade," said Noah, taking a swig of his Scotch. "Jones just pulled the pin."

"Not now, Noah," snapped Denton. "Besides, Gus Reed brought Jones, so Reed has to be in on the deal."

"I'm lost," said Wes, who knew exactly where he was.

*"Something's happened,"* said Denton. "If it's bad, nobody wants to get blamed for it. You know the game."

"What makes you think there's anything like that?"

"Survivin' forty years in this business," drawled Noah.

"You've worked in intelligence for forty years?" asked Wes.

"I lived politics since grade school, *cowboy.* Spook shit is just a part of that." Noah shrugged.

"I trust Noah's instincts," said Denton. "And my own."

"Besides," said Noah, "there's the file."

"What file?" asked Wes.

Noah grunted disdainfully.

"Whether Jones brought up the incident because of a political scheme or blurted it out because of nerves," said Denton, "if I make an issue of it, I elevate it to the Director's level. If it is scandal, then I'm tarred with it. If it's trivia, then I waste my time and am *perceived* as wasting my time. If I ignore it, it might go away. Or explode."

"Why not trust your troops to handle it?"

"They're not my troops. Yet. If any of them has something to hide . . . The old problem, Wes: Who watches the watchers?"

"What about this file?" Wes asked again.

"Two pages of zip," said Noah. "No photo. Says the guy had 'minimal' Agency contact through the Green Berets. If it was so minimal, why the hell did he have the emergency number? Contact severed in the 1970s. Went crazy. A dozen call-ins— paranoia, booze. A 'delusionary pathological liar.' Hands-off instructions. But orders to not piss him off, to log and notify."

"The caller mentioned a bar in Los Angeles. Noah checked with LAPD. The night our man called, another man died in that bar."

"Who?" asked Wes. "How?"

"You tell us," said Noah. "Nobody else wants to."

Wes couldn't wait anymore. "What do you want me to do?"

Denton looked at Noah; got a shrug. And the bulldog grin.

"We want you to ascertain what's happened," said Denton. "And help resolve any problems for America's intelligence and strategic interests that may intersect with that."

"Sir, I'm a Marine officer. What do you want me to *do?*"

"Hell, Wes," said Noah. "We want you to track this som'bitch down. Find out who he is, what's he doing and why he called, and then fix it if it don't sit with the program."

"And do it quietly," said Denton. "Keeping in mind that my profile must remain above any problems. And that absolute confidentiality must be strictly maintained.

"We want you to be our point man," said Denton.

"Bird dog," said Noah.

"Stalking-horse?" ventured Wes.

"Is that what you're thinking?" asked Denton.

"What I'm thinking is there has to be more to this than what you've told me or it wouldn't be worth all this trouble."

"Precisely," said Denton.

"Why me?" asked Wes. "I buy that you won't trust CIA guys for this. Conflict of interest. But why me?"

"The logical choice is FBI," said Denton, "but the Director and I don't see eye to eye. The Bureau would love to go fishing in my agency's business. As for the other civilian agencies . . . I don't have a feel for them.

"Which leaves uniforms. Our man is ex-Army. They can't be objective. Even if they could, the Air Force and Navy would cry foul, the Army getting a special relationship with me. The Marines are lowest in clout and thus nonthreatening to everyone.

"The man you're hunting may be a drunk, but once he was a hell of a soldier. He had to be a paratrooper to be a Green Beret. A general once told me that only guys who fall out of airplanes understand other guys who fall out of airplanes. You had to become a paratrooper for Recon."

"Plus you kinda been playing cop over at NIS," said Noah. "This is close to cop."

"And," added Denton, "you're a lawyer. After Watergate, Iran-contra . . . I'd like to have an attorney's eyes on this."

"'Course," said Noah, "we don't want you tangled up in nit-picker nonsense. 'Legal' has a flexible meaning out here. What's most important is secrecy—and results. That's why we want a Marine. Get the job done. We'll worry about the law."

"We can't make this seem a major effort," said the CIA Director. "Nothing with a bureaucratic identity. Nothing with a future that agitates everyone into circling their wagons. We can just barely get away with turning one man loose."

"Me."

Denton shrugged. "I got you out of Nowhere, New Mexico, launched your career. You've never mixed with Intelligence, so you're clean. Nobody knows you, nobody hates you, nobody mistrusts you. But the NIS, the Laird Commission, Vietnam . . . You're no lamb. You have no family encumbrances, and you're here in Washington."

"You ransacked your files," said Wes. "What if I say no?"

"Then I thank you for your time. And remind you that all this is confidential. That I have keen ears. Send you back to your cubicle where you can stay safe and snug until your pension."

"Hell, Wes," said Noah. "You know you want to say yes! You ain't a cubicle kind of guy.

"'Sides,"—Noah leaned forward—"we're good friends to have. There's colonel up ahead, if you make the cut. You're behind a lot of good men in cut-back times. War College would help. Good word on the Hill. Who knows what could come up?"

"We're making no promises," Denton added quickly. "We want you to do an honorable job. For your country."

The three men stared at each other.

"What if nothing is there?" said Wes.

"If that's what you find—and that's what's true"—Denton shrugged—"then we're all better off."

"What if it is a bureaucratic shot? Zap the new DCI?"

"We'll deal with that," said Noah.

"What if it's something more?"

"Then you'll be there to help us," said Denton. "Help us help our country. You will be there, won't you, Wes?"

Again, silence drifted through the room.

"Understand me," Wes finally said. "I'll do this job—if I believe some answers you'll give me. But I'll do it because it will be my job: no trades. Eagles land on my shoulders, I get them because I earned them, not because I bargained for them. Don't do me any favors I don't ask you for, and I'll work for you."

"Then it's a deal!" Denton smiled.

"What questions?" said Noah.

"Can you square this with the Corps?"

"By Monday morning, I can horse-trade the Commandant to transfer you on detached duty to my personal staff.

"People at Langley won't like it," added Denton. "Trust none of them—not even Billy Cochran. Trust no one but Noah and me.

"Work through Noah. Work it your way. We want no paper on it. No ties to the CIA. Use whatever resources you can scrounge. I can't give you a 'please assist' letter. Tell no one more than you need to. Noah will arrange your expenses."

"Let's be sure everyone knows his place," said Wes. "I work for you. Not Noah. Am I to assume that whatever he tells me comes straight from you? Unedited? Unrefined? And what I send back gets there the same way?"

Denton shifted uncomfortably in his chair.

"Noah has my full confidence," he said.

"I'll assume he speaks directly for you. And if I have any doubts, I'll go straight to you."

The Director looked at his longtime right-hand man.

"I know about deniability, cutouts," said Wes. "And getting left out in the cold."

"Oh, do you now?" said Noah.

Denton waved his hand to calm his men.

"You've got it," said the DCI. "Of course."

"What if I get in trouble?" asked Wes.

"Trouble's not what this is about," said Denton. "If there is trouble, it's to end with you. This is a new era. The last thing America needs is another spy scandal. Understand?"

"Yes sir," said Wes.

"Tell no one about tonight," said Denton. "Be surprised. You'd be a logical selection, even if you weren't who you are."

"Who am I?" asked Wes.

"You're the chosen one," said Denton.

The Director stood and his men followed suit. He shook hands with Wes.

"Leave the uniform in your closet," he told Wes.

Wes's shirt was soaked. He was exhausted.

"Why are we doing this?" Wes asked.

"Nature of the business." Denton shrugged. "Bottom line? I need to know why that guy is so damned unimportant."

‖‖‖‖‖‖‖‖‖‖‖‖‖‖‖‖‖‖‖‖‖‖‖‖‖‖‖‖‖‖‖‖‖‖‖‖‖‖‖‖‖‖‖‖‖‖‖‖‖‖‖‖‖‖‖‖‖‖‖‖‖‖‖‖‖‖‖

# CHINA KINDA GUY

**N**ick Kelley met Jud on a cool April 1976 morning, in Washington, D.C., while working as a muckraker for columnist Peter Murphy. Nick was typing on a battered Underwood manual in his cluttered office at the rear of a mansion seventeen blocks north of the White House, concentrating on his story about a stamped SECRET General Accounting Office study leaked to him by a Senate staff source. The GAO study suggested that the Pentagon was squandering $500 million on a missile system because Secretary of State Henry Kissinger wanted to use it as a bargaining chip with the Soviets at the Strategic Arms Limitation Talks.

"Excuse me," said a man's deep voice in the hall.

Standing in the hall was a man who, unlike Nick, topped six feet tall. They both wore blue jeans. The man's chest and biceps were so muscled his arms curled out from his sides like parentheses. A brown polo shirt strained across his shoulders. The man's hair was ruddy, curly and shorter than Nick's over-the-ears black locks. The stranger's eyes were diamond blue.

"You're . . . ," said the man, hesitated; smiled. "You're Nick Kelley. And you wrote a novel. *Flight of the Wolf.*"

Nick blinked: *How'd this guy get past the receptionist?*

"Am I right or am I right?" said the stranger.

"Yes," answered Nick. He turned away from the typewriter so that his body hid the security-stamped report on his desk.

"See?" The man's grin was infectious. "Told you so. I recognized you from the picture on the cover."

"No one's ever done that before," said Nick.

"Interesting book," said the stranger. "I know a little about that stuff—spies."

"Oh," said Nick, big-time cool.

"Yeah. I was in Special Forces."

"Really," said Nick. In 1976, before he decided the Vietnam war was a tragedy, he'd flunked an Army ROTC enlistment physical. In the haunted world of heroes where Nick lived, he'd fantasized about being in the Army's Special Forces, wearing the elite green beret. He'd read the books. Knew the words to the song about the unit that in 1966 climbed the rock charts. Reporting had taught him military jargon. "What were your MOS areas?"

"I was primarily a zero seven. Intelligence."

"Really." Nick didn't know if "zero seven" meant anything.

"We should get together sometime. Have dinner."

Nick shrugged.

"My name is Jud," said the stranger. "Jud Stuart."

"What are you doing here?" asked Nick.

"Working in the building." He smiled. "See you around."

Then he vanished.

After hiding the SECRET report, Nick circled through the halls of what had once been a Victorian whorehouse.

"Jenny," he asked the receptionist slumped in a cigarette fog, "there's this big guy, polo shirt and jeans, hanging around. Jud something. What's he doing here?"

"He's a locksmith," she said. "Fixing the doors."

There wasn't a door in the mansion Jud didn't work on that spring. One day he'd be there for four hours, the next day not at all. He'd run into Nick in the halls or stick his head in Nick's office. He'd joke and cheerlead Nick and the other reporters into joining his amusement. He'd personalize news events: "Can you believe that shit? Blows my mind!" Then he'd toss a soft question for Nick to knock back with his Washington-insider bat. Jud's questions implied the correct answer: "Was it isolated growing up in a small town in Michigan?" Nick fell into the habit of agreeing with him. And liking him, being charmed by a man who would laugh out loud in a city where everyone else hid their insanity. Most of all, Nick was awed by Jud's churning energy.

"He's like a bear who's swallowed a nuclear reactor," Nick told one of the other reporters.

"Does he glow in the dark?" asked Nick's colleague.

Jud never again brought up Special Forces or spies. Whenever Nick mentioned such topics, Jud sidestepped them.

Besides working at the muckraker's nationally syndicated column to satisfy his curiosity and social conscience, Nick was writing a novel about auto workers to satisfy his demons. Jud regularly repeated his dinner invitation. Nick truthfully kept telling him he was busy. Secretly, he wondered what he'd have in common with a locksmith, whether Jud was a jackal hoping to feed off Nick's fleeting fame. Or crazy.

One 1976 Wednesday morning as April strolled toward May, Nick's ancient Dodge wouldn't start. He was thirty minutes late getting in to work. Nick slumped in front of the Underwood, trying to inspire himself to feed the news machine.

"I was worried about you," boomed Jud from the doorway.

Nick told him about the car.

"So you cabbed it in," said Jud. Nick saw the idea light his face. "I got the company truck! I'll finish about six, same as you. We can get something to eat, then I'll drive you home."

"Well, I . . ."

"We're going to end up doing this sooner or later. Might as well make it easy on yourself, kill two birds with one stone."

And then Jud grinned. "You got a girl, right?"

"Ah, yeah," said Nick. "Yes."

"She doesn't live with you, does she?"

"Around the corner." Nick shrugged. "Her choice."

"Like hell," said Jud.

And Nick had to laugh.

"Must be tough," said Jud. "You meet dozens of women who are knocked out by an author, even if they only know the movie of your book. Plus investigative reporters are cool these days. Am I right?"

Nick blushed.

"You chased her, got her, but longer and more 'n you imagined. She stuck with you when you were nothing, stays absolutely true, right? You don't want to ever hurt her, but you're a man, and from time to time . . ."

"We have an understanding," said Nick.

"Anybody ever explain to you that you could be too loyal for your own good?"

"Nobody I ever believed," said Nick.

"Same here," said Jud. "You can end up bent out of shape by all that though, 'specially with women."

"Don't worry about it," said Nick.

"Hell, I'm stuck, too! My lady's crazier than me! Plus I keep seeing these women around town. Drives you nuts, doesn't it?"

"Can."

"We owe ourselves a night out with the boys, right?"

*I can tell Janey I'm with a source,* thought Nick. *Keep the mute terror out of her eyes. That's potentially true. Why do I have to tell her anything? No more confessions.*

"Okay," said Nick. He'd call Janey, tell her.

"I'll bring a couple things to show you." Jud smiled. "You'll get a kick out of them."

At 6:17, Nick was pacing his office, nervous that Jud wouldn't show. And that he would. Just as he decided to tape a *sorry* note to the door, grab a cab home, Jud loomed in the hall. He'd changed his work shirt for a Hawaiian shirt with white sharks cruising on a blue background. He carried a red nylon gym bag.

"There's a cheap Spanish restaurant over on M Street," said Jud. "What with parking and a beautiful night, we might as well walk. That's okay with you, isn't it?"

"Sure," Nick said politely. "Sure."

They were two blocks down Sixteenth Street, headed toward Scott Circle and the National Rifle Association's glass and steel monolith, Jud laughing and lecturing about everything and nothing, when suddenly the big man halted.

"There's a friend of mine," said Jud. "Got to say hello."

An old woman with a cane tapped her way toward them.

"Mrs. Collin!" called out Jud, leading Nick toward her.

Her cane rose as the two men hurried toward her.

"Yes?" her voice was clear but tentative.

"Don't you remember me?" Jud asked her.

She squinted.

"I should wear my prescription sunglasses," she said as the sunset shimmered on her wrinkled face.

"You don't even like wearing your regular glasses."

"That's right." The old lady frowned. "I know your voice, but . . ."

"Imagine me in a suit and tie," said Jud. "And about forty fewer pounds."

"Oh, my Lord!" A bright smile showed how pretty she once was. "Jud! I haven't seen you . . . why, almost four years!"

"We've both been busy."

"I've retired, you know," she confided.

"No! I didn't."

"Thirty years. People shouldn't work past their time. Block out you young folks." Her lips tightened and her head shook. "Jud, your hair is too long!"

"Gotta hide your losses."

The two old friends laughed.

"I'm sorry," said Jud. "This is my friend Nick Kelley."

Mrs. Collin's handshake was dry and firm.

"Did you read the book *Flight of the Wolf*?" Jud asked. Nick felt his neck flush. "See the movie? Nick wrote that book."

"How very nice," said the proper old woman.

"Thank you," said Nick, certain she'd experienced no consequence of his imagination, bored with this social encounter.

"Mrs. Collin, tell Nick what you did. Where we met."

"I was a White House telephone operator," she said. "Last five years, I was nightshift supervisor."

"Are you guarding the new President?" she asked Jud.

The sidewalk opened under Nick's feet.

"I don't work those assignments anymore," answered Jud.

"You Secret Service agents are all such lovely young men," she said. "Come visit me. I'm in the phone book."

"If I get some time, of course I will," said Jud.

"It was nice to meet you, Mr. Kelley." She smiled. "I shall look for you in the bookstore. I never forget a name."

With a farewell smile, she tapped her way up the street.

"Secret Service?" Nick said to Jud.

"Everyone was somebody before." Jud roared with laughter, clapped Nick on the back so hard Nick staggered.

"Surprised?" said Jud. Then he laughed again and lectured on nothing and everything as he led Nick to the café.

"Really," said Jud when they sat at the table, "*Wolf* was a good book. You wrote it young and made a lot up, didn't you?"

"It's a novel." Nick shrugged.

"But it's about *something*. I hate books that are about nothing."

"Me, too."

"What did you use? Two, three reference books about the CIA, faked the rest, right?"

"I used what I could." Nick wanted to yell that three years earlier, in 1973 when he was twenty-four, there were only three good books on the CIA and no one who'd talk. Certainly not in Michigan.

"Don't get me wrong. I liked it. It had an attitude."

The waiter put chilled mugs of beer on the table. Nick beat back his irrational impulses to storm out or beg forgiveness from this critical stranger. Jud took a long pull from his beer.

"Hey!" said Jud, lifting the nylon gym bag from the floor to his lap. "Almost forgot." He reached inside the bag.

"You're a writer," he said, pulling out a thick gold metal pen, handing it to Nick. "What do you think of this pen?"

"Looks fine."

"No, try it. Go ahead."

Nick sighed: *Get it over with.* He took the heavy metal pen. Twisted the top and the point emerged. He scrawled blue lines and circles on his white napkin.

"Works."

"Does, doesn't it?" said Jud, taking it back.

He unscrewed the top. Unscrewed the cap holding the refill cartridge. Shook half a dozen sawtooth-ended, three-inch strips of metal onto the tablecloth.

"Picking locks isn't like in the movies." Jud held up one of the metal strips. "This is a pick, small, but it'll work. Lock-picking is a two-tooled job. You need a tension bar to pressure the bolt while you use the pick to manipulate the tumblers."

Jud stuck the jagged end of one of the picks crossways in a vise slot of the pen, tighted the grip.

"The picks double as tension bars." He handed the apparatus to Nick. "I made it myself."

*If you didn't,* thought Nick, turning the machine over in his finger, *who did? Why do you have this?*

"I'll teach you how to pick locks," said Jud. "If you want."

"Sure!" said Nick.

Jud smiled. "I need the pen."

The secret tool rested lightly in Nick's hand, real metal of the kind that before tonight—before Jud—he'd only touched in his imagination or spun into his books. Reluctantly, he passed the pen to the man across the table. Jud turned his toys back into innocence just as the waiter delivered two steaming burrito dinners. Nick declined another beer, then so did Jud.

"What did you do in the White House?" asked Nick.

"During Watergate? I stayed out of jail."

Jud laughed; Nick joined him.

"Who'd believe this world?" said Jud.

"Seriously," said Nick. "What about the Secret Service?"

"Want to see my résumé?"

Nick blinked. "Ah, sure."

From the gym bag came a printed sheet, with Jud's suit-and-tied picture in the middle. Nick skimmed the lines: Army, Special Forces, Secret Service. Phrases like "technical security."

"That's a piece of paper," said Jud, folding it into the bag. "I used it once. Have you ever seen one of these?"

Jud passed a hand-sized, red-covered folder to Nick.

Who frowned, said, "A passport."

"A *diplomatic* passport," corrected Jud.

Nick leaned out of reach, opened the folder.

"It's me, isn't it?" said Jud. He held out his hand.

Nick flipped pages. Entrance and exit stamps. Someplace called—

Gently, Jud lifted the folder from Nick's fingers.

"That's interesting," said Nick as the passport dropped into the red gym bag.

A stunning blonde with a whiny coat-and-tied man in horn-rimmed glasses brushed past their table.

"No, *that's* interesting," whispered Jud. He chuckled. Kept an arctic smile on the couple as they sat across the room.

"Women," said Jud. "They're such bullshit, aren't they?"

So they talked about women, how beautiful they were and why the great ones always seemed to end up with jerks. The waiter laid the bill on the table. Jud reached for it, but Nick beat him.

"I'll call it an educational expense," said Nick.

"Submit it to Murphy." Jud smiled when he said the columnist's name.

"This will come out of my other professional pocket. To charge it to Peter, you'd have to help me on some story."

"Ah," said Jud.

Outside, streetlights and neon made M Street glow. Amplified rock music thumped from a guaranteed-totally-nude go-go bar. Nick raised his hand toward a cab but Jud stopped him.

"We agreed I'd give you a ride home."

"Thought I'd save you the trouble."

"No trouble," said Jud.

They walked to a van parked by Murphy's office. The vehicle smelled of oil and rust. Machine parts clanked in bins as they motored toward Capitol Hill. They passed the White House, the Treasury building. The glistening dome of the Capitol came into sight, a view that always quickened Nick's heart. The same scene was on his high school government textbook.

As the van climbed up the Hill, Nick realized Jud hadn't asked where he lived.

"That your place?" said Jud, pointing to the apartment building six blocks off congressional turf. He pulled over.

"Yes," said Nick; thought, *But you already know that.*

Jud shut off the van. "Let's see how my pen works."

At the building's entrance, he told Nick, "You get this door. Don't do your shit on the street if you don't have to."

Even Nick knew the frontdoor lock was simple. He led Jud down the hall. Deliberately didn't check his locked mailbox in the foyer's yellow stucco wall. Climbed the stairs to his second-story rear apartment and double-locked blue door.

"Hold this, will you?" Jud handed him the red nylon gym bag. Zipped closed. It weighed about ten pounds. A passport, a résumé. The pen was metamorphosing in Jud's hand.

"Time me," said Jud. He slid a pick into the lock.

By the sweep of Nick's second hand, thirty-three seconds later came a faint click. Jud grinned.

"Don't stop the clock," he said. "Not till it's over."

The knob lock took Jud fifteen seconds. He opened the door.

"Welcome home," said Jud.

Nick's bowels turned cold.

"Nice," said Jud, standing in the tiled living room, his eyes scanning the museum prints, the stereo and albums, crammed bookcases, and thrift-store furniture. "Your office back there?" Jud walked toward the kitchen, looked in the room with its desk and typewriter, stacks of books and paper.

"Yes," said Nick. He could make it out the door before Jud could reach him. If he had to run.

Jud ignored the dining room and kitchen, came back to the living room. He pointed to a doorway opposite the entrance.

"Your bedroom?" he asked.

Nick didn't reply.

A newly arrived British edition of *Flight of the Wolf* lay on the couch. The jacket was identical to the American edition. Jud grinned at the author's picture, held it up for Nick to see.

"Looks just like you," he said of the photo Janey had snapped one Michigan December morn. "No wonder I knew who you were.

"It says," continued Jud, "you studied karate and judo."

"True," said Nick, who'd regretted telling that to the publisher as soon as he saw the book jacket.

"Tae kwon do?" said Jud, putting down the book.

Nick took a step back. Kept his eyes on Jud, put the nylon gym bag on the floor. "Yes. Some shudo kan."

"How far did you get?"

"Not far." Two years of judo. Two years of karate. It'd been a year since he'd been in a dojo. He tried to relax, wait.

"Tae kwon do isn't bad," said Jud. Six feet separated them. "Dogmatic and linear, but okay. I'm a China kinda guy, Southern Shaolin, mix in other disciplines. Let me show you."

He slipped off his shoes and socks.

*You're still in charge,* Nick told himself. He slipped off his shoes and socks, pushed away some of the furniture.

"Get in your fighting stance."

All Nick needed to do was raise his hands.

*Outweighs me by seventy, eighty pounds,* thought Nick. *Can't all be fat, can't all be slow.*

*Can't all be great, either. If,* thought Nick, *you win or you die.*

"I'll do straight Shaolin, let you see that," said Jud. "We'll take it easy. Don't worry."

Like in the dojo, thought Nick. Nothing to fear. Three-quarters speed. No contact. Pulled punches. To learn. For fun.

Jud stood still, arms at his sides.

"Go ahead," he told Nick. "Take your best shots."

Nick snap-kicked toward Jud's stomach, half feint, and Jud wasn't there. Nick punched for the chest to draw out Jud's block;

did so and snapped back his fist, chopped with his left to block a back fist that turned into a parry knocking his chop away. Nick countered with another right punch.

The bear grabbed it, pulled. Jud's right foot thumped into Nick's chest, then Jud sank into a squat and hooked his right leg behind Nick's, swept Nick's feet into the air.

Nick crashed onto his living room tiles.

Clarity returned. Nick blinked. Saw Jud's hand in front of his face. Froze.

Jud plucked Nick off the floor as if he were a pillow.

"Not bad," said Jud, "but do you see what I mean about linear? This time, I'll mix it up a little."

Nick went full speed. Jud seemed to move slower. He blocked Nick's punch, stuck to his arm, said, "Block, and then aikido," and he led Nick forward. Lightly touched his sternum. A giant hand uprooted Nick, pushed him through the air. He flew six feet straight back, hit the wall with his heels half a foot above the baseboards, then crashed to his hands and knees.

Again and again. Attacks and counterattacks. Nick fought as hard as he could, his body tiring and sore. Carefully lecturing, never straining, Jud would "break" Nick's elbow, tap his throat or eyes or the ribs above his heart, pull Nick's punch into an immobilizing arm bar. Jud turned his fingers into a parrot's beak; drove that hook into a nerve near Nick's collarbone that novaed the world and dropped Nick like a stone. Jud dissolved before Nick's punches, then stole Nick's *chi,* used it to throw him back like God sweeping away table scraps.

Nick refused to show pain. Never said stop.

"What time is it?" Jud asked suddenly. He held up an empty wrist. "I hate clocks."

On the floor, Nick glanced at his watch. "Ten thirty-two."

"Hell," said Jud, "I got to go."

He helped Nick up.

"This was fun," said Jud. "Maybe we'll do it again."

He walked to the door.

"Oops!" He turned back, picked up his gym bag of secret gear. "Wouldn't it have been funny if I forgot this?"

"Yeah," said Nick, his heart hammering his ribs.

He drew a normal breath; another. With that air came the realization that a power in which he'd believed but never known had now been met; hell, the power had held him like a doll in its hand.

"Take care, Bro'," said Jud. As he stood in the open exit, he looked back, smiled. "Be sure to lock your door."

||||||||||||||||||||||||||||||||||||||||||||||||||||||||||||||||||||||||||||||||||||||||||||||||||

# HALO

In the spring of 1990, the road beneath the wheels of Jud's stolen car angled northeast from L.A. The sky turned gray with the coming dawn. He figured he had a few hours yet before this Chevy was reported stolen and logged into the highway patrol's computer. Not much time, and he didn't know if he could stay awake to use it.

A green exit sign said REST STOP. He pulled in, rolled past semi trucks, their drivers napping in cab bunks. A Doberman pinscher poked his head above one semi's steering wheel.

Never liked big trucks anyway, thought Jud.

A man in a cowboy hat shuffled into the bathroom from a cattle truck loaded with battered furniture. No one else was in the truck. Jud parked, grabbed his bags, and hurried toward that vehicle. He'd worn cotton gloves ever since stealing the car in L.A. If he could make this E&E improve, he'd leave no trail. A blackboard blocked the truck's rear window. Jud threw his bags in the cargo box and crawled over the side. He settled in the shadows, between a battered rocker and a musty couch.

*Don't check,* he prayed. Don't check, he willed.

The driver didn't. Came back and pulled the truck into the highway, drove it down the road. Two miles later, Jud stretched out on the couch. He drifted to sleep. Cold wind rushed around him, carried him to dreams of warmer days. . . .

Saigon, 1969. The damp city smelled like barbecuing fish and diesel fumes. And just a whiff of nerves. The enemy's Tet

Offensive was more than a year-gone history. That countrywide chaos was a political victory but a military defeat for the guerrilla Viet Cong and their North Vietnamese Regular Army buddies: this was one tough, strange little war.

But life went on in Saigon, as if Tet had only been a passing show, a bad moment before Act Three when the Good Guys would win. True, there'd been a secret revolt in the American military's high command in '67 because the Joint Chiefs of Staff felt there was no coherent *policy* in this *conflict* they were commanding, but cooler heads had prevailed, the Joint Chiefs called off their mass resignation, and their revolt stayed secret, even after Tet. In Saigon on this September day in 1969, the program was to win the war, whatever winning meant.

But as Jud sat on a couch in the living room of House 12, a mustard-colored dwelling surrounded by a high wall just off Rue Louis Pasteur, sharing warm Vietnamese beer with two other Americans, his mind was on immediate personal survival, not foreign-policy abstractions.

Officially, Jud wasn't in Vietnam. Officially, he was a sergeant in the 5th Special Forces, the U.S. Army's elite Green Beret counterinsurgency unit beloved by murdered President Kennedy and the CIA and hated by the Regular Army. Officially, Jud was stationed with a Green Beret logistics support team in the Philippines.

In reality, Jud was assigned to MACV-SOG—Military Area Command, Vietnam—Studies & Observation Group, a low-profile group drawn from all branches of the military and the CIA that was officially studying the lessons of the Vietnam war. In reality, SOG was an ultrasecret spy and clandestine warfare unit charged with everything from in-country reconnaissance to infiltrating mainland China, from prisoner-of-war rescues to assassinations.

Neither Jud nor the two men he was drinking beer with were in uniform. If they had been, they would all have worn green berets and paratrooper wings, yet another level of sophistication separating them from most of the half a million other American soldiers then in Vietnam.

If Jud and the men in the living room of that SOG safehouse had officially existed.

Jud had only met these men that afternoon. They exchanged

first names and the sly smiles of a fraternity secret even to its own members, kept everything else on the anonymous bullshit level. The closest Jud came to mentioning the incident that he'd been ordered down to House 12 from Da Nang to explain was when he told his two new asshole buddies that this was *one fucking weird war.* He'd started to tell a lie about his romantic conquests during his brief junior-college career when a trim man in a suit strolled into the living room.

"Captain," said one of the men, and they all rose.

"As you were," said the officer. He had blond hair and blue eyes, a small scar on his cheek. He was maybe thirty to Jud's twenty-one. He carried a manila envelope.

"We're ready for you in there, Sergeant," he told Jud, nodding toward the back-room office.

As they reached the door, the captain said, "Don't worry about this bullshit. Piece of cake, pro forma."

He smiled. "And congratulations. Your R and R request has been approved."

The captain handed Jud the sealed manila envelope.

Jud hadn't made a Rest and Recreation request.

"Call me Art," the captain told Jud.

"Come in, gentlemen," said a voice in the back room.

The captain named Art had been right: Jud's debriefing that afternoon had been a piece of cake. Bullshit. Afterward, Jud opened the manila envelope, found the commercial airline tickets, and orders he burned after reading. He had time to pick up his bag, catch the sunset flight.

To Vientiane, Laos.

When Jud arrived, he went to the White Rose bar, where a naked girl danced on tabletops and garnered tips from the sports-shirt-clad Americans by holding lit cigarettes in her vagina. She was up to four cigarettes at once when the captain from House 12 strolled in, wearing a different tropical suit. He glanced toward Jud's table, went to the bar. Had a quick drink. Left. Jud strolled outside in his wake.

"Here," came Art's voice from a bicycle rickshaw.

Art took Jud to Rendez-vous des Amis, Madame Lulu's brothel where that French septuagenarian schooled shy Laotian girls in the art of fellatio. They walked past the downstairs parlor where the pancake made-up proprietress poured Scotch for her customers while they picked their pleasure, climbed two flights of stairs to the roof.

They walked out to the edge. Vientiane smelled of foliage. The lights of the city were scattered and few compared to Saigon. A Ford Bronco was parked in the street below.

A man in a white linen sports jacket stepped out of the roof's shadows and shook their hands with a clammy grip.

He was an American. Art was blond; the man in the linen suit was paler, almost an albino in skin color and translucent white hair, a ghost with blue eyes.

"Look over there," said Ghostman. "Those lights are the Chinese embassy. Russians are here. Uncle Ho's diplomats. There's even a Pathet Lao legation a few hundred meters from our embassy. We're all very polite."

"This is our war, and we're winning it our way," boasted Ghostman. "We're doing a better job with five hundred CIA officers than half a million GIs are doing in Vietnam. They shouldn't have taken that war away from us. Our Laos is cost-effective foreign policy."

Something stirred in the shadows on the roof.

The man in the white linen jacket whirled, jerking a Browning 9mm from a shoulder holster.

"Just a gecko," said Art, shaking his head to Jud.

"I know what it is, Monterastelli!" snapped the CIA man.

And Jud smiled: now he had the full name—Capt. Art Monterastelli.

*We're more equal now,* thought Jud.

"Don't want to kill him," said Ghostman as the lizard scurried away. "The French say that's the start of sickness, the sign that it's time to leave Asia. When you start killing geckos."

"It isn't geckos you want dead," said Jud.

"No shit," said Ghostman. He holstered the pistol, pulled a marijuana cigarette from his shirt. "Want some?"

"I don't smoke," said Jud.

Ghostman laughed. "Of course you don't! You aren't even here! None of us are! There's one senior officer in SOG who knows this nitty-gritty, plus we three stooges on a whorehouse roof."

"Who's the senior officer?" asked Jud.

"You don't need to know," said the CIA liaison. He clicked a

Zippo lighter: Capt. Art Monterastelli and Jud stepped away from that flicker of flame.

"Now who's paranoid?" said Ghostman.

"Sergeant Stuart," he said, "the people who count know what a fine job you've done. Damn good. You're the kind of man America can depend on. We think you're our kind of man. We've had our eye on you. We think you're ready for the big time."

"Is that what this is?" said Jud, resisting the urge to challenge Ghostman's arrogance with a dozen examples of past exploits.

Art kept his gaze flat. He had a boyish face.

"God, this is a backwater!" Ghostman said. "These people believe there's spirits everywhere—in rocks, our airplanes, people. Call it *phi*."

A man moaned in a room downstairs.

"We want you to do something for us," said Ghostman. "It's risky, catch-as-catch-can. It's vital. It's gotta stay buried deep. We think you can do it. If you don't think you can handle it, if you say no"—he shrugged—"we'll understand."

Then they told him what they wanted.

Two months later, Jud was in the belly of a B-52 bomber, 43,000 feet above enemy North Vietnam: 2322 hours, 19 November, 1969. The plane had a skeleton flight crew of four American fly-boys, the right number for this moonless night's mission.

The plane shuddered as its payload sailed down to earth.

*Cold.* Jud was so cold.

Cramped, sitting on the bomb-bay rack, he'd been embraced by the cold, numbed by it and by the drone of the jet's engines. The metallic air he breathed through his oxygen mask chilled his lungs. When the bomb-bay doors cranked open, he'd looked through the steel catwalk under his boots, watched giant, finned barrels roll out into blackness.

One one-thousand. Two one-thousand.

The bomb-bay doors stayed open. In the dim red light, Jud imagined he could see through the goggles and oxygen masks to the eyes of the five men sitting beside him. The four Nungs would show all white. Their throats were dry, like his; their pants wet, like his wanted to be. Next to them was Curtain, the one-one to Jud's one-zero. Curtain was second-in-command. He and Jud filled out the crew's official full-strength quota, in case Uncle Ho's boys got lucky with one of their Soviet surface-to-air missiles and they had to play it as a normal mission. And *don't think* about the Nungs, *don't think* about what would happen to them in the chaos between enemy hit and bailout or impact.

*What are you thinking, Curtain?* Jud wondered. *What's in your heart?*

Twenty-three one-thousand. Twenty-four one-thousand.

Curtain could see no better in the light silence than Jud. He was just as cold. *God knows what the Nungs feel,* thought Jud. *This must be colder than any grave they ever dreamt.*

Thirty-one one-thousand. Thirty-two one-thousand.

The plane arced, turned south and west, pushing Jud back against his main parachute. G forces sucked Jud's aching guts.

Forty-two one-thousand. Forty-three one-thousand.

Back toward the tail, in the swirling blackness below: silent orange mushroom flashes.

*Everything's fine,* thought Jud. He remembered a sign on the door of the restaurant where he'd worked during high school: PROPER ATTIRE REQUIRED. *No shit,* thought Jud.

That night Jud wore full thermal long underwear. Double socks. Nylon gloves covered by wool gloves with the fingers cut out—risky but he'd need the flexibility. Next came black ski gloves. Jud had the sergeant major wrap black duct tape from the nylon cuff of each ski glove to Jud's forearms. They knew about another mission in which the wind had ripped the team leader's right glove off at 40,000 feet. His Number Two had seen it go, seen the leader's hand curl and crack and his fingers freeze solid, snap off. The man went into shock, tumbled in without pulling a cord. No one on *his* team would die that way, vowed Jud. Over his thermals, Jud wore a black jumpsuit with black zippers, Velcro flaps. Jungle boots. Over his head, Jud slipped a skintight black hood, with eye holes and mouth slit. A second hood went over that, then an extralarge jump helmet.

"Your HALO gear costs two-plus grand," the instructor had announced during training. "Secure your DZ, then bury that shit."

Jud strapped an altimeter to each wrist, stuffed a third one into a chest pocket, fastened the Velcro of the pocket shut, and tied the altimeter's cord around his neck. The wind ate the only altimeter carried by Milder, so he'd had to guess when to pull. He guessed wrong, popped open a mile too high (falling at 185 mph, who could blame him?)—which meant a patrol spotted him. The patrol missed seeing the rest of the team drop, and they got Milder back, but it cost the mission and an arm for Milder.

They wouldn't hit the ground. Not at first. First was the jungle, five canopy layers, steam rising from emerald-green trees full of bone-eating bugs and ten-step snakes. Perfumed flowers and rotting swamp. Tigers usually weren't a problem. They'd crash through the trees until the branches grabbed the chutes and left them dangling, swinging in the moonless night while monkeys screamed and birds took wing and God *please* let any patrols think it was just another jungle jump-up and God *please* don't let there be any patrols, there weren't supposed to be. Not tonight. Not according to the briefing given Jud and Curtain.

Jud had strapped a knife to his right boot. A second knife hung butt down from a sheath above his heart. For safety, he carried a razor knife in a zippered side pocket. To cut free of the chute, to let him use the three hundred feet of climbing rope packed ready to spill out from his waist under his reserve chute.

Jud looked over at the Nungs—men whose ancestors had walked from China to Southeast Asia. These four had not done their ancestors proud. Murderers and thieves, they'd looked up from their North Vietnam death-row prison hole weeks ago and there had been Jud, beckoning, the cell door swinging open, their jailer slumped against a far wall. They'd gone, believing there was no worse hell than the cell.

Now, huddled in the belly of the B-52, Jud wagered they weren't so sure. There'd been ten. The handlers washed four out right away; where they went, Jud didn't know. Number five washed out because he couldn't learn enough about weapons. The sixth left when Jud saw the wrong terror in his eyes. That left four, the mission needed four, so Jud made them make it. Babied them through their only other parachute drop: hooked up to an open canopy before dawn when the other troops at the Okinawa jump school slept, then shoved off the platform for a three-hundred foot controlled drop to the sand.

"Tell 'em it's like Disneyland," Jud ordered the interpreter who was coaxing the Nungs onto the jump platform. Jud spoke almost none of the Nungs' dialect; gambled on hand signs, obvious common interest, and their hunger to interpret divine will to get the team through the mission. "Tell 'em anything, but make sure they understand I am head fuckin' Mickey Mouse."

No one mentioned High-Altitude, Low-Opening alternatives.

They'd been on three patrols together, trial runs based from Da Nang, safaris into Indian country. The Nungs showed a crook's instincts for stealth, slaughter, and survival. They slept in a circle with Jud at the center—their choice. He rewarded them with beer and Thai whores who didn't speak their dialect.

Crouched now on the plane, Jud shifted his weight and felt the black canvas bag on his shoulder that held his silenced Russian AK-47. In a shoulder holster underneath his jumpsuit was a fourteen-shot, Smith & Wesson 9mm automatic. A holster on his belt cradled a .45 automatic. He'd rigged a holster next to his naked left thigh for a two-shot derringer guaranteed to put a .22 long inside your skull and keep it bouncing around until your brain turned to mush. The derringer's slugs were coated with shellfish toxin from the same Langley lab that in 1960 dispatched lethal bacteria to an assassination team targeting Congolese nationalist leader Patrice Lumumba. Jud could pull the trigger without drawing the derringer, send a slug into his leg. The Wizards promised him results in sixty seconds and didn't know Jud knew they lied about the agony.

A black nylon HALO chute and special breathing apparatus rode on the team's backs. Oxygen masks had been rigged into the bomb bay for the flight, but no internal radio links.

We have no need to talk anyway, Jud thought, remembering when he and Curtain met the B-52's crew, told them sketchy cover stories, and memorized trivia about each of the fly-boys to con an NVA interrogator into thinking Curtain and Jud belonged on the plane. Photos of Jud and Curtain with girls and football buddies were taped on the plane wall, just as two real crewmen might have done. Faked pictures, faked girlfriends. In case the bomber survived being shot down.

*Don't think about anything you don't need to think about,* Jud warned himself, and he remembered a girl in high school he'd never dared to talk to.

Panic seized Jud: What if he couldn't understand the asset waiting for them on the ground? The asset was a survivor of two groups of North Vietnamese the CIA smuggled out of Haiphong in 1955, trained in Saigon, then sent back to the communist north.

He was supposed to speak French and English, plus Curtain spoke beaucoup Vietnamese, but what if the asset didn't make it to the rendezvous? What if Jud couldn't see the amber light that was supposed to be flashing through the trees to guide them to the DZ? What if the asset had been picked up, hot-ironed, and hell, what if he wasn't an asset? Double, NVA, Pathet Lao, or even Chinese? What if he just fucked up? What if—

*Then,* Jud told himself, pulling it all down to one word he could manage, one word he could keep from mutating into a million shapes and sounds: *then.*

Two red dots glowing in the bomb bay violated light silence and let Jud see not much, not far. But enough to realize the Nungs had joined hands, each gripping the hand of a man from their tribe whom they might not care about but whose fate they were destined to share. Jud reached out, gripped the free hand of the Nung next to him, raised it. The Nungs stared. Curtain made the chain complete. Slowly, all the joined hands rose, triumphant. Jud felt energy flow through their chain, knew the Nungs felt it, too. The right move at the right moment, and even if it wasn't, what the hell, Jud loved the energy, too.

He was already linked to the two Nungs closest to him, as was Curtain to the other two. Two clusters of three men, each cluster bonded with a rope. Jud had tied the Nungs twenty feet apart, giving Curtain and himself more slack. The Nungs only knew they were going to jump, that it would be like on the tower. That they would fall a long time, then Jud would pull himself in close, cut their daisy chain, and jerk their rip cords before he popped himself. Jud knew they thought the free-fall would last about ten seconds. If he'd told them three minutes, they would never have jumped. The plan called for them to panic, falling, blackness all around, the wind rushing, the cold . . . freeze-up. They'd drop like stones. If they didn't panic enough, one of them might find his rip cord, and they'd all be jerked out of free-fall, too much weight for one too-soon chute, tumbling out of control. . . .

*That happens,* Jud told himself, *you can still cut free. You'll have time. Cut free, stabilize, skim away like a bird. Pop your chute, improvise a ground plan. You mind will be clear and your will won't fail you.*

Someone tapped his left shoulder. He looked up into the body of the plane and saw the copilot, oxygen mask, safety line. The copilot made the okay sign, then in the air drew an *L.*

Laos.

Jud stood. Watched his team follow him, watched them remove the plane's oxygen masks and affix their own self-contained breathing apparatuses. Again Jud grabbed the hand of the Nung behind him, had that man do the same, only this time the chain was two separate sections, with Curtain leading the second group. Jud was One-Zero, so first out. The copilot pulled away the catwalk's rope railing. The steel grate trembled beneath Jud's feet. The giant bomber pitched and swayed, dropping down to 41,000 feet. Jud fought to keep his balance and not tumble into the open blackness. The cold rushed in through the bomb-bay doors. Wrapped in his layers of clothing and gear, Jud was sweating. And he was cold.

Down the line, he saw Curtain's black form. Jud pointed his forefinger at him, and Curtain nodded.

*I'll see you on the ground,* thought Jud. *I'll see you then.*

The copilot's hand chopped up and down, a metronome counting off seconds relayed over the intercom to him by the pilot as Jud and his team watched. Beat. Beat. Beat. Beat.

He hit Jud's shoulder.

And Jud rolled off to his left, his daisy chain slipping behind him into the roar of wind and jet engines, followed without a skipping beat by Curtain's group. The copilot watched them spin away into swirling blackness and cold and thought of penguins diving off an ice floe, of lemmings.

Cold. Black, timeless cold.

Jud hit the ground.

*"What hell you doing in my truck!"* roared a God voice in the clouds of Jud's mind. Jud was on his back, on sand, the shoulder of a road, sunshine warmer than his dream, blue sky . . .

*"Who hell you think you are up there anyway?"*

A wiry old man in a battered straw Stetson, faded print shirt, and jeans with their cuffs tucked into scruffy black boots stood beside the junk-filled cattle truck, staring down and screaming at the bum he'd just rolled off his scavenged treasures.

Pain squeezed his whole body. Jud moaned.

"You big bum! Hope ——— Christ you broke goddamned back!"

The sun was two hands over the horizon, burning into Jud's eyes. He squinted at the gap-tooth mouth yelling at him.

The old man was Vietnamese.

In tacky cowboy gear. Jud fought back the urge to sweep the old man's feet, realized he probably couldn't do it anyway.

"Just needed a ride," Jud said, sitting up.

"Need ride! Need ride!" The old man's eyes found Jud's bags in the truck's cargo box. "Hah!" Like a monkey, he scrambled into the cargo box, threw Jud's bags at him. "These need ride, too, yes! Hah!" Scrambled back to earth.

The desert, thought Jud. Flat, scrub brush, brown. Sawtooth, powder-blue mountains for a horizon. A big empty.

"Everybody need ride! Nobody pay! Nobody give me!"

About a mile ahead, across the two-lane blacktop road: a cluster of buildings, a trailer house. Café? Gas station?

"Do you know what time it is?" asked Jud.

"What time? All same time for you. Is now. No time."

The old man tipped back his hat, hooked his thumbs in his belt like he'd seen *true cowboys* do in Caliente, Nevada, USA.

"You pay me, bum, I take you up road with me."

*Dien cai dau!* Jud wanted to say, but his lips were dry. Nature saves your cover, he realized. He floated back to Saigon. Never let the other guy see you lose control. Never dignify him with a curse. Keep your face and rob him of his.

"No thanks," said Jud. "Right here is fine."

"Hah!" The old man spit in the sand between them. "No thanks. You mean no money. No money, no nothing."

He stomped to the cab of the truck, spun a cloud of dirt and sand over Jud as he roared back onto the highway. Gone.

The dust cloud settled. Jud sat by the side of the empty desert road. Tumbleweeds bounced past him. Sage and sand tinged the air. A lake mirage shimmered on the blacktop between his Buddha in the dust and the buildings a thousand meters hence. Something flicked in the corner of his eye—a jackrabbit—then it was gone, back in the scrub brush. The desert. Not like the high dry of Iran. Its own place. This desert. Is now.

He rose, ignored his thirst and his pains, the heat flowing to the land. Bags in hand, shuffle in his step, he circled away from the highway and looped toward the buildings.

Two cardinal rules of Escape & Evasion are Don't Be Seen, and when that maneuver fails, Don't Be Noticed. Jud stopped next to a cluster of brush fifty meters from the café. A wooden sign dangled from a post above the door, black letters burned into weathered pine: NORA'S. Half a dozen cars were parked between the front of the building and two gas pumps. Jud's stomach rumbled. But if that many people saw him, that many people would notice him.

Behind the café, a battered trailer house pointed like a finger into the desert. Beyond it was a squat adobe house, flowers planted beneath brightly curtained windows.

The cars left over the course of what Jud estimated to be a half hour. Five cars carried men, one ferried two women who wore head scarves over blue-gray hair. No new cars arrived. No delivery trucks from bakeries or beer companies. No fuel haulers came to refill the pumps. No station wagon driven by a deserted housemom came by with a fresh load of newspapers for the three metal vending machines by Nora's front door.

The screen door creaked when Jud stepped inside, out of the eye of the world. A woman with curly, faded-blond hair trimmed below her jaw sat at the counter, reading a newspaper. Alone. Swinging doors led back into the kitchen. Her face was tan and pretty, with time lines in the corners of her wide-spaced blue eyes. Her white blouse and pants were not a waitress uniform. Jud filled her eyes, then she looked over his shoulder, saw *no vehicle* out here in the big nowhere.

"I can pay," he said quickly.

"Looks like you already have." Her voice was husky from too many cigarettes. "What do you need?"

"Are you Nora?" asked Jud.

"Sure." She smiled. "What can I do for you?"

"Can I have breakfast? Lots of breakfast? And coffee?"

"Sit down," said Nora, standing. She moved with easy grace. "I'll bring you coffee and a menu."

While she disappeared into the kitchen, Jud took a stool at the counter that let him watch the door. A fly buzzed across the room. From the kitchen came whispers of daytime TV, a portable black-and-white with a coat-hanger antenna. The screen door banged once, twice, hung silent. Jud smelled grease and bacon, fried eggs, beans. Three stools around the horseshoe counter still had dirty dishes in front of them. One of the booths along the wall and one of the small tables hadn't been cleared either.

"'Scuse the mess," said Nora as she pushed through the swinging doors. "My cleanup man skedaddled with the wind."

"Gone," said Jud.

"Good 'n' gone." Nora put a mug of coffee in front of Jud, slid over a creamer and sugar shaker.

"Where . . . ," said Jud, hesitated to not seem dumb (and noticable), then figured what the hell. "Where is this?"

She smiled. "You're on Route One Twenty-seven halfway between Baker and Shoshone. Death Valley's up ahead. Nevada ain't far. I didn't like this place's name, so I gave it mine."

"Good as any."

"That's right." She handed him a menu. "Take your time."

"Can't decide," confessed Jud.

"How's your stomach?" she asked.

"Strong." He sighed. "Whipped."

*Huevos rancheros,*" she told him. "Not too spicy and Carmen can cook that real good. Giant orange juice. Home fries on the side. Run you about six bucks."

She took his order into the kitchen, then turned on the air conditioner above the door and went back to her newspaper. Jud slumped on his stool. A squat Mexican woman in blue jeans and a pink sweatshirt padded through the swinging doors. She wrinkled her nose at Jud, put steaming plates of fried eggs over beans and tortillas and greasy potatoes in front of him. Nora brought him a glass of orange juice, a napkin, and silverware. Jud had cleaned half his plate before Carmen made it back to the kitchen to turn the volume up on her daytime serial in which everyone was beautiful and before Nora finished the wire service story about a new wave of genocide in Cambodia.

When Jud was on his fourth cup of coffee, three aspirin and a trip to the bathroom under his belt, car tires crunched gravel out front.

A white Cadillac parked by the door.

The driver swaggered inside. He was further into his forties than Jud. Like Jud, he carried too much beef between his chin and his hips. His open-collared white shirt showed a gold chain, his sleeves showed the Rolex watch his cousin had snared in a Hong Kong alley for only fifty bucks. His hands were manicured, with one diamond ring. He wore gold slacks suitable for golf course or office, two-tone-brown, Italian-design loafers with tassels. His jowly face was salon and windshield tanned.

"Hi, honey," he called out to Nora.

She kept her eyes on her newspaper as he straddled a counter stool. Jud sat to his left, Nora off to his right.

"You talking to me, Harold?" she told him.

Harold panned the room; did a double take when he saw Jud's scruffy form slumped on a stool.

"I sure as hell ain't talking to *him,*" said Harold.

*Seen,* thought Jud.

"You should be more careful who you let in here," Harold told her, his eyes on Jud. "This place could lose its class."

*Noticed,* thought Jud.

"I can dream," said Nora. "You want something, Harold, or did you just crawl in off the desert to hide from the sun?"

"Oh, I want something, but how about a cup of coffee?"

"I got one, thanks," said Nora.

"What's a guy have to do to get some service around here?" said Harold.

The words that came out of Jud surprised him as much as they did Nora and Harold: "You could try asking nicely."

*Don't,* he warned himself. *Forget it.*

"Nobody asked you anything, *Fatboy,*" snapped Harold. He sniffed. "'Cept maybe when you had your last bath."

Jud dropped his eyes to his dirty plate. Breathed slowly. In, out. In, out. In. Out.

"You want some coffee, Harold?" said Nora, standing, moving behind the counter. "I'll get you some coffee."

"How 'bout sugar?" drawled Harold.

"Your one-cal stuff is on the counter."

As Nora stood at the coffee urn, Harold craned his neck so he could stare at her hips. He made sure Fatboy was watching him. Saw the pig body, matted hair, face bent down—and the whites of two eyes. *Good,* thought Harold. He flicked his gaze back to Nora, wondered if the geek appreciated the way her ass twitched.

She put the coffee in front of Harold.

"Hey, Nora," drawled Harold. "I knows some guys who know some guys in Vegas. Gambling money spills over state lines. I could fix you up with punchboards. The badges around here, they'd understand. They like you. Everybody likes you, Nora."

"Stick to wholesaling women's shoes, Harold," she told him. "I'll stick to Carmen's cooking and my coffee."

"Honey, I can't figure why a sweet woman like you runs a shithole like this."

"Guess it's so guys like you have a place to go."

The air conditioner gurgled, clanked; chugged on.

"So I see," said Harold, pointedly glaring at Jud.

"Come on, Harold"—she smiled—"lighten up."

"Hard to do around you," he said. He sipped his coffee. "You could damn near break a man's heart."

"I aim lower," promised Nora.

Jud laughed.

"What the hell you laughing at, *Fatboy!*" snapped Harold.

*Stop it there,* thought Jud, though he wasn't sure if he was talking to Harold or himself.

His gun was zipped in a bag on the floor.

"Somebody wants something out of you," snapped Harold, "somebody'll pull your chain."

"Harold," said Nora.

"We don't like bums like you around these parts," said Harold. *"Homeless,* my ass: bum. I know your kind. If you were any kind of decent man, you could get yourself a home. This is America, asshole. Not a junkyard for losers like you."

"You done with your coffee, Harold?" said Nora.

"Guy like me, I got a home. I got it all. I got me some friends on the Highway Patrol. And I got me a mind to tell 'em there's a bum loser *Fatboy* dragging his sorry ass around Highway One Two Seven. A walking sack of litter."

*You might do that,* thought Jud. *Burn me to play big man.*

The vision shimmered before him, pure and beautiful.

"We who are called upon to serve," he whispered.

"What did you say?" snapped Harold.

Jud kept his eyes down as he stood. He sensed Harold stiffen. Jud turned the other way, walked around behind the counter as Nora said, "You should have left long ago, Harold."

A gray plastic tub of dirty dishes, glasses, wadded napkins, soggy toast, cups, and soiled silverware sat on a shelf under the counter. Jud picked up the tub, kept his eyes down as he cleared away his dirty dishes.

"What the hell!" mumbled Harold. Nora frowned. Harold said,

"He's the damn hired help! Dishwasher Fatboy. Nora, don't you know business? Never let the hired help bug the customers."

"You're no customer of mine," she said.

Jud moved to the next dirty setting on the counter. He was four stools from where Harold sat.

"Honey," said Harold, "forget him. He's so gone he ain't even here. Carmen in back, plugged into her TV set, all that empty road, nobody else but us two: we could have a fine time."

"On the road, Harold," she mumbled, watching Jud.

"Someday it's gonna happen." Certitude and crumbling caution danced on Harold's face as his eyes ate her. "Nothing you can do about it, so you might as well relax and enjoy it."

"I'll be in my grave first," Nora snapped.

Jud wiped the counter with a rag from the tub. The next pile of dirty plates was on the other side of Harold. Jud put the rag back; kept his hand in the full gray plastic container, slid it along the counter. Toward Harold.

"Oh, hell, Nora!" said Harold, flashing his great teeth his palms flat on the counter. "Where's your sense of humor?"

Jud whirled from the plastic tub, stabbed a dirty table fork into the back of Harold's left hand.

Harold screamed.

And Jud leaned his *Fatboy* weight into the fork, the tongs piercing Harold's flesh. Harold screamed again, clawed at Jud's fist with his free hand only to have Jud slap it away. Jud wanted to push into the fork with everything he had, drive it down to China with his *chi*. Except he couldn't find his *chi* and he felt Nora's eyes on his back; felt her hurry behind the cash register by the door but not reach for the phone on the wall. Jud roared:

*"DON'T! FORK! WITH! ME!"*

"Please! Please! Please!" whimpered Harold. Streams of blood trickled across the back of his hand. Jud eased the pressure, but kept Harold pinned.

*"Please?* Pretty please? Pretty please with one-cal sweetener on it?"

"Yes! Yes! Anything! Anything!"

*"Everything,* asshole!" Jud used his gravel laugh. "You fucked with the wrong Fatboy, didn't you? And you're jerking her around and she's my friend. Now you're forked. Maybe I'll eat this

piece-of-shit hand. Maybe I won't. But you know what you'll be thinking if I let you go?"

"Nothing, honest, mister, I'm sorry, I won't think, I—"

"You better think! You better think and remember. You'll think about your *friends* on the Highway Patrol. Give 'em a call. Send 'em down here. I'll give 'em something to run through NCIC. Then they'll come after *you*. They got some *swell fellas* in San Quentin. You'll all get real tight, *honey.*"

"No! No cops! I won't—" Harold started to cry.

"You say you know some people who know some people in Vegas." Jud's voice dripped bile. He leaned on the fork. Harold paled. Blood trickled to the countertop. "You know Jimmy the Hump?"

"No," whispered Harold.

"You don't know Jimmy the Hump? Such a big man you are, Harold, and you fuckin' don't even know Jimmy the Hump. You've heard of him, though, haven't you Ha-rold?"

"I . . . Yeah, sure, everybody—"

"Everybody who's somebody knows Jimmy the Hump. But you don't. Go see the people you know who know people. Send 'em up the line with a message. Tell 'em I said for Jimmy to fork you good!"

"No, please, don't tell him! I won't—I'm sorry!"

"Sorry?"

"Sorry!" pleaded Harold.

Jud pulled the fork free. Harold moaned, cupped his bloody hand to his chest. His white shirt would be ruined. Jud tossed the fork into the tub. Harold couldn't move his feet.

"If I let you go," Jud explained to Harold, "I'll forget about you. You come back, I—or Nora—gets bothered . . ." Jud shrugged; graveled his voice: "Jimmy the Hump."

"I swear to God!"

"You got any business with him, Nora?" asked Jud. She stood behind the counter, hands out of sight, away from the phone.

"Today finished all our business," she said.

*"Harold?"* whispered Jud.

Harold couldn't help himself: he leaned close to the monster so he could hear.

"Fly," said Jud.

Stumbling, crashing through the screen door, Harold raced

outside. Threw up on the oiled parking lot. Tore away in his Caddy.

A minute of still silence passed.

"Sorry," said Jud. He wiped the blood off the counter, picked up the gray tub, marched it back to its place, rounded the counter, picked up his bags, and headed toward the door; toward the cash register and Nora.

"I'm really very sorry," he told her.

"No, you're not," she said.

"Well . . ." He shrugged. "At least Harold won't bother us."

"Who's Jimmy the Hump?"

"I don't know," said Jud.

Nora blinked. Laughed out loud. So did Jud.

"God!" she said. "I don't know whether to laugh or cry, scream . . ."

"Or shoot me," said Jud, finally figuring her hands, which he couldn't see beneath the counter.

"The thought crossed my mind," she said evenly.

"No quarrel there," he said.

"Who are you?" she asked.

"Just another refugee," he told her. Sighed. Started out the door, then stopped. His abruptness made her jerk, and he quickly said, "Sorry! I almost forgot to pay you for—"

"Forget it." She nodded to the cleared counter. "You worked it off." Shrugged. "Hell, entertainment."

"Thanks," he said. Started for the door again.

"Where you going?" she asked, stopping him.

"Nowhere."

"Without a car. In the desert. Got any money?"

"Haven't spent much so far."

"Haven't got much to spend, either."

"I'm a simple man."

"Spare me. Anybody looking for you?"

He gazed out the windows: a black snake highway through shifting sands, empty blue sky.

"I don't know," he said.

"I hope not." She sighed. "You knew what you were doing— cleaning the counter, I mean. You've worked restaurants before."

"Not for a couple lifetimes."

The air conditioner stuttered; clanked and chugged again.

"Thing is," she said, "I don't have a busboy, janitor. Gas jockey. Somebody good with his hands. And there's more than one Harold on this damn highway."

"That doesn't worry you," said Jud.

"Worry isn't my way of life," she said. "You're trouble. But sometimes . . . Sometimes trouble isn't so bad.

"You got nowhere to go, *refugee*. I need help. Pay is lousy. You get the trailer out back and all your meals 'cept Sunday dinner. We're closed then. Carmen makes good eats. You got trouble, keep it to yourself. I don't even want to know. And you don't want trouble from me.

"Also," she said, "there's no bar walking-close. And you're no good to me when you're no good at all."

"I think I've had enough to drink."

"That's today, but I got a nose. I see the shakes."

"They'll pass. I can make that happen."

"That's your load, not mine. We got a deal?"

Jud again looked out the windows. He ached all over. Out those windows, you could see someone coming a long way off.

"Sure," he told her. Set down his bags.

"Doesn't work out, you can always hit the road."

"Doesn't work out," said Jud, "you can always shoot me."

Nora smiled.

"That all you got?" she said, nodding to the gym bags.

"I travel light."

"Don't deal me cute," she said, then yelled, "Carmen!"

Two wide eyes appeared around the edge of the swinging doors: these were not the beautiful people.

"Enrique got any old clothes to loan . . ." Nora turned back to her new employee. "What's your name?"

"Jud." He didn't want to lie to her.

"Sure," said Nora. "Got clothes that would fit this guy?"

"Guy not big enough," said Carmen. She turned up her nose, but shrugged. Went back to the kitchen; to TV.

"When do I start?" asked Jud.

"Now," she told him. She left the register. Her blouse was out of her waistband. Might have happened in the excitement. Or her blouse might cover a pistol she'd palmed from the till.

Nora picked up her cup, headed back into the kitchen. Over her shoulder, she told Jud, "Don't forget the mess outside."

# WEREWOLF

The Monday morning after CIA Director Denton's party dawned gray above Nick Kelley's blue Victorian house with its black iron fence and more yard than he'd ever wanted to mow. The wind off the Chesapeake Bay some forty miles away was full of the March sea. Nick's windows rattled as he fed Saul scrambled eggs.

"Juanita will be here any minute," said Sylvia as she packed her briefcase with manila files and yellow legal pads.

The kitchen smelled of coffee, cinnamon rolls. Orange juice. The *Washington Post* lay scattered on the kitchen metal table. The big black dog waited beneath the baby's high chair.

Nick stirred Saul's fork in the eggs. The baby watched him warily. A Mozart piano concerto played on the radio.

"Where the hell are my keys?" said Sylvia.

Saul bobbed toward his mother.

Nick shoveled a forkful of eggs into his son.

"Here they are." Sylvia scooped a massive key chain off the kitchen counter. "Been a snake, they'd've bit me."

The baby beat his hands on the high-chair shelf.

"Look," said Sylvia, "I know you're worried about Jud." She sighed. "He's trouble."

"He is that," said Nick. He let Saul hold the fork.

"You don't need that trouble. You don't want it. Those days are over for you, the longer gone the better."

"I know."

"I know you want to help him," she said. "But there's nothing you can do. Nothing you should do. You owe him nothing."

Nick stared at her.

"We've talked about that," she replied.

"I know your opinion," he said.

"I know what I'm right about. You should take care of us. Of Saul and you and . . . This isn't a book you're writing, it's us. Our life. Don't. Just don't. Okay?"

Saul pulled the food toward his gaping mouth, but turned the fork upside down before it arrived at its destination. Eggs tumbled down his pajamas. The dog snapped them up before they hit the floor. Saul exploded in laughter.

"I'm sorry!" she said. "I don't mean to bitch or second-guess you, but you're not part of his bullshit. Never have been, never will be."

"Technically correct, Counselor," he told her.

"But true."

"True for a lawyer. But for these people, in that life, there's more than the law. There's who I am versus what they think I know and what I might do about that."

"But the law's the bottom line," argued Sylvia. "You know that. You believe that."

"*Hola!*" called a woman from the front hall. The front door slammed. "*Señora! Mi amor!*"

The dog barked and charged from the kitchen. The baby screeched in delight.

"*Hola, Juanita!*" yelled Sylvia, her eyes full of her husband and son. "*Estamos en la cocina!*"

She spoke quietly. "I know you want to do what's right, and I love you for it. But I love our life."

"Me, too," said Nick.

"Remember who you are!" she said. Her eyes were moist.

"How are you this morning!" said Juanita. The black dog trailed her into the kitchen. "Sorry I am late."

"We're fine," said Sylvia. "Maybe you could help Nick finish feeding him and—"

"I'll do it, honey. I want to."

Juanita saw a bridge of ice between husband and wife.

"I check the laundry," she said, and hurried to the basement. The dog followed her, paws clicking down the stairs.

"Nick, it's been over a week. Deal with the facts, not what you imagine. Nothing's happened—just another damn phone call in the middle of the night. If it was anything serious, he'd have called back."

"If he could."

She turned away from her husband's steady gaze.

"Don't go looking for trouble," she said.

"This time, I didn't. But I should do *something*."

"There's nothing you *can* do," insisted his wife.

Saul banged his hands on the tray. His parents looked at him; kept their eyes turned from each other.

"Which car do you want?" Sylvia asked softly.

"Doesn't matter. Take the Jeep, the heater is better."

"No, I can take the Ford."

Sylvia cuddled and kissed the baby; told Saul to be a good boy. Kissed Nick on the forehead. Left the kitchen.

Walked back in thirty seconds later as Nick navigated the fork into Saul's mouth for a successful food dump. She put her head on Nick's shoulder, her cheek pressed against his face. He smelled the coconut of her shampoo. He draped his free arm around her. Her hand pressed his back and her breath tickled him.

"Do what you're supposed to, not what I want. But I love you. You and Saul, I couldn't go on without—"

She stopped, kissed his neck. He kissed her lips.

"Go on," he said. "Public policy awaits your arrival."

Sylvia laughed, left.

"And don't worry!" he called out after her.

Nick worked out of an office on Capitol Hill, a twenty-minute ride from his home. As he drove to work that morning, he wondered if Juanita had kept the classical station on for Saul; smiled and wondered if Saul could hear the differences in music yet.

He found a parking space two blocks from his office. He turned the collar up on his Navy pea coat, thrust his gloved hands deep in the side pockets. The icy wind was at his back.

*Nothing you can do,* he told himself.

The top-floor town-house apartment he used as an office had high ceilings, a bay window overlooking the street. Nick tossed his coat and gloves on the worn sofa, put coffee water on to boil, and switched on his computer. The screen lit up.

WHICH FILE FROM MEMORY DO YOU WANT? asked the machine.

"That's not where the answers are," he said aloud.

The kettle whistled.

He kept his mind blank while he brewed coffee. The cream in his refrigerator hadn't spoiled. He took a cup of steaming tan brew back to his desk; stared at the screen, out the window overlooking the tar roofs of Capitol Hill. Across the street, the bare branches of a tree waved in the wind like naked fingers.

The machine held nothing about Jud. As Nick began to understand the world to which Jud admitted him, he'd vetoed any inclination to take notes. It was dangerous for the people Nick met to even think he'd taken notes, kept records.

"Even I wasn't that green," he told the computer.

Of course he'd taken notes on specific journalism stories Jud fed him, including the one that sent a grim Deputy Secretary of Defense scurrying to Peter Murphy's office with a national security plea for Peter to kill Nick's story. Peter did.

The tree limbs waved in the wind, wiped a decade away.

And Nick remembered the ten thousand swimming pools of Los Angeles glistening below his jetliner like turquoise flakes in a gravel patch. The smell of his leather jacket in the cool metal air of the plane. The drone of the engines and the pressure in his ears as the flight sank toward the city.

The fat man sitting next to Nick fanned himself with *Time* magazine. The cover featured the Shah of Iran and the CIA's failure to predict the revolution that deposed him. Nick wondered if Jud would finally tell him about his Iran days; if he was doing anything now about the fifty-two American hostages the Ayatollah Khomeini had grabbed in November. *Time* magazine wondered if the hostages would be home before the end of 1979.

"You going to L.A. for Christmas vacation?" said the businessman, eyeing Nick's blue jeans, sports shirt, and sweater, the leather flight jacket on his lap. "Go to college in D.C.?"

"I'm going out on business," answered Nick.

"Yeah? I work for TRW. You know them?"

"Yes," said Nick. TRW supplied the CIA's spy satellites. Four years earlier, in 1975, a dreamer named Chris Boyce went to work for TRW, saw cable traffic on the CIA's interference with Australian politics and labor movements, grew disillusioned with his country, and along with his friend Daulton Lee, who needed to support his heroin habit, sold American secrets to the Soviets.

The plane wobbled, descended.

"Great place, TRW. Who do you work for?"

"I'm a writer. A reporter, too, but I'm on a sabbatical and I doubt I'll go back."

"Do your own thing, huh?"

"Something like that."

"What's in L.A.?"

"A producer who likes an idea of mine."

"You going to write a movie?"

"I'm going to try."

"Bet you get to meet all the blondes!"

"That's not my end of the business," said Nick.

"You married?"

"No."

"Hell, then you should be in hog heaven in L.A."

A sudden acceleration sucked them back in their seats.

"What hotel are you staying in?" asked the fat man.

"I'm staying with a friend."

How smart was that? Nick wondered. How safe? and could he have said no to Jud's insistent hospitality?

No problem, thought Nick. He knew what he was doing. Sure he did. Seeing Jud . . . That edge, that intoxicating, enlightening edge. Seeing Jud, he could walk along it *cool* and walk away *clean* with savvy and stories he could earn no other way. That was his job, that was what he was supposed to do, wasn't it?

Besides, Jud *was* his friend. On the day that plane brought Nick to L.A., he'd known Jud three years. There'd been three different "bases" for Jud, though he always kept in touch: that first year when he lived in D.C., the next year when Jud was in Miami, and now this third year, when Jud was in L.A. Nick always took his calls, caroused with him during his visits when men in sunglasses and suits followed them until Jud got bored and shook the tail. As a Washington reporter, Nick knew dozens of allegedly powerful, fascinating people, but they all lived and worked in sterile worlds of paper and rhetoric. Jud was a man at the end of their abstractions; his hands were the squeeze of power. Nick's colleagues had begun to warn him about his mystery monster. Nick told them he knew what he was doing; that learning from and about Jud was his job; that Jud was his friend.

Or at least a magnet Nick couldn't resist.

The stewardess announced the final approach. The landing

gear locked into place. Nick watched the shadow of his plane skim over flat roofs, endless streets.

"What's your friend do?"

"Yeah," said Nick.

The plane bounced twice, roared along the runway.

"Welcome to Los Angeles," the stewardess announced over the intercom, "where the correct local time is six P.M."

At the gate, Jud stepped out from the shuffling crowd, big as a bear, broad shoulders and massive chest straining a white shirt, blue jeans and cowboy boots. He crushed Nick's hand in the 1960s brotherhood grip, frowned when Nick said he'd checked a bag.

"Always carry what you got," Jud told him. "But don't worry about it. You didn't know.

"I got things to do before we head home," said Jud as they walked through the parking lot. "Lorri will be there."

"You serious about her?"

Jud laughed, nodded to a midnight-blue Chevrolet Impala parked beside a Mercedes. "In L.A., nobody steals a Chevy."

He threw Nick's bag in the Chevy's trunk.

"Guess who it's registered to?" said Jud.

Nick shrugged.

"The lay leader of a Mormon church!" He laughed, tapped Nick on the chest. "Ain't it a gas?"

As they drove out of the parking lot, Nick asked, "Are you working for the same lock company as the last time I was here?"

"Those days are over," said Jud.

"What are you doing now?"

Jud looked at him sideways; smiled slowly.

"You're still with the Company?" guessed Nick.

"Did you think I ever left them?" said Jud.

They laughed.

"We have an understanding," said Jud.

"Do they know about me?"

"They know what I want them to," said Jud.

"No problems," he added. "Haven't I always covered you?"

The beeper clipped to Jud's belt went off. Jud checked the digital readout as he drove, frowned. He scanned the streets. Saw a gas station in the block ahead.

"Just be a minute," he said as he parked, ambled to the pay phone on the gas station wall.

Sunset colored the world crimson as Nick sat in the car and Jud made his call. Two young gas station attendants laughed and snapped at each other with oil rags. Traffic whizzed by on the busy street leading to the airport. Jud hung up.

Drove back into traffic the direction they'd come.

"We have to meet a man," said Jud. "I don't have time to drop you off."

"Who?"

They drove three blocks before Jud answered.

"One of my men," he said. "Works for me."

"Can I ask doing what?"

"You can ask," said Jud. Nick knew it should have been a laugh line, but Jud's voice was flat. He stared through the windshield. No jokes, no stories, no lectures.

The world rushed past Nick's window.

The road they were on cut through an industrial wasteland surrounded by the glitter of L.A. City blocks gave way to open land imprisoned in barbed wire fences. They drove past white oil tanks. The hills turned gray with the shadows of twilight. Streetlights along the highway glowed. Jud turned on his car lights. He took a right off the main road, drove past green iron oil pumpers, their outstretched metal arms seesawing in a steady, unyielding beat. In the smog rushing past his open car window Nick smelled bare earth. The breeze was cool.

The road curved like a banking plane. Jud took a right onto the paved lot in front of a tin shack. A bare bulb glowed above the shack's padlocked door. In the lot, a watch light on top of an aluminum pole dropped a pale cone of light to the cracked asphalt. A black motorcycle waited inside the light.

"Is that his?" whispered Nick.

Jud parked by the bike, shut off his engine.

Unseen oil pumpers beat a steady *whump-whump whump-whump.*

"Keep your hands out of your pockets," Jud said casually as they got out of the car.

Nick complied. Instinct drew him around to Jud's side.

Gravel crunched in the night. From the darkest shadows at the edge of the shack emerged the shape of a man.

"Be cool!" whispered Jud. Louder, he called, "Dean! It's okay! This is Nick. Remember me talking about Nick? The writer?"

"I remember."

The man shape walked closer, stayed outside the light.

"Nick's visiting from D.C.," said Jud. "Old friends."

"I wouldn't know about that."

Dean stepped into the light. He was about thirty, six feet plus of dense muscle and long simian arms. Nick saw his gun. And his eyes.

The gun was a revolver. Dean's leather jacket was unzipped, clear of the pistol stuck in Dean's black jeans. Guns are the girders of American fantasies, and fantasies were Nick's business. He'd grown up with guns, hunting rabbits in the fields of Michigan. Guns didn't scare him.

"Here we are," said Dean.

In Dean's eyes, Nick heard the crackle of burning flesh.

"You've got trouble," said Jud. "The LAPD knows about your damn hobby. They're watching. They don't have your name, but they want to take you down."

"Their problem."

"*Your* problem. They try it, *my* problem."

"Don't worry."

"I don't worry," said Jud. "I take care of trouble before trouble gets worse. You're fucking up, endangering our operation for nut bar games. I won't tolerate that. Get real."

The two men stared at each other. Dean's face was smooth. Handsome. He smiled.

"Okay," he said.

"I covered your ass on this one," said Jud. "Me. Because you're a friend of mine. Don't forget it."

"Sure."

"Everything else all right?"

"Eddie won't be a problem anymore."

"Good," said Jud. "We'll talk about it later."

Dean's gaze floated in the emptiness beyond Nick and Jud.

"Nice night." Dean sniffed the air. "Cool. People on the streets."

"So what's your new number?" said Jud.

"You got a pen?"

Jud didn't.

"You're a writer?" Dean said to Nick. "Make up books?"

Nick nodded. Dean handed him a pen.

"It's good making it up, isn't it?" said Dean. "Making things be what you want them to be."

"I like my work," answered Nick.

"Yes," said Dean. "Work. Ever go to a morgue?"

The oil pumps kept up their steady beat while Nick groped for an answer.

"No," he finally said.

"Oh." Dean smiled. "Got something to write on?"

Jud slapped his pockets, came up empty. Nick found nothing also, then remembered the address pages of his wallet.

"Here," he said, opening the black billfold.

"It's all right for you to be afraid," whispered Dean.

A tumbleweed bounced across the parking lot.

"He's got me," said Jud. He kept his voice flat, his hands still, and his eyes on Dean. "What's there to be afraid of?"

"Life is a big thing," said Dean.

"Tell us your number," ordered Jud.

Dean dictated a number Nick wrote on the *C* page.

"Somebody's coming," said Dean, his eyes focused on the road.

Nick and Jud stared at the distant headlights.

"Everybody stay put," said Jud.

The oil pumpers beat a steady *whump-whump.*

The air by Nick shifted. He turned, looked: Dean had vanished. He and Jud stood alone in the glow of the yard light; two men, a Chevy, and a motorcycle.

"Shit!" hissed Jud.

The headlights on the road followed the curving loop toward them. When the car turned onto the asphalt lot, they saw flasher lights mounted on the roof, lettering on the doors, and the waving black line of a whip antenna.

"Me," ordered Jud, "it's all me."

Nick's heart beat furiously against his ribs. Dampness cooled his back, but his neck and forehead were hot.

*Play it out,* he told himself. Play it out and it will be fine. Too late for another choice.

The car rolled into the cone of light, stopped ten feet from Nick and Jud, blinding them with its headlights. Two car doors slammed and a radio crackled. The headlights died.

"Well," said the older of the two men who climbed out of the car, "what do we got here?"

They wore gray shirts, badges. Holstered revolvers.

"Rent-a-cops," whispered Jud.

"What'd you say?" snapped the younger hired gun.

The sign on their car door read GUARD-ALL SECURITY.

"What are you doing here?" yelled Jud.

"No, man!" whined the younger guard. In cowboy boots, he was a head shorter than Nick and Jud. His fingers drummed on his holster. "That's our question! This is our job. Our turf."

"Easy, Tom." The older man leaned against the patrol car. "Tom's a tiger. Gotta hold tight to his leash."

"So I see," said Jud.

"You boys are on oil company property," said the older guard. He spit tobacco juice on the ground by Nick's feet.

"We didn't see any signs," said Jud. "Sorry."

"What's the matter with him?" Tom nodded toward Nick. "Cat got his tongue?"

"He's shy."

"What about you, tough guy?" said Tom.

Weeds crackled in the shadows.

Tom whirled, his hand on his gun as he peered through the darkness toward Hollywood's distant glow.

"You hear something?"

"Yeah," replied the older man. "Werewolves."

"The moon ain't right." Tom laughed. "Maybe we should get us some silver bullets."

"So, boys," the older guard said to Nick and Jud, "what are you doing in nowhere-ville?"

"Minding our own business," said Jud.

"What is that, 'xactly?" The old guard spit again. "This close to the airport, you running dope?"

He waited, but Jud said nothing.

"Nah, I don't figure you two pretty boys for that."

"Let me ask 'em, Win," whined Tom.

Behind the two men, by the shack, Nick saw a shadow move.

"I figure you for the bike," said Win, nodding to Jud.

"Sure," said Jud.

"Piece of shit." Tom stepped toward the motorcycle.

*"Don't touch the machine."* Jud's words were jagged ice.

Tom's fingers brushed his gun butt. "You can't tell me what to do!" His whine trembled.

Dean stepped into the glow of the bulb above the shack's door.

Behind the guards. His long arms hung down his sides; his hands were empty. He was smiling.

"What do you want?" said Jud. Nick knew he saw Dean, too.

"We get what we want," chimed in Tom.

"Since you ain't answering our questions," drawled Win, "since you're red-handed caught trespassers, maybe we should radio the sheriff, get a cruiser out here to find out what's what."

Dean slowly drew his revolver.

*Stop it!* Nick wanted to scream. *I'm a reporter! A writer! I'm not in this! They're not killing us! They're doing their job!*

"You don't want to do that!" Jud called out loudly.

"Why not?" snapped Tom.

Gun dangling from his right hand, Dean grinned.

"He, ah . . . ," stuttered Jud. He hung his head, shyly flicked his hand toward Nick. "He's got a wife."

"So what?" said Tom.

"Ah," said Win, narrowing his eyes.

"We needed someplace quiet. To meet. Talk."

Win smiled. "Ain't you heard of the telephone?"

Jud pointed his face to the ground, but his eyes stayed on the two guards; on the man with the gun behind them.

"Please," whispered Nick. Bolster the scam.

"You sweethearts make me sick," said Win. "Too cheap for a motel."

"Creeps!" hissed Tom, getting it at last.

"Seems like there's lots of laws you're bustin'," said Win. "Sheriff will love running you in."

"This is California. Nobody prosecutes that."

"They don't have to prosecute a fellow to make him pay." Win smiled. Spit tobacco juice.

Behind them, Dean let his gun hand float up. He sank into the two-handed-grip, horse-riding combat stance.

*"We're okay!"* Jud yelled.

"Then what the fuck are you doing here?" Win yelled back.

"Ten bucks," Jud said quickly.

"What?" said Win.

"Ten bucks. We're doing nothing you care about. Ten bucks, your boss never knows you've been bonused."

"You think that's what we're worth?" said Win. "Or is that what you're worth?"

Tom snickered.

"So we got a deal," Jud said loudly.

"What are you shouting for?" asked Win.

Dean's face twisted into a slack-jawed grin. His mouth worked as though he were panting or whistling, only no sounds came from his thick lips. He sank lower into his stance.

Thumbed back the revolver's hammer with a loud *snick.*

"You hear something?" said Tom. He started to turn.

"Twenty bucks!" yelled Nick.

Tom locked on him.

"Here!" Hands shaking, Nick pulled a bill from his jeans. "Twenty bucks. Go. Leave us alone."

His trembling hand held the money toward Tom.

"I want the big guy to give it to me." Tom smiled.

Jud slowly took the twenty-dollar bill from Nick's hand. He held it high where Dean couldn't miss it. Jud kissed the bill, crumpled it into a ball, and tossed it to the ground by Tom's cowboy boots.

Nick watched Dean's body tremble; watched his face contort. The gun was steady.

"I'll pick up a fool's money any day," said Tom. He scooped up the bill and stuck it in his shirt pocket.

"Let's go, Tom." Win edged backward toward the driver's door. Tom kept his eyes on Nick and Jud as he backed to the car, climbed in.

Nick glanced toward the shack. Dean had vanished.

"You boys have a good time," said Win.

They roared away in a shower of asphalt chips.

When the headlights were half a mile gone, Jud yelled, *"What the hell are you doing!"*

Dean appeared off to their right.

"Could have saved you twenty dollars," he said.

"Don't bullshit around!" yelled Jud. "I had the play going down! You were out of it! I never sanctioned you for any shit like that! This isn't game time! This is business!"

"Is that what it is?" Dean drifted toward them.

"I am serious as a heart attack!"

"Just practice," said Dean.

"Not on my time," said Jud. "Not on my dime."

Dean smiled. Shrugged. "You're the boss."

He threw a leg over the motorcycle, zipped his jacket over the gun. The bike growled to life. Dean raced the engine twice, let it settle down to a purr.

"We done?" he asked.

Jud handed a roll of bills to the man on the bike.

"Watch yourself," ordered Jud.

Dean grinned; his teeth were ivory. "See you around."

He roared off into the night. Left them alone with the *whump-whump* of the oil pumpers.

"Rough," said Jud, "but I handled it, we're okay, and—"

"He cocked his gun so they'd turn and he'd have an excuse to shoot them!"

"You gotta understand Dean," said Jud. "He loves me like a brother. He'd do anything for me. Balls to the wall, he's one of the guys I'd go to. You have to understand—"

"I understand him down to his bones!"

"I know." Jud's tone deepened, quieted. "But you don't understand just how heavy he is."

"What?"

Jud waited for Nick to come up with the answer.

"You saying he's with the government?" Nick finally volunteered.

"Not full-time," said Jud. "You know that story based on a real-life hit you're here to pitch? The Russian strolls up behind the Bulgarian expatriate in London, zaps a poison pellet into him with an umbrella gun? Dean's less subtle."

"What did he do for you?" whispered Nick.

"Nothing that big," said Jud. "He had to talk to a guy."

"He works for you," said Nick, disgust in his tone.

"Me. Uncle. Guys who need guys like him."

"What's his 'hobby'?" Nick's mouth tasted of bile.

"He breaks into houses when nobody's home. Does things."

"How do you know the cops are on to him?"

"Come on," said Jud, "let's go."

He turned to the car; turned back and found Nick staring at the shack, the dimly lit asphalt lot.

"This is the real shit, Nick. That's what you wanted to know. You'll never get this kind of experience anywhere else. Nobody else would give it to you, trust you enough to bring you out, and be heavy enough to cover your play so you can walk away."

Nick stared a thousand yards off into the night.

"What are you looking at?" Jud asked.

"Someplace new," said Nick.

"Nothing's changed," said Jud. "We're okay. And you did good. Real good."

"No, I didn't," said Nick. "Not *good.*"

He got in the car. They drove away.

On a March morning, thousands of miles away and more than a decade later, Nick stared at his computer screen, remembering. *Why didn't I walk away then?* he asked himself. He didn't have an answer. Wasn't sure one answer would be enough.

He'd seen Dean once more, years later, at a party at Jud's L.A. mansion. Dean had wrecked his motorcycle, mangled his leg. He was a wane ghost on crutches. But he still had cannibal eyes.

*"Balls to the wall, he's one of the guys I'd go to."*

That was years ago, thought Nick. Even before Jud and Nick finally redrew their line, Jud mentioned Dean less frequently. Now they could be enemies; Dean could be dead. If he wasn't, why would he know if Jud was safe? How to contact him?

The top right-hand drawer of Nick's desk glowed. In there, jumbled with pictures of ex-lovers, the keys to his first car, postcards he liked too much to send, and lockpicks given him by Jud, was that old wallet.

Nausea rose up in Nick. He felt as if he were riding a wave toward a shore he'd been approaching for years. On that wave was not where he wanted to be, but that didn't matter.

Outside his office window, tree limbs waved in the wind.

After he met Jud, Nick had finished his novel about auto workers, left Murphy's column, published four other novels, and created an on-the-road dramatic television show that ran for one season. Reviewers called his books street smart; wondered where he found his material.

The computer screen glowed.

The machine held five chapters of the novel Nick was writing about an unjustly imprisoned man. Another deal was percolating in Hollywood. He was busy. Had no time for suicidal quests. No desire to risk his wife and baby, whom he would slaughter thousands to protect.

He remembered one of the early days of madness, whizzing down the L.A. freeway, Jud driving the Mercedes, Lorri between them, her chestnut mane floating in the wind. The radio blasting pounding drums and throbbing bass guitars. They were high on danger and drugs and destiny, Jud shouting explanations of *the life.*

"You gotta know reality!" Jud yelled. "Or you're just another chump!"

Maybe Sylvia's right, Nick told himself that March 1990 morning in Washington. After all these years, maybe the dangers to me are distant ghosts. Harmless. Maybe I do owe Jud nothing.

*Except scars that shaped your vision.*

The first night Nick had ever walked beside the bear who glowed in the dark, Jud had said, "Anybody ever explain to you that you could be too loyal for your own good?"

"Nobody I ever believed," Nick had replied. Proudly.

The wind rattled Nick's office windows.

"What would you say now, Jud?" Nick asked the computer.

But the computer had no answer.

"When it comes right down to it," Jud once asked Nick, "what can you know?"

"That you do something," said Nick, "even if you try nothing."

"So watch your ass, right?"

Then they'd laughed.

In his office, Nick rode the waves. He feared for his family and he feared for himself. What could happen, *if.* If was endless. The CIA motto said knowing the truth made you free. Nick was certain of little, but he felt all he treasured slipping into the hands of faceless strangers and nameless forces. He couldn't merely wait for whatever knock sounded on his door.

"One thing you never need to worry about," Jud had told him. "I'll be your friend. Forever."

They'd shaken hands.

And it all meant what they made it mean, thought Nick.

But he knew that wasn't the bottom line. This wasn't just about Jud. This was about him. And about being sure who he was. About being true to old ideals, no matter how much he'd tarnished them. He knew that even as he opened his desk drawer, pulled the old black wallet out, found the faded number scrawled on the diary page labeled *C.* Numbers change owners. No one would be there. No one he'd ever met. The moon wasn't right.

"Not if I'm lucky," he whispered as he dialed.

# THE ABYSS

**W**es spent the weekend after Denton's party grinding out as much of the work on his desk as he could. Monday morning, he couldn't sleep past three-thirty. He left his Capitol Hill apartment to jog. Winter wind burned his face and lungs as he ran past the Capitol, down the Mall. Frozen earth crunched under his feet. He turned back at the Lincoln Memorial. Close by was the black wall etched with the dead from his war. His *Washington Post* was waiting at his top-floor apartment when he finished his seven miles. He turned on the PBS jazz station, did his twenty paratrooper push-ups. Made coffee, ate Grape-Nuts, read the news, and tried not to worry. He dressed in his uniform, put a civilian suit in his car, and drove down Eighth Street to the Naval Investigative Service's Headquarters at the Washington Navy Yard.

Behind brick walls and guard posts and within cannon range of the Capitol building, the Navy Yard houses dozens of red-brick buildings for high-security operations, ranging from the Library of Congress's Federal Research Division, which produces secret studies of foreign governments, to the CIA's six-story National Photographic Interpretation Center to the Navy Anti-Terrorist Alert Center.

Wes went to Building 111. His ID cleared him through the security guards on the lower floor, then again on the second floor. He avoided his coworkers and closed his office door.

And waited.

At 9:31, a Navy chief rapped on Wes's door: "Commander wants you pronto, sir!"

Two cubicles down the carpeted hall, the Navy officer behind the desk passed a set of orders to Wes.

"You know about this?" said Commander Franklin.

Wes glanced at the paperwork confirming Denton's plan.

"I just read the orders now, sir," Wes deflected, obeying Denton's secrecy mandate.

"Do I smell shit in those papers?"

"No comment, sir."

"You could at least smile," said Franklin.

And Wes laughed.

"If I'd known you wanted a cloak-and-dagger, we could have sent you up to the fourth deck," said Franklin. The fourth floor of the building was NIS's counterintelligence center.

"I didn't go looking for this," said Wes.

"But you're not saying no." Franklin shook his head. "It's tricky out there. Play it tough."

"I'll do my best."

"If you need something, give me a call. That's both official and unofficial."

"I appreciate it, sir."

"My, we are formal today. You're supposed to keep your NIS credentials. Don't smear shit on them, okay? And hurry back."

"I'll try."

"One more thing. General Butler requires your presence at the Pentagon *before* you commence your new detail."

"Did he say why?"

"You and I do not ask Marine generals *why*."

Wes's parting salute was friendly.

"Anchors away," said the man in the white uniform.

Samuel Butler, United States Marine Corps, wore two stars on his starched shirt. His desk and its tidy piles of paper were at right angles with the walls of his Pentagon office. A picture of his wife and three children faced the general's chair at exactly a forty-five-degree angle from the desk's right-hand corner. The wall facing the general held a color picture of the Iwo Jima Memorial. On the wall to his left hung a black-and-white photo of then Major Butler breaking the rules and personally leading a patrol in February 1969. Butler's square-jawed features were barely visible amidst the helmets and flack jackets, the M16s and radios, the nervous faces of young Marines. In that picture, Lt. Wesley Chandler's fatigues were fresh. The coat-tree in the office corner held General Butler's jacket with its four rows of ribbons. His desk drawer contained the Congressional Medal of Honor.

Across from him sat Wes.

"The Commandant told me about your detail," said Butler.

Wes dreaded lying to General Butler. Saying nothing let him keep both his integrity and his promise to Denton. In the instant he chose silence, Wes felt a chill brush his heart.

"See the stars on my shoulders?" asked Butler.

"Yes sir."

"They're on a *Marine* uniform. No better suit. They mean I'm responsible for everybody in olive drab with less metal. You're one of my men. And no Marine knows your marching orders."

"Sir, sometimes national security—"

"Don't tell me about *national security*," snapped Butler. "And don't tell me about *intelligence requirements.*"

Butler shook his head. His silver hair was brushed flat. "Know why I joined the Marines, Wes?"

"No sir."

"Because real *national security* is the damn most important thing a man can do. In a world like ours, that means you need to be prepared to go to war and damn well able to win it.

"But I don't want any more of my men wasted because of politics camouflaged with words like *national security* and *intelligence requirements*. Bunches of tight-assed, ivory-towered politicians playing tough guy. Using my men."

"Sir, I am not at liberty to discuss any details of my current assignment. Like you, I trust the chain of command."

Butler shook his head. "Where you're going, it's not trust, it's faith. And it's not government, it's theology."

Wes risked a smile. "I hope not, sir. Religion has never been a compass for me. I like a good team, but a chance to swing my own bat. And this . . . Sir, I have an authorized detail. A legitimate mission."

"Legitimate? Give me land to seize, an enemy to fight, a war to win. But don't give me any more no-win, no-end *missions.*"

Butler jabbed his forefinger at the man across the desk from him. "Don't end up as another embarrassment to the Corps, whining in front of some congressional committee."

"No sir."

"You might need support," said Butler, "wherever it is you're going and whatever it is you're doing. The Commandant says hands off, you belong to the suits in the woods now."

Butler shrugged. "I can't send air strikes or artillery, but if you holler, maybe I can drop some flares in the shadows."

"I appreciate it, General."

The two men stood. Wes started to salute, but the general extended his hand. As they shook, Butler said, "When you get out there, remember who you are. Watch for mines."

The bare trees along Virginia's George Washington Parkway swayed as Wes drove to the CIA. He'd changed to his civilian clothes in a Pentagon bathroom. At the CIA's chain link fence, guards in a glass booth checked a clipboard, directed him to a parking space by the main doors. Up the marble steps, inside the marble foyer. Guards searched his briefcase, then turned him over to an escort who led Wes to an elevator that whisked them to the seventh floor. The escort nodded Wes toward a deserted reception area, then rode the elevator back down.

A door opened. Noah Hall beckoned Wes. "Any trouble?"

"No," said Wes. The door Noah led him through had no number, no title.

Three of the four desks in the windowed room were bare. Classified reports, file folders, computer printouts, phones, Rolodex files, and a battered aluminum briefcase with combination locks covered the desk nearest the window.

"The boss is mopping up Iran-contra shit," said Noah as he lumbered behind the cluttered desk. "I'll get you going."

The bulldog sat. Wes took a chair from another desk.

"Security will give you a building pass that'll get you up here. If you need to go anyplace else in the facility, give a call to me or the boss's secretary, we'll clear you."

"Why not issue me a pass with building-wide clearance?"

Noah waved his hand. "Too much monkey business."

As he turned the combination locks on his briefcase, Noah said, "When you're at Security getting your pass, see Mike Kramer. He'll play you the tape of your guy's call, plus others from him that they just 'happened' to find."

The briefcase locks snapped open. From inside its scarred metal, Noah took an unlabeled folder.

"That's the pick shit paperwork, my notes," he said.

Noah tossed Wes a heavy white business envelope.

"Fifty thousand dollars," said Noah as Wes counted the used fifty- and hundred-dollar bills. Noah passed him a pad and pen. "Advance on expenses. Write me a receipt—and sign it."

Wes did, passed the pad and pen back, said, "Now you write me a receipt—for my receipt. And sign it."

The CIA Director's bulldog blinked. "We said we didn't want a paper trail, Wes."

"You just had me make one. But it only goes one way."

Noah laughed, shook his head. As he scrawled a receipt, he said, "You might do after all.

"When you leave here today," said Noah, "you got a guy to go see. Somebody to give you a hand when you need one."

"I thought this was a solo mission."

"There may be things you need expertise on, and since we're frozen out of the apparatus here . . ." Noah shrugged.

"Who?"

"Jack Berns," said Noah. "He's a private eye. Nailed a senator in a divorce, fucked up a federal judge. A White House man in Watergate went to Jack for help when the law was closing in. But Jack had a hard-on for the Nixon crowd. Some deal gone sour. Jack had the guy come to his den, law books on the walls, pictures of big shots. Hidden microphones. Jack tapes the shit out of the Watergate guy spilling his guts, then gives the tapes to that fucking columnist Peter Murphy."

"Why do I want to have anything to do with him?"

"Beats me, Wes. You figure it out."

"Has he worked for the CIA before?"

"Our government doesn't hire guys like Jack," said Noah.

They watched each other.

"You want to know what I do with him?" asked Wes.

"All we want to know is what you get," said Noah. "But Berns expects you. I'd hate to see an old friend disappointed."

"I'd like copies of those tapes," Wes told the gray-haired man behind the desk in the blank-walled room. A tape recorder and nine cassettes were the only things on the desk. A purple-coded picture ID was clipped to Wes's suit jacket.

"You don't have clearance for that," said the man. His ID badge had rainbow hues, a dozen numbers, said he was Michael Kramer, but didn't say he was Head of Security, CIA.

"How can I get clearance?" asked Wes.

"Get that other butt boy Noah Hall to do it."

Kramer's gaze was flat.

"I'm not here to give you trouble," said Wes.

"Then why are you here?"

"Ask the Director," said Wes.

"That's not my prerogative, is it, *Major?*"

"What do you want?"

"My pension's guaranteed. I can leave anytime."

"You don't care about your pension," Wes told him.

And saw Kramer smile for the first time.

"What do I want?" said Kramer. "I want this place to run like it should. No fat-cat appointees preening upstairs until something better comes along. No meddlers on the Hill saying don't do this and don't do that but don't let the bad guys win."

"I'm not one of the bad guys."

"Maybe not. But you aren't one of us. You're a toy soldier doing dirty work for the politician on the top floor."

The bare walls held no clock to count the silence between the two men.

"Thank you for your warm cooperation," Wes finally said.

"I do my job," said Kramer. "You want cooperation, get me to trust you."

"I don't care if you trust me." Wes stood.

"One more thing," said Kramer as Wes opened the door. In the hall waited the escort who'd guided Wes to this basement lair. "Deputy Director Cochran wants to see you. You're smart, you'll do what Billy says."

In the hall, Wes tarried outside Kramer's closed door. His escort finally coughed. "Director Cochran is waiting—"

And Wes jerked open Kramer's door.

The security chief had taken a telephone from a desk drawer, was punching in a number.

"Just wanted to say thanks again," said Wes, smiling at the man caught making a secret phone call on a secret phone.

As he left, Wes slammed the door.

* * *

"I appreciate your taking the time to see me," Billy Cochran told Wes.

"No problem," Wes told the man who had souls of a hundred nations reflected in the thick lenses of his glasses. On the Deputy Director's desk, a stack of classified files awaited Billy's eyes.

They sat on padded chairs in a corner of Cochran's office. One wall held five Japanese woodblock prints, ink portraits and still lifes, wisps of blue and red with black calligraphy. The room was quiet and still. Cool.

"The Director informed me of your job," said Billy. "I recommended against pursuing this matter."

"Why?"

Billy looked out the bank of windows.

"You can't see the Potomac," said Billy, "because of the those trees. Most of them are rooted in Virginia, but Maryland is out there somewhere. So, we trust, is the river."

The Deputy Director looked back to Wes.

"The longer I work in intelligence, the more cautious I become. The actions we take trying to acquire data can trigger the catastrophes we fear. Our job is to learn facts, not create them. I don't believe this phone call necessitates an effort by us."

"I'm not much of an effort," said Wes.

"The danger is not who you are," said Billy, "it's what you could become. You must be careful of nuances you might not sense. Both the Director and I agree on the absolute necessity for this undertaking to be as discreet as possible."

"Of course," said Wes. He hesitated, then said, "Do you know anything about Jud Stuart?"

"I know the Agency's data," said Billy.

"I'm only trying to find the truth."

"Then you'll be employed forever," said Billy.

"We're both soldiers," said the three-star Air Force general. "You're carrying out a legitimate order from a superior officer. I want to see you do well."

"Your head of security thinks I'm the enemy."

Billy frowned. Wes told him about his encounter with Kramer, thought, *But I bet you already know.*

Billy walked to his desk. The cold weather made him limp. In 1964, Billy'd been an Air Force intelligence officer whose myopia almost washed him out of uniform. He was at Bien Hoa Air Base on Halloween night when the Viet Cong mortared the runways and sappers penetrated the wire. As two giant planes burned on the runway, unarmed Billy left his bunker to pull a wounded airman from a jeep, grabbed a carbine off a dead air policeman, and fought off the VC. Mortar shrapnel peppered his leg; he lost his glasses. "I shot at blurs," he told the commanding officer. Billy refused any medal higher than a Silver Star: anything else might shine a spotlight on a spy.

"Mike?" said the Deputy Director into the phone. "Please provide Major Chandler with those tapes. . . . My authority. . . . Thanks."

*Now am I supposed to be obligated to you?* thought Wes.

Billy walked Wes toward the exit.

"You might find it useful to check with me from time to time," said Billy. "Perhaps I can open other doors."

At his office exit, he put his hand on Wes's arm. "I'll be sure to stay in touch."

Back at the Pentagon, alone in a windowless office, Wes ate a vending-machine sandwich and drank cold coffee. The lime-green walls were hung with mementos of a nineteen-year Army career. The framed photo on the desk showed a twenty-nine-year-old second wife and a new baby in front of a suburban Virginia home.

A colonel wearing the screaming-eagle shoulder patch of the 101st Airborne Division hurried into the office, carefully shutting the door behind him. He held a file folder in one hand, and with the other signaled Wes to be silent. The colonel unplugged the phone on his desk.

"They can do things with phones," said the colonel as he sat down. He'd gained a belly since jump school. His eyes darted around the room, then locked on the Marine in the visitor's chair.

"Do you know what you've done?" whispered the colonel.

"What's the matter, Larry?"

"This!" The colonel tossed the file folder to the man who'd given it to him. "What the hell is this?"

"It's supposed to be a soldier's service records."

"You're with the *Naval* Investigative Service. This is Army!"

"It's one country."

"Don't give me that. What are you doing?"

"Routine," said Wes. "Trying to understand that file. Blanks on the form aren't filled in. When did he leave the Army? And where was he stationed? Special Forces, but what command?"

"You've got the file. You figure it out."

"The file's bullshit. No photo. And 'Twenty Simulated Combat Jumps.' There's no such designation—and you know it."

"I can't help you, Wes."

"You spent ninety-some minutes with this file. Colonel Whiz, the guy who knows the Pentagon inside out, get you anything, do anything. Your dick gone limp?"

"You've got no right to talk like that to me!"

"Larry: help me."

"I don't know who you are," said the man who'd known Wes for a decade. "You give me a bullshit file and a bullshit story about not wanting to waste time with channels. Send me out like a good dog. My sergeants pop stuff into the computers—all those designations? My stripes have never seen 'em.

"Half hour later, a captain I don't know hands me hard copy of the input, says a major he doesn't know got it from a two-star who ordered everybody not to even think about this guy. And then the captain says: 'Tell Chandler he has all he needs to know.'

"They know your name, Wes!" whispered the colonel.

"I'm flattered. Can you help me?"

Larry shook his head. "They know my name, too."

"Who can help me? Where should I go next?"

"Back to your office at NIS. Home. I don't know."

"It's just brass, Larry. Buckin' the brass."

"These days, I'm a good soldier."

Wes stood and tossed his sandwich wrapper and Styrofoam coffee cup in the colonel's trash.

"Wes," said his old friend when Wes's hand was on the door, "just guessing, but . . .

"That file, that guy: they're off the books. Things happen out there, people . . . You need to know about that guy, find somebody else off the books. Way off."

Jack Berns lived in a suburban Virginia cul-de-sac one price bracket down from and five miles east of CIA Director Denton. Berns was a short man and mostly bald. He wore a lime-green golf sweater and his pants cinched high over a sagging belly. He had tassels on his shoes.

"Glad to meet you!" said Berns as he led Wes inside his home. "How do you like my place? Cost me fifty-two K back in '69, worth a half mil' today, easy. Come on down to my den."

Law books covered two walls of the den. Glass doors and windows overlooking a garden. The wall behind the desk held pictures of Berns with celebrities, framed newspaper articles featuring his exploits, and the first page of a Q&A interview Berns gave a "men's" magazine. Berns had framed the red-headed, twenty-year-old centerfold from that issue next to the article. She wore a black garter belt, mesh stockings, high heels, and a pout.

A pool table sat in the middle of the room.

"Nice place," said Wes. His eyes pointed to the centerfold, but he was looking for the hidden microphones.

"And fully tax deductible," noted Berns.

Colored globes waited on the pool table's green felt.

"Why does our friend think you can help me?" asked Wes.

"Because he's smart," said Berns. "You're looking for a guy— Jud Stuart."

Wes rolled the red 7 ball into a corner pocket.

"What else did Noah tell you?"

"Nothing—'cept that you might need help. And that you'd have cash. What's important is what I didn't tell him."

"What's that?" Wes snapped his wrist: the yellow-striped 9 ball bounced off the cushion, smacked into the solid-green 6, and almost rolled into a side pocket.

"I met your man once."

"When?" said Wes. "Where?"

And Berns smiled. "You got a uniform, I got a business."

"How much?"

"I ain't a nickel-and-dime kind of guy."

Wes tapped the black 8 ball into the corner pocket. While the ball rolled through the table, he got his briefcase from the sofa, put it on the green felt.

"Your business doesn't have confidentiality protection," said Wes, "and I'm a private citizen who requires discretion."

"I can do a whole lot more for you than a doctor or a priest," said the private investigator.

"You take my money," said the Marine, "then we've got a contract. My first rule is you tell no one anything—including Noah. If I see anything about me or my business in any newspapers or magazine interviews or Peter Murphy's column, any government files . . . you'll need more than a lawyer."

"Noah wouldn't send you to me if I couldn't be trusted."

Wes reached inside his briefcase where Berns couldn't see, counted out five hundred dollars, and dropped the bills on the pool table.

Berns scooped them up as Wes continued:

"That's a retainer for your services from me, a private citizen. Whatever your story, telling it won't use up five hundred dollars."

The private eye grinned.

"Before I leave," continued Wes, "I'll get a receipt."

"Noah said that wasn't how this was."

"Noah didn't just pay you five hundred dollars. I'll take a receipt."

"On my business card." Berns laughed. "I can do it all: phone records, tax records. I got people on payrolls the IRS never imagined. You want a wire? I use a guy can tell you when your grandmother farts. 'Course, they all cost. Plus my time."

"Tell me about Jud Stuart."

"It was 1977," said Berns as Wes opened a notebook. "I was trying to broker an electronics deal with a guy named Andre Dubeck, a Czech turned American after World War Two. Dubeck was the technical security adviser to the president of an African country. Who knows what that means. But I knew he had ten million dollars for sophisticated devices I could supply.

"Dubeck was in town. I arranged to buy him dinner. Rented a white Rolls—cost me ninety-five of those days' dollars. Pick him up in his hotel lobby and he's got this clown with him."

"Jud Stuart."

"That's the name," said Berns. "If Noah's looking for a guy with that name, he'd be the kind of guy who might know Dubeck. Anyway, we pile in the Rolls, go to a Georgetown restaurant.

"Fifty-dollar entrées, Dom Pérignon. Those two bullshit, saying a lot and saying nothing. Jud claims he's providing 'technical security' to forty embassies in D.C. Said something about soon getting a change of climate. I figured he was fishing for an invite to Africa from Dubeck. Come to find out over salad, he's a damn locksmith!

"'Course," said Berns, "that's as good a way of getting into someplace as I know. The old fly on the wall trick. I was thinking about putting him on one of my special retainers.

"We finish dinner, I'm setting up my pitch, they order brandy and coffee, go off to the bathroom together like *women* or . . .

"And they skip! Leave me with the check!"

After a moment of silence, Wes said, "That's it?"

"Never saw the son of a bitch again. Until now, there was no money in him. Dubeck's on a plane before dawn, and as far as anybody knows, Africa swallowed him up in '79 or '80."

"That wasn't worth five hundred dollars."

"The five hundred included my retainer—remember? You use me for the other stuff, you'll get your money's worth.

"Oh," added Berns, "I almost forgot about the picture."

"What picture?"

"You think I'd meet a high roller like Dubeck and not be sure I could prove it?" Berns laughed. "In my business, your word is only as good as your proof. Cost another hundred and twenty dollars in dinners plus a big tip to the maître d'. Had me a retired couple sitting close by, camera rigged in grandma's purse—I can fix you up with something like it. Got one nice shot of your boy."

"Where is it?"

"Let's see. The investment expense, storage, my time to dig it out, print it up. . . . Cost you another thousand."

"It's thirteen years old and you've been paid."

Berns shrugged.

"You get five hundred more, and your phone won't ring," said Wes.

The money went into Berns's hand and a black-and-white photo came out from under his desk pad.

"Give you a pocket-sized one, too," said the private eye.

*Big man,* thought Wes. *Broad chest, muscles. Curly hair. Laughing. Wild eyes.*

"Don't forget," said Berns when Wes left with the photos and another secret receipt, "you need me to do it all."

Wes parked across from a row of shops and cafés in Arlington's Little Saigon. Hand-painted black calligraphy signs hung next to multicolored Madison Avenue–crafted posters for beers and shampoos. The late-afternoon light was flat. Wes left his motor running while he leafed through the slim CIA file.

Scrawled on a yellow sheet of Noah Hall's notes was the name of the policeman investigating the death in the L.A. bar.

At the corner grocery store, Wes interrupted Asian chatter between the owner and a compatriot wearing a wool cap.

"Don't have twenty-dollar change," the owner told Wes.

"For twenty-five dollars," said Wes, laying another bill on the counter.

Wes got a handful of coins. The two men shrugged when he asked them for a pay phone. As Wes walked out, the owner said something in French, and the two friends laughed.

The Laundromat at the corner was warm inside. Humid. Dusty yellow. A dishwater-blond girl of nineteen kept her blank eyes pointed at a tumbling dryer while a baby boy slept beside her and a two-year-old girl played with dirt balls on the floor. Wes didn't care what they overheard as he dropped coins in the pay phone.

"Rawlins," snapped a man's voice answering Wes's call.

"Detective Rawlins? I'm calling from Washington, D.C. My name is Wes Chandler, and I'm working with Noah Hall."

"Shit," moaned Rawlins. "Next time your buddies in the mayor's office blow smoke about how come their LAPD ain't winning the war on crack and coke and the gangbangers, you remind *them* we're paying off *their* chits and wasting time with Washington over some who-cares D.U.O."

"What's a D.U.O.?"

"Death of unknown origin. You calling about the stiff citizen in back of the Oasis bar, aren't you?"

"Haven't you determined cause of death?"

"Broken neck, cause unknown. Ask me, a rummy falls down some stairs, then other rummies pick his body clean. 'Course, the coroner said he was well inside the legal limit. Why do you care?"

"Routine investigation. Have you identified him yet?"

"Yeah." Rawlins shuffled through a stack of files on his desk. "FBI made him through his prints and a Navy record."

"He was in the Navy?" said Wes.

"We got an ocean out here. Lots of sailors. The VA has his home address as San Francisco. No next of kin. Hopkins, Mathew J., forty-eight years old. VA lists him as one hundred percent disabled, though the coroner says he's a white male in average health."

"What progress have you made in the investigation?"

"You writing a report?" said Detective Rawlins. "Put in there that with fourteen open-file citizen murders plus six gangbanger bodies, I have progressed to a state of indifference regarding Mathew J. Hopkins—and Washington, D.C."

Wes's call to his old office only cost him a quarter.

"NIS, Greco."

"It's me," said Wes. Frank Greco was an ex-Marine sergeant who spent nine years in St. Louis getting through college and working as a cop. Greco was NIS's head counterspy.

"Heard you're with the import-export bank," said Greco.

"In a manner of speaking. Can you do me a favor?"

"Like what?"

"A complete file pull on a newly deceased Navy vet," said Wes. He gave Greco the man's biography he'd gotten from the L.A. cop. "Don't link it to me and don't red flag it, but don't let the search get lost. I'll call you in a few days."

"Done. What else?"

"Suppose I were tracking a guy who didn't want to be found."

"Best way to play the wolf is to think like the rabbit."

"One more thing. This is just between us, okay? No need to tell Commander Franklin or any of the other squids."

*"Semper fi,"* said the ex-Marine sergeant.

They hung up.

The sky outside the Laundromat was gray.

Inside, the young mother's blank eyes pointed at Wes.

He left a mountain of coins on the ledge by the pay phone, walked out into the wind.

Night ruled by the time Wes reached home. No headlights rode in his mirror during the trip home. No footsteps echoed on the sidewalk behind him as he walked the two blocks from the parking spot he found to his building. His mailbox in the hall was empty.

A strip of fresh white tape with the black-inked letters *B. Doyle* was stuck to the mailbox for the apartment across the hall from his.

The lights he snapped on showed him his home as he'd left it. Nothing changed, nothing disturbed. No surprises.

Most nights, Wes stayed in these rooms that had become his home. Alone. He'd read—most often history. His TV set saw most of its use for baseball games. When he could, he'd drive to Baltimore to watch the Orioles play. He'd go to a movie, have dinner at a coworker's house. Less and less frequently did such an evening involve the colleague's wife having a single or divorced friend with a legendary great personality or sharp mind and the same trapped smile she'd get from Wes as they ate pasta. He told himself he enjoyed not having to share his bed. Lately, he'd taken to reading old letters from his mother—his father had never written Wes. Each day, their images in black-and-white snapshots looked more like strangers.

That night, before he ate a restaurant dinner, Wes visited a photocopying store, copied the CIA file—plus the receipts, Berns's pictures of Jud, Noah's scribbles, and his own notes. At home, he changed his suit for sneakers, slacks, and a sweater, sat at his kitchen table with a tumbler of Jack Daniel's and ice, stared at his copies of official secrets. And wondered if he was sliding from schooled caution to unjustified paranoia.

*Better a scared bureaucrat than a disgraced Marine.*

His photocopies fit inside a Ziploc plastic food-storage bag. He folded that bag inside a black plastic garbage bag, used black tape to make a sealed pouch. From his tool closet came a board too good to have thrown away, a hammer, and nails.

The fish-eye peephole showed him an empty hall.

Wes stepped into the hall, crept up the access stairs to the flat tar roof. The wind swirled blackness all around him as he crouched by the retaining wall circling the roof. Treetop level. Lights glowed from the windows of town houses across the street, but no one was looking out at the cold night. No one was watching him.

The building's air-conditioning unit rested on railroad ties. Wes put his waterproofed stash against the inside of a tie, nailed the board over it to foil the wind and squirrels.

As he tiptoed down the roof stairs, a woman opened the door opposite his apartment.

She took him in with a languid smile. Her shoulder-length brass-brown hair had a widow's peak that swept it up and off each side of her freckled, pale face. She wore a white blouse, black slacks. Her feet were bare. A black plastic garbage bag dangled from her hand. She shook her head—and laughed, a throaty, high-pitched staccato Wes would remember to the day he died.

"Great," she said—her voice was husky, "a man with a hammer when what I need is someone who understands the formulas for posttensioning and prestressing."

*Who the hell are you?* was his first thought. Part of him wanted to lecture her: *I'm a strange man carrying a tool that could be a weapon, don't just . . .* But then his heart smiled: whoever she was, she had a hell of a sense of humor and a nimble mind.

That opened rusted doors in his own memory. Wes asked her, "Do you mean precast or on-site?"

The door closed behind her. "You're not a carpenter."

"You're B. Doyle," said Wes. He joined her on the dimly lit landing. She was more than a head shorter than him, but seemed taller. Lean. Angular yet fluid at the same time. Her mouth was wide, with full lips. Her eyes were well spaced and gray.

"Beth Doyle," she said.

"What happened to Bob?" Wes knew his old neighbor's name, that he was a lawyer for the Justice Department, that he missed the zen of riding his ten-speed bike because of his job's long hours.

"He got transferred all of a sudden because of some work emergency," said Beth Doyle. "Who are you?"

Wes told her his name. "Are you a friend of his?"

"Never met him," she said. "I needed a place right away, we knew somebody in common, so I'm subletting."

"Don't take out the garbage until Wednesday night," said Wes, nodding at the bag in her hand, "or the rats will get it."

"Hate rats."

"Then you should wear shoes and socks if you're going outside. Never know what'll run across your feet. Besides, it's cold."

"Shoes I can handle," she said, "but forget the socks: one more thing to pack. How did you know that concrete stuff?"

"I had to study it once," he said. "There's a fleck of steel sticking in the right side of your nose."

"That's my diamond!" she laughed and touched it. Her finger-nails were chewed low. "Twelve years since India. I don't even see it when I look in the mirror.

"Most people pretend not to notice it," she added. And then looked at him differently.

"Why do you have it?"

"I was terminally naive. Stick skinny—some things never change. Looked fourteen. I wanted to look sophisticated. Older. So it was a carrot and a gold needle. Don't ever let anyone tell you there are no nerves in your nose."

"It's a deal," he promised. "Why were you in India?"

"It was on the road. You ever been to Asia?"

"Yes."

"Do you really know those formulas? Could you help me?"

His mouth opened to say no.

"I can try," he told her.

"I've got bourbon," she said. "If I can find it."

She opened her door. Wes followed her in.

A dozen boxes were scattered around the apartment. The components of a drafting table leaned against one wall.

"Wait a minute!" she said. He stopped in her threshold. "All I know about you is you're Wes Chandler, you've got a hammer and know something about concrete. You could be a stone killer and I'm inviting you in for bourbon. What do you do? Who are you?"

"I'm a Marine officer," he said.

"The first man I meet in Washington is a *Marine?*" She shook her head. "What a desperate town. Should I trust you?"

"No," he said.

She laughed and he had to join her.

"At least you're honest," she said. "Close the door."

She found the bourbon.

They sat cross-legged on the floor, surrounded by half-unpacked cardboard boxes. Engineering textbooks and notebooks lay open between them, glasses of bourbon guarded their sides. From time to time, as she scrutinized her notebook or a text, her hair would slide over her face; without thinking, she'd brush it away, tuck it behind her ear. She smoked Camel cigarettes she lit with the snap and click of a battered Zippo lighter.

"Don't tell me it's an ugly addiction," she said. "Sometimes late at night when you're drafting, it's just you and your cigarette and it's heaven not to be alone."

For once, Wes didn't mind the smoke floating around him.

His memory of engineering problems he'd sweated out at the Naval Academy quickly proved useless.

"What the hell," she said. "I'll unpack tonight, get it in class tomorrow."

"I *know* I know how to unpack," he told her.

She laughed, handed him a taped cardboard box. As they opened her packaged possessions and assembled her drafting table, she told him she was an archivist with the Oriental Arts Foundation, starting work at the Freer Gallery on the Mall, taking engineering and physics classes at Georgetown to make up for a checkered college career at Denison and Barnard.

"I'm going to be an architect," she said. "If I get into school. If I don't work myself to death getting there."

Wes told her he had a desk at the Navy Yard.

She said she was thirty-two. A Catholic girl from Long Island. Single. Germany came up in her stories. Thailand.

"Bangkok was my baptism with reality," she told him after they'd quit pretending to work on academics. "Nineteen years old. I was never so petrified in my life. Millions of little Thai men grabbing at you in the airport. The city is thousands of miles of klongs, canals. They pull bodies out of the klongs every morning. No names, just bodies. Spooky."

Wes opened another box of books, found a battered and water-stained thick yellow volume: *The I Ching or Book of Changes.*

"Is that where you got this?" he said, handing it to her.

"Actually, that's a New York addition."

"I've never been one for superstition."

"That's not what this is about," she said, taking the book from him. "Best therapist I ever had was a Jungian, dream man. Jung loved the *I Ching.*"

"Doesn't it promise you salvation?"

"It promises nothing." She smiled. "Here, I'll show you. You're supposed to have a problem or a question in mind, but I figure you're one big question."

With anyone else, he knew he would have felt foolish, but somehow with her, he felt eager, curious; open. Part of him wondered why he hadn't balked when she'd mentioned a therapist; he dreaded neurotic women. Dilettantes. Flakes. But despite apparent evidence to the contrary, he instinctively ruled she didn't fit in those classes. Nor was she like anyone he'd ever known. His pocket held three pennies. She made him toss them on the floor between them six times, each time ascribing a value to the mix of heads and tails, drawing on a paper either two dashes or a solid line to form a hexagram stack.

"So?" he said as she matched the hexagram he'd made in the index of sixty-four possibilities.

"So the *I Ching* is about now," she said, flipping pages in the book. "This moment. Everything is always changing, and your hexagram can reflect . . . not *advice,* but a *sense* of the changes.

"Oh-oh," she said.

"What?"

"*K'an.* The Abyss.

"Might not be so bad," she said, scanning several pages. "*K'an* means the heart, the soul, light locked up in the dark. Reason. 'Through repetition of danger we grow accustomed to it. . . . By growing used to what is dangerous, a man can easily allow it to become part of him. . . . With this, he has lost the right way, and misfortune is the natural result. . . . What matters most is sincerity.' There's images of water, a river flowing, light."

"I didn't expect danger when you invited me in," he told her, smiling to lighten the moment.

"They were your coins." She smiled. "What do you think?"

"Makes sense," he admitted. "But I wouldn't have used your method to come to those conclusions. I'm more deductive than . . . imaginative. Or intuitive."

She put one of his pennies in his open palm, turned it from heads to tails. The brush of her fingers was electric.

"Same coin, different sides."

Her hand floated away, ground out the cigarette smoldering in the ashtray. Wes glanced at his watch: 11:16.

"I have to go," he told her. "I need to get up early."

"A breakfast meeting?" she asked.

"I have to leave town for a few days."

"Where to?"

"Los Angeles," he said, then immediately regretted it.

"Never been. Bring me back a souvenir of Hollywood."

"Ah, sure."

"And next time, you have to tell me about you."

"There's not much to tell."

"You're a bad liar." She smiled. "I like that in a man."

She walked him to the hall. Stood framed in the door, lithe and vulnerable and smoky while he opened his apartment.

"Don't forget to come back," she said.

||||||||||||||||||||||||||||||||||||||||||||||||||||||||||||||||||||||||||||||||||||||||||||||||||||

# GECKOS

In November 1965, the oil refinery made the guidance counselor's office in Chula Mesa High smell like a burning highway.

"Jud," Mr. Norris told the boy sitting in front of his desk, "your first two years, you were barely here. Last year you pulled your GPA up to a three point four and blew the track coach away. He says it's like you've been running distance for years."

"It's a mile and a half to school, over the hills, through the turkey farm. Until I got fast, I got caught."

Chemistry teacher and counselor Norris didn't want to hear about boys such as this lean, six-foot senior getting pantsed, beaten, and robbed by adolescent wolf packs. There was nothing he could do; that was all just part of becoming a man. And there were worse places to grow up than this southern California town.

The bell rang. Doors banged open. With a roar, teenagers surged through the corridors of American public education.

*Jud's eyes are Bunsen burner flames,* thought Norris.

"So have you given any thought to what career you'd like to pursue?" asked Norris.

"I want to be a spy," said Jud.

The counselor blinked. Then exploded in laughter.

*Stop laughing!* Jud prayed. *I'll say I was joking. Tell you what you expect. Talk about going on the line at Northrop or junior college. Or I'll say I'll wait for the draft. But please,* please *stop laughing at me!*

A girl giggled in the hall. Laughter from a million faceless voices sucked the strength from Jud's limbs. He was dead weight in the wooden chair. His tongue thickened until he gagged. Acid churned in his stomach. The laughter grew louder.

Across the desk, Norris cupped his forehead; his face turned crimson. Tears trickled down his cheeks. His hand dropped into a desk drawer. The counselor's bald head glistened. His tears and sweat beads turned red and rolled to the sea. Flesh melted from his face, his eyes dissolved into black sockets. The skull cackled at Jud. The skeleton in the white shirt and tie raised a revolver from the desk drawer. The pistol's bore stared at Jud, a black eye that grew with each sledgehammer blow of Jud's heart. A bone thumb snicked back the revolver's hammer. Helpless, Jud watched the bleached-bone trigger finger squeeze—

"*Unhhh!*"

Jud was panting, eyes wide open, seeing *nothing*.

A dark room. Bed.

Awake, he was awake, lying in a narrow bed, sheets soaked with his sweat, his skin clammy, his heart slamming against his ribs, his hands gripping the sides of the lumpy mattress.

A blast of a semi truck's horn shook Jud's trailer as the truck roared past on the night highway.

The glowing hands of the alarm clock on the nightstand showed four thirty-five.

Five hours, thought Jud, I slept almost five hours.

He snapped on the lamp, listened to the ticking clock and the wind tapping grains of sand on the trailer's walls.

One of the trailer's previous inhabitants had screwed a mirror in the wall opposite the bed. Jud watched himself stand. He wore green drawstring pants given him by Carmen and the chopped-sleeved sweatshirt in which he had fled L.A.

Four days ago, he thought. In the mirror, he rubbed his stomach—still a big gut, but the bloated look was gone: his liver had shrunk.

*Four days since I had a drink.*

The trailer was bigger than a coffin. Jud fit in the shower stall. A sink and a hot plate were the kitchen. A dying refrigerator served as the shelf for a black-and-white TV. Under the bed, where Jud hid his gun, he'd found a decade-old *Playboy* magazine. The centerfold was a lean blonde with green eyes, wearing a sheer white negligee. She stood in the doorway of a shadowed bedroom, wisps of dry-ice fog all around her. She was smiling.

Quarter to five. Jud didn't need to walk over to the café until six.

In the mirror, a skeleton sitting behind a desk laughed silently.

"He who laughs lasts," said Jud. He turned on the TV.

Phantoms lit the screen, a man and a woman sitting around a coffee table in New York.

". . . and today in federal court in Washington," the TV woman said, "one set of government attorneys will argue against the release of classified documents while another set of government attorneys will argue that they need those documents to prosecute defendants in the Iran-contra scandal. The administration's position in this is—"

Jud snapped off the TV.

In four days he'd cleaned Nora's Café with a thoroughness the business had never known. He rehung the screen door, unstuck windows, even changed the oil on Nora's Jeep.

He paced the length of the trailer. His hands barely trembled. Five o'clock. Dawn would come soon.

His thoughts drifted to a lean sergeant he'd known years before at JFK Special Warfare school.

"Time must be your ally!" shouted the sergeant as he marched through the rows of Special Forces trainees locked in the push-up position, his jump boots barely missing their splayed fingers. "If you want to survive, if you want to win, you must always be gettin' approved rest and rec-re-a-tion, gettin' ready, or gettin' it on! All that gettin's up to you! You don't get it your way, you get it from the other guy!"

*The other guy.* Jud turned out the trailer's lamp, pushed aside the black muslin curtain. In the end of the night, he saw no one.

Yet.

He put on his socks and sneakers. The breeze outside chilled his arms; his pants whipped his legs. The scent of sand and sagebrush filled his nostrils. Packed earth crunched beneath his sneakers as he paced between his trailer and the café. He faced Nora's adobe house.

*Don't think about not remembering,* he ordered himself. *Don't think about whether it's been fifteen years. Don't think:* do. Sand pellets stung his face. *Not important. Not there.*

He raised his hands until his clenched fists reached his armpits, sank into a squat, toed-out his feet, then swung his heels out and settled into a pigeon-toed stance.

A tingle of pride ran up his spine. Jud had to push it aside, not think about the 130 moves left in the beginner's form of *wing chun*. Anyone can begin.

His hands shot down in a cross block. Punches, circle blocks, palm strikes, finger jabs. In a martial pantomine on the night floor of the desert, Jud fought an opponent who wasn't there, who was everywhere; who had no face, who was everyone.

The moves of *wing chun* blurred into blocks and strikes from other systems—and rage. Punch. Block. Grab and trap. Punch. Jud's chest heaved, his skin grew sticky and his arms ached and still he fought. Faster. Harder. Faster. Stylistic orthodoxy was forgotten, but the rage, the rage woke.

And then a hook punch threw him off-balance as surely as if a real opponent had grabbed his arm. He stumbled, staggered across the sand. Felt like a fool, a drunken old man. A clown.

A rosy shimmer outlined the flat horizon behind Nora's house. A lamp's yellow glow silhouetted her in the open doorway.

How long she'd stood there, Jud didn't know. She turned her smile up to the sky; stretched and breathed deeply, sighed.

"Got another one," he heard her tell heaven.

Nora closed her house door and walked to him.

"Do you know what I smell?" she asked, smiling.

Jud shook his head, conscious of his sweaty body.

"I don't smell whiskey in you anymore," she said. "That smells good."

"Better than cheap cologne," said Jud.

"Nothing's cheap." Her brow wrinkled. "You like that tough-guy stuff you were doing?"

"Legend says a woman developed that style."

"Then it ought to work. But if you got tough-guy trouble, you'd be better off practicing running."

"I can do that, too."

She eyed his belly. "Uh-huh."

"I'm not bullshitting you!" he insisted. "I can run."

"Good." She walked to the café. "Coffee when you want."

The café's back screen door banged, and she was gone.

"I can run," he said, but no one was there to hear.

Two gas pumps stood sentry in front of the café. A phone booth sat between Nora's house and the road. Jud stepped onto the black-snake highway. Nothing moved from horizon to horizon.

The asphalt was cool. Lights came on in the café. He sighed, pumped his lungs full of cool air . . .

And ran down the highway. Ten steps and he was panting, thinking about quitting, so he chanted:

> *"Airborne, Airborne, have you heard?*
> *We're gonna jump from the big-assed bird."*

And they had. Into Laos.

Falling, floating, silent stones in the November night of 1969, timeless, brutal cold, Jud and Curtain steering their human daisy chains toward the intermittent blink of an orange light below.

They'd popped the Nungs six hundred feet above the jungle canopy, hit their own silk, crashed into the trees. Monkeys screamed. Bats took wing. They cut themselves free and climbed down, rendezvoused with the ground asset on a midnight patch of earth.

One of the Nungs had lost his mind.

Somehow he'd climbed down the tree. But he wouldn't let go: his arms and legs were locked around the tree trunk. His haunches tried to root in the jungle floor. The man sobbed.

"He's done!" Curtain whispered to Jud as the other three Nungs tried to pry the madman loose. "Punch his ticket."

"He's on the team," said Jud.

The haggard Vietnamese ground asset was fifty-seven, looked seventy. His eyes glistened as he watched the two Americans argue.

"He's dead weight!" insisted Curtain. "He flips out, we're nailed! What will you do with him?"

"What I want, when I want, where I want!" snapped Jud.

Curtain barked an order at the sane Nungs. They looked to Jud—he nodded. They left their mad comrade clinging to the tree.

The team stripped out of their jump gear, dressed in black pajamas unpacked from the canvas bags. Radios, ammunition, food, and medicine were in rucksacks. Jud used his thumbs on nerves in the man's collarbone: he spasmed and fell away from the tree. One Nung helped Jud strip the jump gear off the mental case: he'd fouled himself. The stench made Jud reel. Jud pulled black pajamas over the man's soiled long underwear. As the

Nungs buried the jump gear, Jud put the madman on his feet and strapped his rucksack on him. He slung a rifle on the pack, cut off the man's black pajama sleeve, tied it as a gag in his mouth. Jud tied a rope around the man's waist, handed it to a Nung.

Tears rolled down the gagged man's face—but he followed when his compatriot jerked the rope.

As Jud strapped on his pistols and grenades, checked his AK-47, Curtain told him, "You're as nuts as he is."

"Believe it."

Curtain shook his head, spit. "I got point."

He slid into the jungle night. The Vietnamese asset followed Curtain. The Nungs came next, a single file of three men leading a human mule.

Jud held the rear, his eyes and Russian assault rifle sweeping the bush. He followed the Nung ten steps in front of him as much by internal radar as by sight. Leaves rustled. Night birds exchanged secrets. He heard his own tense breathing and that of the man moving through the brush ahead of him. Something slithered over Jud's boot; something scurried through the tangled roots to his left. An insect buzzed his face. Lit. Stung. His lips burned from his salty sweat; his dry mouth tasted of gun oil.

The jungle at night magnifies the senses. For Jud, each member of the team had his own scent: one Nung smelled like pine, another like lemons, a third bamboo. The madman reeked of shit. The Vietnamese spy who'd guided them in smelled like Saigon: charcoal and barbecued fish. Curtain smelled like warm milk.

*What's my smell?* wondered Jud.

They marched for an hour in dense jungle, twisting and turning, slapping branches out of the way, climbing over felled trees, slogging through mud. Their path sloped uphill, into thinner air. Jud's clothes were soaked, each breath was a rasping effort.

Without warning, the jungle opened up into a clearing sixty feet wide, a cluttered circle of twisted logs and churned earth. The smell of rotting wood hung in the clearing beneath the first stars Jud had seen since they'd landed. An American blockbuster bomb had blasted that hole in the jungle.

Jud took the gag out of the madman's mouth, held the canteen while the Nung drank. No life showed in his eyes. No words came from his lips. Jud replaced the gag.

"Let me keep point," said Curtain. "I been in these boonies before."

"That's right," said Jud, "you have."

"How about you?"

"No," lied Jud.

"Watch the Nungs," said Curtain. "Can't ever tell."

"No," said Jud as the Nungs fell in line, "you can't."

On they marched, climbed. Their rucksacks pressed into their backs. Jud's boots trembled, trees swayed: from far off came the rumble of B-52s unloading on Laos. Two million tons of American bombs rained on Laos between 1965 and 1973—more bomb tonnage than the U.S. used against both Germany and Japan in World War II, dropped on a country smaller than Oregon.

*But no air strikes near here tonight,* Jud told himself. The bomber crews in Thailand, Okinawa, South Vietnam, floating on carriers in the China Sea, didn't have this path of real estate on their mission lists.

Even by SOG standards, Jud's mission was secret. The B-52 crew that dropped them had been briefed on the runway. The sergeant major who was the team's handler was under quarantine in Okinawa: he thought Jud's team was dropping into North Vietnam, as Jud had before. Their ground asset had been activated at the last moment. Jud and Curtain were briefed together eleven days before the mission so they had time to plan, memorize topographical maps, satellite photos.

*And plan on coming back,* thought Jud.

The valley jungle thinned as they climbed along a ridgeline. Jud's compass agreed with Curtain's route. With luck, they'd get through the hills and reach the Plain of Jars by full light. Then the op plan called for them to wait for darkness.

Like a mist, night faded to gray light floating in the trees.

The birds stopped singing.

*What's that smell?* thought Jud.

The brush to Jud's left exploded. A rifle barrel whacked his shins. He fell forward, hands grabbing his arms, bodies crashing on top of him. A machine gun burst cut the night. His face slammed into the mud. A dozen Asian voices shouted. Rifle butts thudded into his back, his shoulders, his legs. They twisted his arms behind him as his pack and weapons were pulled away. They jerked him to his feet.

In front of Jud stood an Asian in a long-sleeved, drab-green shirt, matching pants. He wore a billed cloth cap. A jagged scar ran down his cheek. Scarface speared the barrel of his Czech AK-47 into Jud's stomach. Jud wretched, doubled over despite the three men holding his bound arms. The wooden butt of Scarface's machine gun smashed into Jud's cheek.

A whirlpool sucked Jud into black nowhere.

How long he was gone, he couldn't be sure. He realized he was on his knees, his forehead pressed into the dirt. His face was wet, his jaw throbbed. Blood dribbled out of his mouth. Rope cut his wrists, his hands were numb. The pressure of the derringer against his thigh was gone, as was the flash-encode communicator in the pouch strapped under his black pajama top. Asian voices babbled all around him. Sunlight filtered to the jungle floor. Slowly, waiting for the smash of a gun butt, he raised his head.

Saw a scruffy pair of American jungle boots inches from his eyes.

*We're in a clearing,* thought Jud.

Beyond the khaki-clad knees in front of him, Jud saw Curtain standing at the treeline, his hands tied at his belt buckle. An Asian in a cloth-capped uniform stood next to Curtain. The Laotian wore wire-rimmed glasses and an officer's pistol belt. The round-lens glasses gave him owl eyes. Other soldiers were dividing up the American team's gear.

The man standing in front of Jud poked him with the barrel of his rifle.

"Get up," he said.

In perfect American.

Jud struggled to his feet.

His captor wore a black pajama top with his jungle boots and khakis. A GI web belt hung with grenades, a K-bar combat knife, ammunition pouches for the Czech AK from the arms shipments the Soviet Union started sending to Laos in 1961.

He had ebony-black skin.

The tarnished silver jump wings of an American paratrooper were pinned to a red bandanna encircling the black's forehead. His face was handsome, his teeth white.

He smelled of fire.

"Lisson!" Jud spit the words through his bleeding mouth. "Thank God it's you!"

"God doesn't live here!" snapped the black. "This is the People's Republic of Laos, and you are fucked and refucked!"

"You're Mark Lisson," said Jud. "I was looking for you."

The rifle barrel jabbed the side of Jud's neck.

"Congratulations, honky!" said the black. "You found me."

Owl Eyes yelled something in Lao. The black man glared at him, then told Jud, "Stick around."

And his captor laughed. Scarface aimed his assault rifle at Jud. Lisson and Owl Eyes walked to where Jud's four Nungs knelt in a line, hands tied behind their backs. The Pathet Lao hadn't removed the madman's gag. Two guards watched Curtain as he stared dumbfounded at Jud. Jud counted twenty-three Pathet Lao—and the American.

Owl Eyes drew his Russian pistol, put it behind the head of the first Nung.

*Run!* Jud thought as the pistol *crack!* sliced through the jungle. The first Nung crumpled. *Fight!* His soul ached as they meekly waited for their bullets: *crack!* and the man who smelled like lemons pitched forward. *Crack!* and the pine man flopped on the ground like a fish while *crack!* the madman slumped on his knees.

The Vietnamese who'd guided Jud in was blindfolded, his hands bound behind his back. Blood covered his face.

"You know my name," said the black, ambling back to Jud while Owl Eyes holstered his pistol.

"We're gonna be partners," whispered Jud.

Lisson put his rifle bore inches from Jud's face.

"You are who I tell you to be, white meat," said Lisson.

"Believe me!" said Jud.

"I always believed you, *Mister Charlie.* Call the V.C. 'Charlie,' right? That's what my brothers call our white oppressors. The name of the enemy, right? Only one is the enemy, one is not. I learned that from you capitalist pig motherfucker assholes, didn't I? But you lied about which was which, who was who, I am me, and you, motherfucker, are you."

"You only think you know who I am."

Across the clearing, Curtain shook his head at Jud.

"Fuck me, Charlie," Lisson told Jud. "Fuck me and fuck you and refuck you again!"

He barked an order. The Pathet Lao shuffled into line. Lisson checked one man's gun, adjusted another's pack. A soldier cinched a choke tether around Jud's neck. Curtain's guard nudged him into line behind Jud. Scarface walked by. Jud's holstered derringer dangled from his neck. He spit on Jud.

The Pathet Lao moved out, leading their POWs away.

Curtain hissed, "What do you think you're doing?"

"Nice job on point," said Jud. "The Nungs loved it."

"They were always just meat," said the man behind him. "Why are you dicking the nigger like that?"

"What did you do, Curtain?"

"I got bushwhacked, asshole! Same as you!"

"My ropes are loose," whispered Curtain to Jud's silence. "I get a chance, I'll go for it. If they separate us, I'll circle back, spring you. They'll separate us, but don't worry."

Up ahead, Owl Eyes barked an order. The fourteen-year-old soldier holding Jud's tether ran him up the file. The jungle thinned to forest. They loped past a dozen Pathet Lao. Half the soldiers were no older than Jud's keeper. They ran past the blindfolded Vietnamese asset, ran until they reached the head of the column where Owl Eyes walked with Lisson.

"Figured you'd like it up here, honky," Lisson said. Owl Eyes let the two Americans walk ahead of him. "Leader of the pack and all, a one-zero like you."

"How'd you know I was the one-zero?" said Jud.

Lisson slapped Jud across the face.

"You don't ask questions. You're a flat zero here."

They kept marching.

"And you're number one boy in the boonies," said Jud. "But they keep you in the boonies. With Owl Eyes to watch you."

"He's the political officer."

"I thought you didn't believe in officers anymore."

"A revolution without discipline revolts itself."

"I know you, Lisson. I'm here to help you."

"Don't waste my English on bullshit."

"I stole your files," said Jud. "I know who you are."

"Nobody knows who you are."

"I do," said Jud.

"You do shit!" Lisson thumped Jud with a steel finger. "You're all shit. Pale, white shit, dropped on the people of the world. Anybody who ain't white, ain't right. Con 'em or kill 'em. Selma or Saigon, it's all the same."

"I know who taught you that," said Jud.

Lisson roared with laughter.

*They're not worried about ambush,* thought Jud.

"You guys taught me that!" yelled Lisson.

"I know," said Jud. "How many insertion teams did you hunt down before they trusted you?"

The column paused at the top of a ridgeline. In the distance, Jud saw open grass fields: the Plain of Jars.

"Trust?" said Lisson. "You CIA Green Beret fuck! You know shit about trust. You're rats scurrying before the tidal wave of history. Who's gonna spy to keep the white man on top? Can't slip in a yellow man, because we can't trust no indig. And we don't wanna waste one of the white boys. So let's send in a nigger. We can con the slopes into trusting a black brother. Take a soul man, somebody who . . ."

Lisson started to hyperventilate. He gritted his teeth.

"Two tours in the Nam. Fightin' soldier from the sky. Dumb fuck out of Chicago, man, California Street where the sun never shines, but hey: the U.S. Army gonna make it right. Green Berets gonna let me prove I'm a man. I bought it all the way."

"Yes, you did," said Jud.

Lisson led the column down the hill.

"The worst promises don't have any words, just that look that holds your prayers."

"I know the look," said Jud.

"How many guys you sucker with it?"

Jud didn't answer. Lisson rambled on:

"How you gonna get those clever commies to trust an American so he can spy on them? Give 'em a GI they want: a dude who knows tough-guy secret shit to tell them. Some SOG star.

"And give the spy a legend the bad guys can believe," said Lisson. "You guys taught me Elijah and Cleaver, the Panthers. Che and Mao and Marx. Black power so I'd have a rap and a rep. A reason to fuck up America. Perfect cover. Then last year you shot King. Malcolm. Blew up four girls in a church, sweet fools thought some white God would save them. Fire hoses and police dogs. You're black, stay back, Jack. Oh, you taught me good!

"But you forgot to unteach. California Street. Rats in baby's room and whites only on the Gold Coast. The white boy who slapped Gramma in Biloxi. I used to be ashamed for her. Those villes up by Da Nang where we . . . where I . . . Nobody can forget that."

"I know places like that," said Jud.

"Then I should kill you now," Lisson told him. "Then you're guiltier than you look. White is the color of guilt. Of greed. Of capitalism that oppresses the masses. You got that guilt, you gotta die to get rid of it. Or get the assholes who shit you where you are."

"They caught you like SOG planned. Tortured you—"

"They taught me. Showed me the way of truth."

"You were our double. Became their triple. Gave 'em everything you could. Fight for them, too."

"Bought into the revolution. People of color are one." Lisson jerked Jud's tether. "Who the hell are you?"

"I'm three months short," said Jud. "I've seen all the shit. I want to walk away happy and whole. They sent me out here, so fuck them. I know more of their lies than you do."

"Next you're gonna tell me Lenin is your hero."

"I'm a stone-cold capitalist," said Jud. "And I got lots to sell that your revolution needs."

"What?"

"For starters, the head of North Vietnam's Politburo is headed for a secret meeting with the PLs about twelve klics from here. Our mission was to get him—alive or dead, but get him."

"Just like that, you expect me to believe you?"

"You want to hear the cover story I was supposed to let you beat out of me? About being a SPIKE recon team caching radios and supplies for other insertion teams and downed pilots?"

"You lie good," said Lisson.

"When I have to. But the truth is what'll work now. And it's what you and your dink masters need."

Lisson slapped Jud again, barked an order. Owl Eyes watched the boy drag Jud back down the line.

"Believe me!" Jud yelled. "You got no better choice!"

The boy holding Jud's rope jerked it tight and shoved him into line. Curtain was ten men back.

They marched west.

*They aren't worried about air strikes,* thought Jud.

The column left the hills for the rolling fields and ravines of the Plain of Jars. The natural color of Laos is green: thousands of napalm strikes had charred that land into a blackened abstract smear. Plumes of smoke rose haphazardly to the sky. The surviving foliage was stunted and stained with a dull metallic sheen from defoliants. Bomb craters pockmarked the earth. The air smelled unnatural and dead.

They camped when the sun rose one hand above the hills.

*There's the sawtooth mountains,* thought Jud. To the west, the bumpy plateau was right where it belonged.

"Air-strike time comin' up," Lissen told Jud and Curtain as they were led to a campfire. "This'll be your last hot meal."

The guards made Curtain and Jud squat. Scarface stood nearby, AK-47 ready. Soldiers lit fires, boiled rice. Lisson and Owl Eyes sat around the fire to Jud's right; Curtain was to his left.

"My buddy likes your popgun," Lisson told Jud, nodding to the derringer Scarface wore like a necklace. "You're too smart to pack that prissy piece of nothing 'less it's your 'good-bye guy' gun. You got the balls to shoot your own bullet?"

"I can do what I have to," Jud said.

Owl Eyes kept his face blank.

"He speak English?" Jud asked.

"Damned if I know," said Lisson.

"Damned if I care," said Jud. "What about our deal?"

"Do I smell treachery?" Lisson smiled. "Or bullshit? Same difference, honky: you stink.

"Look at them." Lisson nodded to the eating soldiers.

Curtain watched the fire.

"You got nothing to offer them, white boy," said Lisson. "CIA's been here since it vetoed neutrality in '59. The *armée clandestine.* Meo tribesmen. Don't kid yourself into thinking all fifteen thousand of yours worship you. You control the food supply to their villages, Yale bright boys commuting to work by copter from Thailand. Move whole towns around like checkers. The Company's grand plan. But these yellow brothers knew better than to fall for your bullying or bullshit."

"I told you I don't care about that," said Jud.

The pot of rice on their fire was ready. A guard untied Jud, put a wooden bowl and chopsticks in front of him. His fingers were too numb to move. He stayed on his haunches. Curtain sat on the ground beside him.

"When I knew they were dropping me here, I stole your file," said Jud. A sickly sweet flower smell drifted in the air. "If you grabbed me like you probably did six other teams, I wanted my deal in place."

"And if not?" asked Lisson.

"Doesn't matter now." Jud shrugged. "What did you do with the other Americans you nailed?"

"You already told me your mission," said Lisson, "your backup bullshit. You got nothing left they can't sweat out of you in the bunkers."

"Maybe yes, maybe no."

"Believe it," said Lisson.

Feeling returned to Jud's hands. He picked up the long wooden chopsticks. A guard ladled gooey rice into the bowl.

Slowly, Jud looked over his shoulder. Laughing groups of soldiers. Jud's Vietnamese asset was tied to a tree. They'd taken off his blindfold so he could watch the others eat.

"I have seen the way," sighed Lisson in a child's voice. "I am of the way."

"Then look behind me and see reality," said Jud.

Two Pathet Lao soldiers lounged by a tree, sharing a glass-bowled pipe. The smoke smelled of sickly sweet flowers.

"I got a piece of the poppy trade," said Jud. "The only money crop here in hell. I'm cashing in. Like a good capitalist."

"You and half your damn Meo lackeys. You and all Saigon. Fourteen-year-old girls selling scag at roadside stands on the way to the firebases. How many GI junkies these days, Bro'? Twenty-five thousand? How much heroin you shipping to poison brothers and sisters in New York and Newark and Chi-town?"

"The masses have many opiates," Jud told him. "What do you care which ones, when you can make that work for you?"

"You're scum," said Lisson.

"I'm a pragmatist," said Jud. "You better be. It pays."

"I don't want your death money!"

"Not *you:* your revolution. It's the sixties, Bro': flower power. Hell, in the fifties, French spies used opium to finance their war here, from the poppy fields in the Plain to the dens in Saigon. Called it Operation X. When the CIA found out, they got told to back off."

"Off ain't where they backed," snapped Lisson.

"I got growers in Burma with the Kuomintang Army your

buddy Mao ran out of China," said Jud. "If you protect our caravans to our airfields, we'll take it from there. You get cash. Plus."

"Plus?"

"You get me as an asset," said Jud. "You send me back—help me fake an escape. Maybe they'll make me a hero. I'll re-up. Get a command job with SOG—and do my business till Uncle Ho runs us out of Nam or I get bored. There won't be shit I don't see and know, and that bonus is worth more to you than cash."

His fellow POW Curtain stared at Jud; looked into the fire. Jud worked his chopsticks in the rice, ate a bite.

"You'd be a slimy kind of spy," Lisson said.

"Only kind there is," replied Jud.

"Why the hell should we believe you?" said Lisson.

The chopsticks turned slowly in Jud's hand. He braced the butt of each stick against the heel of his palm. Two ordinary chopsticks stuck out from between his fingers.

Peter Curtain, Jud's fellow POW, his mission number-two, a fellow American soldier, lowered his rice bowl to the ground.

Jud rammed his chopsticks through Curtain's eyes.

Curtain shot off the ground. The chopsticks stuck from his face. Blood sprayed Scarface. A scream gurgled in Curtain's throat; he fell into the campfire, writhing. . . .

Dead.

"No!" yelled Lisson.

Jud fell facedown, his hands crossed over his head.

Owl Eyes screamed.

A dozen Pathet Lao yelled; one accidentally squeezed off a burst from his machine gun. A line of dirt kicked in the air.

Lisson jumped on Jud, beating at the hands over his head. *"Damn you! What did you do? What did you do!"*

Owl Eyes pulled him off. Soldiers jerked Jud to his feet.

"I killed my own man!" yelled Jud. "Now you gotta believe me!"

"You dumb fuck!" Lisson punched Jud in the face. "He wasn't your man! He was *ours!* We owned him! Body and soul, five fuckin' years and you fuckin' killed him!"

"Didn' know," mumbled Jud through the blood in his mouth.

"How do you think we knew you were coming! How the hell did we know where to pick off the other teams! Radio codes and . . . Bought and paid for! Swiss accounts and *nobody* in your fucking CIA fucking Green Beret fucking SOG knew shit and you *waste* it all!"

Jud spit blood. "Now you need me more than ever."

Lisson bellowed and drew his K-bar knife.

Owl Eyes grabbed his arm.

*So you do speak English,* thought Jud.

The black American renegade broke free from Owl Eyes. He charged frantically around the camp. Pathet Lao scattered out of his path. Lisson slammed his boot into Curtain's body; kicked it again. He held his knife high with both hands, plunged it into the corpse; dropped to his knees, screamed words and sentences with no meaning as he stabbed the dead man again and again.

The knife blade came out red and wet. Pointed at Jud.

"We're taking you all the way in," said Lisson. "One way or the other, you'll know the truth. And so will we. But whatever happens, you belong to me."

He yelled an order. Scarface tied Jud's hands behind him, gave his tether to the boy. They jerked the Vietnamese asset into line. Lisson crashed into the jungle; the column followed.

They left Curtain's body where it lay.

Lisson marched the column through scattered grass fields and patches of forest. After an hour, Jud started yelling. The boy jerked his tether, hit him, but Jud kept calling for Lisson. The column halted in a field. Owl Eyes and Lisson walked back to Jud.

"You hit my kidneys too much," said Jud. "I don't pee, I'll black out. Your guys can't carry me far enough, fast enough."

"Piss your pants," Lisson told him.

"If I could," said Jud. "Every jostle makes it stop."

Owl Eyes asked Lisson a question, got an answer. Shrugged. Lisson barked an order. The boy led Jud out of line. Owl Eyes stopped them, summoned the veteran Scarface. Owl Eyes gave him Jud's tether and his instructions.

"Remember, you're nobody in the middle of nowhere," Lisson told Jud. "Do anything dumb, you'll wish I already killed you."

Lisson scanned the exposed terrain, checked his watch and the sky: no warplanes. Yet. He ordered the column to move on.

Scarface ran Jud to a grove of trees, where he undid Jud's black pajama bottoms, let them fall around his ankles. Scarface fixed a bayonet to his Russian assault rifle.

Slowly, he slid the bayonet blade inside Jud's underwear. He yelled, lunged—and cut away Jud's jockey shorts. They dangled from the blade as Scarface walked away, laughing.

"What about untieing my hands?" asked Jud, bending so his question was obvious.

Scarface pointed the bayonet at Jud's naked groin.

For ten minutes Jud shuffled from foot to foot. Scarface sat on a log, smoking a cigarette, the bayoneted assault rifle across his knees. Jud finally relieved himself.

After he'd worked his pajama bottoms down his ankles. After he'd freed his feet.

"Okay!" he yelled to Scarface.

The Pathet Lao put out his cigarette. Frowned at the half-naked prisoner. He put the assault rifle on the ground so he could pull up Jud's pants. Bent down.

Jud kicked him in the chin. Scarface snapped up. Jud's foot slammed into his stomach, doubling him over. A roundhouse kick smashed the guard's temple. Scarface crashed to the ground. Jud stomped on his neck until he was sure.

Time! prayed Jud. Give me time to catch them—twenty-three soldiers, Lisson, my asset; time to surprise *them!*

Three minutes to brace the assault rifle and use the fixed bayonet to cut the ropes off his wrist.

Ninety seconds to dress, scavenge the corpse. Leave the worn photos of a woman and baby, the letters, the blanket, and spare socks. Five grenades, six clips for the rifle. One full canteen, a pouch of rice, some dried fruit, a waterproof tin of matches. Jud pulled on Scarface's pack, took his holstered derringer from around the dead man's neck, strapped it to his left arm.

Owl Eyes had Curtain's flash-encode communicator; Lisson had Jud's.

Three men chattering in Lao walked through the trees.

Jud dove, grabbed the assault rifle, rolled up to his knees, and sprayed half a clip of bullets into the soldiers.

He was running as they hit the ground, scooping up an extra AK-47 and a pouch of clips from their bloody heap.

The patrol was west of him; he ran east. Lisson would have halted the column when he sent the three men; he'd have heard the shots. They couldn't be more than twelve marching minutes away.

Now they'd be running.

Jud raced from one grove to another, up and down ravines, stumbling through bomb craters.

Dirt sprayed into the air to his right; a machine gun chattered. He jumped a ravine, missed his footing on the other side, and rolled down the slope.

A fanned-out line of men ran toward him from a quarter mile away.

He fired a burst, hoping it would make them cautious, slow them down. Scrambled out of the ravine. And ran.

But he'd twisted his knee. The beatings and the pain in his leg drained strength from his stride. His lungs were on fire, his head throbbed. With each step, the guerrillas drew closer.

They kept shooting—short bursts, bullets ripping through brush on either side of Jud. He had to dodge and weave. They could run straight, waste no steps as they closed the gap.

Half a dozen bullets shattered on a rock to Jud's left. Ricocheting fragments sliced his leg, but he didn't stop. They were shooting low: Lisson wanted him alive.

"Gonna die GI!" screamed an Asian voice two hundred meters behind Jud. Was it Owl Eyes? "Gonna die GI!"

Scarred fields stretched in front of Jud for more than a mile: open land. Lisson rated as a sharpshooter.

Jud ran until he thought they'd cleared the trees. He spun around, Scarface's machine gun chattering in an arc along the line of men chasing him. The Pathet Lao dropped as Jud slapped a new clip in the gun, fired it off, catching his breath as they ate dirt. He thought he hit two of them. He rammed in a third clip, fired at a raised head—the gun jammed. Jud dropped it and ran.

"Jud Stuart!" bellowed Lisson. "You're mine, Jud Stuart!"

*You know my name,* thought Jud. *Have you figured out the truth yet?*

Silver dots winked at him in the blue sky.

Something *whooshed* over his head.

Two jets raced toward the other side of Laos, their vapor trails drawing white lines half a mile off the ground.

*I'm down here!* Jud wanted to yell at the Americans in the sky. The Pathet Lao were charging toward him, a ragged line of running men a hundred meters away.

The planes banked through a turn on the horizon, silver dots floating back, coming closer.

Coming to get the enemy soldiers they'd glimpsed running across the Plain of Jars.

A bomb crater was twenty meters in front of Jud. Ten. He stretched his legs, ran with all his might, dove through the air.

Two glistening canisters dropped from each jet, twisting and tumbling through the blue sky.

Napalm.

A roaring orange, soapy gasoline *heat* blew over the crater where Jud burrowed. The warplanes zoomed by, homeward bound. Behind him, he heard the flames crackle, rattling ammunition explosions. Screams. Imagined metal glasses melting in the inferno.

Jud dragged himself to the crater's rim, looked back.

Saw a solid wall of bellowing orange flame.

"Jesus," panted Jud with no disrespect. "Jesus."

In front of the wall of fire, four black silhouettes rose out of the dirt and the ashes of the dead—and moved toward Jud.

The heat wind whipped a bandanna on the tallest silhouette.

The barrel of Jud's second commandeered assault rifle jutted deep into the mud of the crater: blocked, useless.

Jud lobbed two grenades toward the shadows. As soon as they exploded, he ran in the other direction. He didn't look back.

Stumbling, staggering, he made it to another grove of trees. His knee throbbed, his leg and mouth bled. He collapsed, fell on a tree root twisting up from the earth.

*Don't stop. Don't stop.*

When he pushed himself off the root, his whole hand went around it. Quickly, he slid out of dead Scarface's pack. He wedged one of his last two grenades under the root, tied a pack strap to the grenade pin, and laid the pack on top of the booby trap.

And staggered deeper into the trees.

Twenty steps, then came the *whump* explosion. A man screamed. Jud looked back as he heard the man die; stumbled over a log and sprawled face first to the dirt. His last grenade rolled away, lost in the brush.

Footsteps crunched behind him.

Jud scooted on his back until he leaned against a log.

Lisson stepped from the trees. His shirt was soaked. Mucus coated his lips and his chest heaved. His eyes were napalm.

The boy who'd been Jud's keeper staggered behind Lisson, barely able to walk.

Jud pulled his derringer from his wrist holster. Inched the gun toward his own gasping mouth.

"*No!*" yelled Lisson. He charged, reaching for Jud's gun.

And Jud grabbed Lisson's reaching arm with his empty hand, pulled it down and out of the way, flicked the derringer toward Lisson's face. Pulled the trigger.

A *pop!* stamped a red dot below an ebony cheekbone.

Lisson crashed on Jud, dying with a sigh.

When Jud rolled free, the Pathet Lao boy stood ten feet away, his rifle pointed at the ground. Jud aimed the derringer with its one remaining poison shell at him.

Then lowered his arm.

The boy blinked; turned and faded into his country.

Jud's communicator was in a pouch under Lisson's shirt. Nine months after going native, Lisson still wore his American dog tags. Jud dropped them in the pouch he strapped around his waist. He took Lisson's gear, staggered out of the trees.

Black smoke billowed to the sky from the napalmed field. Two klicks ahead of him was a humpbacked hill where he might find shelter from America's steel rain.

He limped to the hill, praying that no American planes would spot his black-pajamaed form; praying that today no other Pathet Lao patrols sought their revolution on this patch of earth. Jud crawled up the slope, hid between two boulders. When his hands stopped shaking and he could control the pain racking his body, he tapped code words into the hand-held communicator.

WATERSHED: the code name of his mission.

MALICE: Jud's code name, known only by the three people who'd sanctioned his mission: Art, the Green Beret captain at SOG/Command Control North in Da Nang; Ghostman, a CIA agent in the Laotian capital of Vientiane whose bottom-line status was hidden from the other five hundred CIA case officers proudly running the Agency's secret war; and a senior military officer whose name, rank, and branch of the service was unknown to Jud.

FLOOD: surface mission blown. Politburo target abandoned.

SHARK: Curtain confirmed as traitor. Terminated.

BARRACUDA: Lisson. Located. Terminated.

WHITE WHALE: the Vietnamese asset. Believed dead. *Blue*

*Whale* would have meant Jud had been able to pull him out alive.

In Da Nang four days after Jud's radio message, someone slit the throat of the prostitute Curtain frequented.

Jud's message pinpointed the humpbacked hill with as many coordinates as he could remember. He wanted to beg for immediate exfiltration, but didn't succumb to that bad strategy. He pushed the transmit button, which sent his message in a microburst up to a satellite, down to CIA headquarters in Langley, to be flashed by cable to SOG/Command Control North in Da Nang and a CIA station in Vientiane. Jud spent the night huddled between the two boulders, shaking with hunger and cold and memories; sobbing. His legs and mouth stopped bleeding, but his whole life ached and he was weak, so weak.

Just after dawn, he heard the helicopters, three gunships chopping their way to his hill. Two copters circled the area, door gunners poised behind their .50 calibers. The third copter sank toward the Plain of Jars, lower, lower . . .

And Jud ran toward the copter, its steady *whump whump whump* once heard, never forgotten, never mistaken. Stiff, cold, shot through with pain, he ran . . .

But it was a car engine, not a helicopter.

Highway, he was on a highway. Desert. Running.

Staggering. His side ached, his knees and back throbbed, he was nauseous and wheezing. Nora's Café was a quarter of a mile down the road. He realized he'd turned around, was headed back.

*Not a helicopter.* A car engine. In the lane to his left.

A battered black Buick with Carmen at the wheel crept past him. She stared at the crazy gringo.

Jud waved his hand, imploring her to stop.

Carmen accelerated, roared down the road to her job.

*The hell with it,* thought Jud. He staggered to a walk.

A rabbit scurried across the empty highway.

*How long?* thought Jud. *How long have I got?*

They hadn't found him in four days. By now, they should have looked. By now *they* should have left a trail.

*If I could find their trail, I could see them,* thought Jud. *And maybe I could keep them from seeing me.*

The telephone booth by the highway outside Nora's Café was a dozen steps away.

*I need an asset,* thought Jud. *A clean asset. Someone to check my trail. Someone whom I can trust enough. Somebody in L.A.*

Dean.

They hadn't talked in years. But time held no meaning for Dean. Jud thought Dean would do it to feed his own fires.

On the edge of a desert highway, Jud caught his breath. He picked up the pay phone.

# THE OLD PRO

The day after Wes Chandler promised Beth a souvenir from Hollywood, Nick Kelley had lunch at the Madison Hotel.

"I was surprised you called," said Nick's companion, a man who'd made it to fifty-six with a horseshoe of hair, a thick chest, and sharp eyes. He lived in a modest Virginia house with his physicist wife and two adopted children. His wife worked for the same firm. Nick had talked to her when he called their home the night before. "Glad, but surprised."

"I appreciate your coming, Sam," said Nick.

"*Appreciation* means this is more than a friendly lunch."

They'd met more than a decade earlier, at the beginning of the era when Sam was allowed to say that he worked for the Central Intelligence Agency.

"During all the years I was covering intelligence for Peter Murphy, I never called you for stories."

"Uh-huh." Sam's repsonse was empty, waiting for Nick's words.

"I've just started a special assignment for Peter."

Four well-fed men in dark suits lumbered past their table. Sam let Nick's image sift through his steady gaze.

"Back to your old wicked ways?" Sam shook his head. "Can't be for money. Murphy is notoriously cheap. Your books keep coming out and you had that TV series. . . . You asked to go back."

"It's a new era. Intelligence is a special interest of mine, and now with *glasnost,* the end of the Cold War . . ."

"That we won," said Sam. "You liberals shouldn't have been so critical of us *cold warriors* all these years."

They laughed.

"But don't worry," said Sam. "If you believe history, you can be certain a new enemy will find us."

He smiled. "Why didn't you ever call me before?"

"I didn't want to have you write me off as a friend. Not for routine muckraking."

"You're a curious sentimentalist for this town," said Sam. "And you went back with Murphy. And you called me. This must not be about *routine muckraking*."

"I'm not sure what it's about."

"I appreciated not getting 'friendly' phone calls. But back then as well as now . . . There are some seven thousand CIA employees. I'm not in the loop of big things."

"Sam, you were in Covert Ops from Veitnam until the early 1970s. You were a presidential briefer. Now you're the top aide to one of the czars out there."

"You make me sound so . . . exotic. Quite the old pro. I must be more important than I thought.

"Actually," he said, "it's all just a matter of watching which chair you sit in at meetings."

"Out there, that's more than standard Washington wars."

Sam laughed. "Are you investigating the new Director? Ralph Denton: the man tragedy elevated—most say beyond merit."

"What do *you* say?"

The old-line CIA executive shrugged. "Denton's a politician. The nature of that beast demands close scrutiny."

"Everybody in this town is a politician," said Nick.

"Of course," said Sam, retreating. "True."

The waiter came over. Sam ordered salmon, soup. A glass of white wine. Nick ordered the first special the waiter mentioned.

"What does your wife think about this career shift?" asked Sam. "Sylvia, right? Works for Congress, right?"

Sam had never met Sylvia.

"She likes my fiction," said Nick.

"Fiction in general or fiction that keeps you away from this topic?"

Nick didn't answer.

"Did you meet her when she was a source of yours?" asked Sam.

"I don't talk about my sources," Nick told Sam's waiting gaze. "No one would ever know you and I talked either."

"Except for the thirty people dining here," said Sam. "But I understand what you mean. You're a good man. And I'm sure you have a lovely wife, however you met her. Many people thought you'd never marry. You were a quiet kind of wild."

"I calmed my life down almost five years ago. Not just because of her, though she wouldn't have bought my bullshit. Plus she has this skin that makes you ache to . . ." Nick drifted off.

"And now you have a son." Sam smiled. "I have other friends from Michigan. We keep up with our *homeboy* celebrity.

"Does your wife know what you're doing?" he asked.

"We're not here about my wife and me."

Nick had told Sylvia not to worry. Explained the wisdom of giving his ex-boss Peter Murphy cheap labor for a free-lance piece to gain a journalistic legitimacy to ask questions.

"There's nothing you need to know," she'd insisted.

"It's the compromise. It's how to handle this situation."

"There is no factual situation," she said. "Not if you don't 'handle' it into existence!"

"It's something I should do!" he told her.

"No more than that," she finally conceded. *"No more!"*

He hadn't told her about his phone call to Dean.

The waiter at the Madison brought Sam's soup.

"Even if I wanted to help you," said Sam, raising his spoon, "I probably couldn't. We function through specialization, compartmentalization. A Team, B Team, different tracks—sometimes one track doesn't even know the other track exists. Not a lot of gossip in the halls."

"Are you saying you'll help me?"

Sam leaned across the table. "What is it that you want?"

"In the last two, three weeks, has something . . . special or unusual happened?"

"Such as?"

"If I knew, I wouldn't have to ask." Nick looked from side to side: no one at the other tables paid any attention to them. "Probably something in the covert ops area. Possibly drugs or dirty tricks. Possibly domestic."

"You're asking me if *something happened?*"

"Something recent. Maybe something involving California."

"Lucky you've got your fiction to fall back on." Sam shook his head. "You're shooting into a black hole hoping to hit something. You might as well be shooting blanks."

"Can you help me?"

"I never pegged you for a conspiracy nut. Are you another sanctimonious ignoramus who thinks the CIA smuggles drugs?"

"No, I don't think you guys smuggle drugs."

"Because we don't shovel dirt like that. It makes convenient fiction but lousy government, and we're not about lousy government. Our kids live in this country!"

"I'm not accusing anybody of anything. I just want to know if something's happened."

"You're not after a story," muttered Sam. He blinked. "What have you gotten yourself into?"

"My kid lives in this country, too," answered Nick.

"Are you in trouble?"

"I'm not. And I want to keep it that way."

The waiter brought their main courses.

"This is about somebody else." Sam pushed salmon around his plate.

"What makes you say that?"

"You say *you're* not in trouble. You're not asking about a particular country or a specific issue. If you're not just fishing . . . If it's not a program, it's a person. How are you involved with him?"

"What him?" said Nick.

"Whatever him there is," answered Sam.

"I thought I was the one looking for answers."

"You came to me," was Sam's answer. "I'm trying to get a fix on who you are these days."

"I'm older, I'm smarter, and I have less time to waste."

"The question is what are you doing," said Sam.

"I've got a journalism assignment."

"Spare me your cover identity." Sam shrugged. "I don't know if I can help you."

"Are you sure it's a question of *can?*"

"Listen," said Sam, "you get something more, you need to talk . . . call me."

"And if you get something?"

"There's nothing for me to get," said the man from the CIA. "Our scandals have all been exposed."

The two men finished their lunch as quickly as they could. They said good-bye in front of the Madison's revolving door. Sam watched Nick walk to the subway. A doorman reached for the parking stub clutched in Sam's glove.

"Could you just park it out here?" said Sam. "I won't be a minute."

The revolving doors spun him back into the Madison. A bellman pointed him to a bank of pay phones. Though only one of the three phones was in use, Sam waited until the fat woman in a fur coat finished chewing out her husband, hung up, and lumbered toward the dining room. Sam dropped a quarter in the phone.

"Emily? . . . Call Public Affairs, tell them I want a press-contact form. . . . I know, but I want *them* to send me one *today*. . . . And call General Cochran's secretary. Squeeze me in to see him."

After the call, he walked back through the revolving doors, turning up his collar against the cold.

# BLOWTORCH

A jetliner brought Wes to Los Angeles before noon. The stewardess had hair that with less blond and no hairspray could have been Beth's color. He rented a car, called Detective Rawlins. They agreed to meet at a Hollywood hotel.

Sunshine and smog enveloped Wes as soon as he stepped out of the terminal: his trench coat went into his suitcase. He drove his rental Ford north on wide city streets.

Block after block of southern California urbanity rolled past his windshield. Minutes, not miles, were the measure here. Everything seemed contemporary and capable of motion: the doughnut shops, the modest homes with green lawns, the sparsely populated sidewalks, the millions of well-cared-for cars.

A red light stopped his progress. A well-waxed black Mercedes with sealed windows pulled beside him in the left lane. The driver was alone, a woman with jet-black hair, wonderful cheekbones, and blood lipstick that matched her fingernails. Surgeons had done a beautiful job on her nose. Her skin was artfully powdered alabaster. She turned toward Wes. Noted his rental economy car. Turned to watch the light change to green.

His road dead-ended into Sunset Boulevard and he took a right. Billboards advertising movies commanded the high ground above the palm trees. He drove past seven guitar shops. A sultry blonde waltzed up the sidewalk in front of the largest shop's long, gray stucco wall. She wore a loose white minidress that could have been designed for a child and strap-on high heels. Maybe she was sixteen, maybe she was a careful and cash-heavy thirty-six. The breeze flapped her skirt to show Wes the white garter belt holding up her patterned white stockings.

And he wondered if Beth ever wore dresses.

He turned left at La Brea. *Are the tar pits around here?* He imagined black puddles bubbling up bones of unwary dinosaurs.

A matted-haired man with sun-leathered skin, a torn brown T-shirt, stained green pants, and wearing one sneaker ran screaming from the franchised burger shop. Wes braked to avoid him, but the screamer didn't care. No one else paid any attention.

Hollywood Boulevard came two lights later. He spotted the hotel, pulled into a parking spot. Two gaunt, denim-clad boys with backpacks, tattoos, and long hair almost as many years out of style as they were old watched him feed the meter. They shuffled down the sidewalk when Wes stared back.

When he was a boy, Wes's mother told him many times of her pilgrimage to Hollywood, of seeing the center of that dazzling universe, Graumann's Chinese Theater, with its red-and-green facade and carved dragons, its pagoda sloping roof, and its sidewalk where the names of the stars were immortally cast in concrete.

Across the street, Wes spotted his mother's memory.

Wes glanced at his feet: he was standing on the star of a person he'd never heard of. Two buses stopped in front of the theater, belched diesel smoke, and disgorged blue-haired American matrons with their sagging husbands and nattily dressed Japanese families in which everyone carried a camera.

A chattering woman wearing 163 slogan and campaign buttons marched up to the tourists. Some of them took her picture; some of them got back on the bus.

Wes walked into the hotel.

A Mexican bellhop nodded to him. A perky brunette wearing the hotel's maroon blazer and a gray skirt gave him a beautiful smile. Another woman wearing that outfit sat at the concierge desk. She had smooth olive skin and was speaking Farsi to a disgruntled man in a three-piece suit.

Two men stood by the dining room. One was fifty, Jewish, with short gray hair and a neatly trimmed beard. He had thick glasses, wore a bulky sweater. His companion was a beefy black man in a two-piece suit and heavy black shoes. He carried a notebook. The middle-aged Jew bid good-bye to the black man, then hustled past Wes, a distracted look on his face.

The black man and Wes sized each other up.

"I'm looking for Mr. Rawlins," said Wes.

"*Detective* Rawlins," answered the black.

"Wes Chandler," he said, and stuck out his hand.

Rawlins had a powerful grip. "You got something besides a driver's license to show me?"

Wes held out his laminated NIS ID for the cop to see.

"That's not a federal buzzer." Rawlins flashed Wes his own badge.

"I'm a lawyer."

"So why ain't you working in Century City, banking big bucks and driving a BMW?"

"My idea was that learning the law would help me understand how things tick. Have a better handle on it."

"You wanna learn how things tick, get yourself a buzzer, a 9mm, and ride around with me."

The L.A. cop nodded to the hotel door.

"That guy I was with?" he said. "Nice guy. TV man, but none of the crap. Couple nights ago, his wife picks him up from work. Good lady. He remembers a call he ain't made, has her park out front. Runs in, drops a dime to some actor with the who-am-I heebie-jeebies, calms him down, walks outside just in time to see a dude *cowboy* the doorman with three blasts from a .45. Going to law schools won't give you the tick on that one."

"What was it?"

"Same gun that nailed a guy on my turf downtown." Rawlins shrugged. "Filipino rock 'n' roll. You had lunch?"

"Airplane food. I'll buy."

"I'll eat," said Rawlins. "We could do it cheap in the coffee shop, but the tables aren't designed for privacy."

Wes nodded to the maître d' waiting by the velvet-roped entrance to the dining room. Rawlins led the way.

"You care if we sit in smoking?" he asked.

"I used to mind." Wes smiled. "I've loosened up."

They took a table by the far wall. About half the other tables were full. A white-coated waiter walked their way.

"You drink on the job?" asked Rawlins.

"No."

"Me either." Rawlins looked up at the waiter as he reached their table. "Vodka rocks."

Wes ordered coffee. Rawlins shook a filtered cigarette out of a pack, tore the filter off, and tossed it in the ashtray. He lit up, nodded to the discarded filter.

"Makes my wife think I'm being cautious. Bumper pads for coffin nails."

A Chinese woman in a tailored suit worth a week of Wes's salary sashayed past the table, ebony hair sleek on her shoulders.

Both men watched her petite hips sway away. Rawlins's eyes were waiting for the Marine's gaze to return to business.

"You never get used to that in L.A.," said Rawlins. "So many of 'em. You married? Kids?"

"Not lucky enough for either."

"This is a hard town to be married in." The cop rubbed out his cigarette. Sipped his vodka. "So how come a L.A. street cop like me with a D.U.O. on ice has a federal case on his hands?"

"I can't tell you."

"I hate the classified blues."

The waiter returned, took their lunch orders.

"Naval Investigative Service," said Rawlins when the waiter had left. "Is that right?"

"Yes."

"You been to more than law school."

"I'm a Marine."

"Ah. With a little rock 'n' roll time. Now you're gumshoeing this ex-sailor—Hopkins."

"Has anything changed?"

"He's still dead."

"You know what I mean."

Rawlins sighed. "Nobody's claimed his body, nobody's called. San Fran P.D. doesn't list him as a missing person and found nobody at his place, so they're done with him. Our coroner says could be accident, could be somebody pushed him down the stairs in back of that bar. The County will keep his body on ice for thirty-one days, then if no other authorities protest and nobody claims him, he'll get a cheap hole at the county cemetery."

"That's it?"

"Hopkins is a case of the *could be's* and *don't cares*."

"What about your investigation?"

"I figure you're the center of my investigation." Rawlins's voice was even. Cool.

"I've got nothing to add to what you know," said Wes.

"You could subtract some of the could be's."

The waiter brought their food.

"I'm just making sure everything is in line," said Wes.

"What line?"

When Wes wouldn't answer, Rawlins cursed, but they both knew it was pro forma.

Throaty feminine laughter came from the table to their right, a steadier-toned laugh than Beth's. A lean, hawk-faced woman with curly brown hair, a tailored jacket, and a midthigh leather miniskirt used humor to insist that the three studio men she was meeting with take her seriously.

"Do you have any suggestions?" said Wes.

"You could go to the Oasis, talk to the night bartender. Guy named Leo. He found the stiff. That's all he told us."

"Was there anybody else there that night?"

"Like who?" asked Rawlins.

"Nobody special."

"As far as we know, nobody special is who was there."

Rawlins told Wes how to find the Oasis, suggested a hotel. The detective agreed to send Wes the autopsy report.

"With Leo," said Rawlins, "try a little lean, try a little green. I ain't had the time or motivation for a second round with the boy."

"Thanks."

Wes gave the waiter cash and took the receipt stub. He stood, looked down at the cop. He liked him.

"There's an outside chance I may need help," said Wes.

"We all take our chances," said the cop. Smiling.

Wes called private eye Jack Berns in Washington from the L.A. pay phone the CIA said Jud had used.

"You said you could provide a service," said Wes.

"I said I could provide *any* service."

"It would be helpful to know the calls placed from a pay phone in L.A. The number called, who the number is registered to."

"'*Helpful*'? You cagey lawyers!" Berns laughed. "Local calls are damn near impossible. Long distance . . . can be done."

"How fast?"

"It's a question of timing. You're in the middle of a billing cycle, so if somebody were to ask the computer, the machine would make a special run, and then that somebody might get hit with questions none of us want asked."

"I don't want to ring any alarm bells," said Wes. "How soon can you get me what I need?"

"I'm betting a couple days—if you can afford to ask."

"I can afford to ask, but not to wait forever."

Wes gave him the number, dates bracketing the night Jud called.

"So you're in L.A.? Where should I call you?"

"Don't try." Wes hung up. He was on a busy road, a second-class commercial strip.

*Why here?* he thought. *Why this phone?*

Leo was polishing glasses at the far end of the Oasis's bar when Wes opened the door. Wes stood in the entrance, giving the bartender a black silhouette in front of the red sunset.

The half dozen drunks scattered through the bar paid the newcomer no mind as he stepped into their dim-lit world. When Leo saw the jacket and tie, the clean-shaven face, he knew.

"You're new," he called out to the obvious cop.

"Same as I ever was," said Wes, leaning on the bar. He casually waved his black ID case, stuck it back in his pocket without opening it, and beckoned for Leo to join him.

"Sorry I didn't come down right away," said Leo. His breath smelled of pizza. "Dozen years after the USC game and the knee still locks up."

"Just tell me the rest about the dead guy," said Wes.

"I told you guys everything. He went out there, he died. I don't know why, I don't know how, don't know him, end of story."

"If it were *end* of story, I wouldn't be here."

"I don't want no trouble. I run a nice place."

"Bullshit." Lawyer Wes held his breath, but Leo didn't object to such arrogance from an authority. "I'm not here to bust you, I'm not here to be your buddy. But I'll do one or the other before I go."

"What do I gotta do?"

"Tell me what happened—all of it, not just the skim you laid on the other cops. Tell me about the dead guy."

"So he and I shot the shit. So he helped me out."

"How?"

"Helped me drag a rummy out there to the bull pen. Didn't mean nothing, so I didn't say nothing."

"What about this rummy?"

"Passed out." Leo's face lit up. "The guy who died? He went back out there to check on him."

"What did he find?"

"The wrong way to go down the stairs."

"What about the other guy?"

Even Leo got it now.

"The other guy came back in first, walked out the front."

Wes knew such a rigged identification would be thrown out of court, but he didn't care about court. He showed the bartender Jack Bern's surveillance photo of Jud.

"Yeah. That's the guy we dragged out."

"You know him? He live around here?"

The idea came slow to Leo, but it came.

"This guy in the picture: if I was to call in what I knew to Crimesolvers, might be a reward in it for me."

"And you'd get busted as an accessory after the fact, plus obstructing an investigation."

The bartender frowned. While he was talking, Wes laid a twenty-dollar bill on the table.

"That guy ain't been back," Leo said, eyeing the bill. "I think he lives at a fleabag up the street called the Zanzibar."

"That's not much for a whole lot."

The bartender licked his lips.

"Maybe his name is Bill," he said.

Wes shook his head, nodded to the money.

"Buy yourself some lying lessons," he said.


"I figured you guys would be asking about him," said the pockmarked man behind the registration desk at the Zanzibar Hotel Apartments. He smelled of violet perfume. With one hand he held a slim cigarillo, with the other he tapped the picture Wes had laid on the desk. "Figured."

"Is he here?" asked Wes.

Beneath the smog of cigarillo smoke, the Zanzibar smelled of dust and mold.

"No. Been, oh, few weeks since he paid his rent. We closed out his room."

"Why did you figure we'd be around asking about him?"

"What am I: stupid? The gentleman's a burglar, right?"

"What makes you think he's a burglar?"

"He's a juicer who jaws your ear off. How *important* he is, how much he knows. He'd get an attitude. Tell me I didn't have a clue. Hah! He's supposed to have this day job? Sure enough, no matter how loaded he got the night before, morning come, he'd crawl out of bed, get a bus to somewhere. But I don't buy it as a *job*. One day he shows me this bag of tools. I seen lockpicks before. Says he's the top locksmith in the country. I say yeah, great, but *I* had it figured."

The clerk blew a cloud of smoke.

"A walking ticky-tocking time bomb, that one." He smiled. "Jud, right? Jud . . . Seward?"

"Something like that," said Wes.

"So am I going to be reading about him in the papers?"

"I doubt it. You said you closed out his room."

"After we didn't see him on rent day, I boxed up his stuff, gave the room to a more responsible party."

Springs stuck from holes in the lobby's sofa. The pay phone on the wall was battered. The muffled sounds of a man and a woman yelling at each other floated down the open stairwell.

"What happened to his stuff?"

"It's in the back room. We're a legit place, so we *must* hold stuff like that for a month. How do you figure the law?"

"I quit trying. I'd like to see the stuff from his room."

"I'd like to see that ID you waved at me again," said the clerk.

When Wes passed the clerk his ID case, a twenty-dollar bill was sticking from it. The clerk slid the bill out, checked it, gave the unopened case back to Wes.

"Nice picture," said the clerk. He crooked his finger.

The back room was jammed with boxes, suitcases, stacks of clothes, and bundled papers. The clerk found a shoebox and two unlocked suitcases, put them on a dusty table, and left Wes alone.

Nothing in the shoebox but toiletries.

The suitcases were made of battered aluminum and had once cost a great deal. The clothes inside them varied from worn-out and formerly expensive to worn-out and formerly dirt cheap.

Wes assumed that any valuables Jud had left behind had long since been appropriated by the clerk.

Wes found a car key with a Mercedes emblem, left it.

In the pocket of a tattered blue Hawaiian shirt, he found two wrinkled and faded Polaroid snapshots.

The first picture was of Jud and another man, sitting on a red couch, smiling for the camera. The other man looked nervous. In the picture, the two men were probably in their thirties. Jud's companion had black hair barbered over his ears, a shirt, blue jeans. He was lean, clean-shaven.

The second picture was of a woman. A gorgeous woman, stunning even in a badly composed, aged Instamatic shot.

She had reddish-chestnut hair cascading from her head like a lion's mane. A widow's peak, like Beth's, but thicker tresses. Her face looked Italian, oval with wide lips, huge brown eyes. Her grin showed innocent embarrassment, thought Wes. She seemed small, though as she turned to be surprised by the camera, her white sweater pulled tight against heavy breasts. She stood on a dune; behind her was an ocean.

Wes kept the pictures.

It took Wes an hour the next morning to find where Jud had worked. Wes used the yellow pages, reached Angel Hardware & Lock on the ninth call, and asked for Jud. The man told him Jud had quit. Wes realized the store was close to the pay phone Jud had used and drove there.

*This guy was born scared,* thought Wes as he interviewed the pudgy owner in the back workroom. As they talked, an old man with a stubbled face disassembled a lock at the workbench.

The owner chewed his lip, confirmed little more than that Jud had failed to show up for work the day after Hopkins died.

"There has to be something you can tell me about him!" Wes insisted.

"No, I, no, nothing, I . . ." The fat man shrugged.

"Was he a good locksmith?" asked Wes in desperation.

"Ah, yeah, as . . ." The owner lost his ability to speak.

"He was not locksmith," said the man at the workbench.

Wes turned around.

"Locksmith?" said the old man, Europe thick in his words. "No.

*I* am locksmith. Jud was an *artist*. He had angels in his hands. This man can manipulate safe. Do you know what this means?"

"No," said Wes.

"Dial," said the old man. "He could dial open a safe. By touch. By sound. By scent. Do you know how rare that is? This is a craft, demanding, ever changing. You must be trained. But few of us are ever more than technicians. To dial a safe like he can . . . perhaps two men in this country. Perhaps one in Europe.

"And I tell you this: wherever he learned what he knew, it wasn't to fix security systems for silly starlets."

"He took things from me," blurted out the owner, afraid to speak, but more afraid to be upstaged by the old man.

"You owed him," said the old man.

"What things?" asked Wes.

"Just tools," said the old man. "Of our trade—yes?"

The owner licked his lips, nodded.

Wes thanked the old man, left.

He went back to the same pay phone and called Jack Berns.

"Good timing," said the private eye. "I think I got what you want: two long distance calls that may be hot."

"Two?" said Wes. Cars whizzed by him on the street. Where had Jud gone? And how had he gotten there? Bus?

"There's one to a special number you may know at the firm where our mutual friend works."

"I know about that."

"I bet," said Berns. "Plus one to Takoma Park, just over the D.C. line. Phone's listed to a Nick Kelley."

"You did good."

"I did more," said Berns.

"I hired you to do what I told you!"

"Then you don't want to hear what I got?"

Wes silently cursed, said, "Go ahead."

"Nick Kelley's a reporter. Or used to be. At my old friend Peter Murphy's column."

"Don't jerk me around, Berns."

"Not unless you pay me to." The private eye laughed. "I recognized the name. Met him a few times way back. My business, you get a hit, you follow through. I dropped by Peter's office—"

"You what!"

"I see Peter a few times a year. I found out that our boy Nick quit reporting way back when to write novels. Wrote a spy book once. Think our mutual friend would like to hear that?"

"He'll hear what I tell him."

"Be sure to tell him Nick Kelley is back on the beat."

"Huh?"

"Peter let it slip that Nick came in, cut a deal to pick up the press pass and do a piece on spooks. He works out of some office he's got up on Capitol Hill.

"Way I figure it," said Berns, "you aren't experienced with reporters, so I'll take a run at Nick and scope out what—"

"Forget it!" Wes felt on fire; his voice was ice. "I told you to get me numbers and names. You went way beyond that—"

"And I scored, *Major.*"

"Your games stop now. Do you hear me? Now! And it all stays just between us."

"Don't worry. I know where my money's coming from. I'll sit right here and wait for it. And for you."

The private eye hung up.

Wes swore, wanted to smash the telephone. A customized 1967 red Corvette roared past Wes, honking its horn at a Japanese family car that was trying to nose its way across the intersection.

*Got it!* He dropped more coins in the pay phone.

"Detective Rawlins," said the voice that answered.

"Can I get a geographic breakdown of reported crimes with the LAPD computer?" Inspiration tingled through Wes.

"There's a guy at a terminal across the squadroom could do just that," said the cop.

"Can you tell me if somebody stole a car?" Wes gave him the address of the pay phone, asked for a six-block-square grid search. "On that night that Hopkins died, the next morning."

"You riding a crime wave, Marine?" said Rawlins.

But he put Wes on hold. Came back a minute later.

"You should play the lottery," said Rawlins.

"What's the license plate and make?" asked Wes excitedly.

"You probably won't care. The Highway Patrol recovered it three days later at a rest stop up north. Vandalized, but what the hell. They didn't turn up any interesting prints."

Wes swore.

"Why don't you drop by my office," said Rawlins.

"Can't," said Wes, "I've got a plane to catch."

*It's late,* Wes told himself when the taxi from the airport left him in front of his Capitol Hill apartment building. He was whipsawed by jet lag into a feeling of timelessness, though he knew that here in Washington, it was half an hour until midnight. The indigo air held a chill. A matron in a topcoat coaxed a wirehaired terrier from lamppost to fire hydrant. Neither woman nor dog looked at Wes as they worked their way down the block. His eyes scanned the parked cars lining his street to be sure they were empty, then he carried his bags of old clothes and new secrets into the building.

*Dear Occupant* junk waited in his mailbox.

The white adhesive tape black-inked with *B. Doyle* had been replaced by one of the typed labels issued by the landlord.

He couldn't stop a foolish grin, climbed the stairs.

The fish-eye peephole in her door betrayed nothing of the quarters behind its convex glass. The molding made it impossible to tell if lights were on in her apartment.

Wes opened his apartment door. The lights he snapped on showed him his home as he'd left it. Another night of no surprises.

The door closed behind him with a solid *click.*

He'd hung his topcoat in the closet, draped his sports jacket on a chair at the kitchen sidebar, and was inventorying his sparse refrigerator when someone knocked on his door.

She stood in the hall wearing a blue blouse, jeans, bronze hair down to her shoulders, and a grin.

"Let me guess," she said, "you forgot my souvenir of Hollywood."

"I didn't forget," he said. "I couldn't find anything perfect."

"That's not a bad excuse." Her face was free of makeup. She grinned. "I have an idea."

She reached around him, turned the button in his doorknob to unlock. He smelled the clean warmth of her skin.

"Give me a minute," she said, hurrying back into her apartment. He saw that her feet were bare.

Wes stared at her closed door, then went back inside his home. His suitcase waited by the door to the bedroom. His briefcase lay on the kitchen sidebar. The pictures he'd taken from the L.A. hotel were in the inside pocket of his sports jacket.

His door opened. She came in carrying a box under one arm, cigarettes and lighter in her other hand.

"This came yesterday," she said.

His door clicked shut behind her.

Beth strolled into his living room. Her eyes roamed over the crowded bookshelves, the stereo system and categorized CDs, records, and cassettes. Paused at the baseball resting on its stand: he'd knocked that grand slam homer into the bleachers and his Academy teammates all autographed it. She smiled at the framed black-and-white photograph of dying Lou Gehrig making his "luckiest man alive" farewell speech at Yankee Stadium, soaked in the framed print of Edward Hopper's *Nighthawks,* a midnight diner scene so sparse and precise it was surreal.

"I like how you live," she told him.

"Practice," he said. Went to her. "What's the box?"

She handed it to him.

"'Fruit of the Month'?" Surprise lined his face.

"It came for Bob," she said. "The guy whose place I'm—"

"I know." Wes shook the box. "Must have been a gift."

"I'd forward it to him, but by the time it got there . . ."

"What do you think?"

"I don't believe in waste," she said.

"So we should—"

"Not give the rot more than we have to.

"Of course," she added. "you're the lawyer."

"Law is just some of what I know," he told her.

"We need to celebrate your return. You owe me a surprise."

He held the box to her. She popped the tape, folded back the lid.

"Pears," he said. "Green pears."

"They're ready."

"I'll get a knife, plates," he said, but her hand on his arm stopped him.

"Don't be silly."

She lifted a pear from its styrofoam cradle, bit into it. Juice ran from the corners of her mouth and she laughed, cupped her hand under her chin.

"God, it's good!" she said.

She held the pear up to him. As he bent to take a bite, he fell into her gray eyes.

The fruit was sweet and wet and dissolved in his mouth. He felt its juice trickle out of his lips.

"I'm getting you sticky," he told her, gently cupping the hand that held the pear for him, moving it away.

Beth laughed. One sharp, husky, honest burst.

The silence rose around them, a pressure roaring and swelling until Wes thought his senses would explode.

Her face tilted up to him, her lips warm. Wide. Parted.

Slowly, carefully, his fingers touched her cheek. He bent down. Kissed her.

And she let the pear fall. Her arms locked around his neck, pulled her body against his, her mouth opening. She tasted like lightning, smoky and fruit-sweet and hungry. All he knew of caution fell away: of the safety of his heart and health. Her hair streamed around his fingers, his hand pressed against her thin-boned back, her waist, the two of them turning, spinning, a *ballet à deux* in his living room. *Is the door locked?* he wondered, and then his hand cupped her hips and she broke their kiss to sigh and arch her back, and he didn't care about anything but her, about them, about now.

She kissed his neck, his chest, her fingers moving down his shirt from button *undone* down to button *undone* down to button. His hand was massive on her chest; her breasts were flat, barely a soft, wonderfully soft, precious soft mound, her nipple stiff through her blouse.

"*Hurry!*" she whispered.

Wes ripped her blouse open and she cried out. She wore no bra and her breasts were white, soft sweet puffs of white, her nipples crimson-brown circles, swollen like pencil erasers, and he brushed his fingers across them, bent, took one in his mouth. She gripped his shoulders, pulled him close. She stood on her toes and he lifted her off the ground, lifted her high, covering her breasts with kisses as she bent over him, her hair draped over his head, panting, her leg wrapping around him.

The chair.

Somehow they were in the armchair. She was pulling off his shirt, shrugging out of her torn blouse. His hands unzipped her jeans. She twisted away without breaking their kiss, stood beside the chair as he pulled her jeans down, stepping out of them, kissing him as she hooked her thumb in her panties, pulled them off. He was half out of the chair, her hands undoing his belt, his button, his zipper. He shoved his pants and shorts off, kicked away his shoes; reached for her, but she pushed him back into the chair. Kissed him, his cheek, his chest, his flat stomach. She took him hard in her mouth and licked him and made him wet, slick. Again he reached for her, and she looked up, kissed him deeply. Pulled him out of the chair. Down. To the floor.

He called her name as they sank to the carpet. Her arms embraced him and he rolled with her push. On his back, he was on his back, touching her, caressing her, her nipples, her face. He cupped her wet groin.

She straddled him, her knees pressed against his sides, strong thighs gripping his hips, her hand holding him, guiding him as she lowered herself slowly, carefully. Together.

He tried to say her name but she bent and kissed him, then arched back, her face turned toward the stars, her mouth open, panting as her hips rubbed back and forth, slammed up and down. She cried out and it was *"Yes!"* or it was *"Wes!"* or it was both or they were one and the same as he yearned for them to be. She shuddered—flamed. Again. He thought he would die and then could not think at all as he surged, as he exploded and cried out: *"Beth"* echoed through his home.

They lay on the floor, curled facing each other on their sides like parentheses, staring, smiling, lightly touching each other, not risking words that can wipe away the wonder. Wes had barely dared to take the chair cushion to put under their heads. Protect this moment. Save this moment. Treasure this moment.

She said, "Your socks are still on."

"No, they aren't," he told her.

They laughed together quietly. Sweetly. Secretly.

"How'd you know I was back?" he asked.

"I heard you in the hall." She grinned. "Welcome home."

"I didn't expect this."

"Sure you did," she said.

This time their laughter was deeper, easier.

"There's a difference between what you hope for and what you think you can get," he said.

"Are you shocked?"

Wes shook his head.

"Sex is like a blowtorch to get to know people," she told him. "I want to know you."

"You're off to a hell of a start." He lightly kissed her lips.

Her eyes bored into him.

"I'm not one for by the book," she said. "Any book. I can't seem to do things the smart way."

"Following the book isn't being smart," he said. "It's trying to be safe. If that's what you try, that's the most you can get."

"That's not how I'd expect a Marine to think."

"That's me," he said.

She grinned. "Me, too."

Beth brushed her lips across the scar on his chin.

"Is it still there?" he asked.

"Sure," she said. "Scars are part of the package."

"No illusions," he told her.

"Just real dreams," she said quietly. Completely.

A strand of hair lay across her cheek. Wes brushed it aside. He let his hand trail down to her shoulder, gently covered her wisp of a breast, the fragile strength of her ribs beneath his fingertips. The palm of his hand traced the slope of her waist, the curve of her hip, the warm flesh of her slim leg. Except for the pinkish-brown circles of her nipples and a thatch of dark pubic hair, she was like snow in the mountains of New Mexico. He ached for all of her beauty; feared his embrace would make her melt.

"What do you want from me?" she whispered.

She brushed the back of her fingers across his cheek.

"I don't know," he lied.

In her eyes, he saw she knew the truth.

Beth laid her hand behind his neck, her grip gentle as she lowered her back onto the carpet.

"Don't worry about it," she said, and softly drew him down to her kiss.

I‖‖‖‖‖‖‖‖‖‖‖‖‖‖‖‖‖‖‖‖‖‖‖‖‖‖‖‖‖‖‖‖‖‖‖‖‖‖‖‖‖‖‖‖‖‖‖‖‖‖‖‖‖‖‖‖‖‖‖‖‖‖‖‖‖‖‖‖‖

# APACHE

**N**ora usually closed her café in the desert at eight P.M. But not on the Wednesday night when Wes first made love with Beth.

The café clock showed five to six. The counter was empty and the only occupied table was the one where Nora and Jud sat in front of finished dinners. Carmen was in the kitchen, watching TV.

"What the hell," said Nora, looking out at the fading light. "Once you know it's a busted hand, forget it and fold."

She told Carmen to go home.

"You sure is all right?" asked the cook, one eye on Jud.

"See you in the morning," said Nora.

"You need me, call. Enrique and I, here in fifteen minutes."

"Your car isn't that fast, Carmen," said Jud.

Nora smiled. Carmen kept her eyes locked forward as she marched out of the café.

"She's starting to like me," said Jud.

"Don't bet on it," said Nora. "Dump the plates, grab us some coffee, and let's get out of here before a customer comes."

Jud carried two tan coffee mugs out to the porch.

"One thing I don't understand about your business," he told Nora as she locked the café door.

"What's that?" she said.

"Your business. This place loses money. You might as well feed dollar bills to the wind. You're too smart for this."

"Like you said: it's my business."

She took a mug from him, looked across the sagebrush flats to the blue-misted hills.

"My partner in Vegas needs the write-off," she said, "somebody to run the café. I get a great wage, any profit I make. A lawyer set me on to this, helped me get out of Vegas."

"What did you do in Vegas?"

"What didn't I do?" she answered.

Out by the empty highway, the phone booth waited for travelers with someone to call. Twilight melted into night. One by one, hundreds of stars dotted the sky.

"It's quiet out here," she said.

The wind came up, pecked sand against the café windows, and chilled Jud's bare arms. Nora poured her coffee on the ground.

"Come on," she told Jud. "I'll make you some fresh."

He'd never been inside her house.

White lace curtains hung from the windows. The living room had a couch, two easy chairs, a television. The kitchen was open. A hall ended at a closed closet door with the bathroom to the right; to the left was the bedroom.

"What did you do in Vegas?" asked Jud again.

In the kitchen, Nora flipped the switch on a coffeemaker. Water trickled through it as she said, "You ask a lot of questions for a guy stingy with answers."

"Ask me a question," said Jud.

She waltzed into the living room and he realized the brass in her blond hair came from impending gray. A desert dweller's tan accentuated crow's-feet beside her pale blue eyes and smile lines along her mouth.

Nora whispered, "Do you miss the booze?"

"Yeah," he told her; guessed, "Do you?"

"All the damn time!"

She curled up on the couch, hugged her legs to her chest then stretched them out, lit a cigarette, and laughed.

"This is a perfect time for a martini, but you can only wake up on a barstool in a pool of your own vomit so many times before you figure what the hell, maybe that isn't such a good idea."

Jud eased down into a chair across the room from her.

"I've been dry eight years," she said. "How 'bout you?"

"How long have I been here again?"

This time they both laughed.

"I didn't figure you'd stay this long," she told him. "Figured you for a couple meals, couple nights, back on the road."

"It's quiet here," he said.

"Doesn't it sometimes damn near drive you nuts!"

"I thought you liked it," he said.

"Yeah, but not forever!" she said as Jud reached for the cigarettes. "There's a whole lot I got left to do in the world."

While he lit a cigarette, she asked, "How about you?"

"You never know," he said.

"I didn't think you smoked."

"I've had my vices."

"Like what?" She grinned.

"You don't want to know."

"It's a big night out there. Might as well fill it up somehow."

"I didn't know you hired me for entertainment."

Her face turned hard. "I didn't invite you in here for parlor tricks."

Their smoke drifted to the ceiling.

"Sorry," said Jud.

Nora shrugged. "You want to start again?"

"How far back can I go?"

She uncurled from the couch, brushed past his chair, and brought their coffee from the kitchen.

"Start with now." She put the warm mug in his hand. As she strolled to the couch, Jud saw the line of her panties under her tan slacks. Her hips were flat, narrow. "And no bullshit."

As she curled up on the couch, she said, "I'm forty-eight."

When Jud frowned, she said, "I knew you wondered. I figure I've got a few years on you."

"Neither of us are old." He shrugged. "I've never planned on being around to collect social security. But don't worry: I won't let my trouble find me here."

"Like I said, a little trouble isn't always so bad."

"Believe me, it's bad."

She lit another cigarette, shrugged. "Okay, I believe you."

"Then why aren't you scared? That'd be the smart thing, and you're smart."

"If I'm so smart . . ." She waved her cigarette around the living room. "I came out here to get away from Vegas. Take a deep breath, get centered before I blossom into whatever it is I'll blossom into next. It's been nine months. Maybe I'm bored.

Maybe I'm starting to blossom. Whatever, trouble's never bothered me.

"Are you a bad guy?" she asked.

"You mean a crook?"

"I mean a bad guy: baby raper or a heroin man or a loan shark, some mob guy with a bad-karma franchise."

"I'm a spy."

Nora shrugged. "What the hell, these days you must be out of work."

Jud laughed with her.

"You married?" she asked.

The room grew warm, close. Jud smelled lemon furniture polish, sand and sage and cigarette smoke, their coffee.

"I was."

"What was she like?"

"Beautiful. Young. She had tawny-red hair. A writer friend of mine said her face was an Italian painting and her body would wake the dead."

"Could have been me, once, only I'm blond."

"And a lot tougher."

"Now. What was her name?"

"Lorri."

"Was she nice? Smart? Funny?"

"For a while."

What happened?"

"She became the effect of the game."

"We agreed," said Nora, "no bullshit."

"No bullshit."

"Mumbo jumbo doesn't make it either," said Nora. "Did you love her?"

"I must have." Jud was having trouble breathing.

"Where is she?"

"Gone." Jud shook his head. "Where's your man?"

"Right now, I'm not in love."

"Don't count on me," said Jud.

"Gosh, mister!" Her voice was a schoolgirl's; her wide eyes belonged to a virgin. "Thanks for the warning!"

They laughed. The muscles in Jud's back relaxed.

"That first day," said Nora, "when you nailed Harold with the fork: the mind to think of that, the heart to do it—do it and walk from it and let him walk, that *style* intrigued me.

"That's not why I hired you," she added. "I need your work. But watching you, the way you make me laugh—hell, even Carmen gets a charge out of you and she won't sleep easy until there's a stake through your heart. Me, I like you."

"Why?" Jud's heart beat against his ribs.

"I figure there's a chance you can understand me."

"Why?" he whispered again.

"That's for you to figure out."

"You think I'm good for figuring?"

Nora smiled and it was sunshine in that dim room. She unfolded herself from the couch, leaned down to Jud. Her perfume was subtle and expensive.

"You're good for a lot more than that."

She kissed him, soft and sweet, and led him into kissing her back. He fought the terror.

"I want you to respect me in the morning," he said.

"We'll see."

She led him to the bedroom. He touched her where he should and she felt good. Her hands floated on him. They undressed in the dark, slid between the sheets. He kissed her, moved his hands on her breasts, her hips, felt her warmth and wetness and he wanted, he truly wanted her: *now,* it should be now. She reached for him. Found him. Didn't shy away, kept kissing him, and he felt as if he could fall into her kiss and never stop and never care and he wanted her *now* and she stroked him and *nothing*. He made himself remember great times, Lorri, other women, women he'd never had, and *nothing*. Nothing. His heart slammed against his chest, his mind burned. He felt small and stupid and wanted to be blind and invisible, to run. Her hair brushed his belly, she took him in her mouth, gently Jesus doing *that* so good.

And nothing.

She stopped.

He lay like a stone beneath the sheets.

Nora curled up on his chest and kissed his cheek.

"Look," he said, then ran out of words.

"We all get headaches."

"If you understood . . ."

"If *you* understood," she said. "There's a hundred reasons why a man can't. It happened, so what, let's talk about it, not be afraid of it, not worry about it 'cause that's not the only reason I got you in here."

"My sense of humor, right?"

"That's one thing," she said.

"I'm not feeling too funny right now."

"Don't use that tone with me," she said. "I don't give pity. If that's what you want, go back to your trailer."

He shifted beneath her weight.

"Don't be so romantic," he said.

She felt his smile. Kissed his cheek. "I can't help it."

"This isn't love though," he said.

"Well, it's something. For you, anyway."

"What do you mean for me?"

"If it didn't matter, you'd be as hard as a baseball bat."

"As a tree," said Jud.

"Probably an oak."

"A giant redwood," he said.

Their chuckle shook the bed.

"Nice springs," he told her.

"We'll see," she answered.

"You want me to go to the trailer?"

"Hell, no."

He felt a thousand pounds lighter.

"Why do you think I can understand you?" asked Jud.

"When I left Vegas, I was dealing twenty-one. Hated it, like everybody. Park your car in the casino lot, walk that tunnel, eat that damn food, turn the cards. A robot in a factory. Everyone wants out but they can't say no to the money. Real-world peanuts.

"Before that, I was a prostitute."

She paused, but Jud said nothing.

"For about eighteen years—not a street girl. And not somebody who gives it away for three squares and a roof either. High class, high rollers. Couple thousand a date. Big time."

In the dark bedroom, Jud felt her breath on his cheek.

"Does that bother you?" she asked.

"No," he said.

"Does it turn you on?"

"No," he said.

She kissed him.

"You *are* a good man.

"So," she said, settling back down on his chest, "even before I knew *what* you are, I could tell *who* you were. I know about being a spy. And I figure, a spy knows about being me."

Her hair smelled warm and good and real.

"Tired?" she asked.

"My boss works the shit out of me," he said.

"You've got a lot to work out."

After they laughed, she fluffed the pillows, pulled up the covers, and settled back down in his arms.

"You don't have to talk," she said.

"Do I have to listen?"

"Damn right!" She poked him. "But not now. Tonight it's okay to just lay here, to just drift."

She sighed and breathed easy. Slid into a gentle sleep, her weight settling off Jud to the mattress, her breath warm on his flesh. He wondered if she'd snore. The house groaned. *How well will I learn the sighs of this home?* wondered Jud. A windowpane rattled in the kitchen. The front door creaked, but he knew the lock was engaged. The muscles in his legs and back relaxed. A coyote howled in the desert night. As he lay there, Jud floated along the border of dreams and slumber with memories of Iran. . . .

One brisk morning in November 1970, as part of a classified mission code-named DESERT LAKE, Jud and eighty-six other Special Forces soldiers parachuted into the Tehran airport. The Shah of Iran was America's favorite and most jealously courted dictator. His country was rich in oil and shared a border with the Soviet Union. The CIA organized the 1953 coup that put the Shah in power and trained his Savak secret police. Savak once told the Shah about a teacher from Tabriz who used vulgarity while criticizing the Shah. The Shah had a private zoo. He jeered while his men threw the screaming teacher into a compound of hungry lions.

DESERT LAKE was a training mission, with the Green Berets scheduled to teach the Shah's army counterrevolutionary warfare and secret operations. The mock airborne assault by the arriving American trainers was officially designed to show the assembled Iranian officers the vulnerability of their capital's airport and unofficially designed to impress the hell out of the assembled Third World Arabs with the United States Army's might.

Jud joined the training team at Fort Bragg, North Carolina, the night the soldiers boarded the planes for the Middle East. The other eighty-six soldiers had been working together for eight weeks. Jud told troopers that his name was Harris and he was a last-minute administrative aide detailed to the team's commander.

"Just a butt boy," Jud said, "along for the ride."

DESERT LAKE's paratroopers jumped on schedule, eighty-seven canopies floating down to a city cupped in a bowl of snowcapped mountains. The concept of the paratrooper demonstration was political and psychological gamesmanship; the reality of the maneuver dropped to the airport tarmac through vicious crosswinds. An acceptable rate of jump injuries for airborne assaults in the sand dunes of North Carolina was 1 percent of the paratroopers injured. That morning in Tehran, the crosswinds twirled the dropping soldiers like puppets. Eighteen of the soldiers—more than 20 percent—crashed to the ground out of control: two of them broke their legs, one broke an arm. The others suffered sprained ankles, wrenched backs, severe bruises, and concussions.

Watching from the sidelines, the ranking U.S. military adviser didn't need to read the after-action report to know that the assault was a debacle. He turned to the Iranian general beside him, grinned, and said, "On target, on time." And stuck out his hand for a congratulatory shake.

All around Jud, paratroopers were reeling in their chutes, checking their gear, helping their injured comrades toward the waiting trucks.

An unmarked jeep driven by a blond man pulled up to the tarmac. The driver wore a sports jacket and black-hole sunglasses.

"Fuck me," muttered Jud when he saw the driver.

Jud dumped his chute and jump gear in the back of a truck, picked up his pack, and walked toward the jeep.

"Where the hell are you going?" yelled a paratrooper.

"Shut up, soldier!" said the Green Berets' CO.

When Jud was ten feet from the jeep, the driver nodded toward the injury-riddled team, the civilian airport's jetliners from fifty countries (including the Soviet Union), the terminal where camera-toting tourists were watching from behind lines of blue jumpsuited airport personnel and uniformed Iranian soldiers: "Crazy way to sneak in-country."

"You should have heard the other ideas." Jud tossed his pack into the jeep. "This way, I'm not on any personnel rosters."

"What else is new?" The blond man in sunglasses drove through the airport exit and onto the highway toward the city.

"Been on any whorehouse roofs lately, Monterastelli?" said Jud, ignoring the driver's status as a superior officer.

"Call me Art."

"Yes sir."

"Anybody from the Company talk to you? Notice you?"

Art steered the jeep off the highway to a construction site where steel girders dangled from lifeless cranes. No one watched as the jeep parked next to a Ford sedan. A locked steamer trunk filled the backseat of the Ford.

"The whole city saw us drop in," said Jud.

"Blue-collar green beanies," answered Art. "The boys from Yale know about DESERT LAKE. No big deal. No CIA reps were in the stands. Maybe some of the Iranians whisper in the Company ear, but even if they noticed me pick you up, they don't know shit."

The two men transferred to the Ford. Jud tossed his pack next to the steamer trunk. Art drove back to the highway.

"You've been busy since Laos," said Art. "Those outside lock men you studied with: will there be any problem with them?"

"No. They think I'm CIA."

"Are you?" asked Art.

"Sure," said Jud. And he smiled.

"Don't fuck with the program, soldier," said Art. "And don't ever fuck with me."

The Ford rolled under an ostentatious arch built over the highway by the Shah that offended the country's devout Moslems.

"Why me?" said Jud.

"They asked for you."

"Who gave them my name?"

"Doesn't matter, does it?"

"How's your Farsi?" asked Art.

"Sixteen weeks at the Defense language school. I can get directions to the piss hole."

Art drove to an underground parking garage. At the entrance, a man in a suit nodded to the Ford. A black Mercedes with smoked-glass windows was parked against the far wall. As the Ford approached, the Mercedes's engine turned on. An olive-skinned gorilla in a suit climbed out of the front. Art stopped the Ford. The gorilla opened the Mercedes's back door.

"Give 'em hell," said Art.

Jud climbed into the smoked-glass sedan. The gorilla shut the door behind him, lumbered over to the Ford. Art kept his hands on the steering wheel. The Iranian's face was impassive as he lifted the steamer truck from the Ford. The boot of the Mercedes popped open like an alligator's mouth. The car sank lower on its shocks when the gorilla put his load in its trunk.

The Mercedes left the garage first. Through the smoked windows, Jud watched his lifeline case officer keep his sunglassed gaze on the empty garage wall; watched Art disappear.

They drove Jud through Tehran for an hour. The streets became more winding. A herd of sheep headed toward the bazaar stopped traffic. The Mercedes's driver blew his horn, cursed at the drab-clothed peasant herdsman, who ducked his head and scurried behind his errant flock. The scent of dust, exhaust, and animal dung filled the car. In this neighborhood, men wore Arab robes. Women veiled themselves with chadors. Pedestrians averted their eyes as the smoked-glass sedan rumbled past.

An ancient mudlike wall loomed ahead where the road split. Twenty feet high, the solid wall sealed off an entire block.

Half a dozen grizzled men in a mix of Arab garb and faded khakis guarded a huge wooden gate in the wall. The guards carried World War II vintage rifles and shuffled with the sullen ennui of irregular troops. When they saw the Mercedes, they scurried into action. Barking orders and laying hold of rusted iron and worn rope handles, they muscled the gate open.

The Mercedes drove into another world.

The wall surrounded a sculptured garden of trees and flowering plants, sprinklers hissing precious water onto immaculate lawns. White swans glided across the rippling surface of a one-hundred-foot-long mosaic-tiled reflecting pool. On each side of the pool was a modern two-story barracks and headquarterslike building. The roofs of the barracks bristled with antennae. On the far side of the water stood a white-columned, Persian mansion.

Trim young men wearing Western suits and Ray•Ban sunglasses patrolled the grounds. They carried slung Israeli Uzi machine guns, and their Italian shoes were spotless.

Jud's driver parked beside half a dozen other Mercedes sedans, three Iranian military jeeps, two trucks, and a Porsche.

A man in a white tunic opened the car door for Jud and bowed him into cool, clean sunlight.

"Please," said the servant in white, "may I direct you?"

Jud followed the servant along a white pebble patch beside the pool. The swans paid them no mind. In his green beret, sweaty fatigues, and dusty jump boots, Jud felt like the wrong package delivered to the wrong place at the wrong time.

The servant led Jud into the mansion. They walked over silk Persian rugs, went upstairs to a reception room with windows overlooking the reflecting pool. High-backed chairs surrounded a table covered with bowls of fruit, platters of smoked meats, dishes of caviar. One end of the table held a silver coffee service and china cups, while ice buckets of champagne and wine sat at the other end. A selection of hard liquor waited on the sideboard.

The servant pulled a chair out from the table.

"If yourself must be relieved after a long journey," said the man in white, "the door in the wall is to a closet of water."

Then they left him alone.

For an hour and twenty minutes.

He sat in the chair. Stared at the banquet. Touched nothing.

Double doors flew open and six men bustled into the room. Leading the pack was an aquiline-faced man in a tan Pierre Cardin suit, a pink shirt, and a silk tie. His black hair swept back from a high forehead.

"How are you? How good of you to come!" called out the man as he circled the table, hand held out to a standing Jud.

The rest of the pack stayed on the far side of the table.

"Sit down. I shall call you Jud, and you must call me Alexi. General this and sergeant that would be awkward among friends. We are all friends here, aren't we?"

"Yes," said Jud, sitting when their handshake ended.

Alexi pulled out the chair next to Jud. He nodded to the men across the table from them, who then pulled out chairs.

"Are you hungry?" asked Alexi. "Try some fruit."

The host bit into a red apple. "Delicious. All the way from Washington State."

"Nice place," Jud told Alexi.

"I designed it myself—one's home and one's office should capture one's spirit. I have heard so much about you."

"From who?"

"Mutual friends. What is important is that our countries remain staunch allies. His Excellency the Shah and I discussed that just last night. We were together. Quite late."

"Yes," said Jud.

"Our governments are alike. Powerful nations with dangerous enemies. But your country has many more complications. So many more competing interests. Here we are all unified under His Excellency's grace.

"You are the only American ever allowed in here."

"I'm honored," said Jud.

"Your CIA thinks of Savak as its child. Such love does exist between us. But a child grows up. The father should help the son—yet respect his independence. Your CIA treats us as the children we are not. They have an observation post, telescopic cameras aimed at my gate!"

"No!"

"Don't worry: the car windows are smoked and my wall is high. Your nonexistence serves everyone's needs and the greater good of diplomacy. I understand how the bureaucracies in a country as complex as yours are forced to compete for the necessity of fruitful corresponding relationships."

"With, for instance, Savak."

"Of course, we all serve the same ends."

"Of course," said Jud.

"Which is why we agreed to help your people with a task and, in return, allowed them to give you to us."

"We are all very grateful," said Jud.

"Let me show you something."

Alexi hurried from the room with Jud at his side, his silent staff trotting in their wake. When the entourage reached the court-yard, the guards whirled to scan the wall, their Uzis ready. Alexi led his parade into a large briefing room on the ground floor of a barracks. Stacked doors and piles of unopened boxes sat against one wall. The boxes contained dozens of varieties of locks and more than twenty different alarm systems.

All made in America.

"Ready for you to begin," said Alexi. "However, a crisis has arisen. One that can only be solved by a person with the abilities your people assure us Jud Stuart possesses."

"Let me help you as best I can," volunteered Jud. There wasn't supposed to be a test.

Alexi led Jud to an office in the basement of the other barracks. The personnel stood at attention as Alexi swept through the crowded outer room to a closed and guarded door.

The windowless inner office contained a desk with a creaky chair, a battered manual typewriter, a worn leather couch. Files were scattered on the desk, its drawers were ajar. On the tile floor between the desk and the door was a dark stain.

A solid steel panel four feet wide and seven feet tall loomed in one wall. A keyhole of a kind Jud had never seen was the only break in the steel's smooth surface.

"A Jew built this years ago," said Alexi. He frowned. "You are not a Jew, are you? You do not smell like one."

"No," answered Jud.

"Pity. Those people." His lips were grim. "The man who had this office was a most trusted servant of the Shah. He guarded sensitive matters—nothing of American's concern. He had custody of the sole key for this safe. Soviet spies took it."

"No!" said Jud.

"Yes. The safe must be opened. Our technicians will not guarantee the safety of any papers inside if they burn through. There is no one who can . . . 'pick' is the word?"

"'Manipulate' is better," said Jud.

"Open the lock. You will do this for us. Before our other arrangement. Before we help you. Now."

"Where is the man who had the key?" asked Jud.

"Unavailable," said Alexi.

Nothing stirred in the basement room for a minute.

"If I do this," Jud finally said, "I must work alone and undisturbed, or I won't succeed." He shrugged. "Concentration."

"The contents of that safe—"

"Will otherwise remain locked up forever."

Alexi hesitated. Ordered Jud to unlock the steamer trunk. Tools lined the walls of the trunk. A bulging green duffel bag secured with a padlock filled most of the space.

"What is in that bag?" demanded Alexi.

"That, Excellency, is only for my end of our bargain."

The lieutenant paled. The gorilla flexed his hands.

Alexi barked an order in Farsi. The gorilla put the duffel bag on the floor. He searched Jud's clothing pack, examined the steamer trunk of tools. When he was done, he shrugged.

"How long?" asked Alexi.

"Could take days," said Jud; thought, *Play to his prejudices.* "They are tricky people."

Alexi ordered the gorilla to push Jud's steamer trunk and pack inside the room—and to lean the duffel bag against a desk in the outer office: "Where it will be safe."

"Ahmed speaks English. He will see to your needs," said Alexi, nodding to the lieutenant.

They left Jud alone in the closed office.

Jud studied the steel panel: he had never seen a lock like that. He had no idea how to open it, no belief that he could.

He stared at the dark stain on the floor.

The desk had been rifled. Jud found pictures of children. A picture of a grave. A wallet with Iranian money, personal papers and photo IDs for a man in his fifties. The man had a wistful smile. The bottom drawer held three empty bottles of cheap vodka.

Jud sat in the desk chair. He stared at the safe; peered over the desk at the dark stain on the floor.

This was the office of a functionary. A trusted functionary, a watchman whose duties were crucial yet mindless, a passive post, an underappreciated job in a numbingly depressing room filled by a man invisible except in the ordinary moments when he performed his mundane task: to unlock the safe.

Jud walked around the desk; stared at the stain on the floor.

Then he opened the office door. Alexi and his entourage had departed, leaving only the office staff commanded by a nervous Lieutenant Ahmed. Jud called Ahmed into the inner office.

"You are the responsible officer," said Jud. Ahmed paled. "It is up to us to get it open."

"Yes, Excellency!"

"No matter what else."

Ahmed blinked.

"The Soviet spies who took the key," said Jud. "Did they use it to take secrets from the safe?"

"No one knows what the Soviets did. Ask His Excellency the General."

"No. For he is above this. In this room, it is just us."

Sweat beaded out on Ahmed's forehead.

"We must pay the price," said Jud. "Of failure. Or success. Not Alexi: us."

Ahmed looked at the stain on the floor.

"The man who kept the key, the man of this room," said Jud. "He was a sad man."

Ahmed nodded.

"And he drank," said Jud.

"This is a Muslim country—"

"We are all men. We all live. We all die."

Ahmed looked at the stain on the floor.

"What happened to the key, Ahmed?"

"He . . . he lost it!" blurted out Ahmed. "He got drunk and he lost it! We searched his office, his apartment, his car. He had nothing to do but sit in there and drink, and he lost one damn key!"

"Where is he now?" asked Jud.

Ahmed stared at the dark stain on the floor, said, "His Excellency the General . . . When confronted with failure, he . . . He is like lightning to implement corrective discipline."

Jud ordered Ahmed from the room. And then tried to imagine the ridiculous: himself as an alcoholic. Nauseous. Clouded mind. Dizzy. Wanting to lie down.

The leather couch.

Jud lifted the cushions: nothing. No doubt they'd done that.

From his steamer trunk he took a long magnetic probe. Carefully, gingerly, he slid it in the cracks of the couch.

And pulled out an exotically cut steel key.

Grinning, Jud started to summon Ahmed. Stopped.

The hollow handle of a metal hammer in his trunk unscrewed to yield a camera. The man in the outer office expected noise, so he didn't worry as he pulled up the floorboards to expose an insulated wire. An alarm: predictable. And antiquated. It took Jud two minutes to splice a bypass device into the wire.

The key unlocked the safe.

He found stacks of American money. Letters from Swiss banks. Three silencers for pistols. Twenty-six passports issued from a dozen countries. Surveillance photos of scenes in the U.S., London, Paris. He photographed the passports and surveillance shots, plus documents stamped TOP SECRET in Farsi. He hid Savak's key with his camera in the hammer, shut but did not lock the safe to secure the alarm circuit, removed and packed his bypass, replaced the floorboards, spread a dozen lockpicks on the floor . . .

And swung open the steel door. The alarm rang and announced to the world the value of a good safecracker.

The Iranians loved him.

Alexi assigned three Savak officers to be Jud's constant companions. The four of them stayed in a lavish apartment on a boulevard named for a British queen. One of Jud's "aides" was always awake. Alexi gave Jud a wardrobe of civilian clothes.

Nights, Jud's escorts took him out on the town. The evenings usually ended in the New City district, an old section of Tehran famous for its bordellos. Jud's companions flashed their IDs and doormen bowed them in. Madames with change makers on their waists presented the *honored customers* with the most expensive colored tokens. The first night, they visited a house offering a selection of boys, but Jud quickly made his preference known. His companions always insisted on Jud's picking his girl first. Wall hangings and mirrors decorated the whores' rooms. Condoms waited on the bedstands. Jud assumed that his performances were being filmed.

Days, Jud trained seventeen Savak agents in picking locks and defeating alarms on doors he engineered from Alexi's American supplies and equipment from the steamer trunk. The students wore beards and long hair that obscured their facial features.

"Speak to them only in English," Alexi told Jud.

The schoolroom was the lecture hall of a barracks inside Alexi's fortress. Jud sometimes held examinations in the basement. During one such underground exercise, screams reverberated down the stone corridor from behind a closed door.

"What is that?" Jud asked his pupils, who were nervously trying to pick locks they'd never seen before.

"We hear nothing," said one student.

"Nothing," agreed another.

The screams continued for thirty minutes. Then, after an hour's silence, came a surreal, rasping, echoed whisper:

*"Krelley harbay"*—please.

Five times a day came the wail of a mosque's loudspeakers calling the faithful to prayer.

During the three weeks he trained his pupils, the closest Jud came to seeing other Americans was the day his escorts were lax and he climbed a ladder to walk along the top of Alexi's wall.

Jud stood above the gate, staring at the jumbled roofs of Tehran, modern skyscrapers, mosques and minarets, hovels and mansions, and open-air markets. The twin towers of the Hilton hotel looked like tombstones in front of the jagged stone wall of the surrounding mountains. Ten minutes passed before the elite guards in the garden saw him and yelled for him to come down. In the street below, the ragamuffins with old rifles sent up a chorus of conflicting shouts; several of them raised their weapons.

The guards immediately took Jud to Alexi.

"Why did you do this?" asked his formerly biggest fan. "You know the CIA is out there with cameras. Even they could spot you on the wall with the baboons at the gate screaming up at you."

"Thought I'd fuck with them," said Jud. "They won't know who I am, and it'll drive 'em nuts."

*And their pictures will eventually get into the right hands,* thought Jud. *Just in case.*

"I am not happy with this, *Sergeant.*"

"Won't happen again, Alexi."

Three days later, Jud told Alexi that the students were sufficiently competent at their studies for Jud's work to end.

"Now it's my turn," said Jud.

"Yes," said Alexi, "perhaps it is."

At first light the next day, Alexi and Jud piled into one Mercedes, bodyguards filled another.

"Remember, Alexi," said Jud as their driver started his engine, "first we drop off the trunk. If I don't return Uncle Sam's equipment, my boss is liable to kill me."

Alexi understood. They met Art in the underground garage. The gorilla carried the steamer trunk to Art's Ford. Jud's locked duffel bag stayed in the Mercedes.

"We haven't much time," said Alexi as he walked Jud to where Art stood.

"I wanted to punch out clean on the trunk and say hi," Jud

called out to the blond American. Art kept his face blank, stuck out his hand. Jud ignored it, gave him a macho hug.

And whispered in his ear, *"In the hammer."*

"Everything's on line," said Art as Jud stepped back.

Alexi led Jud back to their car. The two Mercedes sedans roared out of the garage. Jud didn't look back.

They headed east from Tehran. After three hours, they transferred to army jeeps. Their road degenerated into a rutted dirt trail. Villages grew smaller, fewer, and farther between. The land angled up, from rocky, rolling desert to pyramid hills, eventually stopping at the edge of cold mountains.

It was late afternoon. They climbed out, stretched. The guards walked a perimeter, their machine guns sweeping over the big empty. Jud changed from his city clothes to rugged, nonmilitary wear. Alexi checked his watch.

"We are late, but of course, so are they." He and Jud had said little during the eight-hour drive.

"I do not know why your superiors bargained for us to arrange this," he said, "but I worry for you. As a general, I know that sometimes you must send good men where wise men would not go."

"I've never been accused of being wise," said Jud.

One of the guards shouted and pointed toward a gap in the rugged foothills. A ball of dust rolled toward them.

"Don't trust these people," said Alexi, staring at the coming cloud of dust. "They are not civilized. They are not really people. The rules of modern nations mean nothing to them. They are like your American Indians, your Apaches, *n'est-ce pas?* Only we have yet to be able to put them in camps."

"Reservations," said Jud.

"Yes," replied Alexi. "You should have reservations about this mission."

A hundred yards from where they stood, the dust cloud swirled, parted. A dozen horsemen galloped forth.

"Kurds," said Alexi, shaking his head.

They were stocky men on squat horses. Most of them wore fringed turbans and traditional garb for the extremes of desert and mountains. Their British Enfield rifles predated Hitler. They had fairer skin and lighter hair than Persians or Arabs. Legend says that when Solomon exiled five hundred magical jinn to the mountains of Zagros, the jinn first flew to Europe and abducted five hundred beautiful virgins. From this union came the Kurds.

They reined to stop outside the guards' perimeter. Horses pawed the grounds, snorted vapor clouds. No man spoke.

With one eye on the horsemen, Alexi shook Jud's hand.

One Kurd led a riderless horse. Jud tied his locked duffel bag behind the empty saddle, mounted the animal.

The leader of the Kurds leered at Alexi. The Kurd spat on the ground. He shouted a command and the horsemen galloped back from whence they'd come. With Jud in their midst.

They rode into the mountains, single file over trails visible only to the Kurds. Night fell. Jud feared that his horse would slip and send them tumbling down a rocky slope to certain death. They made camp at midnight, gave Jud a canteen of cold tea and a dry place to sleep. They were back in the saddle before dawn. Daybreak put them at the snow line in a jumble of crowded peaks. The wind was brittle, and breathing was difficult.

Just before noon, Jud spotted a sentry on a crag above the trail. Ten minutes later, he and the man who'd taken charge of his life road into a cluster of fifty small tents. Children ran to their mothers. The men in the camp hefted their guns.

The leader of Jud's band rode toward a tent where a scarred man in his early fifties waited, his sons by his side. The Kurds in the camp circled around the arrivals.

Jud's guide dismounted; Jud followed suit. The guide grunted and jerked his head toward Jud. Spit on Jud's feet.

Jud knocked the man to the ground.

Half a dozen rifle bolts shot home. The crowd murmured.

The scarred man roared with laughter.

"You American! Yes! You American. American only do that! No Iranian. No Savak. Yes!"

He stepped over his unconscious comrade, clapped Jud on the shoulders, and shook his hand.

"I Dara Ahmedi. Learn good English from Brits." Dara spat. "Brits no good. America, very, very good."

He took Jud to his tent, fed him goats' eyes stewed with vegetables and herbs Jud didn't recognize.

During the next nine days, Jud inoculated the children against smallpox with his Special Forces medical kit. In front of the camp's hierarchy, he solemnly gave Dara twenty-five ounces of gold and a new Colt .45 with two extra clips. He helped repair old rifles.

The women and children were fascinated by the warrior-doctor from fabled America. They tried to teach Jud Kurdish songs. He tried to teach them the Beatles, "She Loves You," but the only part the children mastered was the "yeah yeah yeah" chorus. With the women clapping encouragement, Dara taught Jud the dance of Kurdish men. Jud's katas excited the young men, and he taught them commando tricks.

"Teach me American poetry," said Dara.

"Forgive me," said Jud, "but I know too few poems."

"What have you done with your life?" asked the Kurd. Dara recited Kurdish and Moslem classics for Jud. He also tried to educate his guest on the politics of the world.

"You tell His Excellency President Nixon, Shah very bad man," said Dara. "Not trust."

"I'll tell my people," promised Jud.

They broke camp on the tenth day. As Jud and Dara settled on their horses, the Kurd said, "Not for gold we do this. America, Kurdistan: one day they shall rule in justice together."

The caravan set out, winding their way northeast.

Dara made camps at irregular intervals, some days journeying only a few miles, other days pushing his band to the limits of the children and old people. Scouts ranged ahead of the band, and their flanks and rear were always covered.

"The mountains are not for the foolish," said Dara.

All the while, Jud monitored the day-date watch given him before he joined the DESERT LAKE troops.

One day, when Dara gave no indication that camp would be broken so the band could move on, Jud pressed him on their pact.

"How much farther?" asked Jud.

Dara spit in the dust at his feet. And laughed.

They were already in the Soviet Union. The mountains suddenly grew eyes.

"The road," said Jud. "How far?"

"Half days' ride. Here, no helicopters come."

"I must go there," said Jud. "Day after tomorrow. Thursday. Or wait nine more days."

"*Ser chava,*" said Dara: "On your eyes." A solemn ritual phrase used for greetings and farewells. Or oaths.

Shortly after midnight on Wednesday, Jud, Dara, and thirty of the strongest and best-armed men bid their farewells, rode away. The rest of the band melted back across the border into Iran.

Dara's scouts had forgotten more ways through the mountains than modern mapmakers with their satellite photos knew. By dawn, the Kurds huddled along the walls of a gorge leading down from the mountains to a plateau. Below them, the rising sun revealed a dirt road snaking into the heart of Mother Russia.

Even with binoculars, Jud saw no life on the plateau or in the surrounding mountains. He waited until after noon.

A Kurd shaved Jud. From his duffel bag came the uniform of a lieutenant in the Glavnoye Razedyvatelnoye Upravleniye, the GRU, Soviet military intelligence. Jud strapped on a Tokarev pistol, checked his watch, embraced Dara . . .

And walked out of the mountains alone.

When he reached the road, Jud sat down. An hour later, he saw the dust of the approaching staff car. He flagged it down.

The driver was alone. In the uniform of a GRU lieutenant. He got out of the car.

"*Shto vi dielete, zdez?*" What are you doing here?

Jud had studied Farsi for sixteen weeks at the U.S. Army's defense language school—in the mornings. Afternoons, he memorized as many Russian phrases as they could cram into him.

"*Maya mashina nye moshet idyot. Mne ravitza schto vi zdez.*" My vehicle won't work. I'm glad you're here.

The Soviet lieutenant was about Jud's age, a draftee from Georgia. Jud limped around the front of the car.

"*Gdey vasha mashina?*" Where is your vehicle?

"*O menya yest papya.*" Here are my papers, said Jud, reaching inside his overcoat.

The Russian held out his hand for the promised papers. Jud grabbed it, kicked him in the groin, then broke his neck.

Nothing stirred on the plateau.

Jud compared his ID with the dead officer's: the formats matched. Jud hid the body between two boulders, climbed behind the wheel of the staff car, drove away.

The odometer showed he went 42.4 kilometers, through winding hills, up the slope of a mountain photographed by American spy satellites. As he rounded a roller-coaster curve, he saw the prefabricated dome, the spinning radar dish, three wall-sized concave receptor boards mounted on thirty-foot towers, four long-range antennae:

GRU SIGINT (Signals Intelligence) Site 423, a Soviet ear sucking up electronic signals from all over the Middle East.

American intelligence knew a lot about Site 423. Such knowledge came from espionage and mirror logic: a Soviet GRU SIGINT post would logically resemble an American NSA SIGINT post.

American spooks knew that 423 was a *collection* and not an *analysis* site, that it was staffed by eight overworked technicians, three janitor-cooks, two clerks, a master sergeant, a lieutenant who seconded the commanding officer/captain, and another lieutenant who wore a GRU uniform but who actually served the Third Directorate of the Komitet Gosudarstvennoy Bezopasnosti, the KGB, the politically superior civilian intelligence agency. The extra lieutenant made sure none of the Soviet personnel at Site 423 betrayed the interests of the KGB—or the State.

In addition to these seventeen men, six guards were assigned to the Site, for a total of twenty-three Soviet soldiers. SIGINT is a twenty-four-hour job, so at least a third of the personnel were always asleep. If Site 423 needed help, a post of the KGB's crack Border Guards was sixty-three kilometers away. But nothing ever happened at Site 423.

When Jud topped the road's last roller-coaster hill, he saw a dozen troop trucks and six jeeps parked inside the chain link fence. Outside the fence, six squads of men stood in ranks before three sergeants, who were leading them in a karate drill.

Jud slowed his car, blinked, felt his world collapse.

The almost one hundred extra Soviet soldiers were not supposed to be there.

Some of the exercising soldiers showed their toughness by wearing only T-shirts against the cold. Blue-and-white-striped T-shirts, of the kind worn only by Spetsnaz, the elite Soviet troops that are the counterpart to America's Special Forces.

A dozen Spetsnaz faces saw Jud's car. If he turned around, they'd suspect. They'd chase. Radio for helicopters.

*"Shit!"* whispered Jud. He drove forward.

The GRU guard at the gate checked Jud's ID, waved him to a parking spot. A camp guard escorted Jud to the command center. He carried the mailbag from Jud's car, let Jud carry the dead lieutenant's briefcase. The guard whispered a warning, words Jud didn't understand, but a tone he knew to answer with a nod.

Inside the command center, a colonel wearing paratrooper wings had the Site's captain, two lieutenants, and sergeant major quivering at attention as he screamed at them. Three technicians wearing earphones sat in front of the sophisticated console deck of the SIGINT equipment; their faces were pale, their hands trembled.

Jud understood none of the colonel's rapid-fire Russian.

The colonel whirled. Jud saluted, pulled the proper papers from the dead man's briefcase. *"O menya yest papya!"*

The colonel glanced at the paperwork, threw it to the captain. The Spetsnaz officer yelled at Jud for two minutes—and ended his harangue with the unmistakable lilt of a question.

That Jud didn't understand; that he couldn't answer.

The silence between them grew. Electric space heaters labored to heat this room. Sweat ran down Jud's cheeks. He wanted to vomit; faint. The colonel leaned so close Jud could smell his sour-cabbage-and-tea breath.

*"Da?"* screamed the colonel.

*"Da tavarish!"* Yes comrade! Jud yelled back.

"Bah!" The colonel jerked his thumb toward the closed door of the inner office.

And Jud scurried inside, closed the door. He was alone.

His mission was a Skorzeny operation, nicknamed after the Nazi commando who turned deception and audacity into an art form.

The lieutenant Jud had killed on the road was one of many anonymous junior officers dispatched each week from the Soviet bureaucracy. The officer's job was to see that the daily reports of Site 423 had been filled out and to certify them with a rubber stamp. He delivered and picked up camp mail. The Americans knew that the rubber-stamping officer arrived at 423 on Thursday afternoons.

Jud's mission was to replace the lieutenant, utilize the predictable conversation patterns he'd memorized to slide into the rhythm of a routine-numbed base, gain entry to the command center office—and use the camera sewn into his overcoat to photograph the technical manuals stored there. The manuals would give U.S. scientists data on what the Soviet ears could hear, thus pointing the way to countermeasures that might give the Americans a giant lead in the perpetual seesaw intelligence race. Anything else Jud could acquire would be icing on an already sweet cake.

Under the optimum mission scenario, Jud's espionage would go undetected; as he made his escape, he would fake a car accident on the mountain roads, leaving the lieutenant's body in the car. The best intelligence is what your enemy doesn't know you know.

Under the worse-case mission scenario, Jud would be discovered as an impostor while at Site 423. But with only a handful of non-combat-trained technicians opposing him, the mission planners projected Jud's chance of success and escape at 60–40.

No scenario accounted for the presence at Site 423 of a hundred of the Soviet Union's toughest and craftiest soldiers.

The office matched the sketches drawn for the CIA two years earlier by a Soviet Army deserter they'd sucked up in Finland: a small room crammed with files and shelves. Stacks of reports sat on the desk, awaiting the stamp in the briefcase Jud carried. Against one wall was a cement-encased, dull-gray safe.

*Yugoslavian,* thought Jud, secured with the most exotic lock available to the GRU: a standard American Yale.

The manuals were on a shelf, three thick volumes. He had enough film sewn into the lining of his overcoat, but that was a two- to three-hour job. The Site personnel were paranoid, fearful that one of the weekly rubber-stamp lieutenants might be a KGB spy sent to check on them. They avoided the lieutenants. Normally, Jud would have had plenty of time to photograph the manuals, search the office, and stamp the reports before anyone checked on him.

*Today's clock is almost out,* thought Jud.

He stuffed the manuals in the briefcase.

Lockpicks hidden in his tunic let him open the safe in eleven minutes. He stole a highly prized onetime encrypting electronic key shaped like a garage-door opener, files stamped TOP SECRET.

He cracked the office door. The only sounds coming through the opening were the whir and click of computers; static being shifted by electronic ears. He unsnapped his holster.

Jud stepped into the control room. The three technicians and the sergeant stared at him. Jud held his finger to his lips, cocked his head toward the outer door.

Puzzled, but recognizing a coconspirator and an officer, the sergeant eased the outer door open; looked out; nodded to Jud.

He left them with a salute.

*Slow,* he told himself. *Easy. Walk to the car as if Lenin and Stalin and all the other gods have sent you there.*

All around him in the evening light, Spetsnaz troops prepared their vehicles, checked their weapons. A training mission? A cross-border operation? Didn't matter.

Forty-seven paces to the car. Fifty slow-driving seconds to the closed gate.

Where the guard held his AK-47 across his chest. Frowned.

Jud raised his left wrist and tapped his watch.

Hesitation. The guard swung the gate open.

Defeating the impulse to floorboard the car was one of the hardest things Jud ever did. When he rounded a curve and the lights of Site 423 vanished from his mirror, he yelled for joy. And pushed his foot to the floor.

Forty-two point four kilometers to the group. Twenty-five miles over a twisting, roller-coaster road. He was shouting, singing as he fought the steering wheel. Twilight faded. He pulled on the car's headlights. And went faster. Faster.

An old moon lit the high desert sky. Five miles from the gorge, a yellow stream flowed into his rearview mirror.

He beat them to the gorge, jumped from the car, and ran. When he was halfway up the gorge, yellow eyes clustered around his deserted car. Doors slammed. Flashlights winked on, bounced up the trail behind him.

"Here!" Dara's whisper. Hands pulled Jud into shadows.

"Let's go!"

"No," said Dara. "Not yet."

"We don't need this!" argued Jud.

Dara only shook his head.

The forty Spetsnaz soldiers had superior firepower and advanced military training. The Kurds had position and tradition. And surprise. The Russians were clustered together, no scouts, chasing one man, helicopters useless in the mountainous night. Dara's men cut them to pieces in seventeen minutes, stripped the bodies in six. Before the frantically radioed Soviet relief force reached the plateau, the Kurds were in their saddles, disappearing into the mountains they'd won with Solomon's curse.

"See?" Dara called out to Jud as they rode away. "America's enemies—the Kurds' enemies. We forever friends.

*"Kurdistan!"* bellowed Dara.

His victory- and booty-flushed comrades echoed his cry through the stone sentinels of time.

Two years from that night, in May of 1972, President Nixon and his adviser Henry Kissinger would meet with the Soviets in Moscow and agree to defuse tensions in the Middle East. Less than twenty-four hours after that, Nixon and Kissinger would visit Tehran, where the perpetual Iran-Iraq border was again a hot issue. Nixon agreed to the Shah's plan to funnel arms to nationalistic Kurds in Iraq. Better to let the Kurds bleed over borders than Iranians. The Kurds got $16 million in CIA-supplied arms, and promises of U.S. support for their dreams of an independent Kurdistan. Hundreds of Kurds—including Dara—flocked to the insurrection against the Soviet-backed Iraq regime. In March 1975, to promote his position within the Organization of Petroleum Exporting Countries (OPEC), the Shah cut off all American aid to the Kurds. Iraq crushed the rebellion. The Kurds' pleas for help to the CIA and to Kissinger went unanswered. Several hundred Kurdish leaders, including Dara, were executed. Iran turned Dara's refugee family over to Iraq. No Kurd was granted political asylum in the U.S.

Asked about the Kurds, Kissinger told Congress, "Covert action should not be confused with missionary work."

After his mission to Site 423, Jud returned to Art in Tehran the same way he'd left, with a stop at Alexi's walled headquarters to shower and change into "civilized" clothes. When Alexi left the underground garage, Jud gave the Soviet briefcase to two carloads of heavily armed Americans. In thirty-one minutes, the briefcase was on a U.S. jet bound for Andrews Air Force Base.

"Come on," Art told Jud. "Before I take you back to the DESERT LAKE team, I'll buy you dinner."

They drove to the chic Shimiran district in Art's Ford. Dressed in sports coats and slacks, they could have been off-duty oilmen. A locked briefcase rested on the car's floor. Art watched his mirrors, said little to the exhausted man by his side.

They ate in a hole-in-the-wall bistro whose harried owner did everything. The tables had red-and-white-checkerboard plastic tablecloths, candles stuck in wine bottles. Terrible French accordion music blared from a cassette deck next to the cash register. The dour faces of an elderly American couple who were ignorantly overpaying the owner lit up when they saw Art and Jud coming down the narrow brick passageway leading to the café.

"Are you two young men Americans?" asked the old lady.

*"Dien cai dau,"* replied Art.

The old couple blinked at the Vietnamese expletive.

"I'm sorry," said the old man, "no Farsi."

They hurried away in search of a taxi to their hotel

The only other customer was a glassy-eyed, fat African black in an ill-fitting blue suit, tie askew, six empty wine glasses in front of him. Art and Jud took the table in the far corner, sat so they both faced the narrow door. They ordered whiskeys and steaks. The whiskeys came first. The owner laid a serrated-edge steak knife next to each of their glasses.

"You don't have much to say," Art told Jud when the proprietor scurried into the kitchen to cook their meal. Art set his briefcase on the floor.

"Knowing the Spetsnaz were there really helped."

"Ignorance is why we have jobs," Art said.

"Is that why?"

For the first time since the ambush of the Russians, Jud laughed. He drank the whiskey. A European woman in her thirties hurried into the café, looked around. She sat at table for two about ten feet from them, took cigarettes from the big purse she put on the table, lit up, and tried to ignore the two Americans eyeing her. The owner brought her a glass of red wine.

"You're a smart man," said Art. "A young man."

"Please, you're not my type." Jud laughed again.

Suddenly the whole world was funny: this blond American captain who liked dark sunglasses; the American tourists; the owner cursing as he did a thousand things at once; the fat African drunk; the woman puffing on her foul-smelling cigarette; the terrible accordion music in this shabby French café in this absurd Persian city. Mangled Russian bodies strewn through a gorge, Russians who'd been even more surprised to discover Dara's Kurds than Jud had been surprised to see *them* at Site 423. Infiltration via *horses!* It was funny; it *had* to be funny. Had to be. Funny. Had to be. Hilarious. Jud laughed and he laughed.

Laughed. The table shook with his mirth, rattled the whiskey glasses.

"Breathe out," hissed Art. "Again. In. Out."

Jud blinked. Stopped laughing.

The woman was looking at the blank wall beside her. The drunk African's eyes were trying to focus on the mysterious merriment. Two men in baggy suits entered the café, took a table by the door. They stared at Jud.

"You're back," said Art. "You're out. You're clear."

"I'm fine," said Jud. "Fine."

Art had the owner bring two more whiskeys. The owner was from Algiers; he didn't dispute his customers. He scurried to take an order from the men by the door.

"You know," said Art, "you can leave the Army soon."

"You and I aren't in the Army," said Jud.

"We may have superseded the uniforms, but the bond is still there. Do you intend to keep it when your hitch is up?"

"Depends," said Jud.

"On what?"

"On who," corrected Jud. "On the big you."

Art set down his empty glass, picked up his steak knife, and idly used its point to trace patterns on the checkerboard tablecloth. The woman lit another cigarette.

"A great deal of time and money has been spent in . . . *creating* you," said Art.

"Kind of like a tree."

"Any god can make one of those," said Art.

The African belched loudly, shifted in his chair.

"The thinking is that Jud Stuart is just coming into his own. Whether or not you keep the formal tie to the Army."

"What's the thinking on that?" asked Jud.

The African lurched to his feet. He stumbled toward the cash register, fumbling in his pockets and calling for his bill. The two men by the door moved their feet so he wouldn't crush them.

"A uniform is fine," answered Art, circling the knife point on the tablecloth. "As far as it goes." He shrugged. "It's a big world out there. Where we are, life is . . . flexible.

"And what we do," he added, "is the most important work."

"That's what I want," said Jud.

The African pressed some bills into the proprietor's hand,

staggered out the door and up the bricked passageway to the street where Art's Ford was parked. The owner pushed the buttons on the cash register; it dinged open.

"What about you?" Jud asked Art.

"Me?" Art smiled and nonchalantly flipped the steak knife end over end, caught it by the blade.

The woman knocked over her wineglass as she fumbled in her purse, standing, turning, facing the two Americans.

Awkwardly dragging a silenced pistol from her purse.

Jud saw her move in slow motion; saw the black hole of the sausage-barreled handgun seek him. For one shimmer of eternity, that a woman was going to shoot him was unfathomable.

Art threw the steak knife at her. She flinched, twisted her gun arm to block the knife. Its handle bounced off her elbow.

The two men by the door scrambled to their feet, their hands diving into their suits. Jud blinked. Then threw the table at the two men as the proprietor screamed.

The table knocked the men against the wall. One fell. The other lost his orientation as he swung an Uzi from under his suit. His finger jerked in the trigger guard. The machine-gun burst ripped a jagged red line in the owner's white shirt.

Jud charged behind the thrown table, diving beneath the gun, trying to tackle the two assassins, to get in close where he'd stand a chance. The machine gunner jumped back, bumped into his partner, and chopped his gun down on Jud. Jud hit the floor, the Uzi swinging toward him . . .

But Art had grabbed the woman's gun arm, punched her in the stomach, the face, dropped her like a doll as he ripped the pistol from her hand, turned, and squeezed off half a dozen rounds into the two male assassins.

"The door!" yelled Art. "Check outside!"

Jud grabbed an Uzi from a dead man.

"Clear!" he said. "Up to the street!"

"There'll be a driver," said Art. "Maybe a backup team."

He upended the woman's purse. "Get their papers!"

*"Who?"* Jud asked as he took documents from the dead men's pockets. The proprietor lay still, his white shirt now soaked red.

"Alexi doesn't know you fucked him," said Art, reloading the pistol with a clip from the woman's purse. He unscrewed the cumbersome silencer. "Russians. This sloppy, they're second-string. Or contracts. Scrambled fast before you left country. Either one of Alexi's boys sold us out or Savak accidentally got you made, got you followed. Item recovery or payback: either way, same end."

The woman lying facedown on the floor moaned.

"Shouldn't have panicked when you saw me play with the knife," Art told the prone form. "We hadn't made you.

"Get my case," he ordered Jud.

When Jud turned around with the briefcase in hand, Art had straddled the woman. He grabbed her hair with his left hand, lifted her off the floor, and slit her throat with the steak knife.

Blood sprayed at Jud. He yelled, "We could have . . ."

"What?" said Art.

The woman died in Jud's silence. Art let her go.

"There are no losers." Art dropped the bloody knife.

They crawled out the kitchen window, abandoned the Ford. "It's sterile," said Art. Half a mile away, on a crowded street, Art walked up to a cabdriver standing beside his vehicle.

"Taxi?" he said, coming close enough to kiss the man.

The cabbie felt something hard poke his groin. Looked down and saw the barrel of the woman's gun shoved against his zipper. Art's other hand slapped a wad of bills on the cab's roof. The driver swallowed hard. Dropped the keys on the roof, scooped up the money, and vanished into the crowd.

Art drove.

The DESERT LAKE team was bivouacked at an Iranian Army base on the outskirts of town. Half a mile from the lights of the base, Art pulled the cab to the side of the road.

"They finish in twelve days," said Art. "Until then, you don't leave the base, you don't get noticed. You're instructing in the field medicine rotation. Anybody asks, you've been inoculating kids in the countryside. As a favor to the Shah."

He turned off the cab's engine.

"Now's the time to ask to say good-bye," said Art.

The night stayed as it was, silent, still.

"Is there anywhere better to go?" Jud finally asked.

"Not in this life."

"Gone this far," said Jud, "might as well see what's next."

Art opened the briefcase between them. Fresh dark stains marred its surface. He turned on the cab's dome light.

"There's paperwork that has to get fed into the system," said Art. "It's all filled out, but we need your signatures.

"Hell," joked Art, "it's your life."

Jud laughed as he signed dozens of forms: Army discharge papers, secrecy agreements, letters, official and private documents that built a bland legend around his history. He signed a thick application form to the United States Secret Service, Department of the Treasury. A letter dated weeks in the future accepted him for training in the February 1971 class of agents. His training diploma was the second-to-the-last document in the case.

The last document was a set of Treasury Department orders dated five months in the future, May 1971. The orders assigned uniformed Secret Service officer Jud Stuart to the technical security and protective services division and detailed him to the White House.

||||||||||||||||||||||||||||||||||||||||||||||||||||||||||||||||||||||||||||||||||||||||||

# WINTER RAIN

T he day Beth and Wes first made love, Nick Kelley tracked down the hearings of the 1974 Senate investigation into a military spy ring in the White House.

The spy ring came to light in December 1971, when a Pentagon probe of news leaks to a newspaper columnist accidentally revealed that a Navy yeoman assigned to the National Security Council had stolen over five thousand secret documents from such White House officials as Henry Kissinger—and delivered his intelligence haul not to a foreign power but to high-ranking American military officers assigned to the Joint Chiefs of Staff.

Nick leaned back in his chair. He was in the law division of the Library of Congress. Fluorescent lights glowed above thick green carpet. He sat alone at a long wooden table. A frazzled woman in her twenties sat two tables away, surrounded by legal pads and thick volumes. Every so often, she'd groan. Whispers floated to Nick from tables occupied by the law students or junior associates on research errands from the city's one thousand law firms. Librarians worked inside the horseshoe reference station. The scent of ink and book bindings filled the air.

From behind him came the sound of a page being turned.

A white-haired man in a frumpy suit sat at the table behind Nick, reading a book.

*Looks like he's reading a novel,* thought Nick. *A pensioner with nothing better to do.* Nick turned back to the three slim white paper reports of the Senate Armed Services Committee.

The Senate investigation that took place almost three years

after the discovery of the spy ring was the last of three government probes into what became known as the Moore-Radford
affair, named after then–JCS chairman Adm. Thomas J. Moore
and the spy, Yeo. Charles Radford. The results of the Pentagon
investigation in 1971 are sealed. Another secret investigation was
undertaken by the White House "Plumbers" unit formed in the
Nixon administration to stop leaks to the press—a unit whose
plans included burglaries, buggings, briberies, election tampering,
obstruction of justice, political street violence, and the murder of
American citizens, activities whose disclosure forced President
Nixon to resign from office in the scandal called Watergate.

By 1974, when the Senate Armed Services Committee was
pressured into holding hearings on the spy ring, a swirl of
unraveling conspiracies had the country agog at its own reflection. The Moore-Radford affair was a confusing sideshow to the
dramas of corruption in the Nixon White House and revelations
about illegal bombings in the endless Southeast Asian war. The
Committee held four days of hearings. Its chairman told a
reporter that if he allowed the investigation to grow, it "would
destroy the Pentagon."

Nick blinked to clear his eyes for the fine print, reread a page
where a senator was telling the Counsel to the President that an
admiral had testified that "in 'normal times' what Yeoman Radford did would be considered treason."

No one was indicted or tried because of the military spy ring.
The Senate investigation produced no visible results.

Nick couldn't concentrate on the black-ink words.

*What did you think you'd find?* he asked himself. *A line saying, "This
is where it ties into your life?"*

The reports mentioned no other spies in the White House.

*Maybe if I'd paid more attention* then. *Maybe if I'd tried harder over
the years to draw the lines, connect the dots. Maybe if I'd pressed Jud
harder, faster.*

"What difference would that have made?" he mumbled.

The woman looked up from her legal pads, glared at Nick's
disturbance. He shrugged his apology.

Looked around that vast room, with its miles of shelves weighed
down by volumes of America's laws. The verdicts of state and
federal courts were bound and cataloged and properly shelved.

*Where would I look up the verdict on Jud Stuart?* he wondered. *Or
on Nick Kelley?*

He'd long believed there'd be a place and a time when he'd know such an answer. Growing up in boggy, piney flatlands, he'd decided the answer had to be somewhere else beside his hometown.

"I grew up in the hand state," he once told his wife. He held up his left hand, palm out, fingers together, breathing room between them and his thumb. He touched a spot an inch below the knuckle of the forefinger. "Here."

Butwin, Michigan. Population 5,300—when all the farmers came to town. As Nick grew up in the 1950s, the small farmers were beginning to disappear, their wheat and corn patches not economically viable in the modern world.

It was the modern world. Television came to town when Nick was five. Two or three times a week, the sky would crack as a jet from the Air Force base seventy miles away broke the sound barrier and scarred the sky with a white vapor trail. Some of the jets were B-52s pregnant with the hydrogen bombs that would end the world, the bombs that kept the communists in Russia-China-Korea-Cuba-behind-the-Berlin-Wall from marching into Butwin, raping the women, and forcing everyone to worship Lenin. They were coming with a big bang. They were coming one step at a time. Nick planned to take to the pine bogs, hide with his .22 rifle, fight the bad guys.

Summers were muggy and hot; winters long, snowy, and brutally cold, especially when the wind was off Lake Huron. In winter, smoke from hundreds of wood stoves drifted through the town. The railroads quit running passenger trains when Nick was seven, and the terrible/wonderful interstate kept tourists from stopping in town as much as in the old days.

Nick's father managed a freight-hauling company for the Greenough family. He'd come home for lunch when the noon whistle blew on the Borden dairy plant, be back at work by the one-o'clock bell in Nick's school. Nights, he'd work again after two hours off for a six-o'clock dinner. Sometimes Nick visited him in the musty office next to the garage where the trucks were serviced. Nick feared that when he grew up, he'd have to work in a musty office surrounded by ledger books about materials and money that had nothing to do with him and the magic of the world.

And Nick loved the world's magic, mysteries, and powerful forces that swayed life and that seemed to be rooted far from the pine bogs of Butwin, Michigan. His parents wanted him to be a lawyer because he would argue anyone about anything: that's what a lawyer did. Nick wished that being a lawyer meant saving innocent people from execution and catching murderers, like Perry Mason did each week on television. Nick would have liked doing that, but he had a hunch that his parents' view of what lawyers did was closer to the truth than his dreams of Perry Mason.

Nick had no brothers or sisters. He relished the freedom of his solitude. He read mysteries and science fiction. Since his parents thought movies were a fine education for a boy, Nick went to Butwin's one theater two or three times a week. His parents raised him strictly but fairly, with the certainty passed down from the Depression and World War II that Nick was lucky to be alive—luckier still to be living in Butwin, Michigan, USA. He thought so, too.

Because they loved him dearly, his parents insisted Nick work from the time he was ten. Work. Do his best. Do the right thing. Simple rules that kept him in a constant state of self-examination and self-discipline. Rules that cut him off from trivial thrills, rules that made him strong.

His parents never discussed God. The family nominally belonged to the Methodist church. Nick believed in good and evil, that there was something more powerful than man. But he had trouble believing the Bible. What did Jonah eat in the belly of the whale all those days and nights? If Jesus believed in turning the other cheek, why did he attack the money changers in the temple? If God was in charge, why did people go to hell? Such questions widened the canyon between Nick and everyone he knew. Nick's friends were divided up between the other great churches of the world—Lutheran and Roman Catholic. The town had no Jews, and only one childless black couple. There were Chippewa Indians. Nick's mother had their blood in her veins, which made Nick immensely proud.

When he was a teenager, Nick risked negative marks on his *permanent record* by drag racing in his parents muscle-engined Chevy, the radio tuned to WJR rock 'n' roll from Detroit. He hunted rabbits and foxes, but he never jacked deers—blinding them with a spotlight as they fed at night, then blasting them with shotgun slugs. On magic nights, he would drive past the city

limits, pull in Chicago or even New York on the car radio. The
real world. He loved driving, commanding a car to *go,* pushing it
to terrifying limits, shaking and sweating and being alive to
remember death speeds. Many nights, Nick cruised main street
alone, drove through the empty pine flats, looking, waiting,
wanting.

And dreaming. In dreams where he knew the magic of the
world, dreams where he could ride the forces, control them. In
dreams that became stories where choices were found and made.
Heroes. Villains. Right and wrong. Excitement instead of musty
offices or ten-minute end-to-end towns. In the stories that he
dreamt, that he wrote on an old typewriter, the magic worked, the
world made sense; it gave verdicts with clarity.

In 1964, when Nick was fifteen, Joe Barger came back from the
war in Vietnam. In a flag-covered coffin. Nick hadn't liked the
older boy, who'd joined the Marines to avoid the town's wrath for
hooliganism. But Joe Barger had gone where verdicts were clear,
where all the magic was ultimate. Two more boys from Butwin
would die in Vietnam. Larry Benson lost a foot. Mike Cox
returned silent. Nick tried to join ROTC at the University of
Michigan in 1967, but knee surgery after a meaningless play in his
lackluster high school football career kept him from winning the
green beret of a Special Forces soldier. And touching the magic
that way.

Nick's starry eyes bedeviled him. He was invisibly reckless:
secretly committed to a life in which he believed serving the magic
demons that commanded him to write would doom him to a stark
life of bare necessities. He was unfashionably cautious: when he
and Sharon Jones got drunk on Goebel's 22 beer, he rolled off her
naked body, refused to have sex with her. What if he was tricking
her because she was drunk? He wanted it to be real. He also didn't
want to be trapped by another small-town mandatory marriage
that would keep him from getting out.

Into the world. Where things mattered. Where he could make
a difference. Where he could write. Where he could touch the
forces that made things happen. Where he would learn the
verdicts.

*What I ended up with is Jud Stuart,* he told himself. *Hell,* he
realized, *I don't even have that.*

He'd reached Dean at the old phone number, a nervous

conversation in which he told that monster from yesterday that if Dean could, he should tell Jud to call his old friend.

"At work," added Nick. "He's got the number. Tell him not to call me at home, but at work."

"Uh-huh," said Dean.

Dean acknowledged nothing about Jud. Nick asked him no direct questions. Knowledge brought responsibility, exposure. Nick felt exposed enough. He wanted to ascertain how much that window was open, not to open it farther.

"You still a writer?" asked Dean.

"Yes."

"Been to a morgue yet?" When Nick didn't answer, Dean laughed. Hung up.

*That's it,* thought Nick. Dead end. Over.

He closed the Senate report. Enough chasing phantoms. He'd called national-security sources with lame questions about intelligence issues, fishing for leads, anything that might clarify Jud's last phone call. Nick hooked nothing. He had enough clichéd quotes and sophisticated speculation to write a decent think-piece for Peter Murphy, fulfilling the journalistic obligation he'd incurred to gain legitimacy for his personal quest.

*And I can stop not telling Sylvia things.*

His wife knew about the article assignment and thought he was being unwise. She didn't know he'd called Dean. Years before, he'd tried to tell her about Dean, but she hadn't wanted to listen, didn't want to know that the man she loved knew monsters. Nick was guilt ridden by his sins of omission.

The woman two tables away sighed, laid her forehead on the open book in front of her.

*This place is all yours.* Nick put on his coat. As he gathered up the Senate reports, he noticed the white-haired man behind him check a beeper. Nick hadn't heard the device go off.

When Nick dropped the reports on the shelf at the horseshoe reference center, the white-haired man materialized behind him. He smiled at Nick and took a book-request slip from the counter. A blue topcoat was draped over his arm. Nick heard the *click* of a ballpoint pen as he headed toward the wooden door.

The law division was on the second floor of the Library of Congress's Madison building. Nick pushed the down button for the elevator. The doors slid open and he realized where the villain in the novel he was writing had been born; what his grandfather had done. He was the only passenger in the elevator. For a moment, he considered staying in this metal womb while his vision percolated. The bell dinged on the main floor. The vision would still be there after lunch. He buttoned his coat against the end-of-winter cold, walked through the marbled hall.

Sylvia's office was across the street, two blocks down the hill in the Rayburn House Office Building. They could have lunch together. No, wait: her subcommittee had a hearing tomorrow, she'd be swamped today.

As he went through the revolving doors, he realized he couldn't remember the last time they'd made love.

Today was Wednesday. This morning they'd both hurried to work as soon as Juanita arrived.

Tuesday night Sylvia'd worked late, reading draft bills and memos in bed until her guilt at not letting her husband fall asleep made her turn off the lights.

Monday morning Saul woke them at four-thirty. Mom and Dad took turns cooing him back to sleep, succeeding fifteen minutes before their alarm clock went off. Monday night, they were so exhausted that as soon after dinner as Sylvia had finished the monthly bills and Nick had done the dishes, bathed Saul, read him a story, and gotten him to sleep, they collapsed into bed, stared numbly at situation comedies on TV. The most erotic moment came when Nick silently wondered what his wife would look like in a wispy black negligee.

Sunday had been close: in the morning, they'd each tiptoed to the bathroom, then crawled back in bed. Had time to hug each other before Saul's crying became too distressed to ignore. Saul refused to nap all that day. Sunday night Nick had to watch a television movie because his agent wanted him to pitch an idea to the producer; Sylvia fell asleep halfway through the movie, but he'd seen her pull her dress over her head, seen her naked as she went to take a bath.

Friday and Saturday, Nick had been recovering from the cold that Sylvia had been recovering from on Thursday and Friday.

Nick couldn't remember last Wednesday.

That Tuesday he'd been brooding over his novel, Jud's games, and guilt over using disposable diapers. Coming to bed from the nursery, she'd read his vexed mood and checked her advances.

Monday.

Nine days ago. The night after Jud had called.

Saul had fallen asleep early. They'd been undressing for bed, laughing about what Sylvia's mother had said on the phone. He'd been in his shorts, she in her old ivory bra and torn panties. She brushed something off her shoulder. He touched hers, touched her cheek. She smiled. Slid into his arms. He ran his hands up her bare skin. Unhooked her bra. She stepped back, shrugged the bra to the floor. Her breasts were pendulous from nursing. He loved how they filled his hands. They lay on top of the bedspread. Kissing. Touching. Laughing. Shushing each other so they wouldn't wake the baby. He knew where to touch her, kiss her, and she held him. He moved on top of her, like almost always; inside her, warm and wet and sweet, pressed close together, kissing, sighing gently, moving.

*"Nick!"* yelled a man's voice.

And Nick blinked; shook his head.

He was outside the Madison building. Cold, his hands had no gloves. Cars whizzed by on Independence Avenue. The Capitol dome glistened ivory against a gray sky.

"Hey, Nick!" yelled the man's voice again.

A squat man in a leather trench coat was waving at him from the corner of Independence and First Street. He hurried to Nick.

"How you doin'?" The man took Nick's bare hand in a strong, gloved grip. "It's Jack Berns."

"Long time, Jack," said Nick. "What are you doing here?"

"A case. Hanging out in Cannon." Berns nodded toward the white-marbled congressional office building across the street. "What about you? I'll buy you some lunch, we'll catch up. I'm on expense account."

Nick's memories of Sylvia froze, cracked; pieces fell from the portrait like jagged planes of a mirror. Berns loved to brag about forty years of women: his conquests, their failings. Nick wanted the warmth of his memories back, not the jagged edges of Jack Berns's life.

"I can't," said Nick, regretting the loss of a chance to pump this notorious Washington warrior. "I gotta go."

He waved vaguely down toward the row of bars and cafés.

"Going that way myself," said Berns. "Walk with you."

"Okay," said Nick, not sure how to walk away from this friendly figure.

Shoulder to shoulder, they turned their back on the Capitol dome. As they walked into the wind, Nick looked down the block, saw a blue-coated, white-haired man stride around the corner, disappear.

"I was talkin' 'bout you the other day with Peter Murphy," said Berns. "He said you're back working for his column. He said you was doing something on spies."

"Just a think piece. Nothing really."

"I ought to kick Peter's ass," said Berns.

Nick frowned at the shorter, older man.

"Thirty years in this town," said Berns. "I nailed more spooks 'n he knows, and I bet he didn't even tell you to call me."

"No," said Nick. They crossed the street from the Library of Congress block to the café strip. "He didn't."

"Son of a bitch," said Berns. "Can't blame the old guy. Likes to keep the good sources sewed up tight in his own pocket."

"Yeah," said Nick.

"So the boys at Langley ripping somebody off? 'Member how I helped Peter nail that phony business the spooks were running in Miami?"

"That was before my time," said Nick.

"These days, they're jumpy out there. You should be careful crossing the river. Don't go it alone."

"Peter's backing me," said Nick. They reached The Tune Inn, a honky-tonk where stuffed animals mounted on the wall watched congressional aides eat burgers and home fries.

Berns laid a gloved finger on Nick's arm. "You got something, don't you?"

"I don't know." Nick nodded across the street. "I need to get back to my office."

"That's right, you're up here. I should fall by and see your place one of these days."

"Call first," said Nick. "Sometimes I'm out."

"Sure." The bald man smiled at Nick. "We only worked that one story together, but you did a hell of a job."

"It was a puff piece," said Nick. "Nothing to it."

"But you didn't blow it. I appreciate that."

*There was nothing to blow,* thought Nick. Berns sounded like a man on the far side of his own mountain, looking back.

The private detective tucked a business card in the pocket of Nick's pea coat.

"If you're doing what you're doing, you need a guy who knows the ropes," said Berns. "Can't let Peter keep all the good sources to himself. Give me a call. I hear anything, I'll do the same."

"Sure," said Nick; thought, *What the hell?*

Nick shook the man's hand, waved good-bye, and hurried across the street. Didn't look back.

Half a block up from Pennsylvania Avenue, Nick remembered he was hungry; remembered he had no cash. A blast of icy wind pushed against his coat. Icy bullets of rain tapped his face, random rounds fired in advance of a bigger storm. He cut through an alley, turned the corner on Third Street, hugged the building as he scurried back toward Pennsylvania Avenue and the recess in the wall for his bank's automated teller machine.

The smoke-plastic windbreaks of the teller machine sheltered him from the weather. He inserted his card. The green computer screen told him to punch in his personal code. He did so, glanced to the intersection.

A maroon Cadillac stopped for the red light. The white-haired man with the blue topcoat sat behind the window of the front passenger door. Raindrops dotted the glass.

Nick smiled, his imagination stirring with a story about a pensioner killing time in a library.

The light changed, the Cadillac turned left, toward the freeway to Virginia. A grass boulevard divides Pennsylvania Avenue on Capitol Hill; the Cadillac had to stop as it drove through the boulevard to cross the opposite lanes. The windshield wipers swept winter rain from the driver's view.

The driver was Jack Berns.

Traffic parted, and the Cadillac drove off, bearing the old man who'd sat behind Nick in the Library of Congress, an old man who carried an electronic signaling device; bearing the Washington gunslinger who'd stepped out of nowhere to walk awhile and talk awhile with Nick. To ask Nick questions.

The automated teller beeped at Nick, but he stood motionless in the wind, staring down the street, cold and alone.

||||||||||||||||||||||||||||||||||||||||||||||||||||||||||||||||||||||||||||||||||

# MIRROR

**B**eth woke up screaming.

Wes shot out of bed, consciousness roaring into him, eyes blinking, hands reaching for *whatever*. The bedroom was dark, cold.

*"Nightmare,"* she said, grabbing him. "I had a nightmare."

She trembled as he put his arms around her, lowered them down to his bed, pulled the covers over their naked bodies. Beth's thin body warmed, stopped shaking.

"I'm sorry," she said. "I didn't mean to scare you."

"It's okay. You're okay."

Her head nodded on his chest. "Been working too hard. That ever happen to you?"

"Sure."

"Tell me your nightmares," she said.

"Tell me yours. It's what we've got tonight."

"I had this image of a mirror," she whispered. "I was popping back and forth through it, playing with it. I was it, then I wasn't. In and out. Back and forth. Then I went the wrong way, and the glass shattered and shredded all across my body, little tiny pieces of me, bright slivers. Cracking off."

With his hand on her back, he felt her heart racing.

"In my wilder days, I did acid," she said. "Maybe I'm working out that legacy."

"But it's just a legacy," he prompted.

"I might still be wild, but I'm not still stupid."

Lawyer Wes wanted to thank somebody for that truth.

"Wait until I tell you my weird dreams," she said.

"Whenever you want."

"What time is it?" she asked.

"Somewhere between very late and real early," he said. He felt her smile. "Go back to sleep. You're safe here."

"I know."

She kissed the skin above his heart.

A quarter hour later, she was asleep, curled with him like a spoon, her back against his chest. He wanted to stay between her and the nightmares. But his body began to cramp. She shifted in her slumber. And he had promises to keep.

Tired as he was, he knew he wouldn't rest. The luminous hands on his watch showed 4:39. Wes slid out of bed. Beth stirred, but slept on. He covered her bare shoulder. He found his sweat suit and sneakers, eased from the room, and gently shut the door.

Their clothes were scattered on the living room floor. He piled them on the chair. Snapped on the lamp. While the coffee was brewing, he laid Jack Berns's picture of Jud Stuart in the middle of the coffee table. The two photographs he'd stolen from the L.A. flophouse went on either side of that portrait—the picture of Jud Stuart and the black-haired man to the left, and on the right, the snapshot of the beautiful woman.

"Where are all you people now?" he whispered aloud.

He drank coffee and stared at the pictures.

"I'm on the edge," he told them.

Wes knew his law professors and by-the-book fellow military officers would be appalled by the arrogance with which he'd bent a myriad of society's rules. His law school classmates who were now wheeling and dealing in the legal factories along K Street probably wouldn't blink. Marines who'd had to supersede Standard Operating Procedure in combat would probably smile. And his father . . .

*"You're on the horse,"* said the memory of that leather-faced, fire-eyed man. *"Ride it."*

To ride Denton's horse, Wes was certain he'd have to stop bending the rules and start breaking them.

Phone records are protected and private property. While Wes hadn't directly appropriated such property, he had benefited from Jack Berns's acquisition thereof. He had foreknowledge that such acquisition was not legal, paid money to enjoy the fruits of that activity. Classic elements of a criminal conspiracy.

*You're supposed to be a kind-of cop,* he told himself. *You're becoming a kind-of crook.*

*What that's gotten me are two more pictures of people I don't know,* he thought. Plus one more name:

*Nick Kelley.*

Spying on the private records of a public pay phone, playing loose with an L.A. cop, scamming a gin mill bartender and a flophouse desk clerk, stealing abandoned photographs, cadging favors from friends at NIS—no prosecutor would waste time pursuing such activities. His superiors in the Corps or DCI Denton could discipline him, but they'd put him in the field, given him the mission. Their authority required them to understand what a man in Wes's shoes could, should, and shouldn't do. But for them—for most of them, anyway, Wes knew that what mattered most was keeping their suits clean. He neither feared their censure nor craved their approval. They were his commanders, not his judges.

Wes knew little more about Jud Stuart than he did the night of Denton's party. But his instincts told him that Denton was right: the fragments of the life scattered on Wes's coffee table added up to something important—something more important than the hairsplitting legal files on his old desk at NIS.

The best number Wes had in the equation to tally that score was Nick Kelley. Kelley was a reporter, and therefore a land mine. There were a hundred ways he could blow up in Wes's face. Plus Kelley was a private citizen, ostensibly upstanding and within the law. A human being endowed with certain inalienable rights, among them a due level of respect and protection from public employees. Like Maj. Wes Chandler.

"Ride the horse," Wes told his quiet home.

The floor creaked in the bedroom.

Wes stashed the pictures. The toilet flushed. He had time to refill his cup, get back to the couch, and sit down, time to catch his breath before the bedroom door opened and Beth came out, barefooted and wearing one of his long-sleeved, tan khaki shirts.

"I smell coffee," she said.

"In the kitchen."

He liked how she had no trouble finding a cup and saucer,

pouring her coffee; the natural way she came into the living room, moved their clothes out of the chair and curled into it like a cat.

"Good morning." She smiled at him over the steaming cup. "Sorry I kept you up all night."

"Don't worry about it."

She put her cup on the end table, took her cigarettes from his shirt, lit one. The burnt match dropped on her saucer.

"I'm going to have to get some ashtrays," he said.

Her eyes twinkled.

"What time is it?" she asked.

Gray light filled his windows.

"About twenty to seven. Looks like it might rain."

"You can wear that funny hat on your closet shelf." She shrugged. "I was looking for a robe. I get cold."

"I don't use that floppy hat these days," he said. "We wore them in Recon, on patrol. Better protection against sun and rain than a helmet. Lighter. Doesn't stop bullets, but it breaks up the outline of your head in the bush."

"Vietnam."

He nodded, braced for whichever of the dozen clichés she'd hit him with.

"Why are you a Marine?" she said. "Why did you fight over there?"

"For you," he told her.

She looked at him—not stared, *looked,* and he felt like she saw, understood.

"What was the hardest part?" she asked.

"The worst?"

"No," she said. "The hardest."

"The letters."

Beth frowned.

"I'm an officer. When I lost a man, I had to chop a letter to his parents or his wife or his girlfriend. Tell them something. I'd make it back from patrol, sit in a hooch, stinking from the jungle, burned-out and beat-up. Copters flying overhead. Rock music blaring from some radio. Guys laughing. And I had to sit in a sandbagged womb, come up with *words* to put on paper, give comfort and meaning and worth to something as sad and brave as one nineteen-year-old boy taking a bullet while other men and I made it. We don't have the words to do that. We can take the bullets. We can return fire. But we can't write the words to do it justice."

They drank their coffee for a moment.

"What are these?" she asked, fingering the metal maple leaves on his shirt.

"They're my rank insignia. They mean I'm a major."

"Yes, you could be," she said. Then laughed her husky, unforgettable, staccato laugh.

Wes couldn't stop the grin, the blush.

"What time do you have to be to work?" she asked.

"These days, I'm very flexible."

"Sounds like it," she said. "L.A. junket, no clock to punch. Not quite the picture I had of a Marine."

"When do you need to be at work?"

"I usually get to the museum around ten. I've got some studying for my classes I should do first, but it's routine."

She put her coffee cup on the table, stretched her slim bare legs out in front of her. Her thighs were lightly freckled.

*Angel kisses,* Wes's mother would have said.

"You look like a runner," Beth said, eyeing his sneakers, the sweatpants hugging his strong, long thighs.

"As long as my knees hold out," he told her. "Physical conditioning goes with the job."

"The Marines are looking for a few good men."

"We want to keep them that way."

"That's understandable. A good man is hard to find." She stubbed out her cigarette on the saucer, combed her fingers through her long hair, pulled it back from her face and her widow's peak. "So, are you going to go for a run before you do whatever it is a Marine major does?"

"I should stay in shape." Wes's throat was dry.

She leaned forward, and her hair fell alongside her face. Her bruised lips smiled as she whispered, "I agree."

Two hours later, they stood leaning against his closed front door. He was naked. She'd put his shirt back on, held her clothes bundled against her chest. She fingered his shirt.

"I'd say I'd wash and iron it, but I'm a lousy liar."

He kissed her forehead, ran his hand through her hair.

"No pressure," she said, "but when will I see you again?"

"As soon as possible."

"That might not be soon enough."

She kissed his chest, opened the door, and walked across the hall to where she lived. He watched her close her door, watched her not look back.

The phone rang inside his apartment.

"Do you know who this is?" the man's voice on the phone asked Wes.

"Sure," he answered: Frank Greco, the NIS counterspy who'd agreed to get the service records of the dead man in the bar.

"You're gonna make our squash game today, aren't you?"

"When?" asked Wes. Neither he nor Greco played squash.

"I got us a court at that club on the Hill. Third and D, Southeast. Forty minutes."

Wes barely had time to shave and shower, dress. He found a parking spot a block from the three-story red-brick Squash and Health Club he'd never been inside and walked toward its door.

"Hey, Marine!" called a voice behind him. "What a ride?"

Greco, piloting a two-year-old Honda sedan.

They drove to a less crowded residential street and parked. The Navy Yard and NIS headquarters were a mile to their right, the Capitol dome slightly closer to their rear. No one was walking along the rows of town houses. Few cars drove past them.

"Mathew Hopkins," said Greco, dropping a thick manila envelope on the console between them.

Greco's silver hair was thin on top and long on the sides. He was squat and wore suits from Sears Roebuck. Greco had a black belt in judo and could lift as much iron in the NIS gym as most agents younger than his fifty-one years.

"Check the paperwork later," he told Wes. "Hopkins was a radioman, volunteered for Nam, pulled Special Ops. In 1970, he posted to the Naval Field Operational Support Group. Two years, then he's sea-dutied around until he retires out in '79 with a hundred-percent disability. Navy shrinks claimed psychiatric trauma so bad Uncle's gotta pay him off, but not so bad he needs mandatory care. Guy had superior ratings, some commendations, but no hero. Almost nobody anybody would notice."

"Except," said Wes.

"Naval Field Operational Support Group. Sounds like paper-pushers, right? That's the real name for Task Force 157."

"I don't know them."

"They got shut down in 1977. Since the 1960s, they were the Navy's best secret. Civilian contract types, ex-service guys who were bored selling cars, career Navy officers and enlisted men. No diplomat cover, no sitting safe on a ship and intercepting Russian sub signals. HUMINT. Spy dogs. CIA barely knew about 'em. Same for the Navy chain of command. They were the first military group allowed to create real businesses for cover. They had guys everywhere: salesmen, dockworkers. Got people into China. Your pals at the CIA don't want to leave the embassies. The 157 guys ignored the embassies."

"And Hopkins was with them. If they were so good, why were they shut down?"

"Politics." Greco shrugged. "One of their ops was Ed Wilson. He went renegade to get rich. Cut deals with Qaddafi in Libya, making money off Colonel Crazy by selling him assassination gear. Wilson even conned Green Berets into working for his private program. They figured it was all just another deep-cover dodge. Now Wilson's doing thirty years hard time."

"What did Hopkins do for 157?"

"Says radioman. When he was assigned there, we backgrounded him, along with the FBI. Flying colors. Except."

"Except?"

"Except there's a request in our files for us to do another check on him, real deep and real tight. Hopkins still came up squeaky-clean."

"Why the second check?"

"Ask the guy who requested it." Greco gave Wes a piece of paper. "Ted Davis. Retired commander. A mustang who came up through the ranks, did every kind of job before running ops for 157. Davis's good people. He'll be at that bar at three-thirty."

"Thanks."

"Ted's a friend of mine. Even if he weren't, only a fool would fuck with him."

Wes stuffed the manila envelope in his briefcase.

"Looks like you're starting to pack a load, Marine."

"Odds and ends," answered Wes.

The old hand of NIS looked around the neighborhood. A decade earlier, this had been the border of the ghetto. Now, affluent professionals were taking over the town houses.

"I won't ask what you're doing for the boys across the river," said Greco, "but don't let 'em cut you loose in deep water."

"I can swim."

"As raggedy ass as you're looking this morning, I doubt you can even float."

The two men laughed.

"I worked late," said Wes. "But at least my hair is close to regulation, not some gray rope dangling over my ears."

"That's the point," answered Greco.

"What?"

"When I was policing St. Lou, a junkie bit off my right ear. Wear my hair long, I look like a stubby old man who don't know the hippies are dead. Easy to forget a guy like that."

The Navy counterspy dropped Wes off at his car. Wes got out, asked, "What happened to the junkie?"

"I beat the dog shit out of him," said Greco.

Wes checked his watch after Greco drove away: 10:30. The wind stirred dead leaves and paper trash in the gutter. A pay phone hung on the wall of a Veterans of Foreign Wars bar next to the Squash Club.

*Don't cross that line until you have to,* he thought.

The Martin Luther King Library in downtown Washington had three novels by Nick Kelley. The face in the latest book's flap-jacket picture was an older version of the black-haired man sitting next to Jud Stuart in the snapsnot Wes had stolen in L.A.

"Shit," Wes whispered.

He found a bank of pay phones in the library corridor. He got an answering machine when he dialed Jack Berns's number. Wes left no message. He checked his watch: 11:15. Maybe the private eye was at an early lunch. Wes checked out the Nick Kelley novels.

The wind had grown stronger outside the library. Black clouds rolled across the gray sky. A vendor at an umbrellaed aluminum cart sold Wes two hot dogs and a cup of metallic coffee.

"Gonna rain," said the vendor as he made Wes's change.

"Better get inside," said Wes.

"Ain't my job, man."

"No shit," answered Wes.

The Marine carried his lunch to a marble bench in front of the library. The vendor watched his coat-and-tied, trench-coated customer sit down to eat. Shook his head and grinned.

One of the books was *Flight of the Wolf*. Wes remembered the movie. The other two novels were not about spies. While he was reading the inside jacket of the latest novel, a glob of mustard fell from his hot dog and stained the book.

"Damaging public property," he told the wind. He shook his head, unfastened the book's plastic protective sheath, and tore the three-year-old photograph of Nick Kelley from the cover.

His mother had preached that the journey to hell was made one small step at a time.

At a pay phone not far from the vendor, Wes called Jack Berns. Again got the answering machine, again left no message.

*Not quite noon.* He was halfway between his apartment and the bar where he had a rendezvous in three hours. A pellet of cold rain hit his face. The Freer Gallery where Beth worked was almost a mile away. The mammoth gray-stoned National Museum of Fine Arts was across the street. They'd have pay phones in there.

For half an hour, Wes wandered through corridors of abstracts and surrealists. When he found a pay phone by the rest room, got Berns's machine, he left the pay phone number.

As Wes waited by the pay phone, a blue-uniformed museum policeman walked past once, walked past twice, casually checking out the strange man loitering by the men's room.

The phone rang. Wes answered it.

"Wes!" Jack Berns's voice sounded as if he were in an aluminum barrel. "Where the hell are you?"

"I'm at a pay phone."

"I'm in my car. Ain't technology great? I can retrieve your message and call you back, drive and check out chicks, all at the same time. Get a car phone. Portable plus almost impossible to intercept. I can get you a deal, Noah will love it."

The museum cop strolled past Wes.

"Phones are what I'm calling about," said Wes.

"Uh-huh."

The museum cop was ten paces gone.

"The writer you know. He has a home. And an office."

"Nick Kelley. You want tapes on his lines? Or just long-distance records, from that date to when: now?"

"Not the first," said Wes. "Just a list of who and where and when."

"How 'bout if I see if I can find out why?"

"Just do the job I'm paying you for. When can I have it?"

"I'm on the Fourteenth Street bridge. There's the Pentagon—want me to wave for you? Nah, they ain't your boys no more. I'll be home in twenty. I can get it for you by the time you get there."

The museum smelled musty and cool. Footsteps and whispers echoed down marble corridors, and Wes felt a tingle of invisible electricity.

"Berns, did you already do this?"

"Hey, I'm just an order follower."

In the black and white swirls of a canvas mounted not far from where he stood, Wes saw a twisted figure. Screaming.

"Raining like a son of a bitch out here," said Berns.

"What'll this cost?" said Wes.

"Don't worry: you got the budget."

The connection broke off. The museum cop stood at the end of the corridor, watched Wes walk toward him.

"Small steps," Wes said to the cop.

"Have a nice day, sir." The cop's eyes burned holes in Wes's back all the way to the door.

The rain had stopped by the time Wes arrived at the bar in Arlington. He parked his car in the broken-pavement lot next door, checked his watch. He was twelve minutes early.

The four other cars in the lot were empty.

As he walked into the bar, Wes glanced across the street. A bristle-headed man sat in a car parked outside a dress shop.

The only people in the bar were the man in a white shirt and black vest who was polishing glasses and a woman in her fifties playing on the bar's TV. Wes carried a beer to a dark table.

The bristle-headed man entered the bar at exactly three-thirty. He walked to Wes's table, stuck out his right hand.

"How you doing, Wes? Ted Davis."

The bartender brought Davis a clear iced drink.

"Glad to do Frank a favor," Davis told Wes after hearing his thanks. He smiled. "You one of Billy's boys?"

"Billy?" asked Wes.

"General Billy Cochran."

Wes hesitated; remembered Greco's warnings.

"I'm working for the number one out there. And only for this."

Ted Davis nodded, took a pull from his drink.

"You requested a special backgrounder on a radioman who

worked for Task Force 157 from 1970 to 1972," Wes said. "Mathew Hopkins."

"I remember him."

"Why?"

"Why do I remember him or why did I do what I did?"

"Both."

"We ran our own show," said Ted. "Picked Hopkins off a short list the Navy gave us. We had our own como system, separate from everybody—and secure. Encrypting machines smaller than your briefcase, radios, you name it."

"So Hopkins handled message traffic. Any one area?"

"Normally, radiomen rotated. They got stuff as it came, not by area or op. A good radioman doesn't notice what comes out of his encoding machine, once he gets it in plain text. He follows the procedure for that message, goes on to the next one."

"Normally," said Wes. "What about Hopkins?"

"He smoked too much."

"What?"

"He smoked too much. That's why I noticed him. Plus."

"Plus?"

"When Kissinger snuck into China, he didn't trust anybody. Sure as shit not State. Not CIA. He got the Chairman of the Joints Chiefs to loan him the most secure communications system the U.S. had, one even the Chiefs didn't control: us."

"We're talking when?"

"About 1971."

"And Hopkins . . . ?"

"Remember the rotation system. And remember como wasn't my billet. I was ops. But I was between gigs, being useful. I happened to check the como logs. Noticed Hopkins had been swapping duty times quite a bit. Worked out so he always had duty when Kissinger had China shit in the pipeline."

"And he smoked too much," said Wes.

"Frank told me you're a cherry," said Davis. "You take a few more tricks after this one, you'll meet some guy in the trade who's convinced The Bad Joes are targeting him. The guy swears he knows about clearances and ops that nobody else knows.

"You can tell by the paranoia," explained Davis. "A good op makes the right moves, but he doesn't live in fear. The Bad Joes want to hit you, you're dog meat, so you just accept that. Don't be stupid, but don't psyche yourself out. A paranoid is either an op man who's been too long in the field or too long in his head—or an analyst with a wild imagination. Guy like that, they start doing things, seeing things. Big things."

"Hopkins wasn't an op or an analyst, but you thought he was crazy."

"That was one possibility. The Kissinger-China stuff, the too much smoking, I could fit crazy into that profile. 'Course, Kissinger was global politics. Lot of people cared about it."

"So Hopkins could have been a spy."

"A spy in the spies. Best place to have one."

"Was there any other evidence?"

"There never was *any* evidence of *anything*."

"You eased him out of 157," guessed Wes.

Davis laughed. "Maybe Hopkins was right to be paranoid."

"Can you tell me anything else about him?" asked Wes.

"Anything else, he'll have to tell you," said Davis. "Where is he now?"

*Greco didn't tell him,* thought Wes; said, "Out West."

The retired spy grunted. Their glasses were empty.

"Was Jud Stuart ever assigned to Task Force 157?" asked Wes. "An Army guy. Probably loaned out as an operative."

"Nobody by that name with us. We didn't get loan-outs from the Army."

"How about in another group? Anybody have other off-the-books groups?"

"You *are* a cherry. Sure, there were other off-the-books groups. Army had some before they put together the Activity and got into funny-money trouble a few years back—they should have come to us for advice. CIA runs some. Who doesn't? Ask your Marine buddy Ollie North. If they're real off-the-books, I wouldn't know about them. Jud Stuart rings no bells."

Wes handed him the picture Jack Berns had taken.

"Don't know the face," said Davis.

After hesitating, Wes asked, "What happened to you guys?"

"You know the public legend about Ed Wilson, his crooked deals and how he pissed off a certain admiral?"

Wes shrugged, nodded.

"If you want to understand why the Navy got rid of us, the only organization, including the CIA, that was doing secure, productive, legal HUMINT—given that spies are a bunch of thieves and liars and con artists, we weren't jerking around Americans—then you got to understand our friend General Billy, currently Deputy Director of your team."

"He's Air Force, you were Navy."

"Then he was National Security Agency with buddies from his days on the Joint Chiefs. The color of his suit doesn't matter.

"Billy doesn't just have stars on his shoulders, he's got 'em in his eyes. First thing he did when he got to be a mucky muck over Air Force Intelligence was have a clean outside phone line wired to his office. Handy to feed reporters tidbits, get some young press hound on the way up, make him your dog. Keep in touch with buddies on the Hill, help a staffer here, a senator there. Create your own legend. With truth wrapped in shadows. Brilliant."

"If he's so brilliant . . ."

"He's a letter opener. His idea of intelligence is clean and bloodless intercepts. Satellites. HUMINT—street men finding out what's making hearts beat and minds tick—that gets sticky. Sticky gets you trouble, and trouble's no good for Billy. He's a ladder climber. Those thick glasses of his must have steamed up when the President named Denton to head the CIA and not him.

"Lot of people know how to grease skids," said Davis. "Billy helped woo the best guys out of 157. Suggested replacements. He owned 'em or they were so bad they made the team look bad. When Wilson went renegade, the grease was already laid.

"Do me a favor," said Davis.

"If I can."

"Tell Denton that when Billy starts being nice, it's time to put your back against the wall."

Wes made it to Jack Berns's house while there was still light in the sky. In Berns's den, Wes studied Nick Kelley's telephone billing sheets with addresses matched to the numbers. He ruled out the television studio, the publishers, the talent agency. Calls to Michigan to a woman who shared the writer's name—his mother? Maybe the calls to Wisconsin were to his wife's family.

A call from Nick Kelley's office to a Los Angeles number made nine days after Jud Stuart pushed the CIA panic button caught Wes's eye: Dean Jacobsen.

Who the hell was Dean Jacobsen?

Wes scanned the list again; Dean Jacobsen seemed to be the

only unexplainable call. Three and a half minutes, nine days after
Jud Stuart had called the CIA.

"Who's your source at the phone company?" Wes said, looking
at the Xerox copies of billings.

"Hey: fuck you, Major," answered Jack Berns. The stubby
private eye leaned on his desk. "You got what you want?"

"I got what I asked for." Wes yawned. "How much?"

"Figure five," answered the private eye.

"That's steep."

"Cost of doing business."

Wes put ten fifty-dollar bills on Berns's desk.

"Write me a receipt," said the Marine.

"First off, *Wes,* we're talking thousands, not hundreds."

Sunset broke through the clouds outside; soft waves of pink
light flowed through the windows. Wes counted out ten more
fifty-dollar bills, dropped them on the desk.

"That's twice what it's worth, probably four times what it cost
you."

"You're way out of line here, Major."

The private eye glared at his client—who smiled, walked to the
wall of law books, and ran his hand over their spines.

"You think I'm out of line?" said Wes. "I'm an officer of the
court. You've just given me phone company records, illegally
obtained. You're pushing the good graces of Uncle Sam with one
hand, trying to shake him down with the other. I might be out of
line working with you, but you're the one without a safety net."

"You sure about that?"

"Doesn't matter to me." Wes kept his smile.

"Hey!" said the private eye, spreading his arms wide. "We're on
the same team." He chuckled. "Maybe you'll make a businessman
after all."

"Write me out a receipt, and sign it."

With a shake of his head, a patronizing laugh, Berns complied.
When he had the document, Wes headed for the door.

"What next?" Berns yelled after him.

"I need you, I'll call."

Outside, night had fallen. Wes yawned again.

Dean Jacobsen. Los Angeles. Could be Jud Stuart's alias, his
hideout; could be Nick Kelley's college roommate. One call, from
a man who knew Jud Stuart to a man in a city where he

disappeared. Wes could have Greco or Detective Rawlins run Dean Jacobsen through the computers, but that might draw attention to Wes. Besides, *official records* had helped very little so far.

Dealing with a stranger in Los Angeles would be safer than taking a run at Nick Kelley, Washington writer and reporter.

Wes yawned, started his car. He could catch a red-eye. Get something close to sleep on the plane. Be back in twenty-four hours.

Maybe Beth would be home. Maybe she'd drive him to the airport.

# SINISTER FORCE

Friday, June 16, 1972, began as just another muggy, cloudy day in Washington, D.C., for Jud.

Unbeknownst to him, men who embodied the winds of his life were gathering across the Potomac River at Arlington cemetery for the eleven A.M. funeral of John Paul Vann, a key manager of America's ongoing Vietnam war.

Maj. Gen. (Ret.) Edward Lansdale was at the funeral. Lansdale was a CIA saint, the man who'd beaten a communist insurgency in the Philippines in the 1950s, the American intelligence wizard who'd midwifed the creation of South Vietnam.

Lansdale's most infamous Vietnam protégé also came to Vann's funeral: Lucien Conein. Three-fingered *Black Luigi*. The Dark Prince of Ops. As an Office of Strategic Services agent in World War II, Black Luigi parachuted behind Japanese lines into Vietnam when it was called French Indochina. As a cold war CIA agent, he crafted the bloody coup that overthrew the Diem regime.

In that year of 1972, Black Luigi retired from the CIA, and President Richard Nixon drafted him to form a secret Special Operations Group within the new Drug Enforcement Agency. Staffed in part by ex-CIA agents, DEA's SOG worked out of a D.C. safe house, with orders to penetrate international narcotics rings. Rumors claimed that Conein's people were setting up assassination programs to eliminate drug kingpins. Black Luigi denied such rumors.

In the early days of America's Saigon, Black Luigi saved the life of another man who was at Vann's funeral: Daniel Ellsberg. Ellsberg had been part of Lansdale's CIA-based "country team" in Vietnam. Since his Vietnam days, Ellsberg's conscience had changed radically, and he'd smuggled a secret history of the Vietnam war to the press. Published the year before Vann's funeral, that history came to be known as the Pentagon Papers. In order to attend Vann's funeral, Ellsberg had had to fly to Arlington from Los Angeles, where he was on trial for leaking the Pentagon Papers.

Less than a month after publication of the Pentagon Papers, President Nixon's men formed the White House Special Investigations Unit, a covert group to stop news leaks. The secret unit was headquartered next door to the White House in the basement of the castlelike Old Executive Office Building: Room 16—which was actually four rooms equipped with a telephone scrambler whose code was changed daily by Secret Service technicians.

The sign on the door read DAVID R. YOUNG/PLUMBER.

As he sat at his friend Vann's funeral, Ellsberg didn't know that a covert team commanded by White House aides had already twice burgled the Los Angeles office of his psychiatrist, looking for dirt with which to smear him.

Sen. Edward Kennedy sat near Ellsberg. Eleven months earlier, the White House had hired a former CIA agent officially to investigate the Pentagon Papers and secretly to investigate a tragedy in which a female companion of Kennedy's drowned. This ex-CIA agent was one of the men who burgled Ellsberg's psychiatrist.

The most important active CIA official at Vann's funeral was World War II hero William Colby, who helped organize the CIA's Phoenix Program, in which 40,994 Vietnamese civilians suspected of being the enemy were killed. Colby eventually became the Director of the CIA.

Within the CIA on the day of Vann's funeral, two secret investigations were hunting the Soviet mole supposedly burrowed deep in America's security apparatus. One investigation would claim that chain-smoking poet James Jesus Angelton, the CIA's head of counterintelligence and a legendary mole hunter himself, was a Soviet agent. The other investigation implicated Henry Kissinger, the National Security Adviser to President Nixon, as a mole who'd been recruited in post–World War II Germany, given the code name COLONEL BOAR, and catapulted into the power elite of the United States.

On the day of Vann's funeral, Nixon bid farewell to the President of Mexico, who'd been in town for a state visit. A state visit by the nearest Latin American neighbor of the United States was a foreign policy paradox in Washington on that muggy Friday in 1972.

On the one hand, National Security Adviser Henry Kissinger expressed the administration's view of Latin America when he told a Chilean diplomat, "What happens in the South is of no importance."

On the other hand, there *was* Chile.

Three days after Marxist Salvador Allende had been elected president of Chile, the CIA told the Nixon White House that the United States "had no vital interests within Chile, the world military balance of power would not be significantly altered by an Allende regime, and an Allende victory in Chile would not pose any likely threat to the peace of the region."

But President Nixon sicced his CIA Director on Chile with orders "to make the economy scream." The President said that more than $10 million was available for the effort, and that the American embassy in Santiago was not to be involved. Two days before Vann's funeral, the *Washington Post* reported that Allende's cabinet had offered to resign as Chile's economic crises worsened and it renegotiated its $1 billion foreign debt.

After his farewell to the Mexican president, Nixon flew to a multimillionare friend's private Bahamian island for a weekend rest. Where it rained.

Gray clouds left a sheen of precipitation on Washington's black streets that Friday night.

Washington is a political city, never more so than in those days of the Vietnam war, when every step by every citizen was a political compass oriented to the jungles of Southeast Asia. The politics of elections obsessed the city that year, too: the vote to choose who would be the next president was drawing close.

Incumbent President Richard Nixon was clearly destined to be the Republican Party's choice.

Two Democratic senators, George McGovern, an unpopular peace advocate, and Ed Muskie, a more electable middle-of-the-road Democrat, were battling for their party's nomination.

Muskie was making a comeback from a disaster called the Canuck letter, a press-exposed "private letter" that portrayed Muskie as a racist. In defending himself, Muskie cried.

The Canuck letter was a forgery perpetrated by top White House aides. They called such things *rat-fucking*.

On Friday, June 16, 1972, the day Vann was buried at Arlington, sunset came to Washington at 8:35 P.M.

Jud was at work.

When darkness came, the White House glowed.

President Nixon had reversed custom as dictated by such authorities as the *Boy Scout Handbook* and decreed that the American flag should fly twenty-four hours a day, 365 days a year, from the top of the White House. Rain or shine. Day or night.

More than a residence, the White House was an office building for those men and women who governed America's executive branch. Through the tall iron-bar fence surrounding the wide lawns and bushes, up the immaculate sidewalks, inside the closed doors and bulletproof windows, they labored.

And they labored as much as possible in secret.

Six months earlier, in December 1971, Kissinger and Nixon had been caught by a muckraking columnist secretly *tilting* American support toward the President of West Pakistan, who was waging a genocidal war that killed between 500,000 and 3 million people in a land that would come to be called Bangladesh. As a military tactic, America's allies raped women or cut their breasts off with specially fashioned knives. The tilt was partially a payoff for Pakistan's acting as a liaison between Kissinger and mainland China in the negotiations to resume diplomatic relations between the two superpowers, and partially a global chess maneuver based on assumptions that later all proved to be false.

The administration's investigation of the December tilt leak accidentally uncovered military spy Yeo. Charles Radford—but the unmasking of an American serviceman assigned to spy on the White House was still secret from the American public. As was a secret and illegal CIA investigation of the muckraking columnist who broke the tilt story.

There were so many secrets to keep safe inside the black iron White House fence in June of 1972. There was Cambodia, where for fourteen months Nixon and Kissinger had deceived the public, Congress, and high military officers and ordered 3,630

B-52 raids in which 110,000 bombs were secretly dropped on people who knew exactly where the bombs had come from. In America, the White House men had developed schemes for covert political warfare in the U.S., including plans for break-ins, buggings, prostitutes wired for blackmail, kidnappings: "dirty tricks" designed to neutralize Democratic Party candidates and antiwar activists. The President's men were pressuring the Internal Revenue Service to target people on Nixon's enemies list for income tax investigations designed to turn up damaging personal-income secrets useful as political weapons. Some of the White House men were themselves the victims of White House–authorized wiretaps designed to uncover disloyalty.

On that Friday, the men of the White House were awash in money. That week, the press reported that more than $10 million had been contributed to President Nixon's reelection campaign before the new elections disclosure laws had taken effect. Former top cop Attorney General John Mitchell, who was now Chairman of the Committee to Re-Elect the President (CRP, pronounced *creep*), declined to reveal the sources of that money.

What no one outside of those involved knew was that thirteen major American corporations had given $780,000 in illegal campaign contributions to CRP. Milk producers had raised additional millions in exchange for the President's raising the federal price support level for milk. Spooky recluse billionare Howard Hughes funneled $100,000 to the reelection campaign, while Robert Vesco, a fugitive from multiple U.S. charges involving billions of dollars of fraud and a key suspect in a heroin smuggling ring, had secretly given the Nixon team $200,000.

That night, campaign contributions of questionable legality had been laundered through Mexico to fund a group of eight men who were mounting a covert operation from Room 723 of the Howard Johnson's hotel across the street from the Watergate.

And that night at the White House, the glowing White House beneath the flag, Jud Stuart stood watch.

Not upstairs in the family quarters that First Lady Pat Nixon had redecorated in sunny California floral patterns of gold and rose wallpaper, wicker furniture. Jud was downstairs in the White House. The first floor. In the Oval Office.

In the heart.

And he was alone.

Eleven P.M., June 16, 1972.

He had an hour before his shift ended. Less than an hour to do that night's work.

Sweat beaded on his forehead, though the White House's central air-conditioning washed the city's foul air and kept the building cool. Sometimes President Nixon liked to crank up the air conditioner to its maximum cooling potential and sit in front of a roaring fire. The radio mounted on Jud's hip crackled through its earplug. He wore a white uniform shirt, dark pants with a gold stripe down each leg, spit-polished black shoes. On his chest was the gold badge of the Executive Protection Service, the uniformed branch of the Secret Service. The heavy utility belt that held his radio also held a holstered .357 magnum revolver guaranteed to stop a grizzly bear.

Or an intruder into the inner sanctum of America's democracy.

Jud stood with his back pressed against the wall. To his right was the main door with a red velvet rope dangling across its open width. The cold fireplace and mantel were to his left. A portrait of George Washington hung above the fireplace. The black eyes of the first president watched visitors wherever they stood. Whatever they did.

The radio crackled in Jud's ear: Guard Post 23, checking in, confirming all clear. Jud's last scheduled check-in had been four minutes earlier: *All clear,* he'd reported.

Security was tight, rigid with rules and procedures, option plans. That night, the men in charge of White House security, the uniformed officers such as Jud, the suit-and-tie agents of the Secret Service Protection Detail, stood ready but breathed easy: SEARCHLIGHT was in Florida. They didn't need to worry about his being assassinated on turf they were responsible for securing. They didn't need to worry about running into him during one of his late-night meanderings through the presidential complex. He often worked across the street in a hideaway office in the Old Executive Office Building, drinking Scotch and drafting memos for his secretary to distribute during daylight hours. Even with all the presidential tracking systems and devices, in the middle of the night a dark-suited, tightly-knotted-tie, white-shirted SEARCH-LIGHT would sometimes startle a White House guard with a sudden, silent, flitting-eyes appearance.

"Scares the hell out of me," one of the other guards told Jud as they dressed for work in the Security locker room that night. "Who does he think he is?"

And Jud laughed.

The light in the huge Oval Office was dim. Jud's gaze followed the circle of the curved White House wall.

To his left, past the door to the office of the appointments secretary, was a framed, giant color photograph of the earth taken from the moon. Then came the three French doors overlooking the South Lawn and the Rose Garden. The dark night shone through translucent, gauzy white inner drapes pulled closed across the glass. A table sat in front of the French doors, flanked by the American and presidential flags. The table held a pen and pencil set, a black bust of Abraham Lincoln, and a color photograph of Tricia Nixon's White House wedding.

The flags of the Armed Services stood in front of the wall beyond the French windows. Two years earlier, President Nixon and "the King," Elvis Presley, nervously shook hands in front of those flags. They decried the scourge of drugs. The President arranged for Elvis to get a badge as an honorary federal narcotics cop and gave him presidential cuff links. Elvis gave Nixon a gun.

Beyond the service flags and an arched alcove case of porcelain birds was the door to the office of the President's personal secretary. Farther along the curved wall hung a presidential seal embroidered by the President's oldest daughter, Julie. Next came the velvet-roped door.

Then Jud pressed quietly against the shadowed wall.

As quietly as he could. Fifteen months earlier, the Secret Service's Technical Division had been entrusted by the President with the highly secret task of installing a covert, voice-activated tape-recorder system in the Oval Office. The White House already had a hidden taping system in the Cabinet Room down the hall from the Oval Office. Lyndon Baines Johnson ordered it installed when he was president, and it was activated by a switch in front of the president's chair under the long oval table.

Only a handful of people in the world were supposed to know about the new Nixon taping system, a handful that specifically did not include military groups who normally handled presidential communication systems. What Nixon wouldn't learn until it was too late to affect his political survival was that there were two more covert taping systems in the Oval Office, systems that kept complete control of history's record out of the hands of the man whose office this was that June night in 1972.

Jud knew about the Oval Office's three taping systems. He couldn't be sure which ones were turned on, waiting to be activated by any sound other than rustle of air-conditioned atmosphere. Jud knew his survival depended on leaving no more of a trace of his work than absolutely necessary. He was quiet, so very quiet.

The President's desk was close to the French doors. A black phone sat on the desk's left-hand corner. In the front center of the polished flat top was a silver cigar music box embossed with the presidential seal. When opened, the box played "Hail to the Chief." Propped against a pen and pencil set was the green-bound schedule of the President's day.

The black leather executive chair had softened very little after three years of use, thought Jud, who during more than one late-night shift had sat in its comfort.

The Red Phone, the secure-line phone instantly connecting the President to the machinery of nuclear Armageddon, waited in the lower right-hand desk drawer.

A Dictaphone and tape recorder sat on a stand to the right of the President's chair. A brown Samsonite attaché case initialed "RN" stood beside the Dictaphone table. Jud's best time for picking the locks on the attaché case was nine seconds.

His watch showed 11:02 P.M., June 16, 1972.

The radio earphone crackled: Post 12 calling in his *All clear,* the Command Post *Roger*-ing back.

A mile from the White House at the Watergate complex, an ex-CIA agent who was now employed by the Committee to Re-Elect the President was taping open the locks on doors leading into the building from the stairwell.

In the Oval Office, Jud took an ordinary-looking pen flashlight from his shirt pocket. Jud pointed the flashlight at the President's desk: nothing. The invisible ultraviolet light from Jud's torch would have reflected a purple glow on the wood's surface if the desk had been dusted with a powder designed to rub off on the hands and clothing of anyone who touched the desk.

He glanced around the edge of the door, down the corridor beyond the velvet rope: no one.

Quietly, one step at a time, he left the shadows, crossed toward the wall next to the door leading to the office of the President's personal secretary. His flashlight made no purple glow on the wall. He pushed the secret button in the molding. A panel in the Oval Office's wall slid open to reveal a safe whose existence was almost unknown. The light showed no powder on the safe.

Unlike the five men who were at that moment in the process of the third burglary of the Watergate complex sponsored by the President's team, Jud dared not wear surgeon's gloves. A surprise inspection of the White House guard detail that turned up surgical gloves in Jud's possession would spell his doom; the flashlight would pass any routine examination, and the lockpicks secreted in his ballpoint pen did not interfere with its writing. Jud covered his hand with his handkerchief to dial the combination that had taken him six separate nights of patient, fragmented effort to figure out.

His radio crackled: Guard Post 4, checking in.

The flashlight showed no purple glow from the contents of the safe.

Dozens of memos, most of which Jud had seen before, most of them from Kissinger to the President. Some dated back to the early days of the President's term, including TOP SECRET/SENSITIVE memos in which Kissinger bureaucratically knifed the secretary of state. One memo discussed the "madman" strategy of negotiation Kissinger was using with various communist powers. The strategy called for Kissinger to portray Nixon as maniacally out of control, which would theoretically make Kissinger's pleas for the communists to concede certain diplomatic issues more compelling. The "madman" theory of diplomacy was popularized by Hitler in the Munich era of conciliation before fighting erupted in World War II—and had been analyzed in 1959 for Kissinger at Harvard by then–cold warrior Daniel Ellsberg. On top of the pile, Jud found a three-page "Eyes Only" memo from Kissinger to the President outlining strategies for dealing with Premier Chou En-lai that Kissinger planned to follow in his visit to China the next week.

*Infiltrate,* Jud's orders had been. *Monitor. Report.*

He closed but did not lock the safe, closed the secret panel. Getting into the personal secretary's office, photocopying the Chou En-lai memo, took three minutes. One more minute, and he was putting the original memo back in the Oval Office safe.

Jud unbuttoned his shirt.

*Confuse to aid concealment. Provoke to develop intelligence opportunities.*

Such were his orders. *Reconnaissance by fire,* Jud had thought. A common military tactic. But *provocation* was a means to an end that Jud thought went beyond creating "intelligence opportunities." He didn't know every motive that generated his orders, but the words gave him a license for his imagination.

Earlier that night he'd been down the hall, past the Roosevelt Room to the offices of Kissinger and Haldeman. Kissinger's locked files contained FBI reports about his staff and even an "Eyes Only" report from FBI Director J. Edgar Hoover on murdered Martin Luther King's sex life. White House Chief of Staff Haldeman was WATCHDOG. He had two safes: one sat by his desk. The other, a French safe, was hidden in the wall. It had taken Jud five weeks to fashion a duplicate key for the French safe.

From inside his shirt, Jud took an August 9, 1971, White House MEMORANDUM FOR THE RECORD concerning a meeting the President's "plumbers" had had at CIA headquarters. Jud had stolen the memo from Haldeman's French safe. The memo outlined the coordinated strategy between Nixon's men and the CIA.

The CIA liaison officer was named John Paisley. Six years after Jud stole that White House memo, when Paisley was serving on the CIA team analyzing the U.S.-Soviet Strategic Arms Limitation Talks, he disappeared while boating alone on Chesapeake Bay. Days later, a bloated body weighted down with two diving belts was found floating in the Bay and was identified as Paisley. The body was four inches shorter than Paisley's official height. No fingerprint or dental-record check was ever made. The corpse had a 9mm bullet wound behind the left ear. Paisley was right-handed. No gun or expended cartridge was found on his boat. The corpse was ruled a suicide and cremated at a CIA-approved funeral home without the family's having been allowed to see it.

That Friday night in the White House, Jud shuffled that "For the Record" memo in amidst the President's papers.

*So, SEARCHLIGHT,* thought Jud, smiling, *will it wig you out to discover what's materialized in your private safe?*

Jud buttoned the photocopied pages of the China memo from

Nixon's safe inside his shirt. He closed and locked the safe, closed the panel. Turned toward the President's desk—

"What the hell are you doing!" yelled a man from the hallway. Jud whirled, right hand locking on butt of his .357.

*Empty hands,* the man silhouetted behind the velvet rope across the door had empty hands. White shirt and uniform pants. Gold bars on his shoulders.

The Roving Deputy Watch Commander.

With one hand, Jud beckoned for his superior officer to come closer; with the other hand, he held a finger to his lips.

"Your post is the hall!" hissed the RDWC as he joined Jud beside the President's desk. "What the hell—"

"I heard something!" whispered Jud, moving toward the curtained French doors.

"Why didn't you call it in?" The RDWC followed Jud, his eyes darting around the Oval Office, his hand on his own gun butt.

"There wasn't time!" snapped Jud. "Besides, last time I did, the Watch Commander chewed my ass! Said I was hearing ghosts. Said it was Abigail Adams taking in her fucking laundry! He reamed Peters a new asshole for calling in the baby crying."

White House security logs are full of reports of unseen babies crying. Lincoln's son died during his father's first term.

The two Executive Protection Service officers stood in front of the windows, staring out at the South Lawn and the night-enshrouded Rose Garden.

"See anything?" whispered the RDWC.

"Just you." Jud took a breath. "SEARCHLIGHT's not around. We call a *nothing* in, it's paperwork city. Captain's Review."

The two men's radios squawked: shift change in twenty-five minutes.

"Do you hear anything now?" asked the RDWC.

"Just my heart. You."

"Fuck it," said the RDWC. "Two years to my twenty, I don't need this shit. It's nothing, right?"

"Right."

"I'll stick around till shift change," said the RDWC. "Just in case. But we're okay here, aren't we?"

"We're fine," said Jud, his heart slowing. "We're cool."

"This is a weird place," said the RDWC. "Plays tricks on you."

"I know," said Jud.

The RDWC shook his head, nodded toward the night outside the White House windows. "The shit that goes on out there."

When his shift ended at midnight, Jud dawdled in the Security locker room, changing into his civilian clothes, joking with the men around him. His fellow officers were eager to get home or go on shift. When the locker room was almost empty, Jud carefully folded the purloined photocopied memo into an oversize birth-day card, sealed the card in a stamped envelope. He invented a woman's name, addressed the envelope to her at a post office box in suburban Maryland.

A guard he didn't like was about to leave the locker room. The man didn't see Jud shed the pants he'd just put on.

"Hey, Jerry!" Jud called the man over. "Would you drop this in the bag for me on your way? I gotta hustle and get dressed and get out of here, or the woman outside'll skin me."

The guard named Jerry looked at Jud in his underwear. Looked at the greeting-card envelope that bore the name of a woman. Recognized a smile of male conspiracy on Jud's face.

"Yeah, what the hell," said Jerry, taking the envelope. "Bitches, right?"

"Right," said Jud as Jerry left the locker room.

Jud quietly scurried to the door, peered around the corner in time to see Jerry drop the envelope in the outgoing-mail pouch by the Watch Sergeant's desk. The RWDC who'd surprised Jud in the Oval Office was chatting with the sergeant. The RWDC watched Jerry mail the card, watched him walk away. Said nothing. Didn't grab the card, didn't demand an inspection. If he had, it would have been Jerry's envelope, Jerry's word against Jud's.

White House guards use a side entrance to the fence surrounding the presidential grounds. By the time Jud dressed, packed his gear in his gym bag, walked through the iron gate, it was 1:31 A.M., Saturday, June 17.

Nancy was parked up the street in her father's old Chrysler. Even with all the windows rolled down, the car was full of cigarette smoke.

"You're fuckin' late!" she snapped as he settled in the front seat. "You think all I got to do with my life is sit in this shithole car and wait for your ass to get off work?"

Slumped behind the steering wheel, Nancy wore a T-shirt and no bra, baggy shorts. Her brown hair was razor cut in a shoulder-length shag. She had a round face and a squat body, but it was her eyes that marred her looks: she kept them narrow, hard.

"You want to leave, *leave!*" he growled. "I can walk."

She blinked, licked her lips. "I'm . . . Look, it's just hot, you know?"

"Yeah," said Jud. "I know."

"You . . . You want to drive?"

He shook his head. She ground the car engine to life. Nancy was twenty-six years old, flunking out of her fifth year of part-time schooling at her third college. They'd met three months before, when she'd been blind drunk in a bar. Jud had pulled her out of the middle of a fight she'd incited between two conventioneers on the prowl. A week later, Jud gave her her first orgasm.

"I'm tired," he told her as she pulled the car away from the curb. Every turn of the car's tires that took him farther away from the White House rolled a load off his back. "So damn tired."

"You want to go to my place?"

He sighed, nodded.

"How come you're spending so much time in the gym, lifting weights and all that?" she said. "You were strong as hell, but now, you're getting . . . big. You're starting to look different."

Nancy's car rolled into the lower end of Georgetown. Even at this late hour, slick women and well-dressed men prowled the sidewalks between bars. She stopped for a red light.

"I mean," she added, "I'm not complaining, but . . ."

She trailed off, got no reply. The light changed to green. They drove on.

"What time is that party tomorrow night?" he asked.

"Why the . . ." She looked at him; changed her attitude. "After nine. It's no big deal. You don't want to go, do you?"

"You work with them, they invited you," he told her.

"They only invited me because they had to. Because I got that damn stupid job. Because of my *fucking* father!" She pitched her voice to a whining mimic: *"It's a good opportunity! Interesting! Decent money!*

"Stupid damn job," she whispered. "Errand runner with a stupid damn name. They had to give it to his daughter!"

She put a cigarette in her mouth, punched in the lighter of the car that was once her father's. It didn't work.

"Stupid damn car!" she swore.

It was 1:47 A.M.

Jud snapped his lighter, lit her cigarette, one for himself. He blew smoke into the heat outside the open window.

"I want to go to the party," he said. "We'll get there after my shift ends at midnight; it'll still be happening."

"Why do *you* want to go? All it'll be is beer and wine and bad dope and a bunch of hot-shit, kiss-ass, and backstabbing reporters, few years out of college and hustling to get their name on top of some stupid damn story about shit nobody cares about. Wrap dead fish in the damn newspaper!"

Nancy's father was assistant in-house counsel for the *Washington Post*.

"Copy aide," she murmured. "The old man's little girl. Oh, they *really* want me there tomorrow night."

"Don't be late when you pick me up," said Jud. "And don't be drunk. Look nice."

"It's easy for you," she said, driving toward the apartment her trust fund subsidized. "He isn't your damn father."

Jud's voice was fire and ice: "Don't you *ever* mention my father!"

She blinked.

"*Ever!*"

"Okay, okay, baby!" She swallowed. She parked in the driveway of a Georgetown carriage house friends of her father's were letting her use. Tossed her cigarette out the window to where cockroaches scurried over the brick sidewalk. Her eyes were wide as she leaned across the seat toward Jud.

"I'm sorry," she said. Her fingers brushed the gym bag holding his uniform. His gun. Handcuffs. Moved to his knee.

It was 1:52 A.M., Saturday, June 17, 1972. A mile away, an unmarked police car with three plainclothes officers responded to the police dispatcher's report of a burglary in progress at the Watergate complex.

Jud looked at the brown-haired woman leaning toward him across the front seat of her father's old car. Her eyes were narrow, her lips parted; the streetlight showed him her nipples were hard under her dirty cotton T-shirt.

"Just relax," he told her. "Everything'll be fine if you just relax."

*Relax.*

Eighteen years and three thousand miles away from that muggy

Washington night, Jud heard the distant echo of his own words; blinked, and it was 1990. Blinked again, and he was inside a bedroom. On his back in a bed. Naked. The sheets were damp, his skin sticky. The lamp on the bed table glowed. Outside, the desert was cool and dark. Midnight drifted across the packed sand.

Nora lay in Jud's arms.

"I told you, all you had to do was relax and everything would be fine," she said, kissing his chest. "In fact, I'll give you more than fine."

"Okay?" ventured Jud.

"No man wants to know that it was *'Okay,'*" said Nora, raising up on her elbows to smile at him. "You all want to know that it was *great.*"

"Was it great?"

"It was okay," she said.

A heartbeat, then they both laughed.

Nora lightly kissed his lips.

"I told you so," she said.

They laughed again, and she nuzzled back down on his chest. She sighed.

Another night together. Their silent understanding made sure that he brought nothing more than his toothbrush to Nora's house. His clothes, his money, his secret gun—all stayed in the trailer.

"What were you thinking of just then?" she asked.

"I was following orders," replied Jud. To her frown, he added, "Yours. You told me not to think. Just to feel. Relax."

"Not *then.*" She grinned. "I know what you were thinking about then: you were thinking about *then*—if you were thinking at all. This early in it for us, you aren't remembering or fantasizing. Men believe it's a big secret that they're thinking about something else or somebody else or imagining things when they're with a woman. But we know."

"Oops," said Jud.

"I don't mind," she said. "If you think that what's in your head is more . . . *interesting* than what we're doing . . ."

She trailed a finger up his thigh.

"Even my mind's not that crazy," said Jud. "Or strong."

"Yeah, but afterwards . . ." She shook her head. "You guys slip away faster than you slip out. If it's been *okay* for a woman, she hangs around for a while. You guys go."

"Not always," he said.

"Always enough." She brushed her hair off her forehead. Jud adored the wrinkles on her brow, the crow's-feet by her blue eyes. "Were you thinking about your ex-wife?"

"No."

"Someone else?"

"Not really."

"Well, that narrows it down."

She poked him in the ribs. "So then, what do you want to talk about, the tumbleweed count or UFOs?"

"That's it! The reason we haven't seen any UFOs lately is they're disguising themselves as tumbleweeds!"

"Let 'em." Nora propped herself up on her elbow. "How come you never ask me about being a prostitute?"

"I know how that works," whispered Jud.

"'Cause you're a spy." She said it flatly. No trace of condescension, no hint of disbelief. Flat acceptance.

He looked at her. "How did you start?"

"Just lucky."

They laughed.

"Sauk Centre, Minnesota," she said. "My hometown. There's this billboard next to the highway by the city limits. Says Sinclair Lewis wrote a book about the town. I'd see that sign every day from the bus I rode to grade school, and I swore I'd never read any book about that damn place.

"Daddy was fire and brimstone for Jesus, Mom was afraid to be for anybody or anything. Back then, the law had something called 'status offenses,' and my status was offensive. Hitchhiking to town from our farm. All I wanted to do was go to the football game. Where I went was reform school. Twelve years old.

"*Incorrigible*, they said." She shook her head. "Even then, I had tits out to here. *That* scared the hell out of the men in charge, made them think *bad* thoughts—so I had to be bad."

She sat up in bed, stretched. Jud thought her breasts were beautiful, and he told her so, quietly, almost like a boy.

"Not bad for a woman winking at fifty," she said.

"How long did they keep you in reform school?" asked Jud.

"As long as they could. Six years. I lived in a lot of fear. Learned how to survive. You figure out who the ringleaders are, learn what you have to do to get along with them. Learn how to cover your feelings. Only cry in your cell alone at night. Had my first sexual experience there, lesbian. I think that's pretty normal though, don't you?"

"My first was a girl, too," said Jud.

She laughed.

"Then what?" he asked.

"Then I got out. I was intelligent, but not smart. My schooling was a joke—two times two equals four, and that's as far as it went. I had two choices: I could crook or I could hook.

"Tried crook, but if you have trouble reading and writing, passing bad checks is tricky. I got caught. Got another year—this time in jail. Saw some old friends, learned a little more about reading and a lot more about how to stay out of jail. Came out blond and beautiful, schooled and connected.

"I never worked the streets," she said. "Never worked cribs. Lived with a black guy. My lover and business manager."

"Pimp," said Jud.

Nora shrugged. "He taught me a lot. Made me read the *Wall Street Journal* every day. Got me onto the high-class track in L.A. Beat me up some, but I expected it. Wouldn't take it now, but then . . . That was the way things were. I got busted once. Paid a fortune to the right lawyer, everything smoothed out fine. Stay in line with the *real* power structure, you don't get run over."

It was Jud's turn to laugh.

"People liked me," she said. "I was good at getting men to give me money. I ended up in Vegas because a man I loved was there, and because the money was there."

"What about your Johns?"

"I never called them that. I was a working girl, they were dates. They gave me what I wanted, I gave them what they wanted. I didn't hurt anybody, didn't steal or lie or cheat, always gave the bellman his third off the top. I charged a fortune and made a fortune, couple, three grand a night—clear. Men loved giving me money and I loved taking it.

"Wasn't bad work." She shrugged. "Could have done worse. Just . . . turn off your mind. In the middle of the wildest sex scene, thinking about what to get at the grocery store on the way home . . .

"Did you ever use a working girl?" she asked.

"Yes," he said. Waited, then, "Does that bother you?"

She smiled. "No."

Her blue eyes looked toward the bedtable.

"I'm gonna get some cigarettes," she said. She kissed his forehead. "Don't go nowhere."

Barefoot, naked, she padded from the bedroom.

Jud let himself settle back on the pillow. The room smelled like sweat and sex and lilacs from her perfume, and he let himself relax, let himself love it.

There'd been some rough days.

One afternoon, while he was washing dishes in the café's kitchen, he got the booze shakes so bad the two truckers sitting at the counter could hear the plates rattling in the soapy tub. Carmen scurried out front to fill coffee cups whether they needed it or not. Nora sat behind the cash register, reading the Las Vegas newspaper. She said nothing.

"Do you have your car keys?" he'd asked Nora when the truckers left.

"Yes," she answered. "No."

"I have to—"

"Do what you have to do," she'd told him. "But I won't give you my keys to do it. You want to run your sorry ass into town and drink, fine, your choice. But I'm not letting you drive my car drunk, and I'm not making it easy for you."

"I don't need any AA bullshit!"

"That's right," she said, still reading the paper, "you've got enough bullshit of your own."

He trembled: in rage, in need, in fear. He could force her to— No. *No.* Sweating, shaking, gut wrenching, he staggered back into the kitchen. His mind reeled. He held on to the sink until he could finish the dishes, until the sickness passed.

They didn't need to talk about that incident.

She made him keep practicing his katas, though he knew she hated the thought of fighting. "They make you feel safe," she'd told him. She had Carmen bring him an expensive pair of running shoes from Vegas and always had coffee waiting for him when he staggered back down the road.

"Maybe I just want to see how far you'll run," she told him. "Maybe I just like to watch you come back."

She shot a rattlesnake on the road one day. With the café owner's gun, a .25 automatic with a cracked pearl handle.

Using the pay phone by the highway, Jud had reached Dean in Los Angeles.

"Check my tracks," Jud had asked. Dean eagerly agreed.

When Jud called Dean two days later, he learned that the dead man at the Oasis bar hadn't even made the L.A. papers.

"I went there like a shadow," said Dean. "Bartender bragged about the cops doing shit. He probably told them nothing. If you want, he'll tell me—"

"Leave him alone," said Jud.

And Dean laughed.

"Old day, old ways, huh?" he asked. "If you want—"

"All I want is for you to be cool—understand, Dean? Nothing more. Nothing less. Cool. And don't worry."

"*Worry?* I don't *worry*. Did you forget who I am?"

"I know," said Jud.

"I've been waiting. Waiting. Why were you so long gone?"

"Never mind," said Jud.

"Your friend called."

Jud's hand tightened on the receiver.

"That writer. Nick Kelley."

"You gave him your number—remember?"

"Remember. Yes, I remember. So did he." Dean laughed again, high-pitched, intense—then abruptly clipped off. "He wanted to be sure you were fine."

"What did you tell him?"

"Nothing. I didn't know anything. Then."

"Don't have any contact with him—*any*."

Dean's voice was soft, chilly. "Is he a problem?"

"No: he's not a player."

"Oh."

At the pay phone in the desert, Jud wiped his brow, closed his eyes.

"My leg is fine," whispered Dean. "I'm strong."

"Just stay cool."

"Where are you?"

Jud opened his eyes.

"If something stirs," said Dean, "you'll need to know."

Through the windows of the café, Jud saw Nora laughing with Carmen.

"I'm out of touch," he said.

"That's not smart."

He was right. He was wrong and he was right. He was Dean, and Jud knew it. His head ached and rolled with alcoholic waves, his heart said no, but crazy Dean made sense, so Jud made the best play he could think of.

"I'll give you a pay phone number," said Jud. "I'm not there, but I'll detour there every other day at six in the morning. If I don't answer, don't speak."

"Relax," said Dean. "I've got your back."

The pay phone hadn't rung since. Jud made no other calls—not even to Nick. What could he say? Nick was out of it, clear. Had a real life. Jud wouldn't pull him in.

*Relax,* Jud told himself as he lay in Nora's bed. Your trail is clean, your tracks are gone. They can't find you, can't touch you. He glanced toward the curtained window, the night beyond. There was nothing out there. Nothing he could see.

But something bothered him. Something he might have done, some erratic act lost in chemical and battle-battered brain cells, some vibration humming deep in his instincts from a step he couldn't remember, couldn't connect.

*Years ago, you'd have remembered,* Jud told himself. *But years ago, you wouldn't have had a misstep to remember.*

"Carmen brought supplies," said Nora as she walked back into the bedroom. Still naked. She carried a brown paper grocery sack. "Look, everything we could ask for!"

She climbed on the bed, pulled the sheet over her legs.

"The floor's cold," she said, lifting a carton of cigarettes out of the sack. She took a pack from the carton, slit a thumbnail along cellophane, handed him a bottle of spring water.

"And," she said, "we even have"—she pulled a tabloid newspaper out of the bag—"the truth of the world!"

*The American Enquirer.* The nation's largest weekly tabloid newspaper, available with equal ease at a Korean green grocer in uptown Manhattan, New York, or at Manhattan, Montana's, food store–gas station.

"I don't want to see that thing," snapped Jud, sitting up in bed and looking the other way.

"Come on!" Nora lit a cigarette. "It's all just fun."

"I know what it says."

"How? What's the big deal?"

Jud closed his eyes, hung his head. When he looked at her again, she felt a chill in his eyes.

"Turn to page nine," he said. "The astrology column. It's been there for twenty years, always on the same page. Same guy, they never change his picture."

"Okay," she said, turning the pages, finding the feature. "You want to know your horoscope?"

"Today's date," he said. "What's the sign for today?"

"That's . . . Pisces."

"Count that sign as zero. Go chronologically. What's the sign for number seven?"

After a moment, she answered, "Libra."

"Somewhere in Libra it says 'choppy waters.'"

"'Libra,'" Nora read aloud. "'September twenty-third to October twenty-second. Moon cycle high. Romance in the picture. Financial caution wise. Ch . . .'"

She looked at him. His face was impassive.

"'Choppy waters,'" she said. "How did you know that was in there?"

His smile was hard. "Just lucky."

"Because you're a spy," she said.

The forgotten cigarette in her hand dropped a long ash onto the paper with the truth of the world.

"I'm not supposed to ask questions, am I?" she said.

*"Nobody's supposed to ask questions,"* he whispered.

"What are you supposed to do?"

"Follow orders. Get in touch."

"What are you going to do?" she whispered before she could stop herself.

He sat on the edge of her bed. And shook his head no.

For a long time, they sat there. In silence. Nora smoked her cigarette, stubbed it out. She put the newspaper on the floor by her side of the bed. Turned out the light.

# CRACK PEOPLE

In the gentle light of dawn, Nick Kelley watched his son sleep. The baby lay in his crib, snug in his one-piece yellow pajamas, his beloved blue-and-white-checkered cotton blanket bundled beside him.

The baby stirred. Rubbed his nose with a fist that could *just* encircle his father's finger. Blinked his blue eyes open.

*"Hi, Saul,"* whispered Nick.

The child's brow wrinkled as the world came into focus.

They heard the dog bark; the front door open and close; Juanita call out "Good morning" and Sylvia answer as she brushed her hair in the master bedroom. The nursery smelled of dried milk and damp diaper. Warm blankets.

Saul struggled to his feet and padded along the slat walls of his crib toward "Da'y." Almost there, the baby stopped, his attention transfixed by the sun streaming through the window. His tiny hand let go of the crib and opened to catch the light.

The transient beauty of the moment welled inside Nick. His eyes glistened. In these middle years, he felt in his heart the knowledge that as a young man he'd found with his mind: that the cost of joy lies in the luck we inherit and the loves we embrace; that yesterday's choices create today's chances, and that each dawn gives us the terrible freedom to choose again, certain only that we have more to lose. Still, Nick believed in some nameless force akin to gravity that ruled whatever redemption life could offer, a force he felt bound to by common sense and simple honor; a force that required him to be true, to not flinch.

"I'm sorry, Son," whispered Nick. "I'll do my best."

Behind him, Sylvia said, "There are my guys!"

Nick turned to watch her beautiful smile fade as she absorbed the look on his face.

"I need to talk to you," he said.

An hour later, they sat at the kitchen table, the newspapers still in their plastic wrappers, their coffee cups empty. From upstairs came the sound of Saul and Juanita laughing.

He'd told Sylvia everything—everything he could articulate, details colored in to a previously sketchy perspective of his days since Jud's farewell phone call. About Dean, meeting his CIA friend. About Jack Berns and the old man in the library.

"All that wasn't coincidence," he told her.

"It could be your imagination," she said. "Our lives aren't one of your books. I know you want them to be: exciting—"

"Safe," he said. "I want them to be safe."

She shook her head. "It's Jud's fault—whatever it is."

"I've got my share of blame," said Nick.

"For *what?*" she said. "What's there? Paranoia? Mysterious strangers? Politics? Where's a bottom line?"

"My guess is somebody's nervous about what I'm doing—the story, knowing Jud, the link between the two."

"What *story?* That bullshit nothing for Peter Murphy?"

"Nobody knows it's nothing."

"It's all air," she said. "Where's your liability?"

*My wife, the lawyer,* he thought. "Skeletons in my closet. Reporter's privilege should keep me out of a grand jury. Unless they're desperate and know how far over the line I went."

"Nobody knows that except Jud," she said.

"They'd never let him in front of a grand jury."

"So what do you have to worry about? Being unpopular with bureaucrats or that private eye's clients? The hell with them. There's nobody out there who gives a shit about you personally, and professionally, the rules in this town cover you."

"If everybody follows the rules," said Nick. He dreaded putting words to his worst fears; doing so would infect the woman he loved with worry and paranoia. And doubt about him, for Nick knew she didn't believe in the power of shadows over substance.

"Honey . . ." She shook her head. "It's the 1990s. Hoover is dead, Watergate is over. . . . It's a new era."

"And the story is the best shield I've got," he said.

His wife sighed. "You don't need a shield if you stay away from guys like Jud."

"Sorry to have all that history in my bags."

She brushed her hand through his silver-laced black hair, smiled.

"Hell," she said, "you got stuck with my mother."

Their laughter carried tension out of the kitchen.

"What are you going to do next?" she asked.

"I don't know."

Sylvia smiled. "I've got an idea."

Nick and the old woman met for lunch in a Mexican restaurant so far out Pennyslvania Avenue it was almost off Capitol Hill. Soon as they sat down, she ordered a beer.

"American," she said, "one of the real ones, not that light crap. And keep the fruit."

Nick had the same. They both ordered ground beef and cheese in deep-fat-fried flour tortillas, rice, and beans.

She had white hair and a lean face with tanned wrinkles. Her name was Irene and her eyes were amber and bright.

"Thanks for helping me," said Nick.

"I haven't yet," said Irene. "Your wife's a sharp lady. She works for Congress, I work for their library, she called."

"The Congressional Research Service does great work."

"Save the butter for the bread," she said. "I'll give you what I can, which probably won't be much."

The waiter put two bottles of beer and wet glasses on the table. A lime wedge was stuck in the mouth of each beer bottle.

"You can't get what you want these days," said Irene as she tossed the lime wedge into the ashtray. "So what are you after? Something about what'll happen now that the Berlin Wall is rubble? A report card on Ralph Denton, the CIA's new honcho?"

"I'll take a couple fast answers like that, but I'm after something deeper. Only I'm not sure what it is."

"At least Gallahad knew he wanted the Holy Grail."

"I doubt there's anything holy about this," said Nick. "Something has gone bump in the night. I need to know what it is."

"Hey," she said, "I'm a congressional lackey, and Congress is the last to find out what goes bump in the night."

"What about the two intelligence oversight committees?"

"Oversight is a joke," she said. "Congress knows what they tell us. The foxes briefing the chickens on what's outside the coop."

"Where would you look today for something gone wrong?" asked Nick. "Small operation, probably. Off the books, high level, and highly compartmentalized."

"How you *do* talk!"

They laughed as the waiter put their plates in front of them. She ordered another beer, so Nick did, too.

"Do you have an arena?" she asked.

"Could be anywhere. There may be a black-bag angle to it: my guy—the people are B&E experts. But it could be anything from assassination to drugs, and it's gone sour."

"We won't know how sour our spies can go until we make 'em narcs. You got any names?"

"No," he said.

"You bullshit me, I bullshit you," she said.

"The name wouldn't mean anything to you."

Irene took a pull from her beer. "Everybody thinks spooks equals CIA. But look at the Pentagon. All those offices, a dozen agencies, thousands of bodies, and a budget in the billions."

"Makes sense."

"So"—she smiled—"Panama? Nicaragua—even though our guys won the elections, it's a brave new world with lots of turmoil. China, Russia, Beirut, El Salvador—pick your place."

"California," said Nick.

She didn't laugh. They pushed rice and beans around their plates. Nick let the silence whisper to her.

"Domestic spy mess?" She frowned. "We're eating Mexican lunch, and across town, an admiral is on trial for Iran-contra."

"It could be part of that," said Nick, "if there's more still out there than this trial."

"There's plenty there," said Irene. "That was a multi*million*-dollar scam. Suppose something's fallen in the cracks of the investigations. Something or somebody who's still in big jeopardy. You looking for something that went bump in the night, look for the people in the cracks of Iran-contra."

* * *

But first Nick had to look where it started for him. He had to look for Jud.

He wouldn't call Dean again. If one call to him hadn't helped, a second call could only hurt. The nerves in the back of Nick's neck tingled when he thought about Dean.

After his lunch with Irene, Nick sat at his desk in his office, watching the world outside his windows. Green buds dotted the tree limbs. The weather was gorgeous.

There was only one other person who might link him to Jud: *Lorri*, Jud's wife.

*Ex*-wife, thought Nick. For what? Five, six years. He didn't know. But sometime in the mid-1980s, Jud had shed the young wife he'd found in Los Angeles.

*Lorri*. Lost, stolen, or strayed.

Or dead.

Jud had said they'd split, she'd left, deserted, flipped out, run away, been banished by him. High drama. Simple fade. Over the phone, Nick had heard a dozen different versions, but only from his friend Jud: when Lorri left Jud's life, she left Nick's. The two constants in Jud's stories were Lorri's absence and his pain. Who was victim and who was villain didn't matter to Nick, nor was he sure such roles were consistent or free from an inevitability that rendered such labels moot.

God, she'd been beautiful.

Nick remembered—when was it?—1978 or 1979, before the days of madness—or at least before he recognized them as such. In L.A., sweet soul-sucking city of the angels.

Nick had flown to town for a scriptwriting gig. After the first meeting, he knew no movie would be made, but he played the deal out: for the money, for the ticket-punching that made him a *bona fide* screenwriter, for the chance to be in L.A. on someone else's dime. For the chance to see Jud again, and amidst their camaraderie and bullshit, to learn more about the dark world that Jud personified. The glitz of Hollywood tantalized Nick with its allure of creating movies and being loved by beautiful blondes, but he knew he'd get little of either. What excited him was gliding over those same city streets in Jud's slipstream: electric reality, not celluloid, sliding along the knife edge without being scarred.

Jud brought Lorri to Nick's hotel to meet his famous writer friend. Lorri, a mane of tawny red hair, heavy breasts, wisp of a waist, and round hips, clear skinned and with a lopsided smile. She listened while Jud told stores for Nick to ratify.

Nick's meetings were over by three the next day. Jud was *taking care of business.* Lorri drove Nick to the ocean.

"I'm from about as far away from the ocean as you can get," she said as they left a public parking lot at Redondo Beach.

"Where's that?" asked Nick.

"Nebraska." She giggled. "Lorri Lane from Nebraska. What a hick. Sounds like Superman's girlfriend."

"How'd you meet Jud?"

"I was working in a hair-cutting place in Santa Monica. Answering phones, appointments. He was still working for that lock company then, and he came in to change the locks. . . ." She shrugged.

"He was funny. Nice. And he wouldn't take no for an answer. Kept me from doing dumb things. I used to like pills. Jud . . . He took care of me. Pulled me out of that."

Lorri cocked her head. "There's never any . . . It's like he always *knows.* He's never stuck. Or lost."

She lit a cigarette before they reached the beach.

"Forget about me being able to quit," she said.

"I didn't say anything."

"Good." And she laughed. "There's the ocean."

Rolling gray-green waves, only a handful of people on the sand that chilly workday afternoon.

"Jud says he fell for you the first time he saw you."

"Well . . ." She shrugged. "Guess I just got lucky. We laugh a lot. He's real smart. Stronger than anyone I ever met.

"I don't mean just his muscles," she said.

"I know," Nick told her.

"Did he really do all those things?" she asked.

"All what things?"

"Come on," she said, "I won't rat on you to him." She let Nick struggle for an answer, then laughed. "Never mind. He's your buddy, right? He says you understand him better than anybody but me, which is good, I guess, 'cause I don't understand about all that Washington stuff."

"Most people don't."

"Hey," she said, "don't shine me to be nice. I only got out of high school, but I'm not *that* dumb."

"Who said you were dumb?"

"Some people think so."

"They're wrong."

"Yeah. *Yeah*." She smiled to the ocean. "I got out of Nebraska, didn't I?"

"Why here?"

"Here's got an ocean." She lost her smile. "Better chance of being somebody here. Sure certain of being nobody in Nebraska. Being nothing. Or what they let you be."

"Who do you want to be?"

She laughed. "How the hell should I know?"

He laughed with her. They walked closer to the water.

"People back home thought I was beautiful."

"You are."

"Yeah, well, big deal. Here I am. I was going to . . ." She cocked her face and grinned, clicked an imaginary camera at Nick. "Pictures, you know? Hollywood."

She stared at the sea. "I saw the smog, realized I'd never even find the doors. Wouldn't know what to do if I got inside. Other than that, there were just more of the same *offers* I got in Nebraska. Same guys, only they didn't drive pickups or wear caps. But the weather's better, and there's the ocean."

"And then you met Jud."

"Yeah," she said. Smiled. "Then I met Jud.

"Hey!" She laughed, fishing a Polaroid out of her purse. "I'm in Hollywood! Take my picture!"

The night before, she'd snapped a shot of Jud and Nick, buddies sitting side by side on a red couch.

Nick took the camera. For a moment, they were making history or art or at least entertainment. Film professionals. He struck a firm stance. She twirled around on the sand between him and the sea, her chestnut hair floating like waves, snapping around *just so* as she gave a smile to the magic dark eye: not sultry, not taunting, not slick or impersonally perfect. A face of a beautiful girl who'd not been born by these waters.

*Click.*

A minute later, the camera rolled out a warm snapshot.

"It's great," he said.

"What should we do with it?" she asked, looking at Nick.

"Give it to Jud," he answered. "Surprise him with it."

"Yeah," she said after a heartbeat. "He'll love it."

Years later, sitting in his Washington office, Nick wondered, *Where are those pictures now?*

And where's Lorri?

When your life breaks apart, you stumble back to where it all started, call it home, call it whatever; if you can get there, you go back to where you used to be whole.

Nebraska.

Nick took an atlas off his shelf, turned to the map in the middle of the book. The state was white, with red and green and black roads and a thousand towns.

And he *remembered:* Night. Jud and Lorri's L.A. condo. Jud out. Helping Lorri with her new job, lugging a hanging garment bag into the living room, unzipping it to count and bundle three-quarters of a million dollars in fifties and hundreds, cram the lesser bills in the chump-change drawer in the kitchen. They'd smoked a joint, which made their math something to double-check again and again. Laughing, she told him she was from . . .

". . . a piss-ant place so south of Lincoln it's almost in Kansas."

She told him the name, and stoned, he went, "Hey!" and told her there was an author who had that same name.

Whatever it was.

In his office, Nick put his finger on the capital of the Cornhusker State, scanned the white space below it, tiny circles labeled Crete, Cortland, Tecumseh . . .

Conrad.

That part of Nebraska was a 402 area code. The operator told Nick there were three Lanes listed in Conrad: Byron, Mary, and Jack. No Lorri, no *L.*

Nick looked at his watch: noon hour in Nebraska.

Mary's line was busy. Nobody home at Byron's. A man answered, "Yeah?" at Jack's after the third ring. Nick heard kids screaming in the background, a woman yelling, television.

"I'm calling long distance," said Nick: *so take me seriously, help me. I'm looking for a friend of mine, Lorri Lane. She used to live in Conrad.*"

"You lookin' to get money out of her, you're out of luck, and I ain't pickin' up no more of her tabs."

*Big family,* Lorri had told Nick. *All boys. My uncles and brothers used to knock me around some. Nothing special.*

"She doesn't owe me anything," Nick told the man. "I just need to talk to her. Can you tell me where she is?"

"She's here."

"Living with you?"

"I ain't that dumb, mister. . . . *Shut up or I'll knock you on your ass!* . . . Don't mind that: kids. You know."

"Yeah," said Nick, picturing the scene he could only hear. "Where's Lorri?"

"Lives in that dickhead Jensen's trailer out east o' town. Day or night, you want her, she's there, though you won't find a line at her door these days."

"Does she have a phone?"

"How the hell else can welfare make sure to send her checks? 'Sides, she's gotta call Grearson's, get 'em to deliver her macaroni and wine. . . . *I told you to shut up!*"

Over the phone line, Nick heard the *smack* of a blow, a small boy's scream turning to a wail that ran from the room.

"Look, I ain't got all day. You want her number?"

He rattled off four digits: in Conrad, prefixes weren't necessary.

It took fifteen minutes for Nick to dial the eleven digits on his phone. It took six rings for her to answer.

"Hello?" The woman's voice was hoarse, timid.

"Lorri? It's Nick."

"Hello?" In the background, the TV volume faded.

"Nick Kelley. The writer from Washington. Remember?"

*"Ohhh!"* Soft. Happy. "Nick! *Nick!* I know you! How are you? Are you *here?* Are you coming over? What—

*"Did he tell you?"* she screamed. "Does he know where I am? He told you! What does he want? I'm not here! I'm not—"

"Nobody told me anything!" Nick yelled over her panic. "Nobody. Just you. I remembered what you told me, about Nebraska, being from Conrad, the ocean."

"The ocean," she said, calmer. "Yes, I remember, too."

"But he doesn't know where I am." Calmer, colder.

"I don't know."

"Good," she said. "Good. I don't think so. Good."

Nick heard the *rasp* of a farmer's match, the sigh of a cigarette lit.

"So . . . How are you?" asked Nick.

"I'm fine," said Lorri.

"I got married," he blurted out. "I have a baby. A son."

"*A baby,*" she whispered. "A baby."

"I know about . . . the divorce."

"I'm not going back, I'm not, I can't," she chanted. "*No.*"

"Nobody will make you."

"You won't tell anyone, will you?"

"No," promised Nick. "No."

"Why . . . why did you call? Did . . . Did you miss me?"

"I remember the good times," he told her.

"Were they?" She laughed.

"How are you living?"

"Oh, you know." He heard her swallow. "After I got out of the last place, I just . . . ended up back here."

She laughed. "I knew the way. I knew the rules.

"There was this guy," she said, "other guys but then Paul, Paul Jensen . . . This is his trailer, he . . . We . . . Well, what the hell, right? It didn't work out either."

Her laugh turned into a cough, a choke.

"Don't worry," she gasped. "You sign enough papers saying you're sick, they send you money in the mail. Long as you don't get better, everything's all right.

"Just a minute," she said, put the phone down on a table.

Nick her heard footsteps fade, come back. Something clunked on the wood next to the receiver in Nebraska. He heard a plastic *snap,* liquid splashing. He saw his reflection in the window of his office and felt like throwing up.

"Back again," Lorri said into the phone. Another rasp of a match, drawn breath. "Another guy that did the Casper. Remember? Jud used to call it doing the Casper 'cause there was this cartoon, see, and the friendly ghost's name was—"

"I remember," said Nick.

"Long as I remember to keep some money for the phone, don't have to go nowhere. I got a roof. I know the rules."

"That's good, Lorri."

"Why did you call, Nick? We couldn't go to your wedding."

"I'm looking for Jud. I thought—"

*"I don't know where he is!* I told you I don't know and I don't want to know or who he is! Needles or wet sheets or shock machines or nothing's gonna make me know anything! Don't tell me! Don't tell him! *Who the hell are you, huh?* Who the hell?"

"Lorri, if Jud calls—"

"Don't let him! Don't let him get me!"

"He won't get you, Lorri. You know he wouldn't hurt you."

"Who hurts who? Huh? How does it work?"

"Lorri, I don't think he'll come see you. But he might call you soon. If he does, I need you to promise me something."

"No! If he calls, he'll . . . Promise you?"

"Please, it's important."

"You always were important, Nick. You were real, too."

"If he calls, if you talk to Jud, promise me you'll tell him I need to talk to him. Please, Lorri: promise me."

"Promise?" He heard laughter, he heard sobs. "Promise you, Nick? Yeah, okay, I can do that. I can promise."

"Thank you! Thanks, I . . . Lorri?"

"Huh?"

"Is there . . . Do you need . . . Is there anything I can do?"

"Anything you can do." Her flat voice trailed off into silence. A long time passed. He heard her smoking, the rattle of an ashtray.

Then she said, "No, Nick, there's nothing you can do."

# DANCE WITH AN ANGEL

**O**ne look at the house and Wes knew he'd found the right place.

The house was one of ten thousand ordinary houses in a Los Angeles neighborhood known for its ordinary houses. The roof was faded black, the white walls were peeling. Patches of sick grass and packed dirt made up the front yard. A driveway ran along one side of the house. Back by the open garage, a man wearing a denim shirt and jeans tinkered with a motorcycle.

*Dean Jacobsen,* thought Wes. *Nick Kelley didn't call you because you're a movie mogul or a book publisher.*

Despite his excitement, Wes yawned. Beth had kissed him twice when she dropped him at Washington's Dulles airport.

"Once for luck, once for me," she'd said, laughed and driven his car back to their apartment building.

Wes dozed fitfully as the plane carried him westward through the night. He'd dreamed warm dreams of yellow light. In L.A., he rented a car and drove over streets he'd left what seemed like years before, though it had been less than two days.

*B.B.,* he thought. *Before Beth.*

When Wes parked his car across the street from the right house, the man didn't stop working on the motorcycle. He didn't look like the pictures of Jud Stuart.

A raindrop splattered on Wes's windshield. Gray clouds rolled across the sky, absorbing the city's smog. A chilly gust of wind rocked the car. Wes thought about putting on his trench coat, left it on the backseat and climbed out.

No one was visible through the house's windows.

In the wind, Wes heard the babble of daytime TV. A little girl on a tricycle peddled along the sidewalk; she dinged the bell on her handlebars.

Wes crossed the street, walked up the driveway.

"Excuse me!" he called to the man working on the motorcycle. "Are you Mr. Dean Jacobsen?"

"Who are you?" said the man. He was as tall as Wes and heavier in the chest. Dirty-blond hair. He held a wrench.

"I'm a lawyer," answered Wes. "Are you Dean Jacobsen?"

"Why?"

"It's okay," said Wes, "this isn't about you."

The man's bright eyes swept the driveway.

"Seems like it's just you and me." His grin was slow and thin. "So I'll be Dean."

He didn't put down the wrench.

"I'm an attorney." Wes held out his laminated American Bar Association card. The card confirmed only that Wes was a member. As Dean glanced at it, Wes said, "I've got good news."

"No lawyer has good news."

A woman raised a window of the house next door. They looked at her. She shut the window, lowered her shade.

"A friend of yours has come into an inheritance," said Wes. "But we're having trouble locating him, and we hoped you might know where he is."

"What makes you think I've got a friend?"

"My colleague got your name from someone who knows the two of you. I think it was a woman."

"You gotta be careful with the women you believe," said Dean. "Where you from?"

"Pennsylvania." Wes had a Bar membership card from that state that didn't show his place of employment.

"Who's this friend you think I got?"

"A man named Jud Stuart."

"Oh."

An icy water pellet hit Wes's shirt. The sky above the garage churned with pregnant gray clouds.

"I just need to talk to him," said Wes. "Let him know about the inheritance. Straighten out a few details."

"Who died?"

"I'm sorry, that's confidential."

Dean laughed. He tossed the wrench into a tool chest.

"You're lucky and smart, Wesley," said Dean with a grin. He looked around his neighborhood; at the house where the woman had drawn the shade. The wind stirred trash in his garage. From across the street came the dinging of a tricycle bell.

"How so?" asked Wes.

"*Smart,* because like you said, Jud's my friend. And *lucky,* 'cause I'm on my way to meet him. Now."

*Don't let him slip away!* Wes thought. He said, "I'll come along. Save everybody trouble. Get him the good news."

Dean smiled. "If that's what you want."

"We'll take my car," said Wes.

"I'll go inside and get my jacket."

A maroon windbreaker dangled from the fence. Wes pointed to it. "What's that?"

"Ah." Dean shook his head. "How'd I forget?"

Dean slid into the jacket, put the toolbox in the gaping garage. He pulled down the heavy overhead door with one hand.

"Let's go riding in the car-car," said Dean.

On the freeway, Wes asked, "Where are we going?"

"Just far enough," said Dean.

From the first freeway to a second. Traffic was light.

"Where are we going?" Wes asked again.

"A public place. A safe place. Jud is a cautious man."

"He's just a name to me," said Wes. "What's he like?"

"He's the man," whispered Dean. "He is *the* man. Others pretend, he *is*. He knows."

"What does he know?"

"The big secret." Dean smiled.

"What's that?" asked Wes, his heart racing.

Dean's black eyes pulled back from the windshield; fire danced in them as they turned and touched Wes.

"Everybody dies," answered Dean.

Cars whizzed by them. Rain dotted the windshield. The rush of their journey sucked the water droplets up the glass, away.

"Take that exit," said Dean.

The sign said Barham Boulevard. Houses clung to the hills beside the highway. A black tower skyscraper poked the clouds. Roads and houses stretched off into the mist.

"Used to be, I didn't talk this much," said Dean.

A concrete ditch paralleled their path. Beyond it were hangar-like tan buildings. Movie billboards perched on those flat roofs. Wet emerald grass covered the hill to their right.

"How did you meet Jud?" asked Wes.

"People put us in touch." Dean smiled. "He beat me once. At his old condo by the beach. I'd been careless with his trust. Didn't know who he truly was. He took me down to the garage. It was like dancing with an angel. Then I knew."

"That he was the man," said Wes.

Dean shrugged. "Somebody has to be."

"What man is that?"

"If you need to ask, you can't know."

*I don't want to know.* Wes feared he'd flown across country only to cruise aimlessly with a burnt-out case. They drove past Forest Lawn cemetery, with its white stone mausoleums.

"What was he doing back then?" asked Wes.

"Go right," ordered Dean, pointing to a park entrance.

The paved road rose and fell through the park like a roller coaster. They passed picnic grounds and barbecue pits. Wes saw five horseback riders winding their way through the trees. Their leader wore a yellow rain slicker and a cowboy hat.

Dean snickered. "Here comes the cavalry."

A mile later, they reached a chicken-wired field with a two-tiered building at its far end. Hundreds of white balls dotted the ground inside the fence. As they passed the parking lot, four Japanese men in brightly colored pants and jackets and white caps unloaded golf bags from a Toyota.

"I'm about out of time for this," said Wes.

"We're about there," answered Dean. "Go that way."

Down a residential street. They turned right, the road climbing through the hills of elegant Spanish and Tudor mansions. A Mexican gardener clipping grass watched them fade into the mist.

"This is the perfect place," said Dean as they topped the hill. The evergreen trees ended. A massive parking lot waited off to the right. To the left, on the crest of the hill, was a castle.

Not quite a castle. A gray stone building with brass double doors, cathedral windows, a giant green copper dome rising from a tower in its center, and smaller copper domes on each end.

"What is this place?" asked Wes.

"Griffith Observatory."

"Jud is *here?*"

"It's perfect," said Dean. "You'll see. It's all here."

An orange school bus was the only other vehicle in the parking lot. As Wes parked, the bus door opened, and thirty teenagers ran out into the cold.

"Day like today," said Dean, "thought we'd be up here alone."

"Where is he?"

"He'll be around the back. Watching to be sure it's me and I'm okay. When he's sure of that, we'll see him."

"We better," said Wes. "Where's his car?"

"Beats me," said Dean.

As they walked across the lawn, Wes noticed Dean limped. And Dean saw Wes's look.

"Long time ago," said Dean, "I wrecked my bike. Storms make it stiff. Something like that, embrace the pain. Do what you do."

Two teenage girls ran past them, stopped

"Okay," said the chubby girl, "what are we going to do?"

Her friend was pretty, brown haired.

"Like," she said, "you stand there, see, and I stand like this. . . ." She put her back to the hills, cocked her hip, and held her right hand at shoulder level, palm up. "You take the picture, and it'll look like the sign is in the palm of my hand."

Rising from the hills behind her hand were the huge white letters: HOLLYWOOD.

"Come on," said Dean, "we go around to the right."

Side by side, they followed the red concrete path running along the Observatory's white stone wall.

"Where is he?"

"Just a little further."

The path followed the curve of the middle dome. A waist-high, white stone parapet overlooked the city. The Observatory sat on the crest of a sloping hill; the walkway was above the treetops. Dean brushed his hand over a coin-operated brass telescope.

"Hell of a view, isn't it?" he said.

Beyond the edge of the parapet lay an endless urban checkerboard under a cold gray fog. Dean stepped in front of Wes, pointed at a distant building whose top vanished in the mist.

"Used to be they didn't build vertical like that because of earthquakes," said Dean.

Wes glanced toward the skyscraper.

Dean slammed his fist into the lawyer's stomach.

The punch knocked Wes's breath away. He staggered back as another punch rammed into his chest. His mind burned and he collapsed into the other man's grasp.

For an instant, Wes knew nothing. Consciousness returned with his breath. Dean's hands were under Wes's sports jacket, sliding along his sides, his back.

*Gun,* thought the Marine. *He's looking for a gun.*

Dean had braced his prey against the parapet. Wes pushed off with all his strength, driving his shoulder into his attacker's chest, knocking him back into the curved stone wall.

But Dean bounced off the stones, his fists jabbing. Once, twice, three times he landed punches, his simian arms and huge hands keeping him out of the Marine's range. Dean switched to combinations, double shots to the ribs, back to the head.

Primal rage Wes hadn't felt in a dozen years roared through him. He charged through a barrage of fists.

The two men grappled, twisting, bouncing off the dome, off the parapet. The city whirled around them. Dean grabbed Wes's tie; Wes jabbed his elbow into Dean's face. Dean slammed Wes against a column; Wes swung a brass telescope into his attacker's head, then kicked him in the leg he'd favored and thrust his knee up, aiming for the groin.

*Missed.* Dean grabbed Wes's raised thigh. Lifted him off the ground, bent him across the foot-wide stone parapet.

The world reeled upside down, Wes's head and shoulders hung over the stone. His legs scissored Dean, squeezing, holding on as he tried to grab the hands that were pummeling him. Pushing him.

Over the edge.

"You want the man!" screamed Dean. "You wait for him in hell!"

And Dean smashed his fists in Wes's stomach, into his thighs. He pulled Wes's legs apart.

Threw him off the Griffith Observatory parapet.

Twenty, thirty feet West fell. He tumbled through a pine tree, fell onto a thick bush. Slammed into the earth.

Afternoon sunlight drifted through the living room windows of an ordinary house in a Los Angeles neighborhood known for its

ordinary houses. The living room walls were bare, chipped yellow
paint. A ragged couch took up one wall. Across the room sat a
color TV. Newspaper and magazines lay scattered on the wood
floor. A red sock lay crumpled in the hall leading back to the
bedroom and bathroom. A fly buzzed in the kitchen, was silent.

*"Police!"* yelled a voice from the driveway.

The front door crashed open.

First man through came fast and low, pistol clenched in the
two-handed grip. He jumped clear of the door, threw his back
against the wall, zeroed his gun at anything that lived. He had a
beard and long hair and wore a nylon jacket emblazoned LAPD.

Second man through, gun aimed, ran to the door leading to the
kitchen, slammed his back around the corner from its opening.
Third man through the door did the same at the hall leading back
to the bathroom and bedroom.

Fourth man through the door was L.A. homicide detective
Rawlins. The black cop's 9mm was drawn, his face was grim.

Two more cops in nylon jackets ran in behind Rawlins. One
trained his gun into the kitchen, one aimed into the bedroom.

The bearded cop who'd been first through the door whispered,
*"Moving!"*

He jumped into the bedroom. Rawlins kicked open the bathroom door. Another cop searched the kitchen.

A minute later, the bearded man yelled, "Clear!"

One cop reported the news into his hand-held radio.

"Garage is clean," he told the other men in the room.

"Let him in," said Rawlins as he holstered his gun.

The bearded cop emerged from the bedroom, panting and
pale, sweat on his forehead.

Wes shuffled into the house.

His handsome face was an ugly rainbow, black and blue and
red-scraped, disinfectant orange beneath the emergency room
Band-Aids on his forehead, his cheek, his jaw. The old scar on his
chin was a dark line on pale flesh. He couldn't stand straight and
favored his left leg. His breathing was shallow. His tie was gone.
His clothes were streaked with mud and torn.

After the fall, he lay unconscious for what he figured to be five
minutes. His throbbing head woke him. He was facedown on
broken brush. He got to his knees, vomited. Looked up.

The parapet was deserted.

It took him twenty minutes to crawl and stumble and stagger up the slope of the hill, around the edge of the Observatory.

His rental car had vanished from the parking lot.

Inside the Observatory, he begged the woman behind the souvenir counter to call LAPD detective Rawlins instead of an ambulance. She and the old man in a gray suit and thin black tie cleaned the dirt off with towels from the bathroom.

He told them he fell while looking at the view.

They whispered to each other about suicide.

Rawlins drove him to a hospital. Wes convinced him to help, but it was three hours from the time Dean attacked Wes until the bearded cop kicked in the door on that ordinary house.

"You sure you got the right place?" asked Rawlins as Wes looked around.

"My car's ou' front," mumbled Wes. "Hot-wired."

*And thank God I left all my files in D.C.,* kept the pictures of Jud inside my jacket pocket, thought Wes. Dean knew no more from searching the car than Wes had told him. Even the rental car agreement was safe inside Wes's sports jacket.

"Who is this guy?" said the bearded cop. "Junk in the bathroom. Beer in the frig, moldy bread, flies on sardine cans in the kitchen. Dirty sheets and old clothes, tools, cartridges, weird fuck magazines. But hell, shopping-cart people own more shit!"

He kicked the TV. It blared on, startling them all.

"Motorcycle's gone," said Wes. "What 'e had, couple bags, always packed. Gone."

"Don't worry," said the bearded cop. "We'll APB the shit. Assault on a peace officer. Every badge west of the Mississippi will be scanning for his sorry ass."

"No," said Wes.

The bearded cop blinked. "What?"

"No APB," said Wes. "No wants or warrants, no alert. We missed him here, can't turn 'verybody loose."

"Why the hell not?" said the bearded cop.

"Thanks for your help, but—"

"Fuck you, Jack!" yelled the bearded cop. One of his buddies held his arm. "I fuckin' went through a *door* for you! Fellow cop messed up by a freak, fuck that shit! Nail him! Fuck all the *due process* procedure bullshit: kick the fuckin' door! You think this vest would stop a shotgun? An AK-47? My face ain't wearing a fuckin' vest and I went through that door! And now you fuckin' say *forget it?* Well, forget fucking you, Jack, you and your federal fucking bullshit!"

The bearded cop whirled, yelled at Rawlins, "You fuckin' owe me big, me and my guys!"

Back to Wes, he snarled, "And you, you federal fuck, you stay the fuck out of my life!"

The bearded cop led his men out of the house. Wes heard tires squeal as their cars roared away.

The kicked-in door banged in the wind.

Rawlins ripped the filter off a cigarette, threw the filter toward the bedroom. He lit up, dropped the match on the floor. The TV broadcast an ad for laxatives. The L.A. homicide cop inhaled deeply, let out the smoke, and said, "I think Jesse pretty well summed up the sentiment around here."

"Wasn't thinking too clearly," said Wes. "When I asked for cavalry, may have exceeded my authority."

"You sure didn't exceed your bullshit."

"I need your help."

"All this hoorah you started, I gotta answer for it downtown."

"I know that—"

"You don't know shit. You got bruised ribs down your right side, a cracked one on the left. Your left shin should be broken. You can barely stand. Your concussion shouldn't be mild, it should be fatal. Your guts are kicked around, your brain is scrambled bullshit, and you're spreading it on my turf."

"Hasn't been my best day," said Wes.

"It ain't going to get any better. I don't need your permission to APB this joker."

"Don't." Wes swayed. An artfully edited sex scene played out in the TV's soap opera.

"Know why I won't?" Rawlins finally said. "'Cause it'd just roll me deeper in your bullshit and all I want is you gone. There's a dinner flight to D.C. You're gonna be on it."

"I need your help."

"You've had it."

"Nothing . . . Nothing like this. Just some research. We can do it at your office. Then you can follow me to the airport."

Rawlins took a drag on his cigarette.

"Else I gotta stay," said Wes.

The homicide cop watched the injured man swaying on his feet. Rawlins flicked his cigarette to the floor, crushed it with his black wing tip.

"Turn off the TV," he said.

The flight got Wes to Dulles airport at ten that night. A worried stewardess walked him down the ramp, sat with him in the bus that carried passengers from the plane to the terminal.

Noah Hall stood beyond the metal detector, cheap tan raincoat over one shoulder, an attaché case in his hand. The CIA Director's assistant scowled as Wes shuffled through the crowd of arriving passengers and waiting friends.

"Where's the Director?" said Wes. "When I phoned, I said I had to see Denton as soon as I got in."

"Then find a plane to France," said Noah. "He's on an extended classified visit. Come on."

The bulldog led Wes to a row of plastic seats at the far end of the high-ceilinged, black-glass-walled terminal.

Wes dropped into the last chair. Noah sat beside him. He put the attaché case on the tile floor between their legs. Canned music drifted through the airport. In the far corner, a janitor mopped the gray floor with lemony suds. The loudspeaker announced the arrival of a flight from Hawaii.

"I spent all damn day putting out fires you started in L.A.," snapped Noah. "Next time, I'll throw you in the flames."

"I need to talk to Director Denton," mumbled Wes.

"You need to do your job—which ain't to make trouble for us."

"I didn't make the trouble, I found it," said Wes.

"What did you find out about this Jud Stuart guy?"

"That he's somebody. That there is shit out there that somebody besides us cares about."

"That's *all?*"

"I need help," said Wes. "You figure out how to keep the lid on, but I need more official clout, some men, some—"

"I gave you Jack Berns. Set up what you need with him."

"Fuck Berns! You didn't give him to me, you gave me to him!"

"I gave you what you're gonna get. The point of your breathing is to keep all the pencil pushers and form fillers and report writers out of the boss's business.

"What's the matter, Wes? Life get too tough for you? Gotta crawl back to D.C. for Mommy and Noah to dry your tears?"

Wes wanted to hit him, and Noah knew it.

"We thought we were getting a *can-do* guy," continued Noah. "With guts and brains and enough beef to back up his act."

"So far," hissed Wes, "I've found Pentagon shuffles, a wispy link to the White House, L.A. police intelligence files on a psycho who's tight with Jud and who might be a gun for drug dealers and mob—"

"Shut up!" hissed Noah. "Don't tell us about every piece of crap you stick your shoes in! Find out how Jud Stuart is tied to our program, *fix it,* and report only when you're done. We want to know more, we'll ask."

Three Japanese stewardesses rolled their luggage carts past the *gaijin* men. The stewardesses giggled softly. One looked at Wes; blinked. Hurried on.

"I figured you for a right guy," said Noah. "Smart and ambitious. Bored with being a paper pusher. The boss figured you signed on 'cause it's the right thing to do, the thing that needs to be done. Stars and Stripes forever, all that crap. So when the going gets tough, what does our Marine do?"

The loudspeaker announced a flight to San Francisco.

"I need support," said Wes. "Some kind, somehow."

"There's a hundred thousand more in the attaché case," answered Noah.

Wes looked at the briefcase between their shoes.

"Money," said Noah: "it's the big fix.

"The lock is set with your name," he added, "Wes. That's enough to get you what you need, and it's all you're going to get."

Two more departing flights were called.

"This might get stickier," Wes said.

"Just be sure nothing sticks where it don't belong."

"Give me a voucher for the money," said Wes.

The bulldog stood, buttoned his cheap tan raincoat. The piped-in instrumental music played a Beatles song. Noah smiled at the battered man in the Dulles airport plastic chair.

"Fuck you, Major," said Noah.

And he walked away. Left the briefcase beside Wes.

One look at Wes's condition and no one would rent him a car. He made a call, took a cab to a town-house development twenty minutes from the airport. Wobbled up the sidewalk, money-heavy briefcase in hand.

The dark woman in a bathrobe who answered the doorbell caught her breath when she saw him. "Oh, Wes!"

Over her shoulder stood her husband, NIS counterspy Frank Greco, dressed in khakis and a gray sweatshirt. They took him to a wood-paneled office crammed with books and photos, shooting trophies and service awards. Wes sank into a stuffed chair; Greco sat behind the wooden desk.

"You want some coffee?" asked the wife, Latin America in her words. Her father was a Cuban doctor who'd fled Castro's revolution. "Some aspirin?"

"The hurt is what keeps me going," mumbled Wes.

She didn't smile. But she left the two men alone.

"Did you lose an ear?" asked Greco when she was gone.

"Worse. I lost my man."

"This isn't your work. You can take a squad into the boonies, find Charlie, and zap his ass, but that war is over and this is the world."

"And I need help in it."

"We don't work for the same people."

"Sure we do," said Wes.

"Remember what I told you about your friends across the river leaving you in deep water."

"I'm midstream, Frank. And the bad guys threw shit on me. I can't go back, and the mission's out front."

"It ain't the glory days anymore."

"I'm not looking for glory. I'm looking to do a job that needs doing. Will you help me?"

"How?"

"I need a team—for recon. To cover a six-square-block area in Los Angeles. All they're doing is looking."

"For the guy you lost."

"For his motorcycle." Wes passed him the notes he'd made from the LAPD computer search detective Rawlins grudgingly pro- vided. "This bike, with that license plate, picked up six parking tickets in that neighborhood in the last four months."

"He live around there?"

"No, but somebody does. That's Westwood, not far from

UCLA. Mostly apartment buildings, service stores. Some of those are night tickets, so he's not just there shopping."

"Got a picture of the guy?"

Wes handed him a Wirephoto of Dean Jacobsen's driver's license.

"What about Mike Kramer at CIA security?"

"He'd rather nail me," answered Wes. "He's out of it, completely. Everybody's out of it. Officially. No files opened, no designations, no mission. Nothing."

"Wasn't nothing that beat the dog shit out of you."

"I need people, Frank. Off the books, or at least off the official ones. Budget's not a problem."

"Budget's not a problem? Then you must not be working for Uncle Sam anymore."

"He still signs my paychecks. Can you help me?"

The ex-cop shook his head. "You are in the world, aren't you, Wes?"

The digital clock on the desk blinked off three minutes.

"You're my friend," said the master of this house. "The Admiral and Commander Franklin ordered us to provide what assistance to you in your new duties as we can. But you game me, I'll burn you. Burn you down. I'll have to. It'll be my job. And it'll by my ass."

"Thanks."

"Tonight, I can order a surprise crash drill-training mission out of the NIS L.A. region. Search and locate one motorcycle. That should cover us for twenty-four hours. What if we get a hit on the bike or the guy?"

"Observe, follow, report: to me. Especially if he meets another man."

"You won't be in any shape to hear anything pretty soon. I'm taking you home."

"I can get a cab."

"Your place is on the way to the Yard. I need to go in to make the calls, get this 'training mission' on line. The agents in L.A. just *love* bullshit training drills out of HQ."

"Sorry to ruin your night."

"Not the first one." Frank waited, but Wes made no effort to stand. "What else?"

"I need a gun."

When Greco didn't comment, Wes said, "You've seen me in uniform: Pistol Expert badge. Tomorrow, I can get the Commander to authorize me to carry a weapon. But I don't want one of the NIS six-shooters."

"Figured you had your own."

"I always figured the Corps would give me what I needed."

Greco grunted, left the room. Wes closed his eyes. The pounding in his head was terrible. His stomach churned. Every place on his body hurt.

Something clunked on the desk. Wes opened his eyes.

A blunt, black metal automatic lay on the scarred wood.

"That's a Sig Sauer P226," said Frank, sitting down. "A nine mic mic. Fifteen rounds in the magazine, one in the barrel. Two spare magazines. You need more than that, you need a squad. Those green dots on the sights? They're radioactive tritium. Glow in absolute darkness so you can see which way you're zeroed."

Frank put two boxes of shells and spare clips beside the gun.

"One box of wad cutters for target practice. I'll set up the range when you're ready. The other box: Hydra-Shoks, hollow points. You hit him, you'll get him.

"Remember, it's the same paperwork for emptying a clip as it is for shooting once. If you're a fatalist and only fire once, what might be fatal is what you miss."

The ex-cop took a handkerchief from his pocket, wiped his prints off the gunmetal. "This is a clean gun. Sanitized.

"It's been retooled. The trigger pull is only three pounds. You think, it shoots. Faster rapid fire, steadier aim."

Wes opened the briefcase of money.

"I wasn't supposed to see that," said Greco.

"Neither was I." Wes put his new gun on top of the money.

Midnight. Halfway up the stairs inside his apartment building, Wes wished he'd let Greco help him. He was dizzy and the briefcase weighed too much to carry. He sat on the stairs, sagged against the railing, and tried to gather his strength to walk the rest of the way.

Couldn't. He crawled, dragging and bumping the briefcase up the stairs.

Beth's apartment. Beth's door.

Couldn't let her see him like this.

He slid across the hall to his door. Caught his breath, grabbed the doorknob, and pulled himself up. Knocked over the briefcase with a loud *thud*. Fumbled with the keys. Got the right one half in the lock. Dropped them.

Behind him, a door opened, and he heard Beth laugh and say, "What's the matter? Did you forget how to knock?"

He turned to look at her and she was wonderful.

"Oh, Jesus!" she said.

"Had trouble, gettin' you, souvenir this time, too."

She ran and caught him as his leg shook. Got him inside his apartment.

"Don't talk now," she said. "Tell me later."

They made it to his bed. She stretched him out, undressed him. Sighed when she saw the bandages over the two baseballs on his left shin; found the tape on his ribs. She made an ice pack out of a plastic bag and a washcloth, braced it against his shin, and disappeared. It felt so good to be here, to be home, in bed. With her. Falling, Wes remembered falling, and he trembled, his eyes teared up, and then he made it go, let it go.

When she came back, she brought a glass of warm milk, three aspirin, and a Valium from her apartment. Wes wondered what the emergency room doctors would say, swallowed all four pills with the milk while she held his head, the glass.

The sheets, the cool sheets were around him, her light but warm quilt on top of his linen. The washcloth was damp and cool as she wiped his forehead, dried it with her shirtsleeve. She kissed his forehead and her hair brushed his cheek.

"It's all right," she said. "Go to sleep. You're safe."

||||||||||||||||||||||||||||||||||||||||||||||||||||||||||||||||||||||||||||||||||||||||||

# LAST TRICK

Jud and Nora sat in the warm evening sun, a couple of old cats in lawn chairs outside her house, the empty highway off to their left, the café in front of them closed for the day. The sky shimmered pink and purple. Their eyes were shut, faces tilted up.

Nora sighed. "This is how I like it these days. Quiet."

The sand on the desert was still.

"Don't have to be anybody," she said, "don't have to do anything. Just sit. Breathe in. Breathe out. Smell the sagebrush. Know what I mean?"

"Yes," said Jud. And it felt good. So good.

"'Course, I wouldn't mind seeing New York again. But not for a while."

"I don't want to go anywhere," said Jud.

"I don't want you to either."

They let that discovery lay at their feet, unnamed. But the silence was easy, and they both felt that. Their eyes stayed closed.

"Unless," she said, "you happen to be thirsty for some lemonade in the pitcher on the top shelf of my refrigerator."

"Contingency adaptation," he said.

"Whatever. That is, if you happen to be thirsty."

"For lemonade. On the top shelf of your refrigerator."

"Yeah. Just for instance."

"Oh," said Jud. He sighed. "No, I'm fine."

Nora laughed.

A minute went by.

"I've got an idea," said Jud.

"What?"

"There's some lemonade in a pitcher on the top shelf of your refrigerator. Why don't I get you a glass?"

"If you want," she said. "Nice idea."

"Thanks," he said, and she heard him go into the house.

Eyes closed, she chuckled, called after him, "Why don't you have a glass, too?"

The air around Nora tingled with the change from daylight to dusk. She felt the sun's heat still trapped in the sand and rocks, the adobe walls of her house.

Ice-cold, wet glass pressed against her neck.

*"Jesus!"* she yelled, bolting upright in her chair.

"No: Jud," he said, handing her a tall glass of lemonade, sitting down with his and a shit-eating grin.

She scowled at him, but they both knew it wasn't serious.

"I suppose you didn't bring the cigarettes," she said.

"Lord, spare me from a never-satisfied woman," said Jud.

"Climb down off the cross, hon," she said. "We need the wood."

His laughter echoed over the tumbleweeds. When he stopped, he took a drink of lemonade. Made a sour face.

"Not quite that old firewater kick, huh?" said Nora.

He shrugged, sighed. Reached into his shirt pocket and pulled out a pack of cigarettes and a Zippo lighter.

"God, you never make anything easy!" she said as he shook a cigarette out of the pack, handed it to her.

"No, but I share."

One click of the Zippo lit both their habits.

"Ah." She looked around where she lived *now*. "Not bad. Nice day. Enjoy it while you can. Soon, heat'll come. Which reminds me: remind me to call the phone company tomorrow, okay?"

"Why?"

"Somebody screwdrivered the shit out of the pay phone by the road. It's busted all to hell."

*"I didn't know,"* whispered Jud. "When?"

"Beats me. A guy came in while you're dumping trash yesterday. He went to use it and found it pried apart. They even busted the receiver.

"Damn kids," she added. "You think they could come up with more original crimes."

"I hadn't noticed it," he said. "Hadn't . . . I should have been checking it every morning at six, I got . . . I've been . . ."

"Don't worry about it," she said. "It's not your job."

From this distance, the glass phone booth looked fine. His guts felt empty, his mind hollow.

"No accounting for everything in life," said Nora.

*Can't change it now,* thought Jud. *Can't let it matter. It won't matter. It doesn't. Move on to something important.*

"Why did you quit being a prostitute?" he asked her.

Nora took a drag on her cigarette, shifted in her chair, her eyes on him, her eyes far away.

"My last trick," she said.

"When?"

"Nineteen seventy-eight," she said. "August. I was living in Vegas, few but big-time clientele. Raking in the dough. Hadn't admitted yet that it was the booze drinking me and not the other way around.

"I had this customer, regular when he was in town, used to fly me around to meet him. Big shot, picture in *Time* magazine.

"He flew me to Philadelphia. First-class round-trip, best hotel. Twenty-five-minute date. Ten thousand dollars."

The sky was gray, shadows gaining substance.

"What did you do?" asked Jud.

Nora looked at the glowing tip of her cigarette. "I set him on fire."

They said nothing until the light was gone from the sky.

"After that," she said, "I felt this . . . good part of me crumbling. The kind part. The part that could still love. I'd had to think of . . . more exotic, more original things for him each time. After Philly, I knew that where that kind of stuff was taking me, I wouldn't be able to stay me. So I quit."

"Then?"

"Then I got kissed by the tax man. His plan was to make me an example, fine me up the ass. Would have been my ass, too, except for the one decent lawyer in Vegas. He convinced the tax man that if they hit me with everything they could, they'd make me become a criminal again, and that wasn't very smart. Instead, they just took all I had. And I went to dealer's school."

"You don't get to keep the money," he said.

She frowned, but said nothing. The night chill descended on

them. They couldn't make out the lines on each other's face. Their cigarettes glowed orange in the dark.

"When did you start drinking *for real?*" she asked.

"Didn't happen all at once," he said.

"But the first time," she said, "not the first time you partied or got toilet-hugging drunk, but *the first time,* the first time it *meant* something."

"What is this?" he said, making it mostly a joke. "AA?"

"You're not anonymous," she whispered. "And there's always a first time."

A cricket chirped, a trucker barreled past and blew his air horn at the lights of the house by the side of the road. Then he was gone, roaring off into the big nowhere.

"Long ago," Jud said. "Far away."

And as he sat smoking in the cool desert darkness, Jud heard the echo of a man named Willy in a Santiago, Chile, hotel room: September 11, 1973.

"This is an ungood," said Willy. "In the *minus* zone."

It was four in the afternoon. There were three of them in the Santiago hotel room:

*Jud,* standing at the edge of their fifth-floor window, watching the smoke billowing into the sky from the Moneda Palace.

*Luis,* or whatever his real name was—they'd been strangers when they rendezvoused in Miami, and Jud assumed everyone else was also using a work name. Jud claimed to be "Peter." Luis was a gray-flecked Cuban who couldn't be as old as he seemed. He was stretched out on the bed, staring up at the ceiling, the phone resting beside him. Waiting to ring.

*Willy* was a brown-haired, bad-skin-under-his-beard, wiry guy. He was midtwenties, and his syntax said *Vietnam,* but they all knew better than to ask each other any true questions.

Rifles cracked somewhere up the street, answered by a burst of machine gun fire.

Jud looked toward the corner where he'd seen a tank a half hour before, but that street looked empty.

Willy drummed his fingers on the table with one hand while the other turned the dial on the room's AM radio. He got static. He was the commo expert. Such primitive fiddling was far beneath his expertise, but there was nothing else for him to do.

Waiting.

For the fourth man on the team to show up. To call. Waiting to *go,* waiting to *do,* waiting to say *sayonara,* South America, *adiós,* Chile, it's been good to know, better to go.

The fourth man was Braxton, sandy-haired, slow-talking side-of-beef Braxton. He was the boss. Jud was number two. Willy was commo, and Luis was the indig expert, the Spanish speaker backing up Braxton's Tex-Mex fluency. Luis was good with a gun, a bullet counter schooled in the Sierra Maestra with Fidel, then given graduate studies at the CIA's Guatamalan training camp for the 2506 Brigade fighting Fidel.

Their guns were in watertight bags in the toilet tank. Made it hard to flush. The toilet had been getting a workout since they'd gotten *the word* at ten P.M. the night before. They ordered up the last meals served by room service, popped dex pills, and made Jud's room command center. Willy set up his long-range transmitter that had been hidden in a *turista* portable AM/FM unit, but they were in radio silence, no one who'd call them, no one who'd respond. *Shit,* Willy'd said, *so much for advanced technology.*

Braxton was sixteen hours gone, thirteen hours overdue from a rendezvous *out there,* in the city.

Santiago, capital of Chile. An old city of low-slung colonial architecture, surrounded by the *pablaciones,* slums, and offset by *la cordillera,* the mountains. Almost three million people. Rampant poverty, but a country rich in poets, artists, and musicians, a country beloved by Anaconda and Kennecott Copper companies, which found billions in the mines of Chile, and by the International Telephone and Telegraph company, which owned 70 percent of Chile's phone company. In Chile, politics were passionate. Three years before, a Marxist named Salvador Allende had been elected president, a personal political triumph for this man who'd been campaigning for that post since 1952; in 1964, the CIA funneled $3 million to his successful political opponents.

Allende's 1970 election victory sent shock waves through America. Nixon and Kissinger were furious; ITT had spent almost half a million dollars to stop Allende's 1970 election. Executives from multinational companies and high American-government officials wrung their hands and bemoaned a new Marxist regime in America's backyard. ITT pledged $1 million to the CIA efforts to *control* Allende; in the Watergate era, ITT would become famous for such political pledges, including the $400,000 the company pledged to the American President's political party.

After Allende's election in 1970, the American President loosed his spy hawks and diplomatic dogs.

Those men compartmentalized their crusade.

Track I was an anti-Allende propaganda and economic program and diplomatic efforts by the ambassador to keep the Chilean Congress from confirming Allende as president. Although Track I's effects were often visible, its dynamics were kept secret from the American people.

Track II was kept secret from the American ambassador, the State Department, even from the White House–level 40 Committee that supposedly oversaw American foreign policy and intelligence operations. CIA agents using forged passports were sent to infiltrate Chile, contact extreme right-wing military officers, and encourage them to stage a coup if Allende successfully rode his popular election into the president's chair. Track II personnel were allowed to provide direct assistance to any such coup, but it was to be a Chilean affair.

Track III did not exist.

Jud and his team, the Track III group, had been in Santiago for nine days, flying down on documents they'd long since burned showing them to be a film crew for a television company, with delicate cameras that bored customs agents had no desire to unscrew. As he'd gone about his business in this capital city of a country torn by strikes, 300 percent inflation, and political street fights, Jud was struck by the overwhelming sense that this nation was on a train, gathering speed, racing toward some unknown destination.

And he had a ticket.

"Man, this is *fucked* up," muttered Willy.

"Save it," ordered Jud from the window. Like Willy, Jud had grown a beard for the mission, and his hair was over his ears. In Chile in 1973, as in America, long hair was hip. Nonmilitary.

"Braxton is supposed to have come back, Jack!" said Willy. "Without him, we got *zero* cover."

Machine guns chattered outside their hotel.

Braxton's rendezvous promised to deliver credentials for the team to use. In case. For security reasons, credentials in a coup can only be issued just before the coup.

From the bed, Luis said, "These events have a clock of their own. Things happen. Develop."

"That wasn't the plan, man," mumbled Willy.

Their mission had two levels.

There was a political officer on the embassy staff, the spook liaison to Track III, and there was an indigenous asset, a Chilean general. Those two men linked certain elements in the military high commands of each country. Liaisons. Back-channel communications. Just in case. Providing security cover to the American diplomat/spy was the mission's first level. Jud didn't think the embassy man knew who was covering him, or how: deniability, counterintelligence security. Made sense.

Second level was worst-case scenario: scorched earth. *If* a coup went badly, turned into a debacle, Allende rallying the country to rout America's allies, *then* hiding Uncle Sam's tracks would be crucial. Keeping the flag clean. Enforcing deniability. Covering up. Burning. Somebody had to be *out there,* the *stay behind boys,* the rear guard of the retreat. Guys who could do whatever had to be done. The Cleanup Crew.

The phone beside Luis rang. His hand was on it, but he let it ring a second time.

"*Sí?*" he answered.

Jud and Willy watched Luis lay on the bed, phone pressed to his ear. He hung up without saying another word.

"He can't make it back yet," said Luis. "He said sit tight, stay clean."

"Oh, swell!" said Willy. "Why don't we all crawl in the fucking shower! Hell, why not just climb in the toilet? Pull the fucking handle and wash away all our blues!"

"What about the subject?" asked Jud. The diplomat/spy.

"Braxton said nothing," said Luis. "No change known."

"Man," said Willy, "we shadowed his candy ass right to the embassy gate last night! That pussy ain't dumb enough to come out here in the world with the shit flying!"

"So now what?" Willy asked Jud. "Looks like you're the keemo sabe."

"We wait," said Jud.

"I do that so fuckin' well!" snapped Willy, heading to the toilet.

Jud turned back to the window overlooking the city that he'd been watching since before dawn. They'd been waiting since Braxton got the call and left at ten P.M. the night before.

At 5:45 A.M., selected phone lines were cut by rebel Navy commandos. Rebel troops seized strategic posts throughout the country and began rolling into Santiago.

Between 6:15 and 6:20 A.M., a general loyal to the government called President Allende at home to warn him of the coup. At 7:15, in a caravan of five bulletproof Fiats, a truck, and two armored personnel carriers filled with *carabinero* bodyguards, Allende raced to his offices at the Moneda Palace, a two-hundred-year-old Spanish-monastery-style building catercorner across Constitution Square from the American embassy.

At 7:20, a radio station reported "unusual police movements." By midafternoon, most stations were off the air.

Shortly after eight A.M., Allende stepped onto a balcony at the Moneda. A journalist snapped his photo. By eight-thirty, leftist paramilitary snipers were firing on soldiers close to the Moneda.

By nine o'clock, Air Force planes were bombing pro-Allende targets in the city, mostly radio stations. Gunfire filled the streets. Tanks surrounded the Moneda. Troops set up roadblocks. Helicopters chopped through the air. Chilean flags began to appear outside houses, hanging from apartment windows.

At nine-thirty Allende refused repeated offers from the military to surrender and be taken to safety. He delivered a defiant patriotic radio broadcast: "My last words . . ." The Army opened fire on the Moneda. Allende and his men shot back with bazookas and machine guns. The firing raged until about eleven, when the government troops withdrew. To safety.

Two jets appeared in the blue sky above the Moneda and the American embassy, silver birds gliding in formation. The jets arced away, drifted behind San Cristóbal hill.

Roared back. Diving. Dropping lower. Lower. When the planes were over the Mapocho railroad station, they fired rockets. The missiles slammed into the north side of the Moneda. The jets made six more attack runs in the next twenty-one minutes: bombs, rockets, strafing. When they flew away, the Moneda was in flames.

Jud, Willy, and Luis watched from the hotel window.

At 1:33, the coup troops stormed the Moneda.

Gunfire crackled through the city all afternoon. At four P.M., when Braxton was finally able to call Jud and the others at the hotel, the Moneda still burned. Smoke filled the sky from a dozen other locations in the city.

"Here," said Luis, getting off the bed. He handed Willy and Jud cheap crucifix necklaces. When Willy frowned, Luis said, "Communists do not wear crosses."

"Good thing I ain't a Jew," said Willy. He laughed: unwinding, gearing up.

Twenty minutes later, Willy found a radio station that worked. Martial music, carefully selected patriotic Chilean songs, even Sousa marches. A military junta announced that the forces of good had triumphed; that there would be a period of free movement allowed in the city until six P.M., then an inviolable curfew.

At five-thirty, Jud heard a shout from a floor below. Pounding. A crash and screams as first one door, then another were kicked in.

"Yo, *keemo sabe?*" called Willy, poised halfway between the toilet tank and the room door.

"We go!" yelled Jud.

Running, out the door, sports jackets over *no weapons,* racing to the end of the hall, to the window Jud had scouted and unlocked for E&E. Sunset turned the glass red. Somebody screamed one floor down. Somebody shot a gun. Jud and his men scrambled up the fire escape, two floors to the roof; hunched figures running in the fading light, scurrying from rooftop to rooftop, as silently as they could. From rooftops in the distance came the *wink* and *crack* of sniper fire. Helicopters *whumped* through the darkness overhead. Jud peered over the edge of the fire escape at the end of the block: an alley. Smoke filled the air, shouts echoed in the city canyons, but this alley was empty.

"Now!" he ordered.

Down, on the ground, amidst garbage cans. Rats.

"Slow and steady," he whispered, leading his men toward the exit. "Easy, nonthreatening. Smile."

"What the hell is that?" mumbled Willy.

Orange flickering colored the night at the end of the alley.

"Fan out," said Jud. Individuals were less threatening than a group; harder targets to hit.

They stepped into the street of the Santiago coup.

Down the block, a bonfire raged, surrounded by dozens of soldiers with over-the-ears helmets, green uniforms, scarlet neckerchiefs, and black boots, assault rifles slung at the ready. The troopers roared their approval above the flames, their eyes hypnotized by the inferno's glow as other soldiers ran out of a smashed-windowed store carrying more fuel for the blaze.

Books. Hundreds of books.

"They haven't see us yet," whispered Jud.

Down the block the other direction he saw vehicle lights, flashlights, dozens of shadow men; heard shouting. In the alley behind them was the sound of boots clanging down the fire escape.

"Put on your party face," ordered Jud, nodding to the bonfire. *"Viva Chile,* we're joining them before they find us."

"No," whispered Luis.

"It's the best odds!" insisted Jud.

"I have no papers and my accent is Cuban," he said. Smiled. *"Vaya con Dios."*

And Luis quickly walked away, sliding along the walls of shuttered stores and cafés, eyes front, not looking at the soldiers so as not to send a mental signal. Just a half a block to the corner, a dozen locked doors to pass.

"Don't move," Jud whispered to Willy. "Say nothing."

Just seven more doors.

*"Alto!"* yelled a voice by the bonfire.

Luis ran, fast and hard, not looking back. To the corner, at the corner.

A machine gun chattered.

Like a string-cut puppet, Luis dropped. Dead. Gone.

*"Alto!"* screamed a dozen voices. Soldiers raced toward Jud. *"Manos arriba!"* They grabbed him, knocked him and Willy facedown to the cement, kicked them. Rifle barrels jammed in their necks, hands slapped their empty pockets, scooped them up.

"American!" said Jud. "It's okay! I'm an American!"

*"Silencio!"* The officer hit Jud with his pistol.

A cattle truck crammed with dazed people appeared. The soldiers threw Jud and Willy in the back. The truck lurched away, followed closely by a jeep with a mounted and manned machine gun.

The truck took them to the gigantic National Stadium, the outdoor arena where thousands of Chileans reveled in soccer.

That night the stands filled with truckloads of prisoners arrested in sweeps by the military and police. During the coup, seven thousand people would be detained in the Stadium. Soldiers filled the playing field and controlled the entrances to the stands. Training and locker rooms were converted into interrogation centers. Rest-room privileges for prisoners were rare, beatings common, *water treatments*. After many interrogations, gunfire echoed from the Stadium's obscure corners. Everyone was guilty: they were there.

The guards quickly discovered Jud and Willy claimed to speak only English.

The rattle of unseen gunfire in the Stadium ripped through Jud like an electric shock. Each volley was worse than the one before.

"Keep smiling," he hissed. "Show them we know we're okay."

Arc lamps cast ghostly light on the crowded stands, the soldiers pacing the playing field. The two Americans rehearsed their answers. Dozed fitfully on the hard wooden benches. Their lullabies were strangers sobbing around them. The firing squad volleys became nails driven through their nerves: searing at first, then merely one dull blow after another.

Jud's first interrogation came at eleven the next morning.

They marched him down long cement corridors hung with posters of soccer stars and ads for beer. The halls reeked of urine and human shit. They marched through a dozen dark puddles.

To a windowless room that smelled of athletic liniment, a table with an officer sitting behind it, two guards, an empty wooden stool. The sergeant of the guards escorting Jud hit him, sat him on the stool.

"You are American," said the officer.

*A Captain,* thought Jud. *Regular Army.*

"Yes," said Jud, "I'm a—"

The officer nodded. The sergeant cuffed Jud's head.

"Answer questions, no *mas*. Why in Chile?"

"I'm a graduate student," said Jud.

"Student? What? Where?"

"Geology," said Jud. A safe academic discipline. "George Washington University. In Washington, D.C."

"Why in Chile?"

"Vacation. Chile is beautiful."

*"Documentos. Donde estan* your *documentos?"*

"We gave them to the bellhop. He said he'd put them in the hotel for us. To keep them safe."

"You gave *documentos* to a bellhop? Are you *loco?"*

"I'm an America," repeated Jud.

"A man with you when you were arrested. He attacked soldiers. Who was he?"

"He was not with us," said Jud. "We saw him running away in the street, but we did not know him."

"So you say. What did you see in the street?"

"He didn't obey."

The officer blinked.

"Do you know what has happened?"

"No."

"The President is dead. Do you know anything about that?"

"No. But you are in charge, so everything is okay, yes?"

The officer sent him away. In the stands, Jud found they'd taken Willy.

An hour later, they came for Jud again.

Same office. Different officer. A colonel. In a policeman's uniform. He smelled of garlic.

"Your name?" asked the colonel.

Jud gave his work name.

"Date of arrival in Chile?"

Jud told him a week before. Told him his true age. Repeated the lies about being a student.

"Have you ever read or brought Marxist literature into Chile?"

"No."

"Have you ever read or bought literature dealing with Che Guevara?"

"No."

"What do you know about Marxists?"

"What they taught me in the military."

"You were a soldier? An American soldier?" After Jud nodded yes, the cop said, "Prove it."

"My government has those papers," said Jud. "I can tell you what to ask for."

"What did they teach you about the communists?"

"That they are the enemy," said Jud. "They killed some of my friends. In Vietnam."

A gunshot echoed down the corridor outside.

"The war is everywhere," said the officer.

"Yes," answered Jud.

They took him down the corridor. There was blood on the walls. Kept him waiting. When they brought him back into the room, the officer asked, "What have you seen here?"

"Soldiers doing their job," said Jud.

They took him outside the Stadium, put him in the back of a car. A driver and a guard sat up front. A few minutes later, they brought Willy. An officer climbed in back with them. As the car drove away, gunfire rattled inside the Stadium.

They dropped the Americans at their hotel. Drove away.

Braxton was in his room.

"This is a big ungood," Willy told the mission boss.

Braxton smelled them. "You got an hour to get clean. Your rooms are trashed. Grab what you can carry light, meet back here. We got a job."

He handed them yellow police identification cards that the pictures from their burned passports had been glued to.

"Where were you?" said Jud as Braxton picked up the phone. "We lost Luis because you didn't come through."

"He knew the risks," said Braxton. "That's the life. Things got crazy out there, out of hand, off the clock."

"You were in charge," said Jud. "Responsible."

"I still am, *cowboy*," Braxton said as he dialed a number. "And you got fifty-eight minutes to get saddled up so we can ride."

Jud found Willy taking his pistol from the toilet tank. "No more time in this zone with just my dick in my hand."

An hour after they'd arrived, Jud and Willy stood with Braxton at the curb outside the hotel. Willy and Jud had shoulder bags, wore suits but no ties. Braxton's suit and tie were perfect. He carried a briefcase. Three uniformed soldiers standing sentry at the doors paid them no mind. A tank rumbled down the street.

A gray sedan pulled up beside them. Three Chilean men in civilian clothes climbed out. A passenger stayed in the backseat. One of the men handed Braxton a piece of paper and the car keys. As the Chileans walked away, Braxton tossed the keys to

Willy, climbed in the front seat. Jud sat in back, next to the passenger.

The passenger was a man Jud's age. Black curly hair, pasty skin, and a dark stubble. He wore somebody else's civilian suit over a tan shirt. He smelled of sweat and smoke. His eyes were red and his hands trembled.

"You are Americans, yes?" he said, his voice eager yet shaky. "We are allies, yes? That is a good thing. My name is Rivero, Lt. Javier Rivero. *Perdón,* I have been promoted: captain. You can call me—"

"That's fine, son," said Braxton from the front seat. *"Estamos todos amigos aquí."*

"English, *sí, yo hablo* . . . I speak English. I studied with your military. In Georgia."

"Get me on that midnight train," said Willy.

"Roll," ordered Braxton. Willy steered the car onto the empty street. "We're going to an apartment in a neighborhood called Providencia. Then after dark, the four of us are going to take a plane ride to Paraguay. Corporate jet, a favor from some friends."

"Yes, yes, I know," said Javier. "It is important I go."

"One step at a time, *amigo,*" said Braxton. "First we get to a cool-out place, stay low and rest. No big deal, right? Do you know how to get to Providencia?"

"Of course!" Rivero answered. "This is my home! This is my city! This is my country!"

He gave Willy eager and complex directions.

"Anything you need," said Rivero, "just ask. I will help. I will do what must be done. I can. I can."

"Fine by me, Tonto," said Willy, making enough sense out of Rivero's frantic directions to navigate the car.

*"Quien es tonto?"* asked Rivero. "In Spanish, *tonto* means fool."

"Different language," said Braxton. "Different meaning."

Rivero slumped back beside Jud.

"I'm a soldier," he told Jud. "A good soldier. Not fool."

Rivero pulled cigarettes from his pocket. When he tried to shake one out of the pack, his hands wouldn't stop trembling and the white death sticks fell all over his lap. Jud put one between Rivero's dry lips. The cigarette bobbed and weaved in front of Jud's lighter flame as the car rolled over Santiago's smooth streets, but finally caught, smoked. Rivero nodded his thanks.

Willy switched on the car radio. The stations were on again, still only martial or patriotic music. No Beatles, no jazz. Announcements, but no news. Willy drove with his yellow card between his fingers, his hand high on the steering wheel. They were still stopped at police roadblocks—two men in a car with long hair and beards, two men who didn't fit with them—but the magic yellow cards parted all the guns.

They drove with the windows down. The warm air carried the stench of charred stone, napalm.

Chilean flags hung everywhere, from many of the closed shops, from apartment balconies, from light poles. The buses weren't running, traffic was light. A few people gingerly trod the pavement, looking for open grocery stores, trying to get home during the free transit period. Troops and police were everywhere, cruising in jeeps, at roadblocks, squads patrolling the sidewalks.

"We won," said Rivero. "We won. *Viva Chile!*"

None of the Americans answered him.

They stopped for a traffic light. Suddenly, they heard cries, shouts, looked to the left.

On the sidewalk not twenty feet away, soldiers held a woman as an officer used a bayonet to slash her pants legs to ribbons.

"In Chile," yelled the officer, "women wear dresses!"

The soldiers threw the woman into the gutter. The officer looked at the car with four men in it. Braxton and Willy waved their yellow cards. The officer saluted, and they drove on.

Rivero craned his neck to watch as the soldiers tied the hands of the woman in the gutter. The officer spit on her. Rivero's mouth was open, his eyes wide.

They had to detour twice to avoid firefights between leftist sympathizers and junta troops.

The apartment was on the fourth floor of an eight-unit building. The old woman they saw in the lobby quickly looked away as they entered the stairwell running up the building's center.

The apartment was crammed with tasteful family heirlooms. Willy found a baked chicken in the refrigerator. He and Jud fell on it like sharks. Braxton and Rivero said they weren't hungry, but Rivero took one of the cold bottles of beer.

"This dude lives," sighed Willy, sipping his beer.

"There's two bedrooms," said Braxton. "Willy, grab the first shut-eye."

"Gone, keemo," said Willy, disappearing into a bedroom.

Rivero claimed he wasn't tired. Braxton shrugged, told Jud, "I'll be on the phone in the other room."

Rivero sat on the couch, beer bottle shaking in his hands. Jud dropped into an easy chair across from him. Smiled.

"You are American," said Rivero.

"Yes."

"I love my country. Do you love your country?"

"Yes."

"I am a soldier, that's what this is about, yes?"

"Yes," said Jud. "Being a soldier."

"I have a job. A duty." He shook his head. "I don't mind talking about it."

The windows at the end of the living room overlooked the city. A helicopter chopped its way over the rooftops.

"You have been many places in the world?" asked Rivero.

"A few," Jud told him.

"Do you think . . . Would the communists have taken our children to schools in Cuba? Made the women . . . And the church, they would have destroyed the church. They do things like that everywhere, right?"

"I haven't been everywhere," said Jud. He nodded. "They're bad people."

"Yes. *Yes.*"

They could hear Braxton mumbling into the telephone in the other room.

"My countrymen," said Rivero, "some were misguided."

"It happens," said Jud.

"He should have surrendered," said Rivero.

"I mean," he said, a skull grin on his face, eager eyes, "look at it logically. Look at it like a soldier. There was . . . He was surrounded, we had him pinned down. No relief forces for him. Our superior firepower. No advantage to gain, he . . . Logically, he should have surrendered. There was a plane waiting for him, safe conduct guaranteed! The word of the military! He should have surrendered! Taken the plane!"

"Like us," said Jud evenly. "Like we will. Tonight."

"Yes. Yes." He shook his head. "I am a soldier. I follow orders. I do my best. I do my job. I have duty. Loyalty."

His hands trembled, but he lit his own cigarette.

"Your cross," said Rivero. "Do you believe in God?"

"Sure," lied Jud.

"Redemption. Forgiveness. Just as long as you believe." He shook his head. "Maybe you don't even need Jesus as long as you *believe.*"

"Take it easy," said Jud. "You're tired."

"It was a military battle," insisted Rivero. "An air strike, and then I, my men, we were ordered to attack. They shot at us! Machine guns and tear gas, it was all . . . Battle is chaos, you know? Instinct and insanity."

"Yes, I know," said Jud.

"You are a soldier. That is what it is all about, being a soldier. The Moneda, the shooting and fighting and running, I couldn't be sure what I saw and they turned to me—not my uniforms— and I fired. I fired. He fell.

"Later, we found him . . .

"What difference does it make if it was suicide or not?" said Rivero. *"Of course it was suicide!* He stayed in there against overwhelming odds. Wouldn't surrender. He doomed himself. What difference does it make if he put Fidel's machine gun under his chin or . . . or I shot him? Suicide, it was suicide and he is dead."

A great weight rolled through the man on the couch, left him trembling. Jud leaned toward him, but Rivero waved away.

"I am a soldier. I did what had to be done. That is all. I am not an assassin! I am not! *I! Am! Not! An! Assassin!*"

"I know about assassins," said Jud. "You're not one."

Braxton carefully walked into the living room, his eyes on the man who'd been screaming.

Rivero saw the American commander's disapproving look, dropped his voice. "It will be better for history that everyone understands it was suicide that killed the President. Not us. Not me. Suicide. He chose to stay, so he chose to die, and that is suicide. Choosing. Like that. The last choice, eh? We welded the coffin. But it is better, because it is true, it was suicide."

"Yes," said Jud, "I suppose it was."

"That's why I have to go away," said Rivero. "To keep history true. If I stay, I might . . . I could slip or . . . I must go."

"I understand."

"Do you think . . . When will I get to come home?"

"Just as soon as possible," said Braxton.

"I wish I could call my mother. Do you talk to your mother?"

"No," said Jud.

"You should. You should." Rivero shook his head. "There are so many *shoulds*. So many *should nots*."

Willy wandered out of the other bedroom. "Man, I'm all dexed up, I can't sleep for shit!"

"I am tired now," said Rivero.

Braxton whispered to Willy, "Phone in there?"

Willy shook his head no.

"Captain, why don't you go lie down? We'll get you when we need you."

Rivero nodded. Wandered into the bedroom, turned around and looked at these three strangers.

"My country," he said. Then he closed the door.

For a while, the men slumped around the living room listening to sobs from behind the closed door. Braxton made more phone calls in the other bedroom. Willy and Jud stared numbly at the walls, mouths slack, eyes open, minds gone. Time stood still.

"What's that?" said Jud suddenly.

Willy was on his feet, revolver drawn. "What!"

Silence. Rivero's door was locked.

"Braxton!" yelled Jud, and he kicked in the door.

The bedroom window was open.

In the street four stories below lay a crumpled form.

"Dude should have waited for the airplane," said Willy.

"We're out of here *now!*" ordered Braxton.

On the sidewalk, a handful of people had emerged to stare, but not get too close. A squad of soldiers ran toward the disturbance of law and order. Braxton nodded to Jud when they reached the street. "Check it out, be sure."

Jud glared at him. "The man didn't have a chute!"

Braxton looked at Jud's face; barked, "Willy! Do it!"

Without a glance, Willy slid away to follow orders.

"I am in command here," snapped Braxton.

"Of what?" said Jud. "Of who? My orders say I'm to do a job to facilitate a situation. Well, that's done, *boss,* and you've been a great help. But your command is over."

"That man was part of the mission, and until we got him to Paraguay, so were we!"

"So was Luis, and you fucked him up, too."

Braxton blinked.

"Who are you, huh?" asked Jud.

By the body, they saw Willy look toward them, snap a quick thumbs-down, and stroll away. A soldier stopped him, but Willy flashed his yellow card and walked to the car.

"You want to know who we are, hero?" snapped Braxton. "We're the guys scheduled to take a plane to Paraguay tonight. We were supposed to have him in tow. We're the guys who were gonna run a debriefing session with some friends, talk it all out with our no-chute Captain Rivero.

"Only don't call him that," said Braxton. "Call him Lee Harvey. Call us Jack Ruby."

Braxton climbed in the car.

And Jud remembered the Stadium, the firing squads. The woman in the street. The Watergate White House. Being a soldier.

Slowly, Jud got in the car.

That night, after the Gulfstream jet landed the three of them in Asunción—*stand down, all clear*—Jud bought a bottle of Scotch and drank himself into oblivion.

||||||||||||||||||||||||||||||||||||||||||||||||||||||||||||||||||||||||||||||||||||||||||||||||||||

# SUBWAY

Although he completely loved his wife, Nick Kelley was enchanted by the receptionist on the fifth floor of the Washington, D.C., think tank that Watergate Plumbers had schemed to firebomb. She had milk-chocolate skin, black hair that curled to her shoulders, warm ebony eyes, and a smile that never quite stopped. She was lean. Supple. And at least fifteen years younger than him.

"Can I help you?" she asked when he got off the elevator.

"I'm here to see Steve Bordeaux," said Nick, wondering if she realized the balance of guilt and innocence in his stare.

"Do you need me to show you the way?"

"I get lost easily," he said. Truthfully.

He followed her taut hips through a maze of cheap partitions, conference tables, stacks of paper and books. Scotch-taped editorial cartoons, maps of Central America, and charts of America's foreign affairs bureaucracies covered the walls. The people working at computer terminals wore blue jeans and ties. Nick smiled, remembering his rebel days of muckraking for Peter Murphy. *Rock 'n' rolling in the heart of the beast.*

*Most of you were in grade school then.* He wanted to tell them a thousand things; he wanted them to know who he was, that he'd *been there.* Was *there* still. They watched him pass by, a lean guy in a gunmetal sports jacket and not a power suit, a man whose silver black hair and hard eyes put him out of their warless generation, an average-looking guy, not too tall and on the skinny side. His tired face wasn't in their treasured scrapbooks of personas. The looks in their unscarred eyes told Nick that they'd listen to but not hear any wisdom he could speak.

*The old guy,* he thought; then he laughed aloud.

"Excuse me?" said the pretty woman. Her perfume was musk.

"It's nothing," he said. "Nostalgia."

"That's Steve," she said, pointing through the open door of an office before she glided away.

A man all of thirty-four sat behind a cluttered desk, blue shirt and loose tie, dark slacks, glasses, and a cheap haircut. He put down the proof sheets he was correcting to shake hands.

Nick took the chair beside his desk. An intercom announced that Tom and Malcolm were wanted on a conference call.

"Thanks for seeing me," said Nick.

"Hanson said you were a good guy," Steve told him. "You know Hanson, he knows me. In this town, who you know decides where you go."

"My problem is I don't know who I know. That's why I came to you and the Archives."

The National Security Archives is a creature of the 1980s, one of the capital's legion of nonprofit groups struggling to push the Sisyphean boulder of government. The Archives rents space from the older, more prestigious think tank that inflamed the Watergate men, lives off foundation grants, and exists to uncover core data about America's foreign policy.

"I'm after intersects," said Nick. "I've got some topics. I want to check Iran-contra for links. Identify players."

"Anybody special in mind?"

"An old source." Nick shrugged. "I've heard some wild theories I don't buy."

Steve frowned. "Like what?"

"Like cocaine. I don't figure the contras were running it as policy, or the CIA was being that kind of creative to fund their secret war against Nicaragua, but . . ."

*"But."* Steve smiled. "Anytime you get a gang-bang covert operation like the contras, you get guys who cut their own deals in the hush and the fury. Like ex–2506 Brigade members who bought into the latest anticommunist crusade. They used a fishing business to surveil the Nicaraguan coast until Customs in Miami unthawed ice blocks of shrimp and found bags of coke. And some

of Oliver North's memos talk about Young Turks in one contra group being into coke. That the kind of stuff you want?"

"Sounds too normal," answered Nick.

They laughed.

"Who is this guy you're after?" asked Steve.

"Not *after:* tracking. There may be a coke connection involving him, but it'd probably be . . . twisted. And very creative."

"What about the Barry Seal stuff?" asked Steve.

"I don't know the name."

"Not enough people do," said Steve. "Louisiana boy. Like me, only he was Baton Rouge and I'm a Catahoula kid."

"A world of difference," said Nick, and Steve laughed.

"Barry was a pilot. Nicknamed Thunder Thighs. He got jammed up with Louisiana cops who knew he was bringing in coke and weren't buying any of his *undercover agent* or *CIA asset* bullshit. In 1984, he was about to do hard time when he shows up at the Vice President's Florida Drug Task Force, where he claims he can prove the Sandinistas are running coke.

"The White House went orgasmic. Our spooks fitted Barry's plane with cameras. He brought back photos *he claimed* showed a Nicaraguan official loading his plane with coke. Of course, what was being loaded was in bags, and maybe it wasn't an official Sandinista mission, but hey: it was great PR and our Iran-contra boys used it."

"What happened to Barry Seal?"

"The law got pulled off his case for a while. In 1986, two guys machine-gunned Barry to death in his white Cadillac."

"Sounds like business as usual," said Nick.

"There's more. A plane owned by a former CIA proprietary got shot down over Nicaragua while dropping supplies to contras. The Sandinistas caught one survivor. He talked, claimed to work for the CIA, and that started unraveling the Iran-contra scandal."

"I remember the plane," said Nick.

"Barry Seal sold that plane to our Iran-contra boys. He'd used it to smuggle coke."

"Ironic, but nothing for me," said Nick.

Steve shrugged. "What about the other half of the scandal, the Iran stuff?"

"My guy has a link to Iran," said Nick. "But it's old."

"Are you writing history or journalism?" said Steve.

"I'm a novelist," said Nick.

"Then you can just make it up."

"Yeah."

The two men smiled.

"Later this spring," said Steve, "we're publishing an index of Iran-contra. We've got every document cross-referenced, names of almost everybody mentioned anywhere in the six key years of the scandal, organization glossaries—"

"Biographies?" interrupted Nick.

"Brief ones. Couple hundred listings in thirty pages."

"Can I get a copy of that?"

"Sure, but it's easy to check if your guy's profiled."

"He won't show up on lists," said Nick. He hesitated, decided, *What you have to lose is this chance to find out.*

"Do you have anything peculiar about intelligence ops against the cocaine cartel?" asked Nick. "Not busts: strategic. Links to politics, terrorists. Long about ten years ago."

"Ten years ago nobody used the name cartel." Steve frowned. "Give me a minute." He left the room.

Nick stared through Steve's window toward eight-story glass-and-brick warrens he knew were filled with lawyers who worked sixty-hour weeks under fluorescent lights. He closed his eyes and amidst the aromas of ink and paper and dust burning in computer electricity, imagined he could smell musk perfume.

"I found it," said Steve, striding back into his office, a smudged manila file folder open in his hands.

"This is a project I never finished. State Department cables, clipped articles, Hill testimony. Nothing about intelligence *operations,* but some about intelligence *product.*"

"On the cartel?" asked Nick, listening to the researcher as he paged through the file, scanning for Jud's name.

Steve waved his hand. "On drugs *and* terrorists: Colombian left-wing guerrillas doing muscle work for drug dealers. Right-wingers in El Salvador using drug profits to pay for an assassination attempt on the President of Honduras. Reports of Cuban and Nicaraguan officials working the coke trade. The right-wing Gray Wolves in Turkey selling heroin and dealing with communist Bulgarian intelligence services in the same business. Plus some early '82 stuff on the Shining Path in Peru shaking down coca growers."

"Same jungle," said Nick. "Makes sense that spies, revolution-aries, and drug dealers would walk the same trails."

"What's in a name?" said Steve. "Narco king or terrorist, shared tactics merge disparate groups. I toyed with writing a paper showing how the drugs would eventually turn revolutionaries into capitalists—it's happened in Burma with the heroin and the Shans—but . . . other priorities."

"Where did the information for these cables and study papers come from?" asked Nick.

"Since '83, there's been an abundance of it: busts, informants. Looking back, drugs and political outlaws were historical lines waiting to cross. Like you said: same jungle."

"But before that inevitability was clear," said Nick, "where did the *first* intelligence come from?"

"Beats me," said the researcher who'd collated the reported data. "Drugs are an eighty-billion-dollar-a-year business. People pay attention to those kind of dollars."

"Money makes the world go round." Nick frowned. "What about the money in Iran-contra? Close to twenty million dollars. Who got it?"

"The scandal blew up too soon for giant rake-offs. But markups on weapons and food, consulting fees to PR groups and middle-men, padded expense reimbursements—hell, the cachet of work-ing for the White House: we'll never know what it was worth to the bad guys."

"Or what it cost everybody else," said Nick.

He rode the subway to Capitol Hill, his briefcase on his lap. A train wasn't the place to pour over the fifty pages of fine print in the Iran-Contra Names and Organizations Glossaries he'd photo-copied at the Archives.

A black man in a blue suit and white shirt, attaché case at his side, rode across the aisle from Nick.

*Marketing executive,* decided Nick, not sure what that term meant, making up a life story for the man with whom he shared the train. An innocent life story.

A pretty, eagle-faced woman with strawberry-blond hair chopped off at her shoulders got on at the next stop. She was about forty, with bright blue eyes and inexpensive but jazzy clothes.

*Lobbies for a do-good group,* thought Nick. *Lefty, but with a sense of humor. No ring, doesn't look gay, and doesn't look as if she'd be unloved.*

She didn't notice Nick.

Three prep-school teenage girls, backpacks, torn blue jeans, and oh-so-bored faces slumped into the last empty seats on the car. As the train pulled out of the station, they loudly prattled on about how, *like,* stupid some people were and how, *like,* stressed they were, *ohmyGod.* They were each careful to say *fuck* at least once per rambling paragraph.

The eagle-faced woman smiled at the girls' prattle.

Three bulky construction workers stood in the aisle, their thick arms dangling from the overhead aluminum pole, their blue, plastic hard hats jaunty on sweaty brows.

The subway clattered through tunnels beneath D.C.'s streets, a train bearing tourists from Indiana and Kyōto. A Chinese nanny with two tow-haired, giggling little girls. Nick wondered what Juanita and his son, Saul, were doing right then. Briefcases outnumbered shopping bags in this car, and a dozen passengers wore ID badges on silver chains around their neck: this was midafternoon on a Friday in a city defined by work.

Nowhere on the train or the subway platforms did he see a white-haired man in a blue wool topcoat.

Nowhere did he see private eye Jack Berns.

He switched subway lines at Metro Center, shouldering through the bustling crowd, jumping through the doors of the next train just as the warning bell dinged and the doors slid closed. He looked around him, saw no one from his old car: the eagle-faced woman must have stayed on the other train.

A man shaking coins in a McDonald's Coke cup stood at the top of the escalator that brought Nick above ground. Nick had ridden to the stop near the Capitol so he could walk along Pennsylvania Avenue's row of bars and restaurants, see the congressional players strolling in the fresh air. The windows of the well-stocked bookstore where his novels were unavailable reflected no one suspicious behind him.

A woman wrapped in a filthy brown blanket shouted at Nick, *"Give me a goddamn quarter!"* Nick's eyes cut through her. She didn't care. Nick suddenly wished he had all the quarters in the world to give away, the hell if they went for wine or crack cocaine or food for hungry babies.

Three buzz-saw-haircut young Marines in red shorts and gray

T-shirts from the Commandant's barracks a mile away jogged toward the Capitol. None of the pretty girls on the street cared.

The block of town houses where Nick had his office was lined with cars, but void of pedestrians. He climbed the five-stair, black-iron porch, put his key in the locked door to the stairs leading up to his office. . . .

Whirled around: saw nobody on the street.

Nobody.

*Just static electricity in the air,* he told himself.

His office looked undisturbed. The only message on his machine was from Sylvia, asking him to pick up milk on his way home, signing off with a soft *I love you.* He remembered musk perfume, chocolate skin, laughed at his flush of unwarranted guilt.

There was one fresh yellow legal pad left in his stack. He found a pen and took out the photocopied glossaries.

Jud Stuart had not been annotated by the Archives.

The alphabetical Names Glossary had biographies ranging from two sentences to four dense paragraphs. Nick looked for common ground between the names and the legends he associated with Jud: Vietnam, Special Forces or other elite military groups, Iran, Chile (What had Jud done in Chile?), Watergate, drug smuggling.

On the yellow pad he listed the CIA station chief in Beirut who'd been kidnapped and tortured to death, but not the American journalist snatched from that same city. Hostages were the rationale behind the Iran half of the scandal the glossary covered, but Nick didn't associate Jud with random victims.

A CIA agent who'd been tarred by an arms scandal made Nick's list, as did a retired Air Force colonel who formed a host of companies to get contra supply contracts. Two Iranian arms dealers made the list: maybe Jud had known them during his mission to the Shah's regime. An American rancher in Costa Rica who'd been linked to the contras and later fled that country's narcotics cops made the list, as did an admiral who worked for the Joint Chiefs of Staff, the same group that in Watergate had been implicated in the military spy ring in the White House. Nick logged the name of a food store magnate, Vietnam veteran, ex–Klu Klux Klansman who founded a private mercenary group that worked with the secret White House team and sent "missionary-mercenaries" to aid the contras.

A handful of Cuban Americans made the list, mostly members of right-wing groups or veterans of the 2506 Brigade.

A CIA agent with service in Laos and involvement with a now-imprisoned Task Force 157 renegade caught Nick's attention, as did a retired American general who'd consulted on covert warfare training and Iran, formed companies to sell the contras guns. Nick wrote down the name of an ex-major in England's most elite commando unit who'd organized a mission that in 1985 blew up a Nicaraguan military depot and a hospital.

Many of the men on Nick's list had code names; many of them had won fame as criminals in the scandal—admirals, generals, White House aides, military officers, high-rolling political money men, and Iranian arms dealers: guilty of charges such as tax fraud, lying to Congress, destroying government property, bribery, and conspiracy.

Distilling the Names Glossary took Nick two hours. He picked up the Organizations Glossary.

Twelve pages of tightly packed paragraphs on about a hundred organizations, from air transport companies and airlines to CIA proprietaries. From the CIA to a half dozen conservative, tax-exempt foundations and committees that had raised millions of dollars for the contras, sometimes spending it on things such as illegally smearing American congressmen. A handful of Swiss banks made the glossary, as did shell corporations used to sell weapons secretly to the anti-American government of Iran and turn the profits back into the contra war or to other secret operations.

*Complexity aids concealment,* thought Nick. Had Jud taught him that maxim or had he thought of it himself?

Nick rubbed his eyes, checked his watch: almost time to go home. He didn't know how to categorize the organizations.

The afternoon light through his bay windows was gray, like a stream in a steel town. He looked out at the rooftops and budding trees of the world's most successful democracy.

Saw no one in the street below.

But he felt naked. Exposed. Watched. The sensation was so strong it felt like an unseen train bearing down on him; a train he was on, a subway.

In his car, none of the other passengers had faces.

# LOVESICK HEART

Wes spent three days healing.

Beth was there when he woke up Friday; even when she wasn't in the room, he felt her presence, her soothing touch; smelled her skin, her hair.

"I expected our first weeks in bed to be a little different than this," she said as she sat on his bed the morning after he'd returned. She held his plate of scrambled eggs. An ice pack rested on his leg.

"They will be," he said.

"Just so you're around for them." Her eyes went to the window; came back, took in his pale, bruised face.

Wes brushed her cheek with his fingertips.

"The papers say peace has broken out," she said, "but you came back to me wounded. I don't know why or for what. The uniform I can take—hell, you don't know how bad I want *semper fi,* always faithful. True. Maybe I can handle all of it, even if you had to go . . . If it were stopping Hitler, we'd do it together."

"I don't think the Commandant would allow that."

"Fuck the Commandant, I don't love him!"

The sky opened up for Wes. He cupped her face in his hands, felt her tears running over his fingers and whispered, "I love you, too!"

She buried her face in his neck and whispered, "What are you doing? What is this? Why are you hurt?"

"One time," he said, "a onetime thing. Then it's over."

She leaned back, her eyes wet and happy, scared. "What?"

"I have to find something out. Do something."

*"What?"*

"I can't tell you."

"Don't do it," she said. "Don't die. It isn't right."

"I won't die. *Believe me:* especially now, I won't die."

"Yeah, look at you, you're doing so well." She sniffled.

"Honey, I chose the Corps to do what should be done. That's what I want to do with my life. Be part of the solution. Make sure that . . . my folks, my nephews . . . you: make sure you're safe. Make things work. I can't leave that to chance or not pick up my share of that responsibility. I'm part of the right team, and I'm also my own player. I went after the big leagues. If you're going to play, go all the way. This . . . mission: that's what it is.

"I didn't define the battle, but I can't walk away like it isn't there. I can't leave it for someone else to do."

"Why *you?*"

"It's my trail. My jungle."

Someone knocked on his front door.

She left the bedroom. He heard Greco ask for him and Beth introduce herself. Greco told her his first name. Wes covered the ice pack and tried to look better. She led Greco into the bedroom.

"There's coffee on the stove," she told Greco, whose face was polite. "If you two want some."

To Wes, she said, "I've got some calls I have to make."

She kissed him lightly, worry in her touch, left the apartment.

"Who is she?" asked Greco.

"Beth's . . ." Wes grinned. "Somebody special."

"She lives across the hall?"

Wes nodded.

"That's convenient. How long you known her?"

"All my life," said Wes.

"Old friends," said Greco, pulling up a chair, "they're the best. You remember that."

"Thanks."

"Your subject didn't surface so far," said NIS's head counterspy. "I can keep my boys scouting for another seven hours before it starts to smell. After that, you're in luck.

"You ever hear of the Gs?" asked Greco.

Wes shook his head.

"FBI runs 'em. The Special Support Group, SSGs. Civil servant contractors. Too fat or short or too-thick glasses to qualify as agents, but they want to play. They get paid shit. Get surveillance school, camera school, work case-by-case contract. No busts, no guns, no glory. Budget savers on surveillances. Plus they're harder to spot. Bad guys don't suspect fat old ladies.

"They can't work for private concerns. In slack times, the Bureau lets other agencies use them, if they pay the bill."

Greco shrugged. "Your NIS loan-out to CIA is legit: shaky but sanctioned. I made some calls. The Bureau's got Gs in L.A. they ain't using. One of 'em's Seymour, who I've used. He can pull together what you need. If you can pay the bill."

"Sounds perfect."

"If you can pay the bill," said Greco. His tone was flat. He handed him the G's phone number. "My agents can get Seymour copies of that driver's license photo within the hour."

"There's some photos in my suit jacket hanging on the chair," said Wes.

Greco found the pictures. Though not certain of their worth, on principle he asked, "You secure these like that?"

"Turns out that was the safest place." Wes tore a piece of medical tape from a spool by the bed, stuck it over Nick Kelley in the Polaroid of the writer sitting beside Jud Stuart.

"The guy in this Polaroid and that café surveillance photo is the primary target," said Wes. "Could you wire copies of those photos to Seymour? Your guys, too. They spot the motorcycle man, they're to stick with him, but if they have to choose, cover the primary target."

Greco rubbed his thumb across the tape on the picture.

"How many roads must a man go down, huh?" he mimicked out of a song Wes hadn't thought the counterspy would know.

"I need to go to the firing range tomorrow," said Wes.

"I'd keep horizontal for a few more days." Greco shrugged. "You can break it in on Monday."

"I'll be gone, then. Out of town."

Greco stared at the man in the bed.

"Don't worry," said Wes. "No big deal."

"Don't jerk my chain," said Greco.

"I'm not going to the combat zone."

"You taking her?"

"No."

"Then it's the combat zone."

After Greco left, Wes called Seymour the G in L.A.

"Man, are you good news!" said Seymour. He had a nasal voice. "Between *glasnost* and Graham-Rudman budgets we ain't been working a lot. This isn't narco, is it? My people say no to drugs."

"No," Wes told him, shifting in his Washington bed.

"Or gang-bangers. Too many shotguns and AK-47s."

"No street gangs. Strictly fed S.O.P."

"Beautiful. Covering six square blocks in Westwood, two guys, motorcycle, locate and surveil, full-time press."

Seymour tapped a pocket calculator.

"You need two guys at thirty dollars an hour per, twenty-four-hour coverage, equals fourteen forty. Make it fifteen hundred to cover expenses. Two fifty more a day for vehicles and radios—I get a discount from the rental folks because I only take dirty cars." Seymour laughed. "If you issue radios, we don't have to rent."

"Rent," said Wes.

"I got a guy in Torrance. Figure forty an hour for me and my backup at control center—we'll use my apartment, no cost. Ten bucks an hour extra for us because we're field commanding, okay?"

"Okay."

"My backup lives with me, so the radio and phones are covered even when I'm in the tub. Don't worry about any inspector general crying nepotism: we ain't married. Figure we'll give you a flat sixteen hours for the two of us on full-time—fair?"

"Fair."

"Man, you're great! No committees, no Request for Proposals. Did you process the authorization papers yet?"

"They're in the works," lied Wes. Greco would help him create legitimizing documents. "But you'll probably be off-line before the paper comes through."

"Ain't it the way? So we got six hundred and forty dollars a day for me and mine."

"Keep all the receipts, work up documentation for—"

"Man, I bury paper pushers like you wouldn't believe!"

"I hope so," said Wes.

"If you really are the solo center of this, get a portable cellular phone."

"I will."

"So, our end will run Uncle two thousand three hundred and ninety dollars a day. Are we on?"

"I'll FedEx a cash advance of ten thousand today."

*"Cash?* You're too good to be true!"

Wes asked Beth to take the sealed envelope to the Federal Express office. She didn't mind; kissed him good-bye.

He got out of bed, gingerly stretched his long body. Everything ached, but his leg could hold his weight as long as he was careful. He looked in the bathroom mirror. The bruises on his face were losing their color, the swelling was going down. His unshaven skin was pale, and the old shrapnel scar looked like a jagged brown tattoo line. He found a baseball in his closet, took it back to bed with him, and squeezed it as he made phone calls.

At the CIA, Noah Hall was *out.* Mary, the Director's personal secretary was unavailable, as was Director Denton.

At NIS, the commander agreed to issue Wes credentials authorizing him to carry a concealed firearm on *federal business.* Questions echoed in the commander's voice, but the man didn't ask.

Wes slept most of that afternoon. When he woke up, his headache was gone, though his body still ached. Beth cooked him dinner, helped him bathe, changed his bandages. She slept beside him. They were both careful not to say the word *love* again.

*Caution returns,* thought Wes. But he felt curiously free, happy for the risk while terrified at his exposure.

He was out of bed the next morning before Beth woke up, coffee made, paper half-read, a healthy smile on his face. He sent her off to her job, then dressed and drove to NIS headquarters to pick up his weapons permit. At the NIS firing range, a husky instructor who served on the terrorist takedown team and protective services detail spent an hour working with Wes.

The Marines had taught Wes how to handle a pistol in uniformed combat; the NIS instructor worked with him on plainclothes street technique: hip holster and FBI draw, the Weaver stance. Wes squeezed off his box of practice rounds, started good, got better. His left leg could hold its share of weight; his ribs hurt, but he swallowed aspirins and ignored the pain. The pistol felt good in his hand: bucking, roaring, slamming lead into the world with each squeeze of Wes's finger.

He used human silhouette targets.

That night he made love with Beth, cradled her in his arms as she gently slid back and forth on top of him. He called her name aloud and whispered the words in his heart. Sunday they rested, and she failed to talk him out of going.

Monday morning he caught a taxi to the airport, refusing her offer of a ride so she couldn't hug him after he'd strapped on the Sig in the airport bathroom; so she wouldn't see him fill out the *armed peace officer* air-travel forms at the airline counter.

San Francisco is America's most beautiful city, with its bridges, roller-coaster hills, Chinatown and Coit Tower, Alcatraz, its flowers and cool blue skies and smiling people.

San Francisco was where Mathew Hopkins lived, a Navy man who'd worked in the White House and died in the bull pen of an L.A. wino bar.

The VA sent Hopkins's 100-percent-disability checks to a house in Richmond, a quiet neighborhood of attached homes close enough to the ocean to hear foghorns. Wes landed in San Francisco midmorning and before noon, discovered the address was a basement apartment of a gray stucco house. The basement unit had elaborate iron grillwork over all the windows. The barred entrance was recessed under the concrete stairs leading up to the main unit. In the gap between Hopkins's bars and his locked and curtained front door, Wes found a dirt-smudged business card for a San Francisco policeman who'd tried to relay the message from LAPD to anyone who lived there that Mathew Hopkins had died.

"He ain't home," said a woman's voice.

Wes looked out from under the stairs, saw a pudgy woman staring back at him. She flinched at the bruises on his face.

"Do you live in the upper unit?" asked Wes. His Gore-Tex briefcase was in his left hand.

"Who wants to know?" She edged closer to the stairs.

Wes showed her NIS credentials, wished he had a badge.

"Cop, huh? Should have figured. You look like you caught a bad one."

"Yes," said Wes.

"Is Matt okay?"

"Matt?"

"Matt Hopkins, the guy whose door you're poking 'round. I live upstairs, I'm his landlady. A widow."

"When was the last time you saw him?"

"Hell, who keeps track of time? Figure, well, he mailed his rent check, so . . . six, maybe seven weeks.

"He's the quiet type," she said. "Smokes too much, eats too much red meat and frozen dinners, but what's a bachelor to do, huh? Cookin' for one ain't easy. You live alone?"

"Yes," said Wes, "what—"

"You shouldn't. Look at you: you need someone to take care of you. You want some coffee? I got sprout salad for lunch."

"I've got some bad news for you: Mr. Hopkins is dead."

She blinked, said, "Not . . . he wasn't *sick,* was he?"

"An accident," said Wes. "In L.A."

"Shit. No wonder he ain't been around."

"I'm with the federal government," said Wes. "And—"

"I thought you was a cop."

"I'm more than that, I'm a lawyer."

"*Oh,*" she said. And smiled.

"We have to help process Mr. Hopkins estate. Do you have a key to his apartment?"

"Sure. He never lets me go down there, though."

"He won't mind."

"Oh. That's right." She winked. "You wait here."

Five minutes later she hurried back down the concrete steps. She had a ring of keys. She'd brushed her hair.

"He put on all these locks," she said, using three keys. "And you should see the back! Bars on all the windows. I made him pay for them and I insisted on getting copies of the keys."

"That was smart," said Wes.

She laughed. Opened the door.

The air floating out of the basement apartment was stale and thick. Something rotten tingled their nostrils.

The widow sniffed, opened her mouth to speak, but closed it. She put one foot inside the door, pulled it back.

"He's dead, isn't he?" she said.

"Yes."

"I don't like dead." She shuddered. "Gives me the creeps.

"Look," she continued, "could you do this without me? I don't want to . . . Not right away. I'll wait upstairs. I been picking up his mail. Only junk stuff, but you might want it. Just ring the buzzer—Annie McLeod. I'll make fresh coffee. Is that okay?"

"That'll be fine," said Wes, and he gave her a smile that sent her scurrying back up the stairs, happy.

He waited until he heard her door close, then he stepped inside and turned on the light.

Books. Hundreds and hundreds of books, four crammed metal-tiered shelves jutting out from one wall that turned the living room into a library. Stacks of books on the floor. Quality books from New York publishers, green and brown and white paperbound congressional hearings, volumes from publishers Wes had never heard of. A few books in French, Spanish. The books had titles full of words like *spooks, secret, spy, conspiracy, assassination, power, enemies, patriots, lie.* They were dog-earred, yellow highlighted or underlined in ink, with notes jotted in the margins and page-referenced on the inside covers. Between the bookshelves were stacks of magazines and newspapers. Two file cabinets were full of clippings. There was a desk near the curtained bay window, but Wes passed it by to wander back through the apartment—and stare at the walls.

No wonder Mathew Hopkins hadn't let his landlady in here.

Pictures torn from newspapers were taped on the walls next to pictures cut from books. Black-and-white photos of soldiers in jungles, men in front of government-looking buildings. Official portraits. American-looking men, Asians, Africans, swarthy Europeans, Hispanics. Group shots in the boonies or in crowded streets in which a keyhole-sized face would be circled in red ink. White House aides sitting tight-lipped in front of microphones while lawyers whispered in their ear. Defendants waving as they walked from courthouses, newsmen in tow. A shot of a smiling man in a topcoat standing in Red Square. A tall, twisted-frowned man in handcuffs being led past a jail door. Wes recognized a magazine photo of a Marine lieutenant colonel raising his hand to swear to tell the truth to Congress.

But it was the charts that boggled Wes.

Sketch-pad sheets covered with felt-penned notations and names, dates: SOG and CRP and JADE and Project 404. DELTA and B-56, FANK and Raven. White Star. TF/157. Team B. Nugan Hand. Mongoose. YELLOWFRUIT. Castle Bank. VEIL. Charts listed spy and covert warfare agencies, from the Army's Intelligence Support Activity to the Navy's SEALs. Dozens of businesses, foundations, political groups, and lobby associations had places on Mathew Hopkins's wall. The charts listed hundreds of people's names, some famous, some notorious, most unknown to Wes, some with stars or exclamation points inked beside them, some with question marks, some with death dates.

Green and red and blue and black and yellow Magic Marker lines trailed off the charts, tracked across the white walls to connect to names on other charts, to photographs. To nowhere.

The retired spy from Task Force 157 had told Wes how insanity sometimes infected those in the secret professions.

"Who were you looking for?" Wes asked the walls.

Nowhere did he see Jud Stuart's name.

Garbage stank in the kitchen, the refrigerator was icy.

The bedroom was fastidious. Clothes hung symmetrically in the closet, stacked neatly in the bureau drawers. Wes was sure he could bounce a coin off the boot-camp taut bedspread.

His leg and his ribs hurt. He sat on the bed. Heard a *clunk* by the headboard. Wes reached behind the pillows, ran his hand along the edge of the mattress.

Found a hammerless, five-shot revolver. Loaded.

The desk in the living room bay window was a beautiful old rolltop with dozens of pigeonholes. Wes found phone bills with no long-distance calls. He opened the middle drawer.

Found a loaded .45 Colt automatic, the pistol that until recently had been the sidearm for American armed forces.

The L.A. police report noted that nothing had been found on Hopkins's body but clothes. *Did you have a gun with you when you died?* wondered Wes. *Why or why not?*

A thick scrapbook lay under the automatic. Wes put the gun on the desk, opened the scrapbook.

He found an opened envelope addressed to Hopkins, no return address, a Maryland postmark dated a few weeks earlier. The envelope was empty, but paper-clipped to it was an astrology column from a tacky supermarket tabloid. The column had a January 1990 date. Its reverse side had a story about a priest who exploded while performing an exorcism. In the horoscope listing for Aries, the words *lovesick heart* were underlined repeatedly in red.

Astrology columns from the same newspaper were glued to the pages of the scrapbook in chronological order dating back years. In some of the horoscopes, phrases or words were yellow highlighted or underlined, question marks or exclamation points inked in the margins.

The big drawer on the left bottom side of the desk had three other scrapbooks of astrology columns.

The big drawer on the right side of the desk held two thermite grenades, each one capable of turning a room into an exploding inferno.

A framed photograph sat on top of the desk: an impossibly young man in a starched white sailor uniform stood beneath a tree, one arm on the shoulder of a solemn old man, his other arm draped around a plump, old woman in a flowered dress. The camera had caught the old woman with her hand moving, almost to her chest as it rose to cover her nervous laugh.

Wes stared at the picture, the gun on the desk, the grenades in the drawer, the twisted history taped to the walls.

"What were you afraid of?" asked Wes. "What were you doing? What were you looking for?"

A loud buzz came from inside Wes's briefcase. The buzz sounded again before Wes could unzip the briefcase and answer his portable cellular phone.

"Yeah?"

"Bingo!" said Seymour's nasal voice, long distance from Los Angeles. "We spotted your motorcycle man outside an apartment building half an hour ago. Walked to a teller machine, went back inside. Got a backup team there before he came out with the sorriest-looking chick in the world. She gave him keys, he climbed in a black Trans Am, and off he went. We got two cars leapfrogging behind him, a third as a way-back rear guard.

"Hennie followed the chick back into the building. Said the girl was happy to see the dude gone."

"I'll bet," said Wes.

"Her mailbox matched up with the Trans Am registration I got out of DMV. The landlord said that the chick is a paralegal. Landlord don't like the boyfriend. His motorcycle's in the underground garage, in the girl's space."

"Where's he going?"

"He's a rabbit with a suitcase and a shoulder duffel. Wearing an old canvas cowboy duster, driving a black Trans Am."

"I'll call you from the airport!" Wes hung up.

*This place.* He looked at the grenades: one tossed back inside as he slammed the door and ran would wipe out every trace of whatever was here, whatever Wes hadn't seen that no one else should see. One pulled pin, and all of Mathew Hopkins's life was history.

Annie McLeod upstairs making coffee, waiting, wouldn't fare too well either. But the sin of burning away the memories of the dead man was why he put the weapons and the scrapbook back in the desk, locked the apartment when he left to run to his car.

He phoned Seymour from the airport rental-car return.

"He's headed north on U.S. Fifteen!" said Seymour. "We're three deep behind him and we ain't been spotted."

"Where's he going?"

"Damned if I know. He's got about five hours of nothing between him and Las Vegas."

"Don't lose him," said Wes. He hung up.

Across the parking lot from the car rental company's window, he saw a sign: CORPORATE CHARTER AIR.

Two men and a woman were laughing behind the counter at the charter air company when Wes barreled through the door, brandishing his NIS identification like a vampire hunter's crucifix. He pulled a wad of hundred-dollar bills out of his briefcase and said, "I need a charter jet to Las Vegas—now!"

# THE BLACK CAR

J ud saw the black car coming as he stood inside the window of Nora's Café. Like the man in the Oasis Bar, the black car didn't belong where it was; like that killer, Jud knew the black car had come for him.

At first the car was just a shimmer on the horizon at the end of the long highway, a dark core skimming out of a silver lake where the sky curved to touch the earth.

"Nora," whispered Jud softly.

"Yeah, hon?" she answered from the till where she was counting the lunch take. Smoke curled up from her ashtray.

Carmen was in the back, watching TV. Except for the three of them, the café was empty that afternoon.

The black car emerged out of the mirage. Came closer. Closer.

"Did you want something?" said Nora.

Her Jeep was parked by her house. If he made her run *now*, if Carmen waddled out the kitchen as fast as she could, if there was no trouble with the Jeep's keys or the starter, Nora might make it. Carmen, too. If he stayed behind. For the black car.

In his trailer, a blue airline shoulder bag now held Jud's gun and the money he'd stolen in L.A. so long/so short a time ago, plus the cash Nora had paid him. The blue bag hung on a hook just inside the trailer door. If they all ran *now*, they could probably make it *before*.

The black car was only a half mile away.

Jud's hands trembled over the apron he wore for dishwashing; his guts churned. Maybe it was just demons taunting him.

Nora shut the till. "What do you see out there?"

*Too late.* The black car slowed down to forty, thirty miles per hour, cruised along the edge of the café parking lot.

Cruised past it: stayed on the highway, rolled right on by Nora's, right past the telephone booth on the side of the road. The black car picked up speed and roared down the highway, out of sight around a curve on the flat tumbleweed horizon.

Jud laughed out loud.

"What's so funny?" said Nora, joining him at the window, looking out.

Two dirty American sedans, one right after the other, whizzed by the café in the black car's wake.

"Looks like we lost some business." Jud laughed again.

"You got a peculiar sense of funny," she told him.

"Yeah," he said, turning to her, wanting to kiss her.

Her brow wrinkled, but she smiled back, said, "What?"

He just shook his head, watched her. She blushed, turned her eyes to the outside.

"Nope," she said, "looks like we're in luck."

The black car had driven past, circled back. Tires crunched on the pavement in front of the café as it pulled up to the door. The engine shut off. Sunlight bouncing on the windshield made the driver inside a blur of light. The door opened.

And Dean stepped out. He wore a pale canvas duster and an ivory-toothed grin.

"This is for me," Jud said. He stepped outside, leaving her to stare through the glass.

"You're not supposed to be here!" Jud yelled to Dean.

Dean raised his hands to the sky. "So sue me!" He jerked his thumb toward the pay phone. "You weren't answering."

"Come around back," said Jud.

A dirty Japanese sedan slowly rolled past on the highway; its driver watched the two men circle around back of the café.

As they headed toward Jud's trailer, Dean nodded to where they'd last seen Nora. "So how much is that doggy in the window?"

Jud threw a right jab at Dean's face—but Dean caught the punch.

Dean's eyes widened. "Hell, what's happened here?"

Sinking his weight, twisting his waist, Jud jerked his fist free of Dean's grasp.

"Time was, I'd have never seen that coming," whispered Dean. "Time was, when you were the man and I was . . . Who was I?"

Then he laughed.

"I'll be damned," he said. "I'll be damned."

"What do you want?" Jud's hands trembled at his sides.

"What do I want?" Dean shook his head. "Well, right now— right *now,* I don't know.

"I came here 'specting to rock 'n' roll, just like before, you *the man* and me . . . But looks like the *old days* are dead.

"I mean," he said, "nice apron.

"Is this where you been all these years?" asked Dean. "Is this what happened to you?"

"Never mind me," said Jud.

"Minding you is why I'm here. You called me: I was waiting for that call, *man,* waiting *years.* You dropped me like I was dog shit, then *you* call *me,* and it's all supposed to be okay, asshole buddies again. You say cover my tracks, bird-dog my trail, and you were right, there was a suit sniffing 'round after you—"

"Who?"

"—but Dean, he handled that, got the guy gone, no more looking-lawyer *bullshit*—"

"You didn't—"

"I did what Dean does."

"You should have IDed him! Got back to me!"

"He got to *me,* Jack! Way I figure it, somebody popped your writer buddy's phone records and put Dean in the bull's-eye."

*There it is,* thought Jud. The step that had been haunting him, the trail he'd left from the pay phone that first night. And now Nick . . .

"Now what?" said Dean. "Now that you're whoever you are."

"You know who I am," said Jud.

"Maybe I do," said Dean. "Maybe I do."

"What do you want?"

"You owe me," said Dean. "Your trouble bounced me out of L.A. You owe me for that. You owe me for what I did. You owe me for all that *waiting.*"

"I'll give you all the cash I got," said Jud.

"You'll *give* me?" Dean laughed, a dry cackle. He whirled around in a circle, his coat swirling around him.

When he stopped, the smile he gave Jud was new.

"I'll get the money." Jud deliberately turned, gave Dean his back, and headed toward the trailer door; toward the blue bag.

And Dean *pushed* him, both hands slamming into Jud's back, Jud sensing it *too late* to do more than stagger forward and crash into his closed trailer door.

"You're not the man anymore!" screamed Dean.

Pushing off the trailer door, Jud whirled around, hands arcing up for blocks, for snake strikes, balance shaky, and Dean . . .

Out of range, eyes wild and circling away from Jud's charge, Jud circling with him as Dean stepped back, hands blurring under the duster . . .

Swinging out a pump shotgun, its black bore seeing Jud.

*"FREEZE!"* yelled a man by the café. *"DROP THE GUN!"*

*Dropping,* rolling in the dirt, earth and sky spinning for Jud. A tumbling upside-down image of a firing-stance man at the edge of the café; gun, sports jacket, *rolling,* a tall man with short hair.

Shotgun roars and buckshot slams into the back corner of Nora's Café as Jud scrambles toward the trailer door. Dean chambers another shell.

Wes whirls back around from the building's edge that caught the buckshot, snaps *two* from the Sig, close but *duck back quick* . . .

Shotgun blast. Plaster flies off the café wall.

*Inside,* Jud flops inside the aluminum trailer.

The blue bag, grabbing it, sliding the loop over his head as he dives deeper inside and *roaring buckshot* blows out the trailer window, glass shattering, curtain flying.

A pistol barks twice outside. Bullets slam into the right corner of Jud's trailer.

*Dean's there,* he thought. *That's where he found cover.*

One way out, the trailer only has one way out.

Dean's around the corner to the right, he thought. Around the corner *all the way*. With a shotgun. And there's a stranger with a pistol hugging the café wall off to the left.

*He could have shot us both,* thought Jud. *Didn't. Drew down on Dean.*

The shotgun and pistol roared. Another bullet slammed into the corner of Jud's trailer. He heard a *crack*. A jagged line zigzagged through the trailer's blue mirror. In the dim light, Jud saw his image, warped and in two halves.

"I won't die in a tin box," he mumbled.

The short-barreled .38 had six rounds.

*Enough,* he told himself. *Enough.*

Bullets slammed into the side of the trailer. The blue mirror crashed off the wall. The shotgun roared.

His ears rang with gunfire, his heart raced, and *think,* he had to think. Firefights. Alley in Madrid. Café in Tehran. Laos. Bong Sot. Grenades and rockets and don't let them overrun the wire, don't— No, down, stay down, back. *This time,* he said, breathing deep, hyperventilating. *Do this time.*

Think!

*Give the stranger your back. He didn't shoot it once, maybe he won't again. Dean is the killer you know.*

Out the door *fast,* he thought. Zero the corner where Dean is, get out, get close. Lay down suppression fire. Count your rounds. Duck low and jump wide around the corner, then . . .

*Then,* he thought.

Bullets crashed into his trailer and he heard Dean laugh.

*On your feet, soldier.* He climbed off the floor. Held the gun in the two-handed grip he'd learned in the Secret Service, where they'd taught him to stand tall in a gunfight and take the bullet for the Man.

*You aren't the man anymore,* Dean had said.

Shotgun roared.

Yes, I am, thought Jud, moving to the door.

*Yes, I am!* And he kicked the door open . . .

*Out,* sunlight *blinding* sunlight. Gunsmoke. Men yelling. Muffled woman's screams. *Pop!* Muzzle flash by the back of the café, bullet zinging past him, *muzzle flash* and *gun* and *bright white* threat: don't think don't aim don't die point and *fire.*

His .38 roared twice at the threat he hadn't anticipated.

Nora fell back against the café wall, the owner's pistol she'd fired at Dean dropping from her hand, twin red roses blooming on her white blouse.

Dead.

Jud knew she was dead as soon as he recognized her over his gunsight, *two rounds gone.* Knew it before she slid to the ground, eyes gazing in the bright sunlight.

The rattle-*rack* of a shotgun round being chambered to his right and he *didn't care, didn't matter.* A bullet *zinging* across his path *didn't matter* as he stumbled toward Nora.

*"Jud, drop!"* yelled Wes. He squeezed off a round behind the dazed man staggering across the killing zone.

Blood sprayed from Dean's shoulder and he dove out of sight behind the trailer as Wes changed ammunition clips.

*Where'd Dean go!* thought Wes.

Jud, shuffling. Wes knew the look on his face, had seen it on a dazed sergeant, a man blown over the edge, *long gone,* not there, not in the battle, the dust, the gore, not returning fire, not running, not taking cover . . . *gone.*

Wes knew the woman was dead, too. Knew how and knew why and what it had done to Jud—knew all that in a heartbeat, in a crystal moment of clarity snapped into the chaos of battle.

"Take cover!" he yelled to Jud, his eyes never leaving the trailer—which way would Dean go? Wes yelled the only thing he could think of to snap Jud out of it, to get him down, get him safe *until.* Maybe get him to use his gun—on Dean.

"Marines!" Wes yelled to the ex-soldier. "Relief force!"

Jud stumbled toward the dead woman.

*Change position,* thought Wes.

There'd be no relief force for him. The Gs who'd trailed Dean and homed Wes in on this café were parked off the side of the road a mile each direction from the café. They'd follow any surveillance subject who drove past, but they wouldn't help Wes *make contact.* Nor would they come to his rescue.

*Keep your enemy pinned, force him to reorient.*

Gun zeroed on the trailer, West sidestepped through the open toward a Jeep parked between the adobe house and the trailer.

Her blouse was red. Jud reached toward her. Stopped. She was . dead. He'd killed her. His gun slid from his hand.

Revulsion sucked him up like a tornado.

Gone, he wanted to be *never been,* not here. Gone. Nothing else mattered.

The flies were already buzzing her face.

Through the café, past where Carmen was wedged between the refrigerator and the stove: *"Santa Maria, Madre de Dios, ruega . . ."* Door, front door.

The black car.

Beside it, a Chevy rented from the Las Vegas airport. Red. Wes's Gore-Tex briefcase on the front seat, a suitcase hastily thrown in the back. Keys left in the ignition for a quick start, quick pursuit.

Only being gone mattered. Next thing Jud knew, he was in the Chevy, headed down the highway.

Behind the café, Wes heard a car go.

*Screaming,* Dean screaming coat flapping shoulder bleeding handgun blazing charging from behind the trailer firing . . .

At where Wes had been.

Wes shot him five times.

Left him dead on the sand. The woman slumped against the wall—dead. From inside the café came sobbing, hysterical prayers in Spanish.

Wes circled around to the front of the café.

And found only the black car.

|||||||||||||||||||||||||||||||||||||||||||||||||||||||||||||||||||||||||||||||||||

# EXPEDITED DEMISE

This was the third time in his life that Jud had run away.

The second time had been just weeks before, after the man in the Oasis Bar had died. Jud ran then, found Nora, only to have to run again this third time, leaving her dead in the sand.

The first time Jud ran was Miami, 1978.

Miami, the liquid city. Bright, tropical, the big heat. But the running had been clean, because that first time, in Miami, 1978, it had been all business.

"That's why we're here," Art Monterastelli had told Jud as they sat at the white-clothed table spread with bowls of fruit and plates of bacon and eggs. Art tilted a silver pot to fill each of their china cups with sweet Cuban coffee.

"Business," said Art. Whether he was in the jungles of Southeast Asia, on the desert of Iran, or amidst the beaches and sun-bouncing skyscrapers of Miami, blond Monterastelli never tanned, never burned. He wore his smoked sunglasses.

"Aren't we friends?" asked Jud.

In Miami, Art wore his blond hair long and wavy, like a 1950s teenage heartthrob. That day, he wore a pink shirt outside his linen pants. He was thicker in body, more lined in the face.

They sat on the back veranda of Art's Miami home. To be precise, it was Miami *Beach*. Off North Bay Road. They were casual. And too *not-alone*.

In the shadows by the French doors sat Raul, flat eyes, tropical suit, swarthy face. Raul was Art's *numero uno* and an officer in Sigma 77, a paramilitary anticommunist group dedicated to *la lucha*—the struggle. Rumors in Miami said that Sigma 77 helped plant the bomb that exploded that October at a New York City Cuban newspaper that had dared to support *el diálogo*—overtures between exiled Cubans in the U.S. and Castro. A Washington, D.C., policeman once flew down to Miami to interview Raul about the 1976 car bomb that killed the former ambassador from Allende's short-lived Marxist Chilean government a mile from the White House.

In Miami, where a third of a million people were Cuban and from a culture wedded to the romance of *el exilio* and *la lucha,* making Raul his *numero uno* was political genius on Art's part. Raul's Spanish was invaluable in the business. His soul was long gone, lost perhaps when the CIA deserted him with the rest of the 2506 Brigade on the beaches of the Bay of Pigs, perhaps afterward in Castro's prisons. Refugees who knew Raul as a boy in Havana whispered that he'd been a monster even then.

Those Miami days might find Raul whispering with other *exilios* in a mirror-walled Little Havana café or on a shuttle flight to Washington, D.C., or Guatamala. He'd worked for JM/WAVE, AM/LASH and MONGOOSE, the CIA's covert wars against Cuba, helped arrange assassination plots the CIA subcontracted to the Mafia. He knew the Cubans arrested as Watergate burglars, fellow *exilios* dedicated to *la lucha,* all of them friends of men in Washington who went to the streets of Cuban Miami when they needed warriors who wouldn't shirk the crusade. Raul knew people everywhere; more importantly, he was *known,* though no one could ever be sure who he was at any given moment: currents within currents in liquid Miami.

Sitting in the shadows, Raul had his suit coat open. Jud saw the pistol in his waistband.

Behind Jud, leaning against the veranda's thin, black, steel railing, was an ex-biker from Carmel who Art had leveraged out of a jam in Mexico. These elegant Miami days, the biker kept his goatee trimmed and wore a sports jacket over his tattooed arms and a slung Uzi.

Over Art's left shoulder, in the far corner of the veranda, Jud saw a wiry ex–South Vietnamese Ranger coiled in a wicker chair. Art had recruited him out of a refugee camp when he heard how the Asian claimed a berth on a refugee boat.

A wide lawn stretched beyond the veranda to a canal. Green

water slapped gently against the wood of Art's dock. A quarter mile up the channel from Art's shore, charred pilings from a burned dock poked out of the ripples like stubby black fingers. Raul lived on one side of Art, the only Cuban in the neighborhood. The prominent Florida lawyer who owned the house on the other side of Art secretly derived his wealth from Art. There was a chain link fence surrounding Art's property. The real security was invisible, from infrared cameras and motion sensors to land mines that Art switched off when the Haitian lawnboy came to ride the power mower.

Jud sensed more than saw *something* in the shadows of the gazebo on the lawn between the canal and the veranda.

*Kerns,* he thought. The only man in the organization besides Jud who was good enough to guarantee a shot at that range.

Inside the house were a servant and two gunmen Jud had hired for Art. And Monterastelli's seventeen-year-old mistress.

The Miami heat was thick and sweet and as fragrant as the coffee they sipped.

"Friends?" said Art. "Perhaps. But business rules. Your fun days ended when you left the old team."

"I didn't leave," said Jud. "They threw me off. Unstable, reductions in force: which of their stories do you want?"

Art sipped his coffee. "You should have picked your time to leave them, not the other way around."

Casually, as if this were a social breakfast, Art said, "Did the firm pay you much when you were playing locksmith in Washington, black-bagging embassies and other places?"

"I wasn't working for them then," lied Jud.

"Who did you hang out with in D.C.?" asked Art.

"You got a problem?" said Jud. *To defend, attack:* "You want dates with the women in D.C. I fucked or what?"

"If the *or what* matters." Art's gaze was flat. "Did someone send you to look for me?"

Jud frowned. "Are you nuts?"

"That's your reputation."

The two men laughed. The biker behind Jud joined their sanctioned mirth. The Vietnamese and Raul kept silent.

"I found you on my own," said Jud. "You bought that then because it was true, because it made sense, and because I could run security for your program."

"But you're walking away from this good deal, just when we're expanding to ten planes of weed a month."

"Not my fault about the crash," said Jud.

"I believe that," said Art. "It was only a matter of time until a plane went down in the Glades. It was coincidence that you were on it. Or convenience."

"I didn't find it *convenient*," snapped Jud.

"The police did. They found your driver's license on an empty C-130 with enough stems and seeds to make a case. They picked you up in your penthouse, no problem."

"You don't kill cops," said Jud, "you buy 'em."

"Killing's never bothered you before." Art shook his head. "That's so unlike you: in the field unsanitized, dropping nondeniable gear."

He rang a silver bell. The servant cleared the plates. Art leaned back and turned his sunglasses up to the sky.

"Hot," he said.

"It's Miami," answered Jud.

"I talked to the Italians," said Art. "They said no one was ever able to buy that judge before."

Jud's neck tingled. "Nobody ever met his price before."

"How did you come up with a million and a quarter?"

"The lawyer handled it."

"Ah, lawyers. Where would we be without them?"

The two men sat in the heat. Watching each other.

Art spoke first. "So much money passed through your hands and never stuck. You've wasted a fortune—penthouse, Porsches, pussy."

Jud laughed, and Art laughed with him.

"I'll get by," said Jud.

"You're broke, but you want to go."

"I don't want to, I've got no choice."

"*If* you're right about those cops being pissed off because you walked away. That they want revenge or other meat."

"You think I'd roll over on you?" said Jud.

"Would you?"

Art's sunglasses never left the sky.

"I'm not that stupid," said Jud truthfully.

In the shadows, Raul grinned.

For the first time that morning, Art truly smiled. "What would they say about us back on the old team, eh?"

The blond man's smoked glasses stared at Jud.

"You never know what they think," said Jud.

"They're insulated," said Art, "not inscrutable."

Raul spit on the veranda.

"Who ran the show?" asked Jud.

"Don't you know?" asked Art.

They laughed again, neither willing to give an inch.

"You're glad to be done with guys like that," said Jud.

"Who says I'm done with them?"

"You like your own game too much," said Jud. "You're too deep in it, and too smart to mix plays."

"You know that, do you?"

"Yes."

"But do they?"

"What does it matter?" asked Jud. *Change the subject.* "I've got loose ends to tie up. I'll exfilt day after tomorrow."

"Where are you going?"

"Boston." Jud shrugged. "Connections. No heat."

"You should be more of a lizard," said Art.

"Gecko, right?"

"Yes," said Art, remembering with Jud.

Jud stood, carefully keeping his hands in view. He carried no gun, wore no sports jacket over his shirt. Art rose with him. So did the Vietnamese. Raul kept his chair.

"Come by for lunch tomorrow." Art shook Jud's hand with a firm, dry grip. "I want to give you some traveling cash."

"No need for that," said Jud.

"If you don't take care of your people," said Art, "they don't take care of you."

"Yes, Captain."

"Besides, you remember Heather's friend? The redhead with the tight ass?" Art grinned. "I've arranged to send you away with a bang."

All the men on the veranda laughed. Jud waved good-bye, took his time walking through the house with its Baccarat crystal and abstract art. Three Dobermans were locked in the study. The two bodyguards he'd hired for Art wished him well. The teenage blonde who was too cool to have been a cheerleader strolled to the French windows leading to the pool. She wore a bikini.

"See you tomorrow," she said.

*Do you know you're a liar?* wondered Jud.

He didn't worry about starting the silver Porsche. Parked this close to Art's home, they wouldn't have bombed it. Even in Miami, 1978, that was too bold.

Jud drove south on Collins, cut over to Ocean Drive, where scrawny, gray-haired men sat on the porches of tourist homes, staring out at the waves, not hearing the women chatter.

His mirrors showed no one on his trail.

*Be cool,* he thought. *The heat's making you crazy. Art knows nothing. Kerns wasn't in the gazebo, all those guns were there just because. Besides, you'll be gone in six hours, cover Art's curiosity with a phone call: Had to leave early, sayonara.*

He flipped on the radio, cycled the band from the newly labeled genre of light rock to Latin disco to jazz; left it on jazz, a cool saxophone. He rolled up his windows, used the A.C.

*"There are no losers,"* Art had said in Tehran.

The drive between Art's house and Jud's hotel averaged forty-two minutes, from the exclusive homes of Miami Beach, through blocks of decaying grandeur, past downtown's glass and steel buildings that housed CIA airlines and malls where most Miamians couldn't afford to shop. The route passed ornate doors of banks headquartered in Hong Kong and Manhattan and Switzerland. Jud had made the trip a hundred times in the eleven months he'd been in Miami. So had Art.

On Fifth Street, a faded cardboard Santa Claus dangled on a wire strung between a light pole and a palm tree by the freeway.

*Ten minutes,* Jud thought. *I've been driving ten minutes.* He loved his silver Porsche. The radio announced a selection by a group called Hiroshima.

*If* . . .

Jud pulled to the curb a block from the freeway ramp.

*If,* Art wouldn't do it himself. Too risky. A long shot could work, *an Oswald,* but only Kerns had the gun, and if he missed . . . Raul or the biker or the Vietnamese couldn't cowboy it with shotguns and Uzis, Jud might spot them, dodge the play. Same with other guns in the organization. Art could contract Colombian shooters or Raul's Cuban friends, but Art believed day labor was unreliable. He wouldn't farm it to the Italians, give them a handle on a fellow *paesano's* business. As the CIA hits on Castro had proved, esoteric stuff such as poison was for the funny papers.

*"I talked to the Italians . . . ,"* Art had said.

Why? Art wouldn't have asked them *unless* he suspected. He didn't believe the judge buy. He went to the Italians to satisfy his suspicions, one way or the other.

Twelve minutes since Jud had left Art's. Raul's being there made sense. But the biker, the Vietnamese, the regular two thugs, *and* Kerns in the gazebo: too many guns for a friend.

*"Did someone send you to look for me?"* Art craved certainty. He believed Jud wouldn't roll over on him—but Jud was walking away broke. Like a loser, and there are no losers, especially not Jud, which meant . . .

"Ungood," said Jud, remembering.

Thirteen minutes. Jud's mirrors were empty. Heat waves skittered paper trash down the empty sidewalk.

The Special Forces file on Art Monterastelli noted he was trained as an expert in demolitions.

*"Send you away with a bang . . ."*

Fourteen minutes and Jud got out of the Porsche, hurried to the doorway of a boarded-up bar. *Damn it!* He wanted a drink—to pass the time, he told himself, not because of his hands or his thirst. This was the end, the exfiltration blues, the last riff of the sax. He'd play out the paranoia, let it tick off the clock for say, an hour, drive away laughing and pick up—

The explosion blew the doors off the silver Porsche, shattering glass, flying metal, the gas tank erupting with a roaring orange fireball, another black cloud billowing over Miami.

In three hours, Jud had grabbed his cash stash, bought a used car, and hit Highway 1 south to the Keys. Strategic retreat. He went to ground in a seedy hotel halfway to Key West. Bone fishermen filled the other cabins; they paid no attention to him. He coded his report that Monterastelli was a drug dealer *only*, no hostile contacts or connections, no evidence of national security leaks, no hint that he'd betrayed the team to anyone. Other than using his government-perfected skills and experience to smuggle marijuana, bribe, profit, and murder, Art was clean.

In his report, Jud included the story from the *Miami Herald* about a Porsche exploding as it neared the freeway.

*Burned,* he reported. The judge in the scam was probably safe, heavy to hit and no risk to Art, but *watch him, warn him:* Monterastelli craved certainty.

Jud used the motel stationery. *Let them know where I am, let them come see me, face-to-face, let them tell me what to do.* His report requested orders. He mailed it to the Maryland postal box, bought two fifths of Scotch, and stayed out of sight.

A week later, the grizzled motel owner brought him a letter postmarked New York.

The envelope contained a follow-up story from the *Herald* reporting that nobody had been in the Porsche when it blew and a sheet of white paper with three printed words:

*Your option. ED*

Jud sat on the lumpy bed. Art knew he wasn't dead. Art believed in *no losers.* Art craved certainty—the certainty contained in the words "expedited demise." Jud thought about all that. He thought about geckos, when it was time to leave, what was the best way to go. Just before dark, he crumpled his mail into a paper ball in the glass ashtray. Lit it with a motel match.

For two days he cruised the Keys, buying his gear, testing it in the mango swamps off Route 1. Art knew Jud's patterns, knew Jud excelled at close-in work. Jud checked the weather, astronomical charts, drove back to Miami.

Waited until dark. Until midnight. There was no moon, no storm expected.

The inflatable, dark-blue swimming-pool raft buoyed Jud in his black wet suit as he paddled down the canal, past the lights of wealthy homes, past blue lamps marking private docks. Laughter floated over the water; a married couple bickering; the sounds of television, cars. He worried each time he drifted under a bridge, but no one saw him. Once a motorboat, lights out, racing inland, passed within ten feet of him, but whoever was aboard was too intent scanning the shoreline for threats to notice Jud's silent passage.

At one-thirty, he reached the cluster of stubby pilings. The last slab of the burned dock screened him from the lawyer's house. He lashed his raft and waterproof bag to a fire-blackened post with bungee cords, used more bungees to hold the rifle steady against the wood. Jud squinted through the scope sight: Art's windows were dark.

Charred wood, creosote, pungent water, filled Jud's nostrils as the waves lapped around him. Filth floated past. All night Jud rolled with the waves, just enough out of the water to breathe the salty, wet air and watch the dark shore.

Dawn came on time. The heat. Jud's skin became clammy and tepid with the water. Only his head showed above the choppy surface, a black-hooded bump next to stubby pilings a quarter mile up the waterway from Art's dock. From Art's veranda, it was barely possible to see a dark ball bobbing by the charred wood and the flat line of *something* lashed parallel to the gray-green water.

Art's lawn sloped up from sea level. His veranda was higher off the water than a man. The house had two stories above that. At seven, Jud's binoculars showed curtains fluttering on the second floor. They parted briefly, and he saw the girl. Naked. She turned to say something to someone in the bedroom.

At 8:20, Raul stepped onto the veranda. Jud hugged the piling. Raul went back inside.

At 9:11, Raul came back out on the veranda. He scanned the lawn: the mines were armed. His eyes flicked to the canal, saw no boats. He turned and called into the house. Jud hugged the thick piling with his legs, fitted his shoulder to the rifle stock, reached around the wood to push the bungee-tight barrel until the cross hairs in the scope lined up with . . .

Art Monterastelli, former Green Beret captain, former spy, walking out the French doors, crossing to the railing, a china cup of sweet Cuban coffee in his hand as he joined Raul.

The high-powered bullet slammed into Art—a marble going into his chest, baseball blasting out his back, crashing through the French windows, blood spraying the white walls before the *crack* of the rifle shot reached the veranda.

Through the scope, Jud saw Raul's jaw fall open. The Cuban glanced toward the corpse on the veranda; flinched as though he were about to dive for cover.

But instead, Raul froze: no second bullet had come. There'd been time. Jud's finger was damp on the curved metal trigger, the cross hairs were on Raul's heart.

The Cuban stared toward the pilings. Through the telescopic sight, Jud watched Raul turn, nod to the corpse, look back. Shrug.

And smile. Raul fished a cigarette out of his suit jacket. Lit up, stood tall by the rail, smoking: a clean shot and a clear deal.

Raul didn't move even when he saw the dark form swim through the pilings, scurry to dry land, run away.

By sunset, Jud was in North Carolina. By dawn, Virginia. By noon the next day, he'd reached the interstate-highway Beltway encircling Washington, D.C.

Nick Kelley was somewhere in the city.

*Don't let us run into each other,* thought Jud.

He stopped at a gas station for a map, ran his finger down the list of outlying Maryland towns: Bethesda, Chevy Chase, Rockville . . . Saunders.

Saunders, Maryland, was an American classic, a crossroads town with two gas stations, a general store, a dozen houses, some cornfields, and a brick-and-glass post office. In that year of 1978, Baltimore and Washington were growing into one another, swallowing the towns between them that had once been surrounded by cornfields. Saunders had five years left before no fields separated it from the capital city.

The gas station across from the post office was boarded up, a victim of the first Arab oil embargo. Jud scouted the town, then drove to a hardware store where he dipped into his last thousand dollars to buy a ladder, paint, rollers and brushes, overalls.

In North Carolina, Jud had mailed a birthday card in an oversize red envelope to the post office box in Saunders, Maryland. He used too few stamps and counted on the mail's being slow.

The clerk in the Saunders General Store was surprised that someone had hired Jud to paint the deserted gas station, but neither she nor anyone else in the town pursued their curiosity beyond idle gossip about how slowly that man worked, how he always seemed to be watching the post office and not the walls.

At eight A.M. on his third day of painting, a clean-cut, coat-and-tied man in his twenties parked a shiny blue sedan with D.C. plates in the post office lot. The young man put on sunglasses, marched his spit-shined shoes inside. Jud climbed the ladder leaning against the gas station, stared through the government windows as Spit Shine went to the wall where that post office box was. Got something from a box, took it to the postal counter. The clerk handed Spit Shine an oversize red envelope.

When Spit Shine pulled his sedan out of the parking lot, the ladder leaning against the gas station was empty, the paint roller was on the ground. And Jud was in his car, behind him.

*An officer,* thought Jud. *An eager lieutenant. An unbloodied gofer grubbing for brownie points.*

Instead of going to the Pentagon or Ft. Meade, the blue sedan headed toward Annapolis. Country highways, rolling fields, other small towns waiting to be eaten by suburbs. Highways became gravel roads. Jud's heart slammed against his ribs.

The blue sedan went down a long gravel road, pulled into a driveway. Jud rolled past, parked, ran back in time to see Spit Shine standing at the front door of the house, handing the red envelope to a short man in civilian clothes. Spit Shine marched back to the sedan, held the back door open.

The man in the civilian suit put on his glasses. Opened the envelope, read Jud's terse *plainspeak* report:

*Option ED completed.*

Spit Shine drove the man away. Hidden, Jud watched.

He waited until the mail truck made its delivery to the silver box at the end of the driveway. No one came out of the house to get the mail. No one saw Jud steal it.

Circulars, fund-raisers, junk mail, and a personal letter—all addressed to the name Jud had never known.

*Got you.*

Very carefully, Jud opened the personal letter. It was on embossed stationery from a foundation, thanking the general for agreeing to speak at the foundation's Patriotism Day dinner, discussing his honorarium, thanking him for sending his official biography and picture for their newsletter and saving them the trouble of making that request of the Pentagon.

Later that day, Jud called the Pentagon public affairs office, told the officer who answered the phone that he was the editor of the foundation's newsletter, asked for a copy of the general's bio and photograph, and had the PAO release it to a messenger "so we can make our deadline." By the day's close of business, Jud had resealed and remailed the foundation's letter and paid the messenger for the picture and bio of the man who'd commanded Jud's life for a decade.

"No more," Jud told the smiling official photo as he sat in his car. The Beltway was only a few blocks away.

A pay phone hung on a gas station's wall. Nick Kelley was a local call. An old friend. But Jud didn't want to talk to Nick, didn't want to see him. Not until he was clear.

The gas station postcard showed a full moon rising over the Capitol dome and Washington Monument. On its back, Jud scrawled *Sayonara*. Signed it *Malice*. Addressed it to the post office box in Saunders, Maryland.

When Jud dropped the postcard in a corner mailbox, the world fell from his shoulders: no more orders, no more messages in newspapers, no more phone calls, no more illusionary options that all added up to ED—*expedited demise*. He was free, he was done, he was gone. Casper. And now that he had the name of *the man*, Jud was certain he could stay that way.

"Fuck you, General," said Jud. "My turn now."

He pointed his car west, ran away for the first time; ran toward something better.

Twelve years later, in 1990, he ran a second time. To Nora. And then a third.

*In a red car,* Jud realized he was in a red car. On the road.

Nora was dead.

Las Vegas rose out of the desert, neon glittering in the daylight. Jud drove by a casino with a fire-belching volcano constructed in its parking lot. Nora had worked in the casinos, in the hotels. Jud had cut deals with sharp-suited men in the same type of suits where she'd turned tricks.

Airport, he pulled into the airport. Parking lot, the first empty space. A handicapped spot. The blue airline bag with his money was still around his neck. He left his white apron on the red car's front seat, couldn't think clearly enough to search the suitcase or briefcase someone had left in the car.

Jud didn't see the two dusty sedans pulling into the lot behind him, scrambling to find parking places as he stumbled through the sliding glass doors into the air-conditioned terminal.

Drifting, flowing with the crowd, bells dinging from slot machines, the excited babble of tour groups arriving, the quiet shuffle of those headed home.

A bar. Jud bought three shots in four minutes, was about to order again when he realized the bartender was staring at him. *Noticing* him. Jud stumbled back into the stream of airport people.

A counter, a line, a woman in a blue uniform behind a computer terminal asking him questions.

"What?" mumbled Jud.

"Can I help you, sir?" she said, sniffing him: Scotch and a burnt smell she couldn't place. "Do you want a ticket?"

"Where?"

She blinked.

"The next plane," he said.

"The plane to Chicago?" she asked.

"When does it leave?"

"You've cut it close." She punched keys, asked him for his credit card. She shook her head as he counted out the cash. "Do you have any luggage?"

But he only stared.

"Must have been rough at the tables." She handed him his ticket, pointed to a Jetway door. "They're holding the plane."

On board, he couldn't stop crying, shaking. The stewardess wouldn't serve him more than three drinks. Other passengers pretended he wasn't there, counted their blessings.

It was a misty night in Chicago. At Midway Airport, Jud had two more drinks, drifted into a line for a limousine service to swank city hotels, bought the eight-dollar ticket, and got on the van.

Forty minutes later, he was wandering the vast glass-and-steel canyons of a rebuilding city. He answered the blinking red neon summons to an old brick hotel, put enough money on the counter for the sullen desk clerk to give him a room key. Beefy men in leather raincoats and custom-cut suits glared at Jud when he went into the hotel coffee shop. He ate the first thing on the menu, a cabbage-sweet Irish stew.

His room was small and brown and dusty. He stared at the thin floral bedspread. Went back into the night.

The blue bag had forty-six dollars left in it. Eight of them bought a fifth of whiskey. The cork was out of the bottle before Jud was out of the bar. He shuffled through the city, looking for nothing, stepping into the shadows when blue-lighted police cruisers rolled past. An elevated train clattered by. The world spun: he leaned against the board fence of a construction site, threw up. When his eyes cleared, he saw his hand pressed against the brown wood beside black-lettered gang graffiti: *P.V.P.s* and

*Vice Lords.* Farther down the wood, someone had scrawled *Hog Butcherer.*

A civic plaza was catercorner from his hotel. Rising through the night mist from the plaza's marble square was an iron rusted black monster, a looming Picasso beast of poles and wings and eyes.

Jud staggered, his blurry vision full of the beast. His calves hit a chain, and he turned: an orange flame flickered from a burner in the earth. The brass plaque dedicated an eternal flame to the war dead of Korea and Vietnam.

And Jud howled, his anguish and anger echoing through the civic plaza.

The beast was silent.

Until that night, in Jud's dreams, it roared in fire and woke him shaking, trembling, sweating, and filthy, and he knew he couldn't stay still any longer, knew he had to run.

Realized where he had to go. Whom he had to see.

Before dawn, he stole a car parked on State Street, found his way to the freeways of America.

# THE BURNING VILLAGE

The morning after Nora died, Wes charged into Noah Hall's office at CIA headquarters. Noah and Denton's secretary, Mary, looked up from a file-covered desk.

"Where's the Director?" yelled Wes.

Noah hurried around the desk. Mary glided toward a door.

"Where are you going?" Wes called to her. "I want—"

Noah grabbed his arm. Wes knocked Noah's hand away, cocked his fist, and barely checked his swing. Noah didn't flinch.

*"In the hall!"* he whispered, touching his ear, nodding to the walls.

It was 7:47 A.M. Outside, a steady stream of cars checked through the main gate as America's shadow warriors reported for another Tuesday of work. The carpeted seventh-floor corridor was silent. Empty. Except for Wes and Noah, standing toe to toe.

"I need to see the Director," said Wes. "Now!"

"Who the fuck are you?" snapped Noah. "Middle of the night, a Deputy Director at the FBI calls me up, says that *our man* has been abusing Bureau personnel through an NIS loan-out."

"Noah—"

"They picked you up at a diner in East Jesus Nowhere right after some civilians get shot to shit. Bureau said you didn't even stick around to inform the local—"

*"I covered your fuckin' ass!"* yelled Wes, ramming his forefinger into Noah's chest. "I almost had him! This close! They lost him at the Vegas airport."

"What is this?" said Noah. "Post-Vietnam traumatic stress *bat-*

*shit?* You burning the village to save it? We give you a low-profile, fully legal task, and you lay waste to California!"

"I'm doing my job," said Wes.

"Must be," answered Noah, "'cause you ain't doing ours."

A cold chill seemed to sweep down the secret hallway, envelop Wes. Suddenly he felt alone. Naked.

"I'm going to see Denton—*now.*"

"He's at a classified location."

Wes took a deep breath, closed his burning eyes. He hadn't slept on the night flight from Vegas. "What do you want?"

*"We* want this shit *over.* We wanted to know if there was a problem, and brother, you created one. You're done."

"You don't have that authority," said Wes.

Noah blinked.

"Denton hired me, he fires me. Full responsibility, coming and going. You aren't going to buffer him."

Down the hall, a door opened. General Cochran stepped into the hall to peer at them through his thick-lensed glasses.

Noah showed bulldog teeth as he whispered, "Whether you believe it or not, your ass is through. Whether you come out of this *at all* depends on whether we come out of it *clean.*"

"If I don't keep going, *nobody* will come out of this clean," threatened Wes.

Billy Cochran settled his glasses on his nose.

Noah leaned as close as he could to Wes. "You want a stake through your heart, you open your mouth—to *anybody!*"

The carpet muffled Billy's steps as he came toward them.

"Gentlemen"–he nodded—"is there some problem?"

"Don't worry about it," said Noah, his eyes on Wes. "We got everything under control—right, Major?"

Then he smiled and went back into his office.

"You're here early," Billy told Wes.

"Yes sir." Wes saw his bruised, haggard reflection distorted in Billy's thick glasses.

"Come to my office," said the number two official of the CIA. "The galley provides me with fine coffee."

Billy turned to walk away; saw Wes hesitate.

"It's an invitation, Major," said the general, "not an order. What do you have to lose?"

They sat at the small table in the corner of Billy's office, Wes on the edge of the couch, Billy in the chair, a silver pot and china cups between them. Coffee sweetened the air.

"Peculiar weather," said Billy.

"Yes sir," said Wes. *What do you want?*

"'Sir'? Rank has been rendered moot between us. You're out of uniform and not plugged into this command structure."

"Sir, those are the requirements of my assignment."

"This isn't the time to dissect your assignment's requirements. I'm concerned with its consequences."

Billy leaned forward, arms on his legs, frankness on his face. "Just because you were hired by Mr. Denton and Mr. Hall—"

"I don't work for Noah Hall," Wes insisted quickly.

Billy's words were soft: "Something happened near Las Vegas."

"I'm not disposed to talk about that—sir. But I'd appreciate it if you could tell me where I can find Mr. Denton."

"He's finishing up a working dinner in West Germany."

"Shit."

"The menu is more creative than that," said Billy. "German reunification, the fate of NATO, rumblings in Lithuania.

"But here and now," said Billy, "I'm concerned about you.

"This isn't like Vietnam," said Billy, and Wes remembered the general's sometimes-limp, the medals in his drawer. "This business often lacks clarity."

"The jungle was thick there."

"Not as thick as in Washington. That's why there are procedures. Especially since these last few years when men like us got so far out on assignment that unfortunate incidents occurred. We are about national security. What's ultimately crucial to the national security is that the system is maintained."

"What do you want from me?" asked Wes.

"It's not a question of what I want," said Billy. "Being out of the loop is not a blank license or a pardon. If things happened, if there's an ongoing crisis, the best thing would be for you to unburden yourself—through the system."

"Mea culpa," said Wes.

"If a confession is called for." Billy shrugged. "Though I doubt all guilt is yours."

"Have you ever unburdened yourself like that?" said Wes.

"I've never felt the need." Billy shook his head. "Look at you. Battered. Exhausted. That tells me two things:

"First, you're doing something too important to be off the books. Second, your judgment has been stressed—perhaps bent beyond its limits and capabilities.

"Unless you use our communications system, you are unable to securely report to Mr. Denton. I'm second-in-command of American intelligence. Very little is outside my purview. Let me help you. We can bring in the General Counsel. Our security people. You are a part of a good team, Major, trust that."

After a minute, Wes quietly asked, "Sir, in all your operations, did you ever use current or ex–Special Forces men?"

"Major, your job is not to inquire after my history."

"You've been a part of American intelligence a long time, sir. Like you said, very little is outside your purview."

"Apparently you choose to be." Billy nodded toward the door.

The car was parked at Wes's corner, a gray sedan with antennae on its trunk. Three men in suits were sitting in the car.

Wes saw them as he drove up his street; slowed down as he ran the options. Then gunned his engine and parked in the white-striped loading zone. He ran to the building's front doors, ignored a man shouting, *"Chandler!"*

Up the stairs, three at a time. When she was nursing him, Beth had given Wes a key to her apartment. He'd kept it, been proud she hadn't asked for it back. Now it was his luck.

Not knocking, unlocking her door, yelling her name and getting *no answer* as he unclipped the Sig's holster from his belt, put the gun on the table by the door, dropped his briefcase with its money and documents on the floor, and stepped back into the hall, turning the key and locking her apartment.

Downstairs, the building doors opened.

*Ammunition clips.* They weighed down his suit jacket as he hurried inside his apartment. *Prove nothing. Are legal.*

He had time to register the bare facts of *home.*

Pounding on his door. "Major Chandler! Open up! NIS."

He opened it. Credentials out, they stepped inside without being invited. Wes didn't know these agents.

"You didn't stop when we hollered," said Agent One.

"Nobody yelled, 'Halt, police,'" said Wes.

"Where you been, Major?" said Agent Two.

"The CIA—you want to call them?"

They looked at each other. *Bad form*, thought Wes. *Now I know you're not sure.*

Agent Three drifted toward Wes's bedroom.

"Do you have a warrant?" said Wes, halting him.

"What kind of warrant?"

"Any kind," said Wes. "Otherwise, you're invited only into the living room."

"I thought we were all on the same team," said Agent Two.

"I'm on detached duty to a project classified above you."

"Gosh," said Agent Three flatly.

"Where you been, Major?" said Agent One. "Las Vegas?"

"I told you who to call."

"Where's your gun?"

"What gun?"

"The one you brought to the range. The one you got the commander to authorize you to carry."

"That's none of your business."

"Mind if we help you look for it?"

"Got a warrant?"

Agents One and Two laughed.

"Ask him about the money," said Agent One, but Agent Three just shook his head.

"We could help each other here," he said.

"How's that?" answered Wes.

"You're our boy—don't matter about 'detached duty' to anywhere, you're NIS. Hell, you're a Marine: that's Navy. That's us. You fuck up, we clean up. You need help . . ."

He shrugged. "Here we are."

"I need you, I'll call you. You need something from me, run it through Greco, he'll let me know."

"Greco sent us," said Agent Two.

The four men watched each other for a long count.

"You tell Frank to ask his own questions," said Wes.

"Why don't you tell him?" said Agent One. "He's waiting to see you."

"Did he send you three musketeers to bring me in?"

"He knew you were feeling poorly," said Agent One.

"You look like shit," said Agent Two.

Agent One shrugged. "He figured you might need a ride."

"I'll call you if I do," said Wes. "Now your invitation is withdrawn. Get out of here. I need some sleep."

The NIS agents exchanged a look. Agent Two shrugged.

"Sweet dreams," he said, leading the others to the door.

Agent Three was the last one out. Before he left, he looked back. "I'd go see Frank soon. Real soon."

They closed the door behind them.

*How long do I have?* thought Wes. Denton and Noah were waffling, afraid of scandal and anxious for a scapegoat, but if Wes brought Jud in, *justified* the desert fiasco . . .

From his window, he saw that the gray car hadn't left.

*Think!*

But his mind was full of Beth and bullets slamming into Dean, the woman in the blood-soaked blouse sprawled behind the café, the Mexican woman he'd left sobbing in that kitchen, standing in the Las Vegas airport, feeling stupid and hollow, shabby FBI foot soldiers shuffling nervously by his side, and Beth, *God,* how he wanted to hear her voice.

That he knew for sure, Wes had killed six men:

A grenade tossed into a foxhole where two VC were unjamming their machine gun. One man screamed for thirty-four minutes.

Two NVA regulars who'd materialized out of the bush, just as stunned as he'd been by the sight of *the enemy* but slower to swing their rifles up; to fire.

A long, lucky shot across a rice paddy, *bang dead* into an NVA officer picking up a radio phone to report the lost Marine patrol Captain Wes had gone into the bush to find.

Dean.

*No more.* Head aching, sour stomach. *Please, no more.*

Beth.

He lifted his kitchen wall phone, heard the dial tone as his eyes filled with the comfort of *home,* the familiar safety of—

His baseball, the one he'd grand-slam-home-runned into the bleachers at the Army game his senior year at the Academy, the one his teammates had autographed and that he kept on a pedestal next to a row of books on the top shelf in the living room.

It had been moved to the other end of the book row.

*Beep beep beep beep beep*—Wes hung up the phone.

Stared at it. *His* phone. *His* home.

The gray car hadn't moved.

*Beth's.* He was in her apartment in seconds, leaning against her closed door, panting for air.

*Easy.* Easy.

His holstered gun waited on a table by the door, his briefcase was on the floor. A phone sat on the kitchen counter. Information gave him the number of the Freer Gallery.

"I'm sorry, sir," said the Freer switchboard woman, "no one by that name works here."

"What?"

"No one by that name is on our staff list."

"You must be . . . Beth Doyle—*D* as in *Delta.*"

"I know, sir. She's not at the Freer. Have you tried the Smithsonian museums?"

"She's an archivist. With the Oriental Arts Foundation."

"No foundation like that is affiliated with the Freer."

"But you do have an archivist."

"I'll check with him."

*She'll laugh her husky laugh,* thought Wes, joke about bureaucracy and how tired I sound.

"Sir?" said the switchboard operator. "The archivist says Beth Doyle doesn't work for him."

Wes slammed down the phone.

The walls were close in this apartment she'd sublet from a government lawyer catapulted to a sudden emergency *somewhere out of town.* Beth moved in . . .

After Denton created this mission.

Wes blinked; looked with eyes and not his heart.

The apartment smelled of stale cigarette smoke. Her drafting table filled the living room—but she wasn't enrolled in architecture school yet, her classes in engineering were night school, adult ed with no prerequisite background checks. The walls were hung with the lawyer's art—that was his poster of the whale's tail sliding back into the waves. The lawyer's suits still hung in the bedroom closet, pushed aside for her skirts and slacks.

Wes roamed the apartment. There were no pictures of her, none of her family or friends, ex-lovers or ex-roommates. No souvenirs of Thailand or Nepal—he knew she'd been there, she couldn't have faked all she'd told him. No remembrances of Germany, and what had she done there? Worked for discos? She said she'd swum in Berlin's public pool, fat people all around in the cool blue chlorine. Who had she worked for? For who else?

None of the mail on the desk in the living room was addressed to her. Even that month's phone bill bore the lawyer's name: no need to change, as long as the checks kept coming. Wes ripped open the envelope.

The bill covered her early days here: no long-distance phone calls to a foundation or Mother or sisters or brothers or Dad at his office, no trace that she had anyone to call.

Two shelves held her books—physics and engineering text-books, a half dozen paperback novels, an art book on Japanese architecture, poetry books by Emily Dickinson and Carolyn Forche. He flipped the pages in every volume: nothing fell out and he left the books where he dropped them.

Notebooks: sketches, drawings, rough plans—but not too many, none too old.

An address book, she had an address book—that she always carried with her.

He opened the closet: two suitcases and a shoulder bag had her name tags—no addresses. He threw them into the living room, pulled her coats off hangers and searched their pockets, threw them on the couch: spare change, matches, pocket litter.

In Recon, Wes always made sure his patrols carried nothing that would betray them.

Kitchen drawers full of knives, desk drawers with only the lawyer's papers, sparse supplies in the refrigerator. Back to the bedroom, her landlord's clothes in three drawers, tossing out her underwear—no bras, just panties, soft and pink and white. Socks, a couple pair of panty hose, two silk scarves. Where was her jewelry? Sweaters on the closet's top shelf: he mashed each one, tossed them onto the bed. Nothing hidden in the toes of her shoes. He threw them aside. The bed table: books, an ashtray, coffee congealed in a cup. Nothing under the bed, under the mattress. The bathroom: few cosmetics, a brush, comb. Aspirin in the medicine cabinet, a bottle of Valium prescribed by a New York doctor and birth control pills.

A long brown hair lay in the white sink.

But nothing to prove who she was, nothing to prove who she wasn't. Didn't matter if she'd given him a key.

The bathroom was bright: white walls, the sink and the shower stall, the chrome drainpipes. The mirror on the medicine cabinet showed him his face, bruised and pale and haunted.

The toilet lid was closed. Wes collapsed on it.

And cried. Silently at first, a tear trickling down his cheek, then a gasp and he couldn't stop, shaking, hugging himself, trembling against the wall.

Ten, fifteen minutes. He caught his breath. Felt his cheeks dry, felt the tile pressed against the side of his head. Tasted the salt and the phlegm on his lips, the tang of lemon-scented bathroom air.

Heard the *click* of the front-door lock.

He was in the living room, watching her back into the apartment, a grocery sack in each hand, turning, seeing him . . .

"Wes!" She smiled. "When did you . . ."

Then Beth saw her coats heaped on the couch, the books on the floor, her sketches scattered across the drawing table. The grocery bags slid to her feet. She wore a belt bag for a purse. A briefcase hung from one shoulder; it fell beside the grocery bags. She wore corduroy slacks and a sweater, a long black coat. Her brown hair was brushed, her widow's peak prominent, and she wore no makeup on her wide gray eyes, no lipstick.

"What . . ." She shook her head. "What happened?"

"Who are you?" whispered Wes.

"What?" She frowned at him. Stepped closer.

His gun was on the table just behind her.

"Who are you?" he said, louder, keeping her eyes on him.

"I don't . . ." She drifted closer to him, her gaze flitting from side to side, seeing the chaos of her home but still not seeing the gun. She blinked. "Did . . . Did you do this?"

"Why did you come here?" he said.

"I live here." She shook her head. "Wes, what's wrong?"

"You tell me."

They were close. She reached out to touch him. Stopped.

"You aren't here," he told her. "There's nothing *real* of you here: no pictures, no letters, no *life*. It's all props. Usable. Functional. Believable."

"You went through my things!" she whispered. She shuddered. Her hand fell to her side, and she shrank back.

Like a Marine officer, he said, "Who do you work for?"

"You know! I—"

"I called the Freer. They've never heard of you."

"What?"

"They never heard of your 'foundation' either."

"I was there today! I'm getting groceries during lunch!"

Wes shook his head.

"Jeannie," she said, "the switchboard lady—she's a ditz! An officious ditz! You don't ask her exactly right, she doesn't tell you! She's a slot machine, a crazy—"

"The archivist said you didn't work for him."

"I don't! I'm on a fellowship and I've barely met— Did you talk to him?" When Wes didn't answer, her face lit up. "You didn't! If you would have—"

"You're good, aren't you?"

*"Good?"* She shook her head. "I love you!"

"Was that your idea? Or were you just supposed to fuck me?"

Beth covered her mouth; her eyes glistened and he heard her gag.

"You went through my stuff when I was asleep," he said.

"I . . . You *asshole!* I went through *your* stuff!? What were you . . . What are you looking for? Is this . . . sick, kinky, crazy . . . What did you expect? What do you want?"

"Who's paying you? How much? Civil service? Contract? Off the books? Or did you get jammed up in Thailand or Germany or New Jersey and they bailed you out and you're working it off?"

"Jesus!" She backed away from this bruised stranger. The fire in his deep-set black eyes flushed her face. "You . . . I thought . . . And I was worried about whether you'd *run,* whether you'd find somebody else or fuck somebody else or I'd drive you crazy . . ."

She shook her head. "Is that it? You're crazy? Some sick Marine *fuck* who gets his kicks, control . . .

*"Damn you!"* she yelled, and ran at him, slapping him, hitting his chest, his face, his arms, as he grabbed her shoulders and pushed her away and she staggered back toward the door.

"Going to beat me?" she said. "Rape me? Wasn't it good enough when I wanted you?"

A coolness flowed through Wes, a pain, doubt, and he reached for her. "Beth . . ."

She backed away. Closer to the door.

"What's my crime?" she said. "That pictures lie and I want to remember the truth in my heart, not what some camera traps?

That trinkets get lost or stolen by a Baghdad window crawler or burn up and then it's worse than never having them? That my mom and sisters have been too busy to write me? What about my dad, huh? He's never written. Oh, that's a real sin! Let's beat the shit out of Beth. What did I do, scare you? Is that it? Love equals risk equals fear equals destroy?"

"I don't want to destroy you!" said Wes. "You . . ."

"Me?" She shook her head. "No, you: who *are* you?"

"What happened . . . ," he started to say as her eyes darted from side to side, seeking safety, seeking certainty.

Saw the gun.

Wes knew that she saw the gun, but he was rooted to the spot.

Slowly, she took a step. Reached out—plenty of time, Wes had plenty of time, but his feet were locked to the earth, his legs couldn't move, his arms too heavy as she *reached out* and picked up the gun.

Slid it from its holster.

"Is this it?" she whispered. "Is this what you do?"

She looked at him, her eyes wide. She held the gun toward him—held it awkwardly. The bore pointed into the kitchen. She took a step toward Wes.

"Is this for me?" she whispered.

*Nothing;* he tried and he could say *nothing.*

She was close. Close enough for him to grab the gun. He couldn't move. He couldn't speak. Couldn't take his eyes off her.

"Is this what it's all about?" she said. "This is for me? From you?"

The gun turned in her hand.

"Like this?" she said, and she held it by the barrel, its bore staring back at her. "Is this how it's supposed to be?

"Here?" she said, and slowly brought the barrel of the gun up until the bore where the bullets came out kissed the forehead below her widow's peak.

"This way?" she asked. "Is this what you meant when you said you loved me?

"Here?" She held the gun bore in front of her lips, so close her breath fogged the black metal Wes had polished.

"Here?" She pressed the gun bore to her heart, then lowered her arm, the steel trailing down her chest, her stomach.

"Here?" She pushed the gun bore against her vulva.

When she moved again, he thought eternity had passed. She pressed the gun into his grip.

"Then do it," she whispered, tears running down her cheeks. She turned and slowly walked to the door.

Stopped. Without looking back, she said, "You were right. This isn't my life."

Then she was gone, the door clicking behind her.

When he could move, he went back to his apartment.

The gray car was still parked out front.

He'd left his suitcase in his car. There'd be tickets on it by now: too long in the loading zone. He changed into jeans, sneakers. Packed clothes and toiletries into a duffel bag that he could carry in the same hand as the briefcase of money and documents. The holstered gun was clipped on his belt, covered by a black wind-breaker. He took a last look around this apartment.

Someone else lived there.

Wes went to the roof.

He stayed low, out of sight of the street. His stash of duplicate documents looked secure. The surveillance team would figure out he'd left this way. Perhaps some *they* would find his stash. Maybe Greco's people. Friendlies. Maybe. He crawled and climbed over the block of town-house roofs, dropped to an alley garage, then lowered himself to the pavement. And walked away.

There was nowhere left to go but forward.

Private investigator Jack Berns wore a silk bathrobe over his undershirt and jockey shorts when he opened his front door to Wes's repeated knocks.

"I ain't home," said Berns, swinging the door shut.

Wes slammed his shoulder into Berns's door and sent the private eye stumbing backward into his house.

"Sure you are," said Wes. "You been up all night, too?"

"You are fucking *gone*, Marine!" yelled Berns, pulling his robe closed. "You're history!"

Wes grabbed a fistful of bathrobe, pulled him close.

"I'm your history," he hissed at the smaller man.

"What the hell do you want?"

"You work for me—remember?"

"Are you an idiot? Don't you know?"

"Tell me," said Wes, keeping his grip on the bathrobe.

"There's a burn notice out on you," said the private eye. "All your spook friends, they'll get it today!"

"But you know now," said Wes. "How's that?"

"I, uh . . ."

"Who called you?" When no answer came, Wes slammed the smaller man against the wall. *"Who called you?"*

"Noah," blurted the detective, "last night, after you . . . After the FBI tweaked him. Damage control, you know?"

"I know a lot," said Wes. He pushed the man deeper into the house. Berns glanced at a table. An alarm, thought Wes, or a gun. But he knew Berns would try neither. "Down to your office."

"I told you—"

"I told *you*," said Wes.

Downstairs, the bathrobed man stood in his law-book lined study, trembling. Wes slowly circled round him.

"Noah called you," said Wes. "But you've been calling him, haven't you? All along. Everything I hired you to do, you reported to him."

"What's the big deal, huh?" said Berns, trying to keep his eyes on the crazed Marine who'd probably killed someone the day before. "He's your boss, he's—"

Wes's push almost knocked him over.

"I told you not to!" yelled Wes.

Berns regained his balance. Watched the madman circling him like a shark.

"Look," said Berns, "a guy's gotta do business."

"So you played me for Noah." The idea came slowly, grew as he walked around Berns's wary eyes: "Who else?"

"What?" Berns licked his lips.

"Who else did you sell me to? Sell whatever it was you knew I had, knew I was doing?"

"What do you—"

And Wes hit him, knocked him to the thick carpet.

Berns pushed himself along the floor until his back was against his desk. He wiped blood from his lip.

"You're through!" Berns spat through the blood. "Done! You're—"

Wes kicked him in the chest.

Wheezing, gasping for breath, Berns feebly batted at the arms that pulled him off the floor, bent him back across his desk.

*"Who else!"* bellowed Wes. "There's three people dead so far. You want to be number four? *Who else?"*

"I know 'eople all over," sputtered Berns. "People inside, people outside, people you can't even imagine. People who can get to you. Count your days, Major. Count your time."

"Not my job," said Wes. "But you . . . your *job:* you got the assignment from Noah to be my legman—and to spy on me for him. But that wasn't enough: you shopped around, found somebody else who cared. Or maybe they heard Agency gossip about us, came to you with a proposition. That doesn't matter. But *who?"*

"Fuck you. Goody flag boy like you won't kill me and you can't hurt me enough."

For a moment, Berns was wrong and they both felt that. But only for a moment. Wes jerked him off the desk and threw him against a book shelf.

"Denton and Noah are going to love it when I tell them you sold them out, too," said Wes.

"They're big boys, they knew me. I'm too valuable to lose and too slippery to squeeze. Besides, after your messing around, all they care about is putting the lid on. Loudmouth like me, they won't jerk my chain."

"What else have you done?" said Wes.

"Count your blessings, Major." Berns straightened his robe. "You might not die. Whatever this is, you fucked it up all to hell, but if Noah keeps it quiet, you might stay out of jail. Might even get to keep your uniform. If you keep your mouth shut and do what you're told. If I don't decide to fuck with you."

. . . *whatever this is* . . .

"You don't know," said Wes. "You don't know what this is all about."

Berns shrugged. "If you've got some ideas, know something . . . I'm the kind of guy who knows how to wheel and deal your way out of trouble."

"No," said Wes, "all we got left is simple business."

"We're through."

"You've been on Nick Kelley," said Wes. "How close?"

Berns wiped the blood from his mouth with the back of his hand. Shook his head no.

"You're right," said Wes, closing the distance between them. "I won't kill you. It's my weak heart. But I've got a strong stomach.

I've already lost more than just a few qualms about how I'll get where I'm going and what that'll cost a slime like you. I'll buy that you won't tell me everything. But you're a businessman. You'll sell me what you can to buy what you want. What you can buy is a lot less pain."

When Berns laughed, Wes hit him in the stomach. It took the private eye a full minute to regain his ability to talk:

"Close 'nough, know he's pokin' round. He doesn't have nothing. Couldn't."

"Then you'll leave him alone?"

Berns looked up. "Not my show, is it?"

"Come on," said Wes. "You got one more card to play."

Wes sat Berns at the desk, pushed the phone toward him.

"Your source in the phone company," said Wes. "I want all of Nick Kelley's long-distance calls since we last checked."

"Can't. This time 'month, he won't dare pop up the—"

Wes grabbed the private eye's left hand; broke his little finger. Berns threw up. Made the call. After he'd cajoled the source into risking a computer search, Wes took the phone and pushed him away. Wes listened: he was on hold.

A man's voice came back on, dictated a series of calls Wes wrote down: from Nick Kelley's office, calls to Nebraska.

When he was finished whispering the list into the phone, the source said, "Do you know what a risk I took? If—"

"Don't hang up!" said Wes. The man on the other end of the line froze at the sound of a stranger's voice. "I'm a federal law enforcement officer and you're in violation of privacy and tele-communications laws. That's between us, but you talk to Jack Berns again, you give him any of this data, I'll send you to jail."

"How . . . Who . . ."

"Doesn't matter," said Wes. "You're burned."

He hung up the phone.

"Do you know what that cost me?" cried Berns.

"One finger," said Wes. "So far."

He searched the house, took voice diaphragms out of all the telephones. He called a taxi from the private eye's car phone, then broke that phone and took the engine's distributor cap. When the taxi came, Wes left the private eye tied to his couch with his bathrobe belt, swearing and staring at his swollen hand.

All flights to Nebraska were booked or had left for the day by the time Wes got to National Airport. Under a false name, he caught a flight to Nashville, where in the morning he could make a connection to Lincoln. He checked his gun and cash in his duffel bag, gambled that his wouldn't be one of the bags airport security randomly x-rayed.

The sky slipped past the window of his plane.

# STOLEN CAR

Jud took the wrong road in the dark. He cruised past Gary, Indiana's hulking steel mills and the dark sheen of petrochemical lakes before he realized his error. He exited the interstate, parked on the crumbling asphalt of an abandoned gas station. Under the front seat of the car he'd stolen was a screwdriver and a torn map.

Outside the car, he urinated in the predawn shadows. He found a rusted gas can in the weeds, used the screwdriver to chop the hose from the dead gas pump. Most of the nearby homes were still dark. He switched license plates with a parked car and used the chopped hose and rusty can to siphon fuel.

Back on the road, he found U.S. 80 West. Gas fumes and bile filled his mouth. Chicago's whiskey cut the taste. He had to stay sober enough to drive, drunk enough to keep going.

The cities of Illinois rolled past his car. Joliet, with its gray prison walls. La Salle. Annawan. Truckstops with cherry pie, coffee. Towns where no one would answer his knock at a lonely house. The door would be unlocked, there'd be fifty-one dollars in a desk drawer, a toothbrush still in its plastic case. A Dodge without a locked gas cap. Whiskey in a cupboard, beer and leftover roast beef in the refrigerator.

*Keep going,* he told himself. *You can do it. You can do anything. You can face anyone. You can make it.*

Laos and SOG, Iran, Watergate, Chile, Miami: they were nothing compared to this interstate humming beneath the tires of his stolen car. Only twice before had Jud so desperately needed to believe in his own righteous invulnerability:

Once was the last time he saw his father.

The second time was when he seduced America.

Phantom operas flowed around him like fog as he tried to keep the car on the road.

*You've done this before,* Nora had said. *Worked in restaurants, I mean.*

In 1964, when he was sixteen in Chula Mesa, perpetually one step ahead of the sheriff's cruisers and truant officers, Jud worked as a busboy at a seedy Italian restaurant, supplementing his cash from anger burglaries with money he could account for.

It was October, a cool night for southern California, a Tuesday. Jud remembered every day that mattered. It was on a Wednesday that his kindergarten teacher made him stand in the corner so long that he wet his jeans. It was on a Thursday that he killed his first man, a VC sentry, slit his throat, black blood in the moonless night. The last time he'd seen his father was an October Tuesday, 1964.

A slow night for Enzio's Italian Palace. Jud practiced being invisible as he cleared tables and loaded dirty dishes into a gray rubber tub.

"Hey, you!" said a woman's nasal voice behind him.

She was more than twice his age, red lipstick, dyed hair sprayed into a brass swirl, a fake silk dress that was tight across her chest and tighter still across her hips. She wore high heels and waved a lit cigarette as she spoke.

"Yeah," she said as Jud turned around, "I *know* you."

"I don't think so, ma'am." Part of Jud feared she'd seen him in some illegal escapade and the police were just a dime drop away; part of him feared/hoped she wanted him for the big mystery.

"What's your name, kid," she said.

"Jud."

She rolled her eyes to the plastic chandelier.

"Jud Stuart."

She blinked; grinned. "No shit. Come on, there's someone I want you to meet."

"I'm Myra." She winked, led Jud to the raised platform against the back wall. Jud watched her girdled hips as she said, "There was something about your hair, the way you walked."

Up the three steps to the balcony where *someone* sat at the table beyond her and she turned, said, "Jud, meet Andy."

There *he* was: eyes wide, mouth open, hands trembling around a tumbler of iced vodka.

"Stuart and Stuart," said Myra. "Father and son."

Jud's stomach fell away. A freight train roared through his head. He was clammy all over, cold and flushed.

"Aren't you two going to say anything?" chimed Myra.

"So, ah," he said, and it was *that voice*, "you're Jud."

"No, dummy," joked Myra, "he's your other kid."

Andrew Stuart gulped his vodka. His hands trembled. He glared at Myra as she circled around the teenager in a busboy's white fatigues. She sat behind the drink she'd left.

"I always find pennies," she said, lighting another cigarette. "No matter where they roll. Thought you should remember that, Andy. Thought it'd be nice for the two of you to say hi."

Smoke rose from the table. She filled her lungs four times in the silence.

"So . . . ah . . . you work here?" said Jud's father.

Barely, Jud whispered, "Yes."

"Good, good." The man had waves in his brown hair. *Like me,* thought Jud. His father said, "Good job?"

"You're a barber," said Jud.

"'Do a lot of things, kid."

"He sells cars now," said Myra. "Don't you, honey?"

"You left when I was three," said Jud. "Got in the red car, drove away and it was a long time and you never came back and I waited, you said we'd play ball. It was a Friday."

"Tuesday today," said Myra.

"Look," said the man who was still handsome. Broken veins on his nose. Jud's knees were water. "Nothing personal, right? A man's gotta do what a man's gotta do, so . . ."

"Do you have another son?" whispered Jud.

"Wouldn't make that mistake twice," mumbled Andy.

"I don't like kids," said Myra.

"Hey, but look at you," said Andy. "Handsome, healthy. Got a good job. I couldn't have done that good for you."

"I'm in high school," said Jud. "A sophomore."

"Education is very important," said Andy.

"He always says that," added Myra.

"So, ah . . ." The father glanced at Myra. A slow smile came to his lips. He watched her as he asked, "How's your mother?"

"She pushes paper for the state," said Jud. He could breathe now. In, out: he could do it, he could breathe. "Sits on the couch with a six-pack. Watches TV."

"I couldn't take that shit," said Andy. "It's her fault I had to leave you."

"She says she should have beat you to the punch."

Andy shook his head. "Told you so."

"You got a girl?" said Myra, leaning back against the padded booth. "Gotta watch you don't tangle with the wrong girl."

"I have to get back to work," said Jud.

"Sure," said Andy. "I understand. A man's gotta do."

Jud stumbled back to the table where his gray rubber tub waited. He wiped the tablecloth, pushed the chairs into place. Kept his eyes on the kitchen's swinging aluminum doors as he carefully marched toward them.

Through them. In the kitchen, Jud dropped the dishtub on the counter beside the chef, who was chopping up a chicken. Enzio was chewing out the Mexican dishwasher. The black-tuxedoed owner turned to yell at his busboy, but Jud ran out to the alley.

The dark, unseeing alley, with the burning stench of the oil refinery and a sickly sweet cloud above the dumpster.

Dizzy, he was sick, threw up, sobbed and cried and beat his hands against the metal dumpster as he sank to the tar-sticky earth amidst broken glass and torn paper.

How long he huddled there, he didn't know.

*Get up,* he told himself. *You can do it. Keep going. You can do anything. You can face anyone*—fuck *them! Fuck him. You can make it.*

Jud's *hwarang-do* teacher was a struggling Korean immigrant. "Be wind," the mystic karate *sensei* would order Jud, trying to get the boy to channel the fire inside him. "Be water!"

*Be ice,* Jud told himself.

He got off the alley floor. Wiped his eyes.

Back inside the kitchen, Jud grabbed an empty rubber tub. He'd go back out there. He'd do his work and he'd do it *great* and he'd do it right in front of that man. He wouldn't look at him and he wouldn't look away; that man was *nothing.* Make him do the looking. Never let him see. He pushed through the swinging doors.

The table at the back of the room was empty.

*On the road,* back on the road. White letters on a green sign: MOLINE   10 MI. Iowa wasn't far.

His father died in 1973—Jud manufactured an FBI inquiry that found the report. Cancer. Jud never mentioned his father to his mother. He seldom spoke to her after his year of junior college, after joining the Army. She died in 1975, a heart attack while Jud was doing a crash *clean & burn* job in Africa, covering up a mercenary project gone to hell. He visited her grave in Chula Mesa once. To be sure.

In the stolen car, Jud heard Myra's laughter, smelled her cigarette smoke. Smelled Nora's smoke, ached for her smile. The landscape outside his windows was green and rolling, not the flat, brown desert by Death Valley. A black African arms dealer in a French suit sat by the side of the road, his head lolling at a peculiar angle; his eyes were open and he saw Jud coming, which was more than he had in Zaire. Jud drove past him; they didn't wave. A road mirage shimmered up ahead; beyond that lake Jud sensed Art—sprawled on his back, chest blown to gore, smoked sunglasses to the sky. Jud drove on. The lake disappeared. He drank the last of the whiskey; it was good, and he wanted more, needed more.

He'd needed a drink the day he decided to seduce America. By then, the thirst was steady. Saturday. He couldn't remember dates, but he never forgot days. That was a Saturday, a summer Saturday in 1979, Los Angeles.

Jud had been in L.A. five months, Miami behind him, not checking supermarket tabloids to learn what the stars wanted for his fate. He'd walked into a locksmith shop and after twenty minutes of showing his skills, won a job. Three weeks later, he'd been dispatched to a hair salon. He stepped into the perfumed atmosphere of blaring rock music, clicking scissors, and vapid chatter, saw the girl who was answering the phones: cascading chestnut hair, a sweet face with eyes like the ocean, firm swelling breasts, no waist; tiny, fragile—innocent.

"How are you?" she said, and thunder rumbled in his head.

"Finally great," he told her.

She'd laughed, told him she was Lorri.

*No,* he wanted to tell her, *you're my payment due.*

Within a week he'd overwhelmed her, within two days they were renting a house together in a blue-collar zone. They laughed and she listened. He told her so many things, and she heard him, though not with the informed ear of his friend Nick Kelley. Her ear cared about Jud, not at all about the world he revealed. They laughed and they loved and they worked hard.

But it wasn't enough.

That summer Saturday, he had to face that truth: it wasn't enough, and it wasn't right.

He was working overtime, retooling doors on homes he couldn't afford to sleep in. He finished the last job at four; Lorri was a hundred blocks away, scheduling beauty appointments for rich bitches who'd buy the hair off her head if she'd sell it; their husbands would buy the rest, if they could get away with it. Jud drove to a main drag, defiantly chose a fern bar where the waiters wore white shirts and bow ties. The customers were in tennis togs and beach casuals, young and clean and no better than him; their eyes whispered that his blue jeans and work shirt were in the wrong place. But they didn't dare refuse him a table. He ordered a Scotch and saw the world.

He'd conceived and executed ops involving hundreds of men and millions of dollars that wrote hidden lines in the history books. Now he did nickel-dime jobs for a mom-and-pop store, took orders from bosses who'd never decided who would live and who would die. He'd rock-'n'-rolled in the White House, went toe-to-toe with heavyweights shown on the evening news. Now pencil-necked geeks in cheap bars lectured him about politics. In Miami, he drove a Porsche, lived in a penthouse, wore tailored suits, had the finest food and priciest whores. Now he drove a rattletrap van painted with someone else's logo. His jeans and shirt were two years old. His rent was due on a house no better than the one his father fled. He had as much specialized training as a Harvard law school graduate; such lawyers were whores who were called Mister. He'd worked for *national security* and *patriotism* and *honor,* and he was Joe Shit The Ragpicker. He'd been shot at, beaten, he'd lied and been lied to, he'd bled and been sick from bad places and bad times. Risked everything. He'd killed—God, how he'd killed.

And nobody saw him when they looked.

What could he do? Be a throwaway, a denied *never was*. Or be back at the end of their whip, waiting to be snapped onto whatever line they wanted.

A man laughed at the bar. He was Jud's age, with soft hands and a great tan, *prep school* written all over him as he leaned on the mahogany and made time with two beach bunnies.

*Did I do it all for you?* thought Jud. *So I could sit here and worship you and smile and be thankful for my Saturday overtime and bar-brand Scotch?*

*This damn town,* thought Jud. It was worse here than anywhere else, worse than Miami or D.C. Or maybe everything was just clearer here. *Los Angeles,* his friend Nick had said, the city of perpetual dissatisfaction. The *never enough* town.

What was he going to do? Wait for Nick the writer to make him famous? To make all *them* understand? Nick couldn't do that. Even if he tried, it wouldn't be Jud on the billboards or the screen, getting the handshakes, getting the applause. Nobody was going to come down and make it all *worth* it, not even Nick.

Joe Shit The Ragpicker.

*Lorri.* How long could a mere Joe Shit keep her happy? How long before the daily grind wore down the special look in her eyes when she saw him? How long before the *nobody nowhere blues* soaked into her eyes and drowned her heart?

How much longer could he take all this *not enough* before he blew apart? Snapped some geek's neck or spilled his guts?

*No more bullshit from assholes,* he swore.

"So, do you want another drink?" sighed a slim waiter who kept his eyes at a languid half-mast.

"Bring it to me," said Jud.

When the waiter swished away, Jud saw Wendell at the bar.

Saw Wendell watching him.

*Wrong place, wrong time,* thought Jud. But with a wink and a nod, he told Wendell it was okay to come over, okay to sit down.

"*Man,*" said Wendell, "I ain't seen you in *light-years!*"

Since Miami: Wendell had been a two-pound-a-week dealer way down the corporate ladder built by Art Monterastelli, a simple man who let his love of smoke lead him into buying and selling it. Normally, Jud would not have associated with someone of such low rank in the organization, but Wendell's confined ambition gave Jud someone to jive with who wouldn't circle back.

Or so Jud had thought.

"Man, how are you?" said Wendell.

"Surprised to see you here," answered Jud.

Wendell leaned close. "*Amigo,* I'm going to lay it out *straight,* because I like you and I know you and you got the wrong toes to step on."

"You always were smart, Wendell."

Wendell cleared his throat. "Miami went nuts. Colombians, feds. You were cool to boogie when you did and while you could."

"Like you?"

"The shit was flying." Wendell licked his lips. "Thing is, I relocated here—didn't know where you went, knew better 'n to ask. I don't *comprendo* all of what went down and don't enlighten me, okay. But Raul, Cubans: world of their own. So, I'm here today. *Working.*"

Jud nodded.

"I got a sliver of the cola trade," said Wendell. "Few ounces a week, clear about a thou. Hell, bunch of my customers are hanging here."

"Then you shouldn't be," said Jud. "They get careless, you could be a proximity casualty."

"My man!" Wendell shrugged. "I had to deliver to one of my guys—imagine that: me with guys on a payroll!"

"Even worse," said Jud. "Don't be there when they do business. Cutouts, Wendell: work smart."

"That's why you're the man," said Wendell. "It's like you went to school for it."

"Yeah."

"Look," said Wendell, "flat out: you here working?"

"Yes," said Jud.

"No offense, I didn't know. If I'm dancing on your turf, tell me and I'm *gone!* This cowboy is not that dumb!"

Jud smiled. "It's a big city."

Wendell grinned. "Let me buy you a drink!"

The waiter arrived with the refill Jud had ordered. Before he set the glass on the table, Jud told him, "Chivas Regal."

The waiter stared at the glass of cheap Scotch on his tray. "What will I do with this?"

"Drink it yourself." Jud dismissed him with a wave.

"Crazy world," said Wendell. They drank to it.

"Look at 'em," said Wendell, nodding to the beautiful crowd at the bar. "More money than they need, everybody wants to be cool, sexy . . . *dangerous*. Ride the edge, get pumped up . . ."

Wendell raised his beer glass. "Riches to come."

Jud drank with him.

"Hell," said Wendell, "right time, right place, right product. They're bored with grass. Besides, the badges are so down on it that you can't ship enough to make it pay. Booze is for squares. Cola is *it*: makes you better 'n you are and who doesn't want that? Doesn't hurt. Who's going to tell the people no?"

This was 1979—after years of mistruths in the name of drug education, after a generation came of age paying price-support taxes for a killer addictive drug called nicotine; after thousands of Americans *privatized* LSD experiments begun by the CIA in the 1950s and found that not everyone hurled themselves from a hotel window as had the doctor who'd didn't know he'd been dosed with LSD in a CIA experiment. Cocaine had been used by Freud, the guru of mental health. Nobody died, nobody became addicted: nobody in 1979 knew those were lies. In 1979, nobody imagined a cut-rate refinement from hell called crack or the political consequences of buying a gram of snow, or how at the end of one white line there could only be another. And another. And another.

"Weird business, man," said Wendell. "Down in Colombia, everybody's getting into it. Army, politicians, the whole jungle."

"What about the guerrillas?" said Jud.

"We aren't talking about *Africa!*"

They both laughed.

"They got guerrillas down there?" said Wendell.

"Sure," said Jud, not remembering the name of M-19 or Shining Path or any of the other Latin Marxist groups.

"Fighting commies was never my gig," said Wendell. "I figure if the money's good enough, sooner or later, everybody will go for it. Capitalism rules, man, the dollar is the bottom line."

Wendell wiped his lips.

"Look," he said, "this is . . . don't get me wrong, okay?"

"Don't worry," said Jud.

"I'm a good man, but I don't want to be *the man*. I ain't cut out for tycoon shit. The business we're in, that happens fast. You know that. Look at you: highflier in Miami, out here before the wave crests, all set up and low-key . . .

"*Proposition*," said Wendell. "I like what I got just fine. Suppose I fold my action into yours? I can double my business, take the same rake or more, you get the skim."

"And what would you get?"

"You," said Wendell. "The cats crawling around Miami now will pop up on Sunset Boulevard. I need somebody who can keep their claws off my back. Somebody who knows how to play the law. Somebody to watch the big picture. Somebody who I can trust."

For a long time the two old friends watched each other.

The man at the bar laughed, walked out with his arms around two young girls. He didn't give Jud a glance.

"We'd have to see how you worked out," Jud told Wendell.

"No problem! You call the shots!"

"You say you can move an extra ounce a week," said Jud.

"Easy."

"Show me," said Jud. "This one we go fifty-fifty. The future we work out then. Do this right—no flash, no strangers, no funnsies, strictly business."

"No problem. My connection says his people are a clear pipeline, no supply woes. I'll need eight hundred—"

"You front this one yourself," ordered Jud. "I don't pay for your audition."

Wendell blinked; shrugged.

"Give me your phone number and address." Jud passed Wendell a pen. "You don't tell them *shit* about me or any deal. Secure communications. You work out, I'll let you bring them in on it. Everything goes all right, you get everything you want."

"How about the waiter?" said Wendell, smiling.

"That's your problem," said Jud, "not mine."

"I always thought that was too bad."

"It always will be," said Jud. "Get our tab, show him some flash, leave a big tip . . ."

They laughed. Jud stood.

"One thing," said Jud, leaning close. "You're a friend. But you fuck up, you front me out—you pay the tab."

Wendell's eyes said he *understood*.

Jud could barely concentrate enough to drive to Lorri's salon.

She frowned while he told her boss they'd be glad to close the place up, but said nothing: Lorri had an instinct for a riff.

"I don't get it," she said when they were alone. "You made me stop popping pills, now we're going to deal cocaine?"

"Whole different league," said Jud. "And we're doing business, not pleasure. It's our way out of the shit. Besides, they owe me. This is how they'll pay."

"Who are 'they'?"

"Don't worry, baby. It's okay. I love you."

"What if we get busted?"

"I got that covered," he said. "I got that covered."

She looked at him, laughed. "What the hell, everybody's doing it. Even Marie who does perms sells grams on the side."

"Already you're earning your way," said Jud, his subconscious scheming for ways to pull Marie under his umbrella.

Lorri called the L.A. *Times,* charmed a weekend editor with a story about her UCLA term paper's needing a few details about communists and guerrillas in South America. The bored man checked the clip files, read her a story, told her about sushi at a great place on Sunset. Lorri lied and agreed to meet him there for dinner, hung up, and laughed with Jud. They drank beer from the salon refrigerator. She read fashion magazines while he coded the message:

> Previously highly reliable source informed this agent re: involvement in cocaine trafficking of communist terrorist groups possibly M-19, others, in S.A. armed and hostile to U.S. international and domestic interests. Follow-up reaction penetration initiated. Advise operation, complete penetration, maximum cover, deniability. Zero cost projected, minimal contact, minimal support. Operation Plan upon sanction.

*Just enough,* thought Jud. A polygraph would say he didn't lie. He signed it *Malice,* the code designation of a veteran American intelligence agent of the highest sensitivity.

"What did you just do?" asked Lorri after he mailed the envelope to a suburban Maryland post office box.

"Don't worry," he said, though his heart trembled.

*He'll take it and use it in his hand, deal it around his table,* thought

Jud, remembering the face of the general he'd glimpsed months before. *It's too sweet to turn down.*

Three weeks later, in the supermarket tabloid, Gemini's horoscope said "rainy days": activate. Contact. Go.

He was already gone. America couldn't imagine how far.

Jud flipped his profit from Wendell back into the market.

Ounces became pounds. Marie joined Jud's team. She and Wendell recruited customers who Jud screened into associates.

Pounds became kilos. Marie and Wendell introduced Jud to their connections. In four months, he was their only outlet; in five months, they were working for him. Jud and Lorri quit their straight jobs, moved into a beach condo. Jud enlisted managers to handle the actual sales. He found Dean: between the two of them, corporate discipline became tight and rip-off artists got the word.

Kilos became loads. Jud did business with *the boys from Illinois,* with *the guys from Vegas,* with *the families back East.* Jud dealt with the bikers, barrio brothers. Big men in Miami vouched for him. Nobody asked about Art Monterastelli, and Raul sent his regards. Jud forged alliances; where hostilities appeared, federal busts materialized.

Loads became shipments. Jud organized safe houses, bankrolled a mescaline anarchist whose imagination and computer skills were light-years beyond law enforcement budgets for electronic intelligence. Jud bought money counters, a secret interest in a Florida bank, two Mercedes sedans, and a Porsche convertible. When his gold Rolex broke, he dropped it in a panhandler's cup on Sunset Boulevard, got another one. He bought $500 bottles of wine and carryout dinners from French restaurants, complete with gold-inlaid china that went into the trash. Jud met with men who controlled planes flying the Gulf of Mexico, trucks rolling across the Mexican border, cargo from Alaska.

He and Lorri bought a Spanish mansion on a hill overlooking the ocean. There were cases of Chivas in the pantry and a crystal decanter in Jud's office. The big-screen TV was always on. Lorri roamed the house, from the bedrooms to the Jacuzzi to the TV. The women she knew were like Marie, or crystal-slick women on the arms of men like Jud. A Mexican maid who feared Immigration and loved a hundred dollars a day took care of the house. Lorri could drive her black Mercedes anywhere she wanted, as long as she followed security procedures. She wore silk blouses, tight jeans, high heels, kept her purse with her, her compact full of white powder in case Jud played a power trip and locked up the house supply. Uzis and magnums and 9-millimeters were stashed in every room; there was an alarm system, a Doberman, and a bodyguard who stayed awake all night. Outside, peacocks roamed the streets.

Jud became a wild man: restaurant scenes, racing through the streets, buying shopgirls flashy gifts, flirting with them for weeks, demanding their adoration, never seeing them again. He gained weight, fat around a wall of muscle. He was a gorilla striding through discos, alone or with dead-eyed men who laughed only with their mouths. Sometimes Nick was in L.A. and cruised with him; for a while, a famous Hollywood director who loved cocaine rode along, but the movie man's promises of redemptive *deals* never came through. Those *in the life* knew Jud as a legend, believed that somehow he had it all *wired,* and that somehow that wire would not tighten around their necks.

"I hold it all together," he once told Nick. "You don't know. I'm doing it, I'm making it, I'm covered and it's cool and it doesn't bother me—fuck 'em—but you just don't know."

"I don't think I want to," replied Nick. He shook his head. "These are the days of madness."

In November 1980, on a Saturday, Jud married Lorri in a chapel by the sea, tuxedos and no visible horror-show. Dean flipped his Harley and missed the ceremony. Lorri's family came from Nebraska skeptical; went home scared. By then, her smile was a sly grin, her skin was pale and she had black holes in the oceans of her eyes. At the service, the Hollywood director was an usher and Nick Kelley was Jud's best man.

Once a week, Jud locked himself in his study and coded a report to the Maryland post office box. At first, he reported only *infiltrating.* He sometimes requested information, never reported names of his allies or details of his operations: the other end didn't need to know; didn't want to know. Jud assumed that when a cop typed his name into the computer, someone visited the cop and erased the entry. Sometimes a coded letter in his post office box that not even Lorri knew about warned about someone or something; identified specific intelligence needs.

Nine months after his wedding, Jud began meeting *down South* with the marketplace czars who would soon dominate cocaine production in South America. He began to report substance akin to the hypothesis he'd raised in his brief Operation Alert: arms shipments, warfare and cooperation between the coca industrialists and the entrepreneurs of revolution. He gleaned tidbits from the swirl of black-market secrets and gossip: what foreign minister was owned by whom, what Middle East arms dealer was prospering in Paraguay, who the Cuban attaché in Bogotá was courting, what the Israeli advisers were doing in Panama, which Chinese tankers in Argentina had captains with hungry eyes.

Each time he looked in the mirror of his mansion's ornate bathroom, he told himself this life was *justified*. If it hadn't been him, it would have been someone else, some independent who gave nothing for what he got, a creep who didn't care. Outside, a white blizzard swirled through his country. He told himself it didn't matter, that the cries beginning to echo in the snow-burned streets came from losers who would have fallen to booze or to heroin, if they'd been brave enough for a needle. Cigarettes, hell: he'd quit smoking. He was a businessman providing a product; he wasn't to blame for its abuse. The intelligence gained justified the means expended, plus he was finally getting paid for years of terrible risks. He'd gotten a sanction. So what if it was a seduction.

Then he'd have another drink.

*I'm owed,* he swore.

*They* slipped up. Three coded messages ordered him to provide funds: $20,000 each time. Each time he mailed the cash to the Maryland post office box. The fourth time, he sent the cash—and requested a receipt covering all disbursements.

No receipt ever came. And no more requests.

*Got you, General,* thought Jud. *Even you.*

In October 1981, Nick came to L.A. He asked Jud to meet him at the hotel he'd insisted on taking instead of the room at the mansion Jud offered. Jud didn't like the tremor in Nick's voice. The night before the meeting, he had the anarchist put a tap/trace on Nick's hotel phone. Three of his men whom Nick didn't know staked out the writer and his hotel room.

Before the meeting, Jud checked with the anarchist.

"He called some producer's office where he's got a two-o'clock; his agent, who wasn't there; and some chick in D.C. who wants a gold ring, which I don't think she'll get."

"I know about her," said Jud. "She'll be history soon."

Nick had dined alone. No one suspicious had a room anywhere around him. He'd met no one, was not surveilled. While Nick was eating, Jud burgled his room, found nothing incriminating.

They met in the hotel restaurant. It was sunny, between breakfast and lunch. Nick had coffee. Jud had a Bloody Mary.

"Look," said Nick, "this isn't easy."

"Don't worry," said Jud. "Everything's fine."

Nick shook his head.

"You leaving me for another girl?" joked Jud.

And Nick had to laugh.

"I love you like a brother," said Jud. "We've been through a lot together. I know it hasn't been easy on you, but—"

"You're my friend," said Nick. He sighed. "I don't like what's happening to you."

"What do you mean?" Cool, Jud was very cool. And friendly. This was the only man not *in the life* whom Jud could trust—which meant he was the only man Jud could trust at all.

"Used to be once, twice a month, a late-night call—"

"I'm sorry about that, it's just the pressure—"

"Now it's every night. Usually you're drunk, crazy. I keep expecting to hear UFO stories! Spirit-world shit!"

"I live in California."

"Wherever you are, it's gone bad. It's eating you up."

"I got it under control."

"Then you've lost control of something else. This shit you're doing: it's wrong."

"You never complained before," said Jud. "You like the product."

"Those are my sins," said Nick. He looked into Jud's eyes. "I don't do coke anymore."

"Did you find Jesus?"

"No." Nick shook his head. "Coke's . . . *intoxicating*. Exciting. I don't think it would hook me like I've seen it hook a couple people."

He paused, said, "People we know."

Jud's gaze didn't falter.

"But bottom line," said Nick, "when I get high, I support goons and corrupt politicians and killers, prop up people and things I've spent my life fighting or hating."

"Like me," said Jud.

For a long time, Nick didn't answer.

"I don't know what you're doing here," said Nick. "I tell myself it's more than it seems. You tell me that, too. I can't afford to know. If you're my friend, I guess it has to be enough for me to believe. But that doesn't mean I like it."

"So what now?" asked Jud.

"I don't know," said Nick. "But you know where I am. And it can't be as close to you as it was."

They told each other they were still friends; swore to keep in touch. Nick insisted on paying their bill.

From then until he became a gutter drunk, Jud called Nick only about once a month, and then usually during the day.

November 1981. The Tuesday before Thanksgiving. Out the mansion's picture windows, the sun hung low and red above the sea. The TV was on. Jud slumped on the couch, flicking channels. Perched in the steel chair, Lorri used a glowing butt to light a fresh cigarette.

"You smoke too much," said Jud.

"What the hell else do I got to do?" she intoned flatly.

"You got a problem?" he snapped.

She laughed.

"You think that's funny? You got more than you ever wanted. There's a million women who'd trade places with you!"

"You been taking names?"

"I don't have to take names, they're given to me."

"Oh, right, I forgot who you were."

"You never knew who I was."

"Really?" she said. "Who else has heard you cry?"

"I guess that was my mistake."

"So that's what it was." She sniffed, scraped the last of the coke off the saucer with a playing card, hit both nostrils.

"You're a fucking junkie," said Jud.

"We don't fuck anymore," she said, staring at him flatly. She watched him watch her lick her numb lips.

"At least I don't," he said.

"You going to tell that to the bitch you got stashed at the beach? I'm not complaining. She saves me the trouble."

The plastic channel wand cracked in his grip. If she heard it, she was past caring.

"Your men are too afraid to fuck me," she said. "They might shoot me, but they won't fuck me."

She stood, stared out the window. The sky bled.

"Why do we live like this?" she said.

"Would you rather go back to Nebraska? You want to go back to making hair appointments and two-dollar tips?"

"Rather?" She shook her head. "I can still *rather?*"

He heard her crying, but all he could think about was when would she stop.

"I'd rather . . . ," she began—then she lost the thought, her mind slipped gears. Wistfully, she said, "I'd rather we'd had the baby. You said it wasn't the right time, it wasn't safe. You said I hadn't been clean enough long enough, the baby would be . . . You said you were worried."

And he couldn't stop, "I was worried whose kid it was."

*Awareness* slammed back into her face, her features hardened as she turned toward him. Her cheeks were wet, but the razor was back in her voice.

"You've got your secrets," she said. "I've got mine."

"I did all this for us!" he yelled. "And for things you can't understand! Don't know about!"

"Honey, that's a sad lie," she said. She swirled around as she had in the picture Nick had taken of her. This time, her smile was empty. "Congratulations. You're brilliant. You won."

"What do you want?"

"Me?" She looked around the empty mansion. "I want to be gone." She laughed. "I want some more coke."

She smiled slow and sweet, leaned toward him, her thick hair cascading, her body still young and lush, said:

"I'll pour you a drink."

Jud threw her the keys to his office where the drugs were. He heard her climbing the stairs as he walked out.

The Porsche took him across town. He stopped twice for a drink. The post office he used gave its boxholders twenty-four-hour access. There was a letter in his box.

He knew something was wrong the moment he opened it. The envelope contained two sheets of paper, one small folded square, one carbon-copy sheet of a typed, encoded message.

*A carbon copy.* There should never have been any copies of anything; that he'd been sent a carbon was a message in itself: *the team had lost autonomy.* Jud stood at the postal table in the deserted government building, decoded the message:

Sanction withdrawn effective 12/20/81 . . .

A month. They were giving him a month. They claimed.

Exit clean. Prepare full final report. Identify Assets, Targets, Personnel. Turn over material, operational funds. Debriefing to be scheduled. Inform fully.

*Something's happened,* thought Jud. He unfolded the second piece of paper. That message was hand printed in plainspeak, a private communication:

### REMEMBER MONTERASTELLI

*Blown,* thought Jud, then he corrected himself: *Discarded.*

He'd become a liability—the general's or the general's general. The rules had changed. Carbon copies: suddenly they wanted a record to cover their asses. *Identify Assets, Targets, Personnel.* Finger your people. They'd roll up Wendell, Marie, others. Put the screws to them. The big boys would have another line entered in their file folders—the big boys had lawyers and connections and could keep the cops away no matter what a roll up of Jud's network yielded. *Turn over* . . . everything. Be Joe Shit The Ragpicker. And just to be sure, we'll polygraph you and dope you and microscope you until you are.

*Sanction withdrawn.* If he ignored them, every cop who'd been warned away and every tax man who'd been told to mind his own business would be loosed on Jud. His picture would join the mug shots on the wall of this post office.

And if the law didn't get him . . . *Remember Monterastelli.*

Don't talk. Don't piss us off. Or you'll die.

*Something more,* he realized. He looked at the two messages. Sending Jud a carbon, sending him the personal note, the general had to realize Jud would figure out . . .

That was it: the general and the team didn't want Jud to come in any more than he did. But somewhere someone had gotten

JAMES GRADY

scared or changed his mind, and as long as Jud existed, the renegade dope spy, he had to be pulled back into line.

As long as he existed, they'd have to try.

Joe Shit The Ragpicker.

*For nothing*, he thought. *I did it all again for nothing.*

What he kept would be the measure of their revenge.

The scream roared out of him, echoed off the empty post office's green walls and brass boxes.

Two hours and five drinks later, he was back at the mansion. The bodyguard was awake. He was a Korean with dubious papers. The Doberman liked him. Jud ordered him to pack.

Lorri was passed out across their king-size bed, a bottle of Valium by her side. She used them to bring her down so she could sleep enough to get high again. While she lay there, Jud packed two suitcases with her less flashy clothes. He packed two bags for himself, went into his study hung with the fourteenth-century Japanese-samurai woodblock-print collection he loved.

His green beret, a 9mm Smith, and $50,000 in cash went into his briefcase. His practiced eye told him there was about $70,000 left in the safe. He put $10,000 in one envelope, the rest in a shaving kit. The safe held about a kilo of cocaine. He put two cupfuls in a plastic bag, dropped it in the shaving kit.

It took him an hour to make the rest of his preparations.

"Come on," he said then, shaking Lorri into a semiconscious stupor. She was sluggish, but he got her downstairs, into the garage, into her black Mercedes. The Korean loaded her bags in that car, loaded Jud's in the Porsche along with a case of Scotch, drove it up the block, and walked back.

"Take this," Jud said, handing him the envelope with $10,000. "Go to your cousin's in San Francisco, use what you need. If I haven't contacted you in two months, it's all yours."

Jud tossed him the key to the second Mercedes.

"Take the dog."

A slow bow, and the Korean obeyed.

"Never liked that dog," said Jud as the Korean drove away.

Lorri was in a stupor. Jud drove the black Mercedes down the hill three blocks to the parked Porsche; later he'd ditch it for the low-key Dodge he'd kept stored at a safe house. They could see the glowing mansion. Neighbors they didn't know slept in palaces around them on this pinnacle of American success.

"Wake up!" he said. He used his knife to give her two hits of coke from the shaving kit. She snorted them automatically.

Blinked, shook her head; looked around and saw her bags, the shaving kit with money and drugs he'd left on the floor, the keys in her Mercedes.

"Wha . . . What th'hell . . ." Her eyes widened.

A black box sat on the car seat between them. Jud pointed back to the mansion with all their expensive frivolities and fineries. He turned a dial on the box, flipped a switch.

Radio bombs exploded in his office; in the kitchen; in the basement; in the living room where the giant-screen TV still played. Each bomb was taped to a full can of gas. Fireballs novaed through the oak-paneled mansion: drapes, electronic spy gear, paintings, computers, guns, ammunition, clothes, drugs, piles of cash abandoned in kitchen drawers—all fed the inferno.

The peacocks in the street panicked; stupidly ran toward the exploding house as lights came on all over the hill.

"You want to be gone," Jud hissed to Lorri, "*go!* Go now, go fast, and go hard. Don't look back. This is all gone. It never was. There's nothing here for you. Not in this town. Not in this life. Forget my name and don't ever forget not to fuck up!"

The burning mansion was reflected in the black dimes of her eyes. He saw she'd been waiting for this, expecting this.

From farther down the hill came the sound of fire engines. House doors slammed nearby.

Jud got out of the car. Lorri hesitated, then slid behind the wheel of the Mercedes and drove away.

She didn't look back; Jud watched.

Nine years later, he was driving a stolen car west on the interstate highway crossing Iowa. Headed to Nebraska.

He knew where she was—a cousin of hers still thought Jud could send him money so he still sucked up. Jud even called her trailer once, heard her say "Hello." Heard her hang up.

The stolen car turned south, crossed the Missouri River. The afternoon light made shadow patterns in the trees along the road. Jud hadn't expected Nebraska to have so many trees.

Not that he was going to stay. Not that he had any expectations, any idea of where he was going next. He knew she'd have *not much* to say and cared not for words he didn't have anyway. But he had to see her, just one more time. Just to say one thing.

A flash of white, walking in the trees; it was Nora.

When Jud cut south on the state road outside Lincoln, the VC whose throat he'd cut was standing by the curb, crusty black pajamas, empty eyes. Jud half expected him to stick out his thumb: hitchhiker. Jud roared on by.

*Can you apologize to all your victims?* Jud wondered.

Maybe Lorri would say, *Where you been? Where'd you go?*

*Low,* he'd tell her. Maybe she'd laugh.

Maybe he'd tell her everything. Maybe he could and maybe now she could understand, maybe they finally knew the right language. Maybe she'd be proud of him:

*They activated me one more time after our fire,* he'd tell her. *Horoscope horrors. They didn't know how low I'd fallen. Autumn, 1984, and I got them to brief me through the mail and I told them no.*

*So?* she'd say.

But maybe she'd say, *What the hell.* And smile.

And then maybe she'd let him go.

Conrad, Nebraska, is a dirty little town. Couple hundred houses, half of Main Street boarded up, grain elevators by rusted railroad tracks where trains don't stop anymore. More gravel than pavement in the streets. Satellite dishes to bring real life into drab living rooms. Pickup trucks parked outside the two bars that Jud forced himself to drive past. The blue airline bag by his side still had thirty-two dollars in it, plenty enough for a bottle or maybe two. But he could wait. He could make himself wait.

The trailer was east of town, a quarter mile from any other houses. A row of trees cut it off from prying eyes. A mile on the other side of the trailer were the sewer lagoons. They only smelled on really hot days, and by the time Jud got there, the sun was setting. It was spring, anyway.

Two mongrel dogs circling the trailer loped off when Jud drove up. He didn't like their look. He grabbed the blue airline bag. Got out of the car, road stiff, nothing else to do but walk up to that closed metal door.

Knock.

# THE YELLOW DOG

Wes found the trailer outside Conrad, Nebraska, before noon the next day. The sun was warm, the sky blue. He parked his rental car a hundred meters up the empty road from the trailer, used binoculars to scan the curtained windows, the splotchy pastel paint on the metal walls. A rusted pickup with Nebraska plates slumped beside that now-immobile home.

Three mongrel dogs paced the dirt yard, sniffing, trotting around the aluminum box. The yellow dog scratched at the trailer door. No one let him in.

Wes ran his hand over his unshaven stubble. He wore a black windbreaker, shirt, black jeans, sneakerlike black shoes.

*Not an official image,* he thought.

The Sig rode on his right hip. Chambered. Ready. During his Nashville layover, his sleep had been deep and dreamless.

Nothing moved at the trailer. Except the dogs.

*Twelve o'clock,* said his watch. *Straight up.*

Slow and steady, he drove down the dirt track to the trailer, his eyes focused on the door, the curtained window; his right hand in his lap, heavy with the Sig.

The dogs barked; trotted out of kicking range, barked some more. Watched the strange man.

He parked ten feet from the door. Shut off the engine.

The curtains didn't flutter. The door didn't burst open.

"Hello!" he yelled out the car window.

Flies buzzed. The yellow dog barked.

Wes got out of the car. He held the Sig behind him.

"Anybody home?"

The breeze stirred the dust at his shoes. Wes sniffed: a sweet-sour scent, like ham and cabbage. The man at the gas station had said the trailer was near the sewer lagoons.

Two steps closer. "Hello?"

From inside the trailer came soft tinny laughter: people?

*No,* he realized, *television.*

A dog growled, but Wes knew it was a bluff and didn't look: the trailer door was unlatched.

He stood wide of the door when he knocked.

No reply.

He knocked again.

The yellow dog barked.

Wes raised the Sig, stood clear, and swung the door open.

No one yelled; no one charged out. He stepped inside.

Flies buzzed over dirty aluminum frozen-dinner plates in the kitchen sink. The tiny refrigerator groaned. Clothes, magazines, and beer and wine bottles covered the floors. Ashtrays held pyramids of cigarette butts.

The eyes of the woman slumped on the couch stared at the portable color TV set mounted at the far end of this metal box; a contestant spun a wheel in a game show while the gorgeous hostess clapped. Pale and slack as it was, the face of the woman on the couch showed the ghost of a beauty greater even than in the picture Wes carried of her. Her chestnut hair spilled around her like a shawl. The gashes circled her wrists like gaudy ruby bracelets.

Her hands lay in her lap; a dark splotch spread out from them, over her blue jeans, the couch, down its side to a black smear soaked into the cheap industrial carpet.

Between the couch and the door was a wicker coffee table with a glass top. On the table was a dark-stained wine bottle, two prescription pill vials, a tin of aspirins, a cigarette pack, and an ashtray. A finger of ashes trailed to the edge of the table from a lit cigarette that had been dropped, burned itself out. Not far from the ashes was a crusty razor blade. A makeup brush lay in the center of a dark smear on the table. A pattern of streaked dark lines waited on the smudged glass.

Letters. Words.

Jud I couldn't stand waiting for you to
come finish
me so ha ha
PS Nick Ke

The Sig dangled in Wes's limp hand.

When he could open his eyes, when he could look at her again, he whispered, "I don't even know who you are!"

*Too late,* he thought, shaking his head. Too late.

The gun was heavy. He was too dizzy and nauseous to trust his hands, so he turned to watch himself holster it. As he glanced at his belt, he saw a blue airline bag on the floor.

*Jud,* he thought, remembering his first sight of that man in the desert, remembering the description of the Gs who'd lost Jud at the airport in Las Vegas.

The bag lay forgotten on the floor's clutter.

Wes looked at the woman again. He'd seen enough death to know she'd been dead several days. Dead before Jud got here.

*Too late,* thought Wes, *you got here too late, too.*

Inside the bag was a new toothbrush, almost no money.

"When were you here?" said Wes. "Where did you go? How?"

The woman on the couch said nothing.

The air inside the trailer was close and thick. The TV played commercials. Wes felt sweat trickling down his spine as he stared at the dead woman, forced himself to breathe, to think.

Outside the trailer, the dogs whined.

Then Wes knew what he had to do.

||||||||||||||||||||||||||||||||||||||||||||||||||||||||||||||||||||||||||||||||||||||||||

# THE BIG CLOCK

Two mornings later, Nick Kelley sat on the couch in his Capitol Hill office, staring at the notes he'd made from the glossaries. He was no closer to getting out of the jungle than he had been the day Jud dropped him in it with a phone call.

*Maybe there is no jungle.* He looked out the window. *Maybe they're gone. Maybe there is no they.*

The phone rang.

"Nick," said a man's voice he'd never heard, "it's Lorri's friend. I'm calling about our appointment today."

Nick knew no friends of Lorri's, had no appointment with anyone. Before Nick could reply, the man said:

"*Think about it:* don't you hate phones? You never know who's there."

The two men listened to each other breathe.

"Like now," Nick finally said. He could barely talk.

"Yes. But calling was better than coming to your office."

"Oh?"

"We need to meet earlier than lunch."

"What?"

"Twenty minutes. Union Station." Nick knew the way, but the man told him the exact route to take.

"Don't look back," said the stranger.

The phone clicked: dead.

Oh shit.

*Think!* A killer would be a fool to alert him. This was too complicated for a setup like a drug frame. A ruse to get him out of his office for a black bag job was unnecessary because he was gone all night. If they needed to get him out of the office for any other reason, this was an iffy way of doing it.

He stared at the phone. *You never know who's there.*

If his phone was hot, the wiretappers had heard the call. The man hadn't wanted to come to Nick's office: did that mean he *knew* someone was watching Nick?

*"Don't look back."*

The stranger had Lorri's name. Which meant Jud. Somehow. And maybe some answers, a way out of the jungle.

*One thing moves, all things change.* Whatever the stranger had started, if Nick hesitated, all the other players had a chance to regroup.

The silence of his world pressed in on Nick. Vertigo swirled through him and he was nauseous. A thousand regrets found voice in his heart: he should have been more careful, should have stayed clear of Jud, should have not—

*Stop it!* Regrets were worthless now.

The big clock was ticking.

Everybody knew who he was. That he was in his office. With no witnesses. If he didn't act, he'd surrender to whatever someone else chose.

A nylon backpack from Nick's college days was buried in the closet. He stuffed the glossaries and his notes in the pack, strapped it on, and felt foolish: a backpack over a sports jacket. But his hands were free.

*Sylvia:* Nick looked at the phone, ached to hear his wife's voice. Call home, have Juanita hold the phone for Saul.

Not a secure move. Not enough time.

He locked the office door behind him.

Capitol Hill is a beautiful neighborhood of flowering cherry and crab apple trees, dogwoods rising from brick boulevards. Nick's office was in a blue town house on Southeast A Street, six blocks from the Capitol, another four blocks to Union Station.

*Who's out here?* thought Nick as he stepped onto the concrete stoop of the town house. *What do you want with me?*

Sunlight glistened off parked cars. A woman walked a yippy dog, a closed umbrella in her hand. Rain wasn't expected until that night. A man got out of a Toyota: Nick flinched. The man walked the other way. To the west was the back of a Library of Congress building.

No old man with white hair.

No Jack Berns.

*Casual,* Nick told himself. *Quick, ready, but casual.*

He locked his eyes forward: a homicide cop once warned him that halfway measures get you killed. Long ago, Nick's karate *sensei* had shouted to the class: "If you move, *move!*"

The idea struck him when he was a block from his office. He checked his watch, quickened his pace. Nick was loping when he reached the kiosk at the end of the street, hands shaking as he dropped a quarter in the pay phone.

The homicide cop's home answering machine had an anonymous greeting followed by a quick beep.

"This is Nick Kelley." He rattled off the time, date. "I'm going to Union Station to meet an unknown male call-in source about a CIA story. I think my phones are hot, so I'll call you. If I don't . . . You know. Thanks."

He checked his watch: he had maybe a minute to spare.

Nick called columnist Peter Murphy's office, wouldn't let the receptionist take the time to switch him to anyone else, dictated a version of the same message he'd left for the cop.

Hung up and hurried on. Didn't look back.

But thought, *Now it's my game, too.*

Gray clouds drifted across the sky. The air was cool. The trees had budded out green. Two Library of Congress workers in brown uniform shirts and pants laughed as they walked past him.

Nick followed the route given him by the stranger: one block north on Third Street to East Capitol, left to face the glistening-white-icing congressional dome. A red cardinal flew down the street, chased by a diesel-belching Metro bus.

*Sit back in your eyes. Open your ears. Keep walking.*

Don't look back.

A fire engine siren wailed behind him and to the right; Klaxon honking as it raced the other way. *Don't look!* He always checked out siren-screaming police cars; so did his baby son—*God,* he loved his son!

Coming toward him, a loud-voiced middle-aged woman at the head of a two-by-two column of children. The kids held hands. A black man was the caboose, guarding the children's rear, making sure they were safe and that they all got where they were going.

One of the boys waved at Nick; a little girl giggled.

At First Street, he turned right, walked between the wide lawn of the Capitol and the white marble steps leading up to the Supreme Court's columns and ivory facade etched with the motto *Equal Justice Under Law.* Tourists took pictures with drugstore cameras, automatic flashes wasted in the daylight and at any time worthless at that range.

On he walked.

Cabs and open car, blue-and-white tourbus trains rolled by. On the sidewalk, he passed men and women in serious suits who glanced at him, saw a harried man with silver-streaked hair and a backpack strapped on over a sports jacket. Skinny, tense, rushing along to a rhythm they didn't hear. Their eyes judged that he was a blink away from being one of the screamers shouting about Martians and justice on the Capitol steps. Nick wanted to yell that he was sane; that he was walking in *the real world* that they with their heavy briefcases didn't see.

Don't look back.

The traffic light at Constitution Avenue was red.

Green, and he walked between the Dirksen and Russell Senate office buildings. The sidewalk sloped downhill. Less than half a mile away, he saw Union Station, massive gray and concrete, big as a baseball stadium, draped in red and white bunting to celebrate its renovation from a corruption-mauled train depot to a giant indoor mall and transportation hub. He saw the curve of the white marble fountain in front of the station, cars whizzing past.

With binoculars, he could have discerned the lines and angles of the ant people leaning against the fountain wall.

He reached the station seventeen minutes after the stranger called. Stepped on the main entrance's rubber mat. Electronic wooden double doors swung open before him.

He stared at the shadowed opening.

Went inside.

Union Station is like a cathedral, with high domed ceilings, soft light, mahogany railings and information desks, chessboard marble tile, white tablecloths and wine cafés, multicolored computer screens and loudspeakers announcing trains. Corridors lead to colorful jewelry and clothing stores, a bookstore. Escalators cycle down to thirty food stands, nine movie theaters. Nick could smell coffee and spices and pine-scented suds from the janitor who was mopping the tiles by the rest rooms. Hundreds of people streamed around Nick. They carried suitcases, cameras, anxious looks, or eagerness for commercial excitement.

*"Take the escalators up to the top parking level."*

As Nick walked through the crowd, no one called his name.

*Bump,* a woman brushed his side: whirling, left hand circling up to block, right fist cocking to strike. But she was two steps away, gray-flecked hair, jabbering about St. Paul to a granddaughter who would graduate from high school in a few weeks.

Nobody, she was nobody. Innocent.

Keep walking.

Don't look back.

The cacophony of the train station rang hollow in his ears; he heard everything and nothing, as if he were sinking deeper underwater, pressure building. The people around him moved in slow motion. Their features were razor precise. It was cool beneath this beautiful arched ceiling; his shirt stuck to his sides, the backpack rode on him like a cancerous hump. His feet and hands and head were boulders, yet inside he felt weightless, floating.

Union Station has four levels of parking stacked like giant concrete pancakes at the rear of the building. Escalators lead to the parking levels from the safety of the shops and trains. Each level has two escalators up, two escalators down.

The first set of escalators was crowded: businessmen; a laughing married couple, holding hands as they stole a movie out of the workday week. He and Sylvia had done that; there were so many movies he'd never seen, her skin was so soft. They'd never gone on a picnic. A herd of yelling teenagers ran up the escalator rising alongside Nick's, charged into the parking lot where their bus from Maine waited.

The second set of escalators was only half as populated, more by people riding up than arrivals riding down. Nick glanced to his left: an acre of parked cars sandwiched between a cement roof and a concrete floor. A sign on the wall read: PUSH RED BUTTON FOR EMERGENCY ASSISTANCE.

There was nobody he could call for help. No *authority* could rescue him.

The third set of escalators was empty when Nick got on at the bottom. No one rode on either side; he heard no one behind him.

A nun stood at the top of the escalators. A nun in full black-and-white penguin habit, hair and forehead covered, hands hidden in the black folds. She got on the downward stairs.

*Why isn't she holding on to the rubber rail?*

Closer, they slid closer together. The nun was on his left. His heart side. An old and pasty-white, lined face. Closer. The nun had wary eyes that pointed straight ahead. Nick knew she saw his every move. His mouth was dry; his heart raced. He rode the stairway toward heaven and tried to be loose, ready as they slid closer, closer together. Side by side.

Past.

Nothing cut into him.

The last set of escalators were empty. Through the open walls to Nick's right were the brightly painted town houses of Capitol Hill, a jumble of rusted railroad tracks snaking from the heart of the city.

Risk it.

He locked his gaze on a black town-house roof. The escalator carried him up and forward. His face slowly turned . . .

A man in a sports jacket rode the escalator thirty feet behind Nick. The man was checking his watch. Nick could only see the top of his head: a bald spot spreading out from a crown of black hair. The man had tan hands.

End of the escalator.

Nick left the escalator platform for the concrete parking lot. In the sunshine, no one stood amidst the parked cars.

*"There are three concrete stairwells,"* the stranger on the phone had said. *"Ride the escalators up to the top, go to the middle stairwell, walk down."*

The middle stairwell was a room-sized gray concrete box with a giant ventilator mounted on its top. Nick turned the knob on the metal door: unlocked. The landing inside was lit by bare ceiling bulbs. A steel staircase led down.

The stairwell was empty.

*Is the escalator man behind me?* thought Nick. His guts were like lava. He stepped inside the stairwell, closed the door.

Took a breath; heard nothing—water dripping.

One landing down, he found a line of orange rubber cones

barring the door to the next level. A DETOUR sign was taped to the metal door and lumber had been wedged across it.

Dead end. Trapped. The cinder-block walls closed in on Nick: *Run.*

Back, three steps at a time up the first set of stairs, turning the corner, nine more to—

The metal door burst open. The man from the escalator flew inside, staggering, slammed against the wall, turned back toward the door. His face was gashed, bloody, his hand reached under his sports jacket . . .

But the man in jeans and a black jacket who'd thrown him through the door was there, grabbing the escalator man's hand, whipping *black metal* across Escalator Man's face. He staggered. The ambusher hit him with the black metal again.

*A gun,* recognized Nick. *Gun.*

That locked on him as Escalator Man collapsed in a heap.

"Don't!" yelled the man with the gun. "Just *don't!*"

Nick kept his hands in sight. There was nowhere to run. He was too far away to charge the gun. The gunman was big.

The gunman kicked the man crumpled on the floor in the leg; he didn't move.

"You're okay!" the gunman told Nick. "You're safe!"

*"Fuck you!"* yelled Nick before he thought.

"You'll have to stand in line."

"You going to do me now!" bellowed Nick.

"Quiet!" The gunman's shout echoed in the concrete and steel box. "I'm not going to do anything to you!"

"You got a gun!"

"For him, not you."

His feet turned the unconscious man's face toward Nick. "Do you know him?"

"I don't know you either!"

"I called you, got you out of there so I could shake anybody off your ass. I'm Wes Chandler."

"All I know is you're the man with the gun," said Nick.

"That's right," said Wes.

He holstered the Sig, heard his rasping breath in this concrete box where with stolen orange cones and lumber he'd set up his ambush. Wes saw Nick sneak his foot up one step; saw Nick calculate the distance, the odds.

"Don't," said Wes. "Even without my gun, you don't stand a chance."

"Sure," said Nick, biding his time.

"If I wanted you dead, you would be."

Nick blinked. "Who are you?"

"I'm your way out. Your only way out."

The man who said he was Wes Chandler held a Polaroid photograph like an ID for Nick to see.

Squinting, climbing two slow steps closer, Nick saw a photo of himself, sitting on a red couch. Next to Jud.

Nick whispered, "Where did you get that?"

Wes pointed to the unconscious man. "He was following you."

"Why? How do you know that?"

"Because I disappeared and they didn't have any other choice," said Chandler. "I didn't give them one."

He bent and searched Escalator Man's clothes.

*No,* Nick told himself when Wes dropped his attention to the man on the floor. *Wait.*

"I didn't know if the CIA had targeted you," said Wes. He pulled a revolver from under Escalator Man's jacket.

"If it would have been official, they'd have had a team on you. A tap and a team dispatched ahead. They didn't. I tracked you with binoculars. This guy followed you by himself."

"He heard the phone call? Was waiting outside?"

"Doesn't matter." Wes took the man's wallet. "Solo tail, small op. Whoever they are, if it's official, it's way off the books."

The man on the floor moaned. Still holding the revolver, Wes told Nick, "Let's go."

They left the stairwell. Wes directed Nick to a rental car, walked around to the driver's door.

"Get in," he said.

"You must think I'm nuts!"

"I *know* you're in trouble. Way over your head. If you didn't think so before . . ."

He pointed the gun back to where the man he'd beaten was regaining consciousness.

"I'm under the same shit," said Wes. "We've got a chance to get out of it—together. On your own, you've got nothing."

"At least I know where I'm going and who I am."

"Do you?" said Wes.

The revolver he'd taken from the ambushed man hung in his hand. He slid the gun across the hood of the car toward Nick.

"Your choice," said Wes.

He got in the car. Started the engine. Watched Nick staring at him through the windshield.

*He's the chance I have,* thought Nick. He picked up the gun, got in the car.

They drove to the National Arboretum, a 444-acre preserve of rolling trees, flowering bushes, and deserted paved roads just off Capitol Hill. They parked not far from a Japanese gazebo where an old woman in a wide-brimmed hat painted at an easel.

Wes talked like a machine gun: told Nick he was a Marine assigned to the CIA, detailed to investigate Jud after a phone call to the CIA's panic line. Told him about the pictures he'd stolen in L.A. Explained how phone records had linked Nick to Jud.

"I need to talk to Jud," insisted Wes. "He's the way out of all this. He knows it, he's got it or he's it. He can set the ground rules. He knows I don't want to hurt him. I had a chance, in the desert. There was some trouble."

"Where is he now?"

"My guess is he's headed here. To you." Wes swallowed. "Lorri is dead. Suicide. He found her, she'd left . . . kind of a note. Mentioned your name."

"I called her," whispered Nick. "Last week. She was alive just . . ."

"Don't worry," said Wes. "I cleaned up."

"What?" Nick's mind reeled. She's dead. She was alive and then I called her.

*And then she killed herself,* he realized. I told her Jud was coming, I was back in her life. Then she killed herself.

Nausea and guilt swirled through him.

"We don't have much time," said Wes. "There's a burn notice out on me. The firing squad is forming, and I'm against the wall. Jud's out of control. They'll put him against the same bricks."

"For *what*? You bushwhacked that guy, not Jud!"

"You're right beside us," said the Marine. "Jack Berns put you there. My guess is that's how that guy got on your tail. Anyway, you're the last one alive at the end of Jud's rope."

The car was close, small. Nick put his hand on the door.

Wes opened the wallet of the man he'd ambushed.

"Virginia driver's license." He read, "'Norman Blanton'—mean anything?"

"No," said Nick. *Where was Sylvia? Was she okay?*

"Credit cards, traveler's checks—why the hell does he have traveler's checks? No government ID, no . . ." He pulled a crinkled business card out of the wallet. "'Norman J. Blanton, Executive Vice President, PRS—Phoenix Resources and Services.'"

"Wait a minute," said Nick.

He pulled the names glossary from his backpack.

"No Blanton," he said, explaining the names glossary.

But Phoenix Resources and Services (PRS) was listed on page 9 of the Archives' Iran-Contra Organizations Glossary:

> A Virginia-based company founded in January 1985 by
> BYRON VARON, a retired general. PRS served as a minor
> subcontractor in both official and extraofficial efforts to
> aid the contras, including providing a conduit for funds,
> middleman functions for small-arms sales, and air logis-
> tics.

"Where does an arms company fit in?" asked Wes.

"Not where," said Nick, pulling the set of photocopied pages from his backpack. *"Who."*

Nick paged back through the names glossary:

> VARON, BYRON R., Retired Lt. Gen., USA, service in
> Vietnam, Laos, later served as deputy adviser for military
> assistance programs in Iran and headed up low-
> intensity-warfare group for Joint Chiefs. Varon was
> honorary chairman of the AMERICAN LIBERTY MOVEMENT
> and raised funds for the contras as well as arranging
> purchase of arms and participating in planning of off-
> the-shelf operations for the secret White House team.

"You're the white knight," Nick told Wes. "Now what?"

# MONKEY MAN

Ten minutes before noon that day, the chairman of Sylvia's congressional committee visited her jumbled office on his way to the Cloakroom and told her to take the rest of the day off.

Actually, what he said was, "Get your ass out of here. When we start conference committee next week, I don't want to look behind me at midnight, see you sitting against the wall, *my poor family* written all over your face."

"As soon as I draft our response to the Senate staff proposals—"

"Fuck the Senate staff," said the chairman of a powerful House committee. "If you feed dogs when they bark, they start thinking they're in charge."

He walked to the door, winked at her. "You owe me one."

Sylvia laughed and picked up the phone.

Got Nick's machine. *He must have gone to lunch early.* After the beep, she told him she was going home; told him to call. "Want to see a movie?" she asked her husband's office machine.

Raindrops tapped her car's windshield as she drove to the suburbs, sacrificial scouts for clouds beyond the horizon.

When she got home, Saul was down for his nap.

"A good boy," said Juanita. "All time, he wants only to walk. No more crawling."

Again Sylvia called Nick. No answer. They could still make a late-afternoon movie. She remembered the chairman's wink.

"Juanita . . ."

It was a simple deal between equally agreeable parties. For the rest of the day off, Juanita would baby-sit Friday night.

"For a date," she said. "For you and Nick, a real date."

"Yes," Sylvia smiled, dreaming ahead.

When she walked Juanita to the door, she noticed the wind had turned cool. The clouds looked thicker, grayer.

*Alone,* thought Sylvia. With Saul asleep for probably another hour, she was as good as blissfully *alone* in a quiet house. Except for the dog, the big black rottweiler who padded from room to room with her. She could even take the phone off the hook.

*No,* Nick might call. She half hoped he wouldn't.

Upstairs, she checked on Saul: curled on his side in the crib, ribs gently rising and falling, precious hands up by his face. She pulled his bedroom door shut to preserve his quiet rest.

As her baby's door closed, she remembered the smile her boss had given a freshman congressman from Ohio, the smile and an agreement not to oppose a floor amendment from the freshman that would give a $6-million tax break for his district. In turn, the freshman gave her boss his marker for final passage of the bill. What the freshman hadn't known is that her boss already had a deal with the Rules Committee to send the bill to the Floor with a no-amendments rule. Her boss kept his promises, but he'd snookered the freshman. "Procedure beats substance," her boss said. Now if they could get labor to squeeze the senator from—

*Stop it!* she ordered herself. *It's your day off.*

In her bedroom, she kicked off her shoes and found a hanger for her suit, slipped off the jacket. Unzipped the skirt, clipped it to the hanger. There was a coffee stain on her blouse. She shook her head as she tossed it in the dry-cleaning hamper: another $1.50 accident. She peeled off her panty hose, tossed them toward the bureau. They floated to the floor. She laughed and accidentally looked in the full-length mirror on the bathroom door.

Saw her reflection. For the first time in months, she stopped and really *looked*.

Lines of gray streaked her black hair. Her bra was faded white with torn lace. The elastic in her cotton panties was shot; she could see flesh through the thin material over one cheek.

The extra weight from the baby had melted off six months after his birth, but her muscle tone had never come back. The waist was there, no roll, but her belly bulged. Her breasts filled the C cups, but when the bra came off, the flesh sagged.

"What do you think?" she asked the dog. He didn't answer. She hoped Nick was blinder than her mirror. Often as not, women were beautiful in the novels he wrote.

She saw stretch marks. Forty merciless years.

"But I'm here Monday mornings," she told the mirror.

And she thought about the coming Friday night; smiled.

Her old blue jeans felt good, the long-sleeved pink top was comfy. She liked her feet bare.

It was her afternoon off, and she was blissfully alone.

One of the few points of contention in her marriage was that she loved to read in bed and Nick didn't. But Nick wasn't there. As the dog curled up on the bedroom carpet, she piled the pillows against the headboard, snapped on the bedside lamp. She snuggled into the pillows, picked up the biography of Martin Luther King she'd been savoring in snippets carved out of busy days, and lost herself in the panorama of real politics and true heroes.

The dog growled as Sylvia read about the sixteen-year-old girl defying conventional wisdom in 1951 and rallying her high school classmates to break the chains of segregated schools.

"Quiet!" ordered Sylvia.

The rottweiler flowed to his feet, a hill becoming a muscular river of black fur, flashing eyes, and white teeth.

"There's nobody here," she muttered, her eyes clinging to the words inked on the book pages. "Saul's sleeping."

The dog barked, a guttural bass explosion.

"No! You'll wake—"

The doorbell rang.

*A mailman*, she thought, swinging off the bed. *Special package, probably from a grandparent or her sister in Milwaukee.*

God, *don't let it be a salvation squad: old ladies wearing hats and bearing* The Watchtower, *Bible-toting young men in white shirts and black ties.*

She hoped the dog wouldn't scare them—too much.

"Coming!" she yelled as she hurried downstairs. She grabbed the choke-chain collar, pulled the dog back from he front door: 120 pounds and the vet said there was more to come. "Sit!"

*Why the hell couldn't Nick have wanted a cocker spaniel?*

Their dog had a diploma from obedience school.

"But no summa cum laude," she'd complained to Nick.

"*Sit!*" She jerked his collar. He calmed down enough to back away from the door. He strained against the choke collar, the metal cutting into her hand as she opened the door.

Found him standing there.

Big and crazy, matted hair, stubbled face. His shirt was stained with road filth. Greasy jeans. Battered sneakers. The chilly wind carried his stench of sweat, bad breath, and sour whiskey, and he wobbled as he stood before her.

"I'm sorry," he said.

*That voice:* five, six times she'd answered the phone for late-night calls that all her pleas to Nick never seemed to end.

"I'm sorry," he said again. "You're Sylvia. I'm Jud."

"H . . . Hi."

Her smiling response was automatic. But her heart and head reeled. This man was important to Nick, his friend—a man whose problems Nick had taken on. And here he stood on her porch, clearly needy. But no one in their lives troubled her more. His specter had haunted them. As a ghost, he was an abstract worry; on her porch, he embodied dangers she never let herself name. The choke collar cutting into her hand felt welcome.

"What are you doing here?" she asked, though she knew.

"Nick, I need to see Nick."

"He should be at his office," she said.

"I can't make it there," he said, and she saw that was true. "Car smoked up, died in Pennsylvania. Stole a bus ticket to West Virginia. Hitched to Maryland with a minister. Let me off at the Beltway sign that said Takoma Park. Rest of the way, I humped it. You're in the phone book, gas station knew the street.

"I can't hump it anymore," he said.

Low in his throat, the dog growled.

"I'm sorry." Jud's face lost the little color it had. "I don't want to be trouble."

His eyes were moist. Raindrops dotted the sidewalk behind him, falling faster, harder.

"I can wait on the porch," he said. It was covered. He shrugged. "They might see me sitting out here."

The Washington suburb of Takoma Park is filled with trees, winding streets—America's Azalea City, with acres of pink- and red-dotted bushes. No one watched from her neighbors' closed windows. No one sat in the few parked cars. It wasn't a busy street. Nor was it a hard street to find.

Propriety and compassion overrode Sylvia's caution. "Don't be silly. Come inside. But don't move fast. The dog doesn't like strangers."

"Smart dog," said Jud, shuffling with her as she backed into the house, her hand tight around the collar.

She kept ten feet between them, led them past the full book-cases of the living room, past the fireplace with its mantel of happy pictures to the open dining room and its round oak table.

"You can sit there," she said.

Jud collapsed onto the chair.

The dog strained against Sylvia's grip.

"Easy," she said. "Easy."

She let him go. He trotted to Jud, smelled him, then moved between his human and the stranger.

"Long as everything is fine, he won't hurt you."

*Why are you talking so tough?* she thought. But then she looked at him, saw he didn't care: Jud's eyes were lost in the table's brown mirror finish.

Sylvia propped the kitchen door open. Her view of Jud was blocked as she moved to the wall phone, but she could see the dog; she'd know if Jud moved.

Nick's machine answered her call: "Come home right away!" she told the tape.

*Juanita.* She was going to her cousin's. Sylvia called that house. A man answered, and Sylvia told him, *"Dígale à Juana que venga à mi casa lo mas pronto, que pueda por favor."*

She hung up, walked back to the dining room.

"You're Spanish is still good from Mexico," muttered Jud. "The Peace Corps."

"How did you know about that?" she asked.

"Nick."

"What else did he tell you?" She crossed her arms over her chest; felt the touch of unseen eyes.

The wreck of a man shrugged. "That he loves you."

"Oh." She shook her head, pressed her hand over her eyes. "Look, I don't mean to be so . . ."

"Paranoid," he finished for her. "That's smart."

"That's not the most reassuring thing to tell me."

"I don't want to lie to you," he said.

Her neck felt cold. She blurted out, "We don't want your trouble."

"Me either." Yet again he said, "I'm sorry. I need to talk to Nick. Tell him . . . bad news."

"What?"

"I don't want to say it more times than I have to."

"Is that all you want?"

"I don't want to hurt him. I never did. Or you."

"Then maybe you should have stayed away from us."

"Yeah."

*Why doesn't the phone ring!* she thought. *Where's Nick?*

"You can't stay here tonight," she said, hating herself for fears she didn't understand but couldn't ignore.

"Okay."

The dog finally sat, but kept his eyes on Jud.

Suddenly she felt too cruel.

"Do you . . . Are you thirsty?"

"Got a drink?"

"We don't have any liquor in the house."

"Oh," he said, and they both knew he recognized the lie.

"Do you speak Spanish?" she asked.

"I can order beer and say *gracias*. Tequila. *Señora and señorita.* Eat the worm."

"All we've got is milk," she blurted.

"Milk?" He shook his head. "I'd love a glass of milk."

As she gingerly sat a cold glass of milk on the table, a baby's crying floated downstairs to them.

"That's Saul," said Jud.

*"No!"* snapped Sylvia. "I mean, stay here. I'll go . . . take care of him. Stay here."

"Whatever you want."

The dog came with her. She wasn't sure if that was a good thing or not.

Saul smiled at her from his crib. He wore overalls and a Mickey Mouse sweatshirt, socks. He was standing without holding on to the bars. He reached out for Mommy.

Probably he was wet, but she didn't want to change his diaper, risk *exposing* him. Not even for a minute.

When they came downstairs, the dog led the way. He kept between his baby and the stranger.

"He looks like Nick," said Jud of the son the mother carried into the dining room.

"Yes." Saul clung to her neck: *Who was this guy?* "I have to fix him something to eat."

"Sure."

"You . . . Are you hungry?"

"Been awhile." His milk glass sat on the table. Empty.

*Shit,* she thought. *I should have asked sooner and I shouldn't have asked at all.*

In the kitchen, the baby held on to her leg as she opened cans of tuna fish. But by the time she dumped the tuna into a bowl and started mixing in mayonnaise, he'd wandered to the door. Sylvia kept an eye on him as he held on to the doorjamb and stared at the man sitting where his daddy always sat.

The dog moved close to his boy.

"Hi, Saul," said the gravel voice in the dining room. "How you doing?"

Saul stared, drooled.

Jud smiled. Saul smiled back. Jud made a monkey face, an orangutan. Saul blinked. Jud scratched his arms and mouthed simian noises, bounced around in his chair. The baby's smile became a grin, and he pointed at the funny man. Jud covered his face with his hand; peeked through his fingers. The boy giggled. One after another, Jud slapped his hands down his own face, a surprised monkey grin showing between blows.

Saul laughed, hit his own face. Jud laughed with him. Excited, Saul ran into the kitchen, to Mommy.

Jud laughed again, shook his head at the son.

Then he cried, quietly and completely, tears running down his cheeks as he stared at the empty doorway.

*She must have heard me crying,* he thought, because she called out, "Here comes your sandwich," but waited a minute before she walked into the dining room bearing a tray with two tuna fish sandwiches with lettuce and tomato on whole wheat bread, potato chips, a fresh glass of milk.

A baby boy who adored his father toddled behind his mother, who loved them both.

Jud had time to wipe his cheeks.

As she sat the tray down, she asked, "Are you okay?"

"Sure." He forced the words out, got his breath back. He could smell the bread, the tuna. "Sure.

"I was just being a monkey," he said. "For the boy."

He looked at the wide blue eyes beside her knees.

*"Monkey man!"* Jud said. Made the face. Made Saul giggle.

Sylvia sat at the table, that brave with the dog nearby. She scooped her son to her lap. Spoon-fed him from a bowl of tuna.

"Who are you?" she asked Jud.

The food melted in his mouth. His stomach rumbled with denial, with anticipation. One sandwich disappeared in five bites.

"I'm your husband's best friend," he said.

"I don't think so," she said.

Half the second sandwich went inside him; his guts struggled with the abundance of riches. His hands trembled, and he wondered where they kept the liquor.

"Guess not," he said. "Guess I was just dreaming."

"Not with my family," she whispered, embarrassment at her anger flushing her face. She could feel the paring knife she'd hidden in the right back pocket of her jeans. She hated herself for doing it, found comfort in its pressure.

Jud heard the love in her words, wanted to weep; coveted her devotion. He finished his sandwich. Held out a potato chip.

"Here," said Jud. Saul took it. "I'm the monkey man."

# THE INSIDER

**W**es had called ahead after leaving Nick, so they were waiting for him at the main gate. An escort car led him along the road winding through the trees, around the massive building, down into the CIA's underground garage.

They drove slowly through that dank concrete cavern. By an elevator at the end of a row of cars stood Kramer, head of security. Two men with wary eyes and loose suits were with him. The escort driver motioned for Wes to park.

"Leave the keys in it!" Kramer yelled as Wes climbed out of his car. He carried his attaché case of money and documents.

"Give me your gun," said Kramer.

"That's not in the deal," answered Wes.

Kramer kept his eyes on the big man and angled his head toward his two aides. "You'll never even see Andy's hands move."

"I won't be watching him."

"We don't need his help to get it," said one of the suits.

"Never mind," said Kramer. "The major might be a fool, but he's not a fanatic."

The four of them rode elevators to the top floor. The carpeted executive corridor was empty. Kramer led Wes to the unlabeled brown door. Knocked. They went inside.

Air Force general and Deputy Director of the CIA Billy Cochran sat behind his desk. He peered through his thick glasses.

"He reads clean on electronics scan," said Kramer. "He's carrying a gun, but no wire and no recorder."

"Thank you, Mr. Kramer," said Billy. "You'll handle the rest?"

"Personally. And my men are just outside the door."

Kramer left them alone.

"Where's Director Denton?" said Wes.

"Is answering that part of our deal?" said Billy.

"Just tell me." Wes took a chair in front of the desk.

"He's attending a conference at the State Department, with his secretary. And Noah Hall got an urgent call from the White House just before you arrived. A political crisis that required him to leave the building."

"You handled that nicely."

"Those men are your superiors—not me. You spurned my help before. So why are you bringing me your 'deal' now?"

"They're politicians, but they play minor league ball: all careers and no risks."

"What does that make me? And who then are you?"

"I'm a soldier."

Billy's voice dripped sarcasm. "Selfless in the service of your country."

"You took the deal," said Wes.

"I lifted the burn and alert notices so you could come in. Like a stay of execution, my intercession can be reversed. You are a man in a world of trouble."

"You ought to know. It's your world, *sir.*"

"I don't kill people in the desert."

"Really? Well, that's not important now. Denton and Noah didn't trust me. They screwed me up and deserted under fire. But I should have expected that when I took their job. Maybe I did, and maybe I didn't care. I can't remember, it doesn't matter. I needed a mission, they gave me one. Now it needs finishing, and they can't do it. Wouldn't if they could. I came to you because you're the insider, and that's where the answers are."

"To what? Your wounded phantom, Jud Stuart?"

"This isn't about him. He's just the body in the bag."

"Where is he?"

"The deal was you'd have Kramer run three names for me."

"You've been given everything in the system about Jud Stuart."

"We'll skip past that lie."

"I do not lie." A sentence as flat and hard as a saber.

"But you're a genius at structuring the truth: *in the system.* What does that mean?"

"Ask your names," said Billy, picking up the phone to where Mike Kramer waited in front of a computer terminal plugged into the greatest network of information in history.

"Beth Doyle," said Wes.

He gave Billy what other data he could remember, and the general relayed it to Kramer. Billy hung up.

"This will take time. Now—"

"We can wait."

In silence, they did.

Wes tired of watching the thick glasses of the man behind the desk. On the walls hung Billy's collection of Japanese woodblock prints from the era of emperors. The prints were beautiful, the warriors bold with their drawn swords and wise as they knelt to work on their calligraphy, swords sheathed by their sides.

Twenty-two minutes later, the phone rang. A fax machine behind Billy's desk hummed. Billy answered his phone, listened. He hung up, tore a freshly transmitted sheet out of his fax machine, and passed it across the desk to Wes.

An old passport photo.

"Yes," said Wes.

"There are legions of Beth Doyles," said Billy. "But your data indicated her. No arrest record or warrants. A lot of foreign travel: visas for Asia, Europe."

"Who does she belong to?"

Dryly, Billy said, "The records indicate she's single."

"You know what I mean: is she one of you?"

For a heartbeat, Billy didn't answer.

"There is no indication," he said, "that she has ever been employed by a government security, intelligence, or law enforcement agency. No indication of contact, no registry in an active file or a cross-reference in anything other than routine customs and State Department records for travelers."

"What else?"

"What else could she be?" Billy's hands spread wide. "All that travel? She could be a recruit of a foreign agency."

"That wouldn't matter for this."

"But if there is any chance of that," insisted Billy, "our CI people and the FBI should be notified."

"No chance. Keep her out of their files."

"Then you shouldn't have had us run a check on her."

Wes shook his head, sighed. "Would it show if she worked for a private eye named Jack Berns?"

Billy polished his glasses with a tissue.

"Our files contain the license records for this area. Nothing showed up, but my understanding of that *profession* is that its regulation leaves something to be desired."

"No," said Wes, "she wouldn't work for him."

A great weight floated from his heart; another one settled in its place.

"Give me your second name," ordered Billy.

Wes handed him the driver's license of the man who'd followed Nick Kelley, the man Wes had ambushed at Union Station.

The number two man at the CIA frowned. He telephoned the data on the Virginia driver's permit to Kramer.

During the ten-minute wait, Wes closed his eyes. He imagined Beth, her hair, her mouth, her smoky taste. Her look as she held his gun, as she walked out the door. He heard her laugh and remembered how it filled his heart.

The phone rang.

"Yes?" Billy listened to the voice from another room. His eyes withdrew behind the thick glasses. "I see . . . Thank you."

After he hung up, Billy frowned, then pushed away from his desk, turned his back on Wes, and walked to the windows. Today his limp was noticeable. He stared out the glass at the rain-gray sky and the tops of the trees in the Virginia forest.

"Aren't you going to ask me for the next name?" said Wes. He waited like a fielder, eyes on the man at the plate.

"How far gone is this?" Billy finally said.

"Too far to stop."

"You've done a good job, Major. You should be proud."

"Fuck you, *sir*," said Wes.

The expletive turned Billy from the window.

"If we were in uniform," he said evenly, "I could throw you into hell for that."

"Yes sir," Wes told the man silhouetted against the sky.

"I respect uniforms," said Billy. "As, I suspect, do you. For their precision. Their sense of purpose. They represent an extension of our institutions, and our institutions are us at our best. They are our salvation."

"Don't you want to know the third name?" said Wes.

"I did not intend to make intelligence my career," said America's most respected spy. "The military, yes. But here . . ."

His gesture swept beyond his office.

"I dislike HUMINT," he said. "Agents in place, legends instead of identities, floaters, contracts . . . covert operatives. Covert operations. They breed a culture and a mind-set that dulls the precision of institutions. Means can become ends. Men can be seduced by that, lost in it. Perhaps like Jud Stuart."

"Forget about him. You know the third name."

"Varon," said Billy. "General Byron Varon. Retired."

"What do you know about him and Jud Stuart?" said Wes.

"Knowledge is a precise term, Major."

"Don't bullshit me, *General*. I'm a lawyer. I know all about exactitude and fine lines and how only God can't hide behind ignorance. We're not talking about the law here. We're talking about truth."

"The truth is that our job is to preserve this country," said Billy. "Democracy stands or falls on its institutions."

"It stands or falls on its people," answered Wes. "I told you this was gone too far to stop."

"But not too far to avoid more damage. Not so far gone as to start witch-hunts."

"I don't know about that," said Wes.

"I do." Billy shook his head. "This business is secrecy and secrecy breeds fantasy, even among the most brilliant of minds. The things I've heard! That people believe! *Grand conspiracies.* There is no grand conspiracy. Just small whirlpools."

He walked back to his desk, took an unmarked file folder from the top drawer, and handed it to Wes.

"How long have you had this?" whispered Wes.

"It's not an Agency file," said Billy. "It's mine. I worked for the Joint Chiefs with General Varon. He served there when he got back from the Middle East and before he went to the Pentagon. His Special Forces experience made him useful in low-intensity-conflict projects like the aborted second rescue mission to get the hostages out of Iran, certain aid programs.

"Varon excelled at doing what people wanted done but were too cautious to do themselves. And he was *politically correct*—vocally anticommunist with just enough foam in his mouth. In addition to his stated duties, he ran a few operatives, a team he kept isolated after Vietnam. An off-the-books apparatus. Never admitted or logged into the system—wiped out of it, in fact.

"I learned about it quite by accident. My prejudices against such things were well-known, so some of them were isolated from my purview. Various projects skimmed back funds for him—he didn't need much. He relied on patriots who trusted that whatever irregular service they performed helped the country. Maybe he paid bribes. Here, there, instances I couldn't be sure of, he'd help. Provide product to selected allies in agencies like DEA and the FBI as well as CIA, DOD."

"So you started a file on him."

"He was in the cracks of the institutional process," said Billy. "A man with an independent agenda and personal power base. That seemed prudent."

"And Jud Stuart?"

"He's been calling in since the mid-1970s. Burned-out, lost. But obviously somebody. When I saw those reports, checked his files . . . He seemed likely to have been one of Varon's men."

"How many more are there?"

"I have no idea. The man on that driver's license is linked to one of Varon's businesses. He's been a contract agent for various official entities in the past. That company was involved in Iran-contra. As was Varon, in several ways."

Cochran shook his head. "In the early 1980s, Varon retired from the Army under a cloud. A surplus-weapons sales scandal. A prosecutor looked into it, but couldn't find enough evidence to bring charges."

"Damn!"

"Yes. Whatever he's done since then has definitely been off the reservation. You ask about Varon's associates? Ours is a deep but small sea. The same fish keep swimming by. You learn to wait. Watch. Listen. I'd heard once that Varon hired a private eye to help him with a business deal."

"Jack Berns," said Wes. "Did Noah Hall know that?"

"Noah works the electoral back rooms. He knows less than he thinks he does." Billy shrugged. "You harness the horse you know. Berns makes a point of being known."

"Would Berns have known about Varon's network?"

"I doubt it. But Berns is in the information business. He knew Noah and Denton were interested in Jud Stuart—and that their interest was not protected by normal channels. He might have offered the trust bestowed in him to other old customers."

"Berns is crazy to double-deal them."

"Only if he gets caught. And only if they succeed in making him pay for his betrayal."

"Who else is in this?" said Wes.

"I don't know," said Billy.

Slowly, Wes opened the manila file. Plain sheets of paper, no letterhead. Typewritten on different machines. Precise paragraphs of supposition, analysis of covert operations and intelligence supplied to various agencies from unknown sources. The particulars blurred in his eyes: Iran, Chile, cocaine.

"You've had this all along," he whispered. He glared at the man in thick glasses. "You knew all along!"

"I *knew* nothing!" Billy leaned toward Wes. "My first recommendation was to let sleeping dogs lie. This is history—Varon is an old man. Sick, I hear. His power all but gone. His exposure in Iran-contra was his second slip and he knows he'll get nailed in a third. I knew no good would come out of chasing phantoms and stirring up ghosts. Jud Stuart might have been important once, but he'd become a broken record of no value to the Agency's legitimate business.

"My superiors disagreed," he continued. "Fine. That's the way institutions work. But did they follow procedure? Did they pursue their goals through channels? No: they brought in you. They cut me out and brought in you."

He leaned back in his chair.

"That's *my* file, *my* unofficial speculations. My orders were to stay uninvolved. I bent those orders, offered you help, but you turned it down. Just like Varon and all his people, you were off the books, out of the loop, off the shelf, off the reservation. Cowboy. Not my concern."

"Well, you're in it now, *General!* You and your institutions! I don't care if you've covered your ass, somewhere out there, you and yours are responsible. There's corpses all across this country and—"

"They appear to be in your trail, Major."

"That's right!" Wes jammed his forefinger at Billy's desk. "And my trail leads right here."

Billy took off his glasses, wiped his brow.

"Jud Stuart may be a broken record," said Wes, "but he's got some song that's worth something to Varon. Something that started this whole thing. Something that sent a sailor who worked in the White House—and who I bet was on Varon's team—from San Francisco to L.A. I don't know why. But Varon does. And whatever it is, it's not about history or institutions, it's about today."

"Today is my concern," said Billy. "That file, Varon, Jud: the world has changed out from under all that. The Berlin Wall is gone! KGB headquarters gives tours to American newsmen! But the need for this institution, for my CIA, is just as great: trade wars, terrorists, nuclear proliferation . . . I don't know where we'll have to go, but if we get torn apart by another scandal, by the sins of good intentions or bad ops that Jud Stuart and Varon represent . . . today is what will suffer. And tomorrow."

"Fuck it," said Wes.

"How noble of you to incur that debt for the country."

"Let's get out from under all this bullshit," said Wes.

"How?"

"I'll bring Jud in. You protect him. Immunity, whatever he needs."

"You're a lawyer, you know I can't give that."

"Of course you can. One phone call."

"What else?"

"Whatever Varon's done, nail him for it. I've lost too much to let that son of a bitch slide."

"You? I thought this was about America."

"I'm a United States Marine."

"Who's been operating in a dubious fashion."

"Prosecute me for what I did. Give me my day in court."

"There are other remedies."

"That's a two-way street," said Wes. "I know a writer with an ax to grind. He's already involved. Lot of ways I can help him."

"What do you get out of all this?" asked Billy.

"Out of all this," answered Wes.

"And?"

"That's it." Wes paused, said, "Anything more, I'm stuck for good."

Gen. Billy Cochran leaned across the desk. "Major, you are

already stuck. The only question is how hard and how deep—and if you screw with me, if you fail . . ."

"I know my chances," said Wes.

"Be careful with your choices," said Billy. "What about Director Denton?"

"You'll finesse him," said Wes. "You're the inside man, the pro. He wants to stay up there high and mighty and loved, with a spotless record. You'll figure a way to give him that. Or scare him enough so he doesn't mess us up."

"When can you get Jud Stuart here?"

"As soon as possible," answered Wes. "If you keep the dogs off my back."

"I can contain the interest of the federal agencies—if it's no more extensive than I know about and if your sins are no more heinous than you imply. But no group will help you. I can't authorize aid from this agency without Director Denton's approval, which I won't get. Noah will tell him I betrayed them when I lifted the burn notice, conspired against them in this meeting."

"You can take care of yourself. When this is over, none of that will matter."

"And you are in your own hands, Major. Remember: Varon is an experienced strategist who deserves his combat medals."

The Marine shook his head, stood.

"You'll just be doing your job, Major," said the Deputy Director of the CIA, already spinning a new web in refined light. "The one Denton gave you. Bring in Jud Stuart. And do it quickly. We'll work it out."

Billy held out his hand. "The file is mine."

The unlabeled manila file folder was light in Wes's grip, full of notes he ached to study. This was a file folder no subpoena would ever find, a file Billy wouldn't routinely keep in his desk. How many more like it were there somewhere else?

"What were you going to do with this?" asked Wes. "What would you have done if I hadn't uncovered Varon or come to you with this deal?"

"Whatever was necessary and prudent," said Billy. His hand hung empty in the air. Waiting.

Wes dropped the file on the desk.

|||||||||||||||||||||||||||||||||||||||||||||||||||||||||||||||||||||||||||||||||||||||

# THE TUNNEL

All Nick wanted to do was go home.

As he drove through afternoon traffic, the Capitol dome in his rearview mirror, he didn't care about Wes Chandler, USMC. He didn't care about Jud or the CIA or villains who betrayed America's trust. He wanted to go home, hear his wife laugh and feel her embrace, to watch his son toddle across the living room. The dog would lick Nick's hand. He wanted to call his mother in Michigan, hear about hometown weather and her Monday-night bridge game, his crazy aunts. He wished his father were still alive. Nick was drained and battered, and all he wanted to do was go home.

Traffic was tense: cars hurrying to get where they were going before the storm broke and the streets turned slick.

Their Jeep was in the driveway: *Sylvia was home early.*

The dog barked as Nick walked up the sidewalk. *He always barked.* Sylvia opened their front door, a stern look on her face. Nick hurried toward her to say that everything would be all right. He hoped that he wouldn't be lying.

"*He's here!*" she whispered as he bounded up the porch.

"What?"

"*Jud,*" she said. "Inside."

"Dad'y!" Saul charged behind his delighted squeal, grabbed Nick's knees for balance and love. "Dad'y!"

The dog trotted behind the baby. Made sure it was his master at the door. Looked back into the house.

"I've been calling you all day!" said Sylvia as Nick scooped Saul into his arms.

"I—"

"I told him he couldn't stay." She felt embarrassed shame equal to the pressure of the paring knife in her back pocket. Nick was here, everything was fine. She smiled weakly at her husband, but his answering gaze was empty of joy or relief.

His son in his arms, his wife by his side, his dog leading the way, Nick walked into the dining room.

Saw Jud sitting at the table. In front of him were a cup of coffee and a banana peel.

"Long time, Bro'." Jud smiled. His voice was tired.

"How did you get here?" muttered Nick.

"Best I could." Jud sighed. "There's no one on my tail."

"Yes, there is," said Nick.

"Yeah," confessed Jud. "But nobody followed me here."

Nick sat at the dining room table, Jud to his right. Sylvia sat to his left. Saul squirmed in his arms, watched the big people, his eyes wide, his head pressed back into Nick's chest.

"You said you had bad news," Sylvia told Jud.

The two men looked at her; she stared back, unflinching.

"I'm part of this, too," she insisted.

"Tell me," said Nick.

"Lorri's dead," said Jud.

"I know," said Nick.

It was a toss-up who was more surprised, Jud or Sylvia.

"How did you—" began Jud.

But Nick interrupted, "How did she die?"

"She . . . Suicide. I found her. In Nebraska."

"Jesus," whispered Sylvia. Fear crept into her dining room.

"Are you sure?" said Nick.

"What do you mean is he sure?" The wife stared at her husband.

Who wouldn't look at her; repeated, "Are you sure?"

"She did it herself. Alone." Jud shook his head. "But I put the razor in her hand a long time ago. Figure I killed her."

"No," said Nick. "Not by yourself."

"No matter. Doesn't clean my slate."

"What do you two mean?" said Sylvia. "Jud, I never met her, but I'm sorry, I . . ." Her look expanded to include both men. "What do you mean?"

"How did you know?" Jud asked his old friend.

First Nick, then Jud looked at Sylvia.

"No," she said.

"Honey—" began Nick.

"*No!*" she insisted. "You're my husband! That's my son you're holding! This is our life and *you two* can't toss it around in some macho bullshit that—"

Mommy yelled so Saul cried. The dog got to his feet.

"Sylvia, let me just . . . figure out where we are, what—"

"We are in our *home!* With your damn secrets! I'm your wife: that gives me privilege. I can't be forced to testify—"

"I'm not worried about testimony." Nick rocked his sobbing baby.

"Then what are you worried about?"

"It'll just be better if you give me and Jud some time alone," said Nick.

"Better for who?" she asked.

"For everyone," said her husband. "When I can, I'll tell you everything, and it'll be okay. Trust me."

"Like you trust me now?" she said.

The baby howled.

"That's not the issue," said Nick.

"No," snapped Sylvia, standing, bundling Saul into her arms. She nodded toward their son. "He is."

Sylvia glared at the stranger who'd brought legends of death under her roof; glared back at her husband.

"*Forsaking all others,* right?" she said. "We should have stuck with the traditional vows instead of writing our own."

The mother picked up her son and headed upstairs. The baby's cries grew fainter. The two men seated at the dining room table could hear the ticking of the grandfather clock in the living room. The dog stayed downstairs, with them.

"I like her," said Jud.

"Me, too," whispered Nick.

"How did you know about Lorri?" asked Jud.

Nick hesitated.

"You have to trust me," said Jud. "I've never done you."

Nick told Jud about Jack Berns and the Marine named Wes, about the ambush at Union Station. But he didn't mention Iran-contra, or a retired general named Varon.

"How do you know this guy Wes Chandler is who he says he is?" asked Jud.

"Besides his ID?" said Nick.

"'ID' stands for 'Idiot's Deceit.' You know how many people I've been, complete with IDs? So why do you trust him?"

"He had a gun." Nick didn't mention the ambushed man's revolver, now in his backpack. "He didn't have to let me walk."

"Wheels within wheels," said Jud. "Don't you remember what I taught you?"

"That ambush wasn't faked."

"You mean some hero wouldn't volunteer to take a few punches to establish that Marine's bona fides with you? So he could find out what you know and *then* take you out of the box?"

"He found out enough of what I know," said Nick. "And he didn't take me out of the box. So I trust him—at least a little."

"What does he know? What do you know?"

"No," said Nick. He felt the flow between them change. "All these years, you called the shots. I never demanded answers you wouldn't give. And that was fine, because I was just along to learn the ride. I wasn't part of it. At least, so I thought.

"But not now," said Nick. "When you called the last time, you tied me up in it. That's how everybody got to me. No matter if I'd done nothing, they'd have come after me to get to you. You made me a player, and I'm not going to just ride along."

"What do you want?" said Jud.

"To walk away safe, but that's something you can't fix."

"Maybe I—"

"No maybes," said Nick. "I know this guy. He's not a *maybe* you can control."

Jud sighed, rubbed his brow.

"Why'd you come here?" said Nick.

"Lorri . . . She—"

"I know about her . . . note. You put the razor in her hand, I tipped her it was time to use it. I know I'm probably the last friend you got who would help you and not cut a deal out of your hide. But why else did you come back to D.C.?"

"Aren't you reason enough?"

"For you," said Nick, "it's always wheels within wheels."

The clock ticked. Nick felt it like a heartbeat.

"I have to see the man who started it all," said Jud.

"Your case officer. The head of the team you were on."

"All those labels fit," said Jud.

"Why?" asked Nick.

"That's what I have to find out," said Jud.

"But you already think you know." Nick's look forced the answer.

"There was a job he wanted me to do," said Jud. "In '85 or '86—these days, sometimes . . . I started drinking heavy and . . ."

"I know," said Nick. "I understand."

"I didn't do it," said Jud. "It sounded like a setup, and I'm *nobody's* sucker."

Again he laughed. "Or everybody's."

"What job?" said Nick.

"No," said Jud. "If I tell you . . . then you know."

"Maybe I do already," said Nick. "Iran-contra."

"Just because you're in the stands doesn't mean you know the play," said Jud.

"If they sent someone to get you in L.A., if the job you turned down was a setup . . . what the hell do you think you'd be walking into now? If they're after you, why walk right in to them?"

"Where else can I go? What else can I do? Besides, they don't know when I'm coming. They don't know *I* know who he is."

"Who is he?" asked Nick. "What can he give you?"

"I can see him," was Jud's answer.

"Meet the Marine," said Nick. "Wes Chandler. He'll do it by your rules. Talk to him. Let him help you—help us."

"He's one of them," said Jud. "Even if he's not lying to you, he's one of them. He could be the Erasureman."

"The what?"

"When they want to clean up a problem, erase it, hit somebody, they have a meeting, a chat with Dr. Gunn, who's the expert. Then they send the Erasureman." The growl that always chilled Nick's blood came into Jud's voice. "I ought to know."

"He's not the Erasureman," whispered Nick. "If he were, he would have sat on me until you showed. He knew you'd come to me. He'd have had people on the house. He'd have . . . finished by now."

Jud's hand trembled as he touched the stubble around his dry mouth. He licked his lips. Maybe Nick would give him a drink.

"It's not one big *them*," said Nick. "I know who your 'he' is. So does Wes Chandler."

"What?" Jud's hand rattled the coffee cup and saucer.

"Varon," said Nick. "General Varon."

Jud couldn't keep the truth off his face.

"He's not God," said Nick. "He's not invincible or invisible."

"Who told you? Who broke security?"

"He did," said Nick. "When he started serving himself."

"He knows? The Marine?"

"Yes. And he's finding out more." Nick leaned across the table and grabbed his friend's arm.

"It's coming apart," he said, "the whole damn thing. Your only chance is to come in. Chandler's cutting a deal for you with the CIA."

"Oh, *shit.*"

Jud stood. This octagonal, bay-windowed dining room with its lace curtains and shiny mahogany table, its china cabinet and paintings, this house in a quiet suburban neighborhood: everything whirled around him. He caught his balance, saw the door to the kitchen, the refrigerator, and he was there, finding two bottles of Peruvian beer. He chugged half of one. The cold, tangy shock cleared his eyes. He walked back to the living room, a bottle in each hand.

He leaned against the doorjamb, finished the first bottle in a long swig.

"When is he doing this *deal?*" asked Jud.

"He's there now."

"Shit." He tossed the empty bottle into an open trash can in the kitchen. *Two points,* he thought as the beer warmed his stomach, hit his blood.

"With who?" he asked. "The hack the President put in?"

"No. With General Cochran, the number two. The pro."

"*Shit.*" This third time the expletive was a drawl, not a whine. "Billy C. When he was at NSA and the Chiefs . . ." Jud shook his head. "A deal: Billy C. knows how to deal."

"My phones are hot," said Nick. "Varon's people. But we don't think he has many. When Wes makes the deal, he'll call and—"

"I'll be gone."

"You can't run forever!"

"I'm done running," said Jud.

"Come with me," said Nick. "To Wes."

"I'm done with deals, too."

"You put me in this," said Nick. "You owe it to me."

*The last one,* thought Jud. *Nick's the last one left.*

"Okay," he said. "I owe you. I'll see your Marine. After Varon."

"That's not—"

"That's the only way!" snapped Jud. "I don't give a damn about any *deal* with the CIA! What can they give me? Can they sew Lorri's wrists back up? Make Nora alive again? Give me back everything I fucked up and heal every fucking I've gotten?"

"Don't you get it? If I don't do it myself, face him *myself*, it's all their game, and I'm a waste, all for nothing."

"You do that, he'll . . . You can't . . ."

Jud shrugged. "Besides, if he's still got some sanction and I go around him, I'm the traitor."

"You know he's not legit."

"None of us were ever *legit.*"

"Don't," said Nick.

Jud smiled. "I love you like a brother."

"Then treat me like one and trust me."

"You, I trust. But this isn't about you." Jud winked. "Don't worry: he can't beat me."

"He can kill you."

"No, he can't," said Jud.

The doorbell rang.

The dog barked.

Sylvia's footsteps sounded on the stairs; Saul's laughter came closer.

The dog charged the front door.

The doorknob turned. . . .

Nick and Jud raced to the front hall. Nick snatched his backpack off the floor, clawed at its straps as he saw Sylvia coming down the stairs, Saul in her arms, as the door swung open. . . .

"*Hola!*" called Juanita, hurrying in from the rain. "*Sylvia! Soy* . . ."

"Me," she said, slipping into English as she saw Nick. The dog licked her hand. Nick waved Jud back.

"My cousin told me you called," said Juanita, the worry clear on her face.

"Take Saul," said his mother, pulling a yellow rain poncho over the baby's head, pulling the hood's drawstrings tight, kissing his forehead. *"Por la noche."*

"Sylvia," whispered Nick, "what are you . . ."

"What I have to," she said.

Juanita saw Jud's shadowed hulk backing into the dining room, whispered, *"Señora, tu quieres la policía?"*

"No," said Nick.

*"Gracias, no,"* said Sylvia.

Juanita looked at her friends, the parents of her *amorcito*. She hugged Sylvia. More shyly, she hugged Nick.

The parents knelt, kissed their perplexed child, held him, and made their good-byes gentle. Juanita shouldered a diaper bag.

"It's okay," said the Mommy, "you're going to be fine, baby baby boy. Mommy and Daddy love you. We'll see you soon."

Saul grinned: he liked going in the car.

Sylvia cried as Juanita led the yellow-slickered child into the rain.

"He's never been away from us at night," whispered Nick. "He'll be so scared."

The look Sylvia gave her husband could have frozen the rain. "My baby isn't going to be in this!"

Nick put his hand on her shoulder; she was tense, but she didn't shy away. They closed the door.

Wandered back into a living room that seemed empty and bitter. Jud waited for them by the mantel with its pictures of Saul in swaddling clothes, Saul taking his first step, Saul getting licked by the dog.

"What are you going to do?" Sylvia asked them.

"I've got to go see a man," said Jud. "Then there's somebody Nick wants me to meet."

Outside, the rain fell.

"How are you going to get there?" asked Sylvia.

"I'm driving him," said Nick.

*"What?"* Sylvia and Jud said together.

"Yes," said Nick.

"No," said Sylvia.

"I can borrow your money, get a cab or—"

"If you vanish," said Nick, "I'm who's left for them."

The couple glared at each other.

Jud coughed. "Look, I don't have any fresh clothes, but—"

"Wait a minute," said Sylvia.

After she scurried upstairs, Nick told Jud, "Don't give me any argument."

"Okay," he said, "but I'm in charge."

"Bullshit," said Nick.

Sylvia came back. "There's towels and a toothbrush in the first bathroom. Nick's pants won't fit you, but one of his aunts sent him a shirt for his fortieth birthday that might. There's clean socks, underpants a friend of ours left who's . . ."

"Big," said Jud.

"Soap and shampoo," she said, her eyes on Nick.

"Don't do this to us," she told her husband when Jud closed the upstairs bathroom door.

"I'm doing it *for* us," said Nick.

"And what do *we* get out of it? Widows and orphans?"

"I fixed that," said Nick. "Now isn't the time to explain—"

"He's in the shower!"

"If I get polygraphed, I don't want to flunk questions about who knows what."

"I'm your wife. The lawyer. Polygraphs are always voluntary. Who are you going to be talking to?"

"Nobody, I hope. This time tomorrow—"

"Today!" She choked down a sob. Fear overcame anger, and she slid into his arms, crying. "My baby's gone and you're doing something stupid you won't tell me about, and I can't—"

"*Shh,*" he whispered. "*Shh.* It'll be all right."

"Says who?"

"I'm just giving him a ride, then turning him over to a guy I know. An official who—"

"Who better get rid of him for us!"

Nick turned her face up to his. "Who'll do the right thing. And then we're out of it. Clean. I promise you."

"That's what you mean. You can't always be right."

"This time I am," he said.

A thousand thoughts swirled through her, but she could only hold him close, sob, and tell him she loved him.

Jud coughed before he walked down the stairs. A snap-buttoned, cowboy printed shirt strained across his chest and belly.

"My blue Gore-Tex mountaineering coat should fit you," said

Nick. He found that coat in the closet, switched his sports jacket for a dark red nylon windbreaker.

"We might not be back until tomorrow morning," Nick told his wife, certain that he'd be home by midnight but not wanting to terrify her if he wasn't.

"No problem," said Jud.

"For you," snapped Sylvia, then instantly regretted it.

"The phones," said Nick, and he remembered he had to call his homicide cop, clear the Union Station meeting alert and set him up for this move. "Don't say anything on them."

Sylvia's red-streaked face paled.

"What is this?" she whispered.

"Just a road trip," said Nick. "A couple of guys."

Jud emptied the blue Gore-Tex raincoat's pockets of all pieces of paper, all traces of the coat's owner.

"Where are you going?" said Sylvia.

"Better you don't know," said Jud.

"Damn you both," she whispered.

"We could use a map," said Jud.

"There's one in the study," said Nick, leading the way up the stairs, around the corner; leaving Sylvia in the hall.

She waited until they were out of sight, then quickly tiptoed up the stairs. Pressed against the wall, she heard their voices murmur.

Jud: ". . . there once. Off Route Fifty by Annapolis . . ."

Nick: ". . . dozen exits."

Jud: "Multiple . . . remember multiple . . . Four Twenty-four. Highway Four Twenty-Four."

She heard the map being folded.

Sylvia raced down the stairs, made it to the couch in the living room in time for them to see her rise from it. *As if I'd been sitting there, waiting,* she thought.

Jud looked at her, shook his head. "Guess the best thing you can hear from me is good-bye."

He walked out into the rain.

Nick's arms held her tight. "I love you. I'll be back."

And then he left, too.

Rush hour in the rain. By the time they got to the Beltway, the cars were bumper to bumper at thirty miles per hour, a chain of yellow headlights crawling over a mirrored highway. They'd taken Nick's four-door family Jeep. Their windows were open to keep the windshield unfogged. The wipers beat a quick-march cadence.

"You've never met Varon?" said Nick.

"No. Made sense. Security, need to know. Deniability."

"There's some documents in my knapsack," said Nick.

Jud found the revolver, stared at his writer friend.

"We took it off the guy at Union Station," said Nick. "You better take it."

The gun was a familiar weight in Jud's hand.

"No," he said.

Jud scanned the Archives documents. "The Marine knows all this?"

"Yes." Nick put on his left blinker, eased into a lane where the cars crawled faster. "He says you know you can trust him because of the desert, when he could have killed you but didn't."

Jud's eyes floated beyond the windshield.

"Tell me," said Nick. *Before*, he wouldn't have pushed.

"Dean."

"Shit," said Nick, another notch on his conscience.

"You did what you had to do," said Jud. "We all set it up. Dean pushed it over the edge."

The windshield wipers thumped for half a mile. Tears streaked Jud's cheeks.

"What happened in the desert?" asked Nick.

Jud shook his head, wiped his eyes. "I say what I did, it's all over. Give something a name, you die with it."

"What about Dean?" asked Nick.

"If the Marine made it, Dean didn't."

A passing truck splashed water over the Jeep.

"You know the ultimate truth about us?" said Jud.

Nick drove, waited.

"You always wanted to be me," said Jud. "A spy, a tough guy like in one of your books. Out there, on the line. Dark knight for a good cause. *Dangerous*."

And Jud laughed. "What romantic bullshit.

"And I always wanted to be you," Jud added. "A straight fuck who was his own somebody. Who people knew. Picket-fence parents, clean hands, easy sleep, a wife, a kid . . . A life."

"And you for a friend," said Nick.

"I targeted your ass." There was ice in Jud's words; warmth, too. "My mission was to tag your columnist boss's sources. You were there. You wrote a novel about my world, were a journalist, had some legal immunity. I profiled you, folded you in . . . I thought you would be my—"

"Your redeemer," interjected Nick. "That I'd write something because of knowing you and that would redeem you."

"You've thought about it, too?"

"No," said Nick.

They laughed.

Jud shook his head. "You were my confessor. And I taught you about hell. But you never got your wish, *Mr. Dangerous*. Congratulations."

They rode in silence for a moment.

"Neither did I," said Jud.

"Is that what you want?" said Nick. "Straight life?"

"I gave up wanting the impossible in Nebraska," said Jud.

"Then what?" asked Nick. "You can't stay in this life. You lost your stomach for it. If spy games don't kill you, the booze will. Both are shit ways to go. What do you want?"

Jud said nothing for ten miles.

"All these years," Nick finally asked him. "How much of what you told me was true?"

"I don't know," Jud honestly answered.

They followed Nick's headlights and the compass of Jud's memory. The map lay between them. Their route circled D.C. toward Annapolis. Traffic was thick as commuters shuttled along the Washington-Annapolis-Baltimore corridor. Exit 424 was a two-lane state highway through cornfields and groves of trees. This land held too many houses with twinkling lights to be pure country, too few homes to be suburbia or a town of its own.

Their rearview mirror was empty.

"You're sure you know the way?" said Nick. If they got lost, he could convince Jud to turn around; link up with Wes.

"There's a bar up ahead somewhere."

The white lines in the road arced to the left. A red neon light glowed along the road a mile beyond the curve.

"We're not stopping to drink," said Nick.

"Just a landmark."

They whooshed by the tavern, where four cars were parked.

"What do you want from Varon?" said Nick. When Jud didn't answer, Nick said, "What if he's not there?"

"He's got nowhere else to go either," said Jud.

"We could . . . ," began Nick, and then he caught Jud's stare. Nick sighed, said, "No, I guess we couldn't."

"Up there," said Jud. "Turn left at that general store."

Later, they went left again, then again, and then a right that Jud decided was a mistake. They backtracked to the preceding intersection, made a left off their original route.

The compass on Nick's Velcro watchband spun.

This road was only two lanes and erratically striped. At every intersection, Jud made Nick slow the car to a crawl while he peered through the rain and darkness.

"Here," Jud finally said. "I remember that basketball court where the streetlight is shining down on the road."

A battered green road sign read AULDEN DRIVE. They left paved highway for its bumpy gravel path.

"It's a straight shot," said Jud. "Down this road maybe four, five miles. The house is on the right. There's a mailbox."

The path was a tunnel through swaying sycamore trees; their bark shone black and pale gray in Nick's headlights. Shadows of pines and scrub brush waved behind the sycamores. Rain fell through wisps of fog.

"The Chesapeake Bay is close," said Nick. "When I was in fifth grade, we had to trace it over and over for history."

"Stop," said Jud.

A mailbox stood sentry by the road. Nick braked the car, turned off his headlights. The wipers kept up their heartbeat. He pushed the button, and his electric window slid down. The air was cool, damp, smelled green and wet and gravelly. The rain in the forest sounded like a thousand rushing streams.

Through the woods, Nick saw the glow of house lights. A chipped-rock driveway led toward the house in the trees.

"It's about a hundred feet off the road," said Jud. "The trees have grown up around here. I'll hump it in. You go home, I'll—"

"No," said Nick. "We have a deal."

"I'll keep it," insisted Jud. "But you're not coming with me—that would be stupid. When I'm done, I'll call a cab or—"

"A cab? *That's* stupid! Cabs don't—"

"Go home, Nick," said Jud. "You've done enough."

"I didn't get in this car to drive away," said Nick. "I'll buy that you go in alone, but I'll be right here. On the road. Waiting."

Jud looked at his old friend, saw enough not to argue.

Nick held out the revolver. "Here."

"No," said Jud. "Not now."

"You're just going to walk up to the front door?"

"Balls to the wall." Jud opened the Jeep's door. "Stay in the car."

He laughed. "If shit happens, somebody has to go get the Marines."

"Sure," said Nick.

"See you later," said Jud.

Then he was gone, a hulking form slogging up the driveway through the rain. Nick strained: through the storm and the trees, he thought he heard a doorbell, thought he saw a shaft of light escape into the night as a door opened. Imagined he heard voices, questions asked and answered. Then the light vanished; he was alone in the tunnel with only the sound of the rain.

# YELLOW SNAKE

**B**ad weather's rush hour traffic trapped Wes; it took him an hour to get into D.C., another half hour to get through it and find the Maryland suburb. The Beltway would have looped him around the city, but he preferred the straight line to the curve, even if it wasn't the easiest way.

The house looked wonderful, even in the dark: big, rambling, blue. Gables, covered front porch. Oak trees. A yard for kids. *Did Beth like this kind of place?* He parked, took his attaché case, and hurried up the sidewalk through the rain.

*Like a husband home from a hard day's work,* he thought.

A dog barked inside the house. A big dog.

She didn't answer the first time he rang the bell. Nor the second. When he didn't leave, he heard her quiet the dog behind the wooden door.

"What do you want?" came her muffled voice.

"I'm a friend of Nick's!" said Wes. "Please open the door: the dog sounds like he can keep me out, and I hate shouting our business for the neighbors."

The door swung open. She was pretty: black hair, smile lines on a grim face. She held tight to the rottweiler.

"Who are you?"

"Wes Chandler, a friend of your husband's."

"I don't know you."

"I'm new," said Wes. "Is he here?"

"He'll be right back! You can't wait!"

*Right back?* Nick had said he'd go home, wait. "Where did he go? Does this have something to do with Jud?"

"I don't know what you're talking about." Her face said she lied. "Now please leave."

"You've got to trust me, Mrs. Kelley."

"Why?"

"I'm a Marine officer. A lawyer and—"

"I'm a lawyer, too. Big deal."

Her hand grabbed the door: he was losing her.

"You work for a congressman!" blurted Wes. "Nick said!"

She frowned, stayed her push.

"Suppose the congressman vouches for me?" said Wes.

"If you knew him, I'd know you."

"Wait." Wes took his cellular phone from the attaché case. "We can't use yours."

He saw her blink.

"What's the congressman's name?" When she didn't answer, he said, "I can call and get your listing in a staff directory."

She told him.

Wes called a number he'd been given weeks before. "General Butler, it's Wes Chandler. A while back, you told me that if I needed help, you would send up some flares."

"From what I hear, you've been burning up the sky yourself," said the Marine who was Wes's mentor.

"Not enough, sir. There was some confusion the last few days. I was reported AWOL. That report has been corrected."

"Shitty business, Major."

"Yes sir. And I'm taking fire. Flares, sir."

"What?"

"I need you to call a congressman—now. Vouch for me."

"What the hell are you doing, Wes?"

"*Semper fi,*" was his reply.

General Butler sighed. "Which son of a bitch do you want?"

Sylvia made him wait on the porch. They didn't try small talk. The dog waited by her side, mouth open, eyes on Wes.

Seventeen minutes later, the cellular phone buzzed.

"Who's this?" growled a man when Wes answered.

"Congressman?" asked Wes.

"I know who I am, who the hell are you?"

"One moment, sir."

Sylvia hesitated; took the phone.

"Yes?" she said. "Yes. . . . I appreciate it. . . . No. . . . I can't tell you now. . . . No, it won't affect you. . . . Thank you. . . . Okay."

She handed the phone to Wes. "He wants to talk to you."

"Major," snapped the congressman, "Sam Butler played a chit for you. I don't know your bullshit, but I've got your name, rank, and serial number, and *you've* got *my* word that if Sylvia ends up with so much as a frown on her face, you'll be bulldozed so deep you'll forget you ever saw sunshine!"

The connection died.

"You can come in," she told Wes.

The dog stayed between them as they stood in the hall.

"Where's Nick?" said Wes.

"He left." She licked her lips. "With somebody."

*"Jud Stuart?* He was here?"

Sylvia nodded.

"Why didn't they wait?"

"Nick wanted him to—Nick's doing what he thinks is right! He has no knowledge of or active participation in—"

"I'm not a judge," said Wes.

"Then what are you?"

"Where did they go?"

"I don't know. Nick drove him in our Jeep. Jud went to see somebody, then he's agreed to meet a *friend* of Nick's: you?"

"Did they say who they were going to see?"

"They wouldn't tell me." She hesitated, bit her lip.

"Mrs. Kelley, if you know anything . . ."

"This is how it starts, isn't it?" She shook her head. "I *spied* on them. I snuck up the stairs, listened to . . . They went to somebody's house. Jud had been there before. They took Route Fifty. I heard them say something about Exit Four Twenty-four.

"Now I'm just like all of you, aren't I?" she whispered.

"Where off of Four Twenty-four?" said Wes, who'd gone to the Naval Academy not far from that road.

"I can't give you an address," she said.

"But somebody can." Wes pushed REDIAL on his phone. After his call, he asked her, "You heard me mention General Varon?"

She nodded.

"If something happens—"

*"What?"* said Sylvia. "If *what* happens? What kind of—"

"You'll know," said Wes. "General Byron Varon. If anything

happens, call your congressman, tell him Varon is the one. Tell him he'll need a giant bulldozer."

"What are you doing? Nick— When will . . ."

"Give us until dawn," said Wes.

And then he was gone.

Sylvia walked through her home, turning lights on. The dog padded beside her. After the Marine left, she'd let the dog outside to pee. Now the house smelled of wet dog. She locked the doors and windows. The nursery was empty; she left Saul's ragged stuffed monkey where he'd dropped it in the middle of his map-of-the-states rug. The bed in their room was too soft for Nick. She'd meant to get a new one. *This is where I dream beside my husband.* She hurried downstairs.

Her limbs were heavy rubber; her flesh tingled and she was nauseous. She didn't dare turn on the TV or radio—she needed to be aware of the creaks and moans of the house. Three dining room chairs were pushed out from the table. *Are they still warm? Could someone tell they'd been used?* She quickly shoved them back in place, hid Jud's dirty dishes in the dishwasher, ran that appliance to wash away his fingerprints.

The grandfather clock ticked as though this were normal time. Visions of her life were everywhere; she backed up until her shoulders hit a corner of the dining room.

The Peace Corps in Mexico showed her the futility of the past and the future, the unrelenting randomness of fate. She'd learned what law school ignored: that laws are hollow vessels empowered by the blood poured into them. On the Hill, she'd watched unseen forces rewrite the best of plans. Yet still she believed, hoped. She trusted. She asked for only what she earned. And it had all come to this: she was trapped in her house, the night and the storm cradling all she loved most.

Tears streamed from eyes she forced to stay open. She slid down the corner until she sat on the wooden floor. There were dust balls under the china cabinet. The knife in her back pocket dug into her hip. She laid it on the floor; light glistened on its blade. There was a phone on a side table. She lifted it down to her side: traitorous machine, her compromised lifeline to no one who could help. The black dog curled up beside her, huge and wet.

She sank into the hardwood floor, her back against the corner. Waiting. Crying.

A yellow snake of headlights crawled in Wes's rearview mirror. Traffic thinned by the time he reached the Beltway. Most people were home, having dinner or watching the evening news, scolding the children or worrying about the rain as they got ready to go out for social events, to a movie. He couldn't remember the last movie he'd seen, wondered if Beth . . .

*Don't think about her!*

When he left the Beltway for Route 50, few of his fellow travelers came with him. Traffic on that highway was light.

*When did I start on this journey?* he thought. *Was it twenty days ago, when Denton summoned me? Or was it twenty years ago?*

*How much time do I have left?*

Twenty minutes later, he found the 424 exit. As he drove east on that two-lane road, his mirror showed two pairs of headlights take that exit, fall in behind him about a mile back.

*Couldn't be a tail.*

When he'd left the CIA, he'd cut and woven his way through rush hour traffic. No surveillance team could have seen through the Metro buses as he turned sharp corners or caught up to him with blind luck when he'd blown through red lights.

*Probably young professionals,* he thought. *High-powered D.C. jobs, a daily hour drive to a home by the Bay.*

This was his college turf: he remembered day trips off campus and away from pressures of academics and rank. General Butler had given him the address, but Wes wanted to check the map in the glove compartment. He couldn't read it while driving.

Up ahead, left side of the highway: a neon red sign. A roadhouse. Rain pounded four vehicles pulled close to its door. Wes pulled off the highway, parked alongside a black Porsche, two Toyotas, and a battered pickup. His trunk pointed toward the tavern door, his windshield toward the dark road. He turned off his headlights, unfolded the map on the steering wheel.

But he watched the highway.

*They'll pass by in a minute. Two cars, commuters headed home. They're only a mile or so back, and there were no turnoffs between here and there. They'll pass by in a minute.*

Two minutes. Four. Six.

He couldn't believe in flat tires, Good Samaritans. They were out there, stopped along the road. Waiting.

The Sig was on his hip, spare clips in his black jacket. He took the attaché case in his left hand; his gun hand was empty as he opened the car door and stepped into the wet night.

Eight minutes. No headlights passed. The neon sign on the tavern's roof cast a red glow over him as he stood beside his car in the rain. Nine minutes.

He opened the trunk of his car. *Nothing.*

A car drove past—from the wrong direction.

He crawled on his hands and knees in the wet gravel and mud, ran his hand along the car's undercarriage. Found it stuck out of sight beneath the back bumper: two red lights glowing on a magnetic box the size of a paperback book. A small antenna.

*Electronic tracker.* They didn't need to see him with their eyes to follow where he went.

He grabbed the box—froze.

*There's more than one. They'd plant one for me to find—if I were that smart. They had this car the whole time I was upstairs with Billy. The other transmitters would be impossible to find in a field search. If I pull this one, they'll know I know.*

Betrayal flooded over Wes as he knelt in the mud. He scrambled to his feet, hurled gravel at the empty highway.

Rain beat down on him.

The light inside the tavern was yellow and shadowed. The bartender watched Wes walk in, then turned back to the TV's basketball game. The tables were empty. A couple huddled in a booth. Their eyes were wide and nervous as Wes entered, softened when they saw only his drenched form. They went back to holding hands. Wes guessed their wedding rings weren't a matched set.

A man talked on the pay phone by the rest room. He wore a flashy sports jacket, a tie. His haircut cost fifty dollars.

". . . so it ain't enough I got to eat shit from the D.C. Realty Board," he said. "Their bullshit rules. I drive out here to nowhere in the fucking rain to show a house, and my shithole client decides he don't want to come get wet!"

Outside the tavern's windows, the road stayed empty.

*What am I going to do?* thought Wes.

"Don't talk to me about money!" whined the salesman. "More

guys got paper on me than I got bills in my wallet! The bottom falls out of the housing market and lands right on my head!"

In the TV set, the ball game's time-out buzzer rang.

"One day at a time?" said the salesman. "I'm working on *last year!* Pick up the phone today and it's the car dealer. Loved me when I came in and made his commission, now he's digging me because I'm a few weeks late! Hell, the insurance premiums on the Porsche are killing me and he wants his damn monthly vig!"

*Whatever their agenda is,* concluded Wes, *they don't care about me. Or Jud. Or Nick. All they care about is keeping their marble walls clean.*

"I got a half a mind to call our friend in Baltimore," said the real estate agent. "Tell him where to find the Porsche, let the insurance company feed the dealer his nut, and cut me the change."

*Billy told the truth,* thought Wes. *As far as he went. But he didn't trust me. He set me up, put his people on my tail.*

"Gotta sell, right?" said the man on the phone. "Gotta move, gotta sell. But ain't nobody here buying *shit!*"

The broker lifted his Scotch rocks off the nearby table, knocked it back, said, "What the hell's a guy supposed to do?"

Ice rattled in his glass. He groped behind himself to put the glass on the table. Something *thunked* close to his hand.

A wad of money lay tossed next to his glass. The salesman raised his eyes. Saw a big guy in a black windbreaker, water dripping from a cheap short haircut. The cop stare. He was closing an attaché case, smiling at the wad—shit! Five, six hundred dollars showing! More under that!

"Ah, Lewis," said the salesman, "let me call you back."

Nick sat behind the wheel of his family Jeep, engine off, staring through the rain toward the house behind the swaying trees. He kept the Jeep windows rolled down so the glass wouldn't steam up; so he could hear. The revolver filled his hand.

Jud had been gone seven minutes.

*Behind me!* Noise inside the rain: an engine whine, coming closer. Gravel crunching. Coming closer . . .

No headlights in the Jeep mirror. Nick stuck his head out the window: rain batting his eyes, the night, trees swaying. . . .

Behind him: a dark shape. Coming closer.

Jud had said *stay in the car.*

*Sitting duck.*

Nick bailed out of the Jeep—*forgot about the interior light's flashing when the door opened!* He scrambled across the slippery gravel road to the barrow pit as the dark shape whined closer. Nick ran, tripped, staggered, and fell, rolled prone in the ditch across the road and twenty feet behind his vehicle.

A dark coupe, headlights out, stopped a car length behind the Jeep. The coupe's engine chugged, died.

Water and sweat streamed down Nick's face as he aimed the trembling revolver at the coupe, at the shadowed human being silhouetted in the driver's window. Nick's guts were on fire, his trigger finger ached. He clicked back the gun's hammer and tried to breathe air thick with wet trees and rain, gravel and fear.

A thousand heartbeats, a handful of time.

The voice of the coupe's driver cut through the rain. "Nick: I saw you when you got out. It's Wes. I know you're out there. I'm alone."

*The right voice.* Nick licked his lips, swallowed. Kept the gun zeroed on the Porsche.

"I'm opening the car door."

The Porsche's interior light winked on: the Marine, unzipped black jacket, hands empty as he stepped into the rain.

"It's okay, Nick." His words were hushed, but firm.

Gun aimed at the coupe, Nick stood. Wes didn't move as Nick came close, peered into the Porsche.

*Empty.* Nick lowered his pistol.

The rain fell on the two of them.

"Jud's in there," said Wes, nodding toward the house.

"About ten minutes," confirmed Nick.

Wes wiped his face. "We don't have much time. I ditched the CIA, but they'll figure it out soon, put where they lost me together with where I could have gone, and come up with here. What about Varon's men?"

"I don't know who's in there," said Nick.

"We're exposed here," said the Marine. "There's a basketball court at the turnoff from the main road. Parking lot beside it, in the trees, out of the light. Follow me there and stash the Jeep. Can you drive a Porsche?"

"Had one once. But—"

"You'll bring me back here," said Wes. "Drive back there, wait."

"That's four miles away," said Nick. "I won't do any good there."

"That's the only place you *can* do any good." Wes nodded toward the gun in Nick's hand. "This isn't your job."

"This isn't about work."

"It's about duty. Yours is back there. Jud and I will walk out, rendezvous with you. If you don't make it by dawn, if shit flies . . . Somebody has to be left to put it straight."

"That's not my job."

"Has to be," said Wes. "You're who's left."

|||||||||||||||||||||||||||||||||||||||||||||||||||||||||||||||||||||||||||||||||||||||||

# HEARTBEAT

Jud pulled off the blue jacket's hood when he reached the house. The rain beat down on his head. He stared at the white door for a long time before he rang the doorbell.

The man who answered the doorbell lost his smile. He was a squat man, with gray brush haircut and flat brown eyes. He wore a green cardigan sweater over a white shirt, dark slacks, and ratty black bedroom slippers. Uncertainty flickered across his face. Then the smile returned, and his eyes hardened.

*"Jud Stuart."* He had a deep voice. "Good to meet you."

Varon's hands hung by his side; strong, empty, hairy.

The hall behind Varon was empty. Somewhere in the house a radio orchestra tinkled through an elevator rendition of "New York, New York."

"It's wet out there," said Varon. "Come in."

"Just like that?" whispered Jud.

"You rang the bell, I answered. I'm alone—are you?"

"I know who you are." Jud didn't move from the stoop.

"If you didn't, you wouldn't be worth the trust I gave you. Your training. Your scars. Now come in out of the rain, soldier."

Varon gave Jud his back and walked away. Jud hesitated, then obeyed. *I came here for this,* he told himself.

"Don't push any buttons," warned Jud, shutting the door.

He heard it lock.

Varon laughed. "Who could I summon? I retired."

"Bullshit."

They walked past stairs to a silent second floor.

"Yes, bullshit." Varon's nod directed Jud toward an open room, couches. Jud smelled wood burning in a fireplace. "Pentagon paper-pushers. Shoe clerks at the CIA—though I still have friends out there. Politicians at the Justice Department running scared of idiots in Congress. They pushed me out."

"What about the White House?"

"They're useless these days. The old people developed amnesia and the new ones embrace ignorance."

The unseen radio played *Theme from A Summer Place.* Jud's head spun with 1960s' celluloid images of a blond girl, not blond like Nora, not as beautiful as Lorri—

He blinked and was back. An open door in the hall showed him an empty sitting room; another door revealed an empty bathroom.

Step by slow step, Varon led Jud deeper into his home.

"Last report," said Varon, "you effected an E&E from a CIA ambush in the desert near Las Vegas. How'd you get here?"

"Stole a car," said Jud.

*"Appropriated,"* corrected the general. "A soldier in the field does not steal, he *appropriates."*

"I'm not a soldier anymore." Jud's hands trembled.

"No one has relieved you of your duties."

The hall led to a sunken living room where couches and easy chairs circled a coffee table. A battered leather briefcase yawned beside the table; file folders and yellow legal pads waited on its dark wood surface—as did glasses and a bottle of Scotch.

The fireplace crackled.

"I love a fire," said Varon. "This might be the last one of the season."

He strolled down into the sunken room.

"I'm having a drink," said Varon. "Want a Scotch?"

Light from the fireplace danced off the bottle of amber liquid. Jud could taste the liquor's burn. Somehow he shook his head no.

The wall beyond Varon was glass. Spotlights illuminated grounds sloping down to a treeline. Beyond that, the night seemed to part: out there, through the rain, Jud saw a long, dark shimmer.

As he poured a drink, Varon followed Jud's gaze. "The river's down there. If the rain weren't so thick, you could see the blue light at the end of my neighbor's dock."

One wall was covered with plaques and signed pictures of Varon with presidents and kings, Iran's former shah, TV evangelists. There were more than a dozen military and combat citations: Korea, Vietnam. Award certificates from patriotic groups. Pictures of a younger Varon, in the bush.

"To live this good," said Jud, "you must have *appropriated* a shitload from the field."

"I've never gotten *half* of what I'm owed!" snapped Varon.

"Who owes you?"

"Everybody who sent me into combat," said the retired general. "Everybody I ever sent good men out to kill and die for. Everybody I ever took shit for. They all owe us—you, and me."

"How much?" whispered Jud.

"How much can we get?" said Varon.

Jud shook his head. "How much did you do?"

"Enough. *Damn!*" Varon swore at the glass in his hand. "I forgot you didn't want a drink. I already poured that one on the table."

Amber liquor swirled in the glass Varon held. "Once it's out of the bottle, you can't put it back.

"Tell you what," he continued. "I'll drink this one, and leave that glass there. In case you change your mind."

Jud smelled the booze all the way across the room and . . .

And Varon had moved, was over by the wall to the left, his back to Jud, reaching toward a table . . .

*"Don't!"* yelled Jud.

Varon froze. Jud focused on Varon's hands: one held his drink, the other rested on an FM receiver. Varon turned a knob. The radio died.

"That's better," said Varon. "Maybe the music was why I didn't hear you drive up.

"Did you come straight here from Nevada?" asked the master of the house, moving back into the circle of sofas and chairs. "That writer: have you talked to him since then?"

"He's not a player," muttered Jud.

"Nick Kelley." Varon settled on a couch. "Does he know you're here?"

"Why did you send someone to kill me?" asked Jud.

"I never sent an operative to kill you."

"That man in the L.A. bar."

"Mathew Hopkins."

*Hopkins:* Jud remembered the name from the driver's license he'd taken off the dead man behind the bar. "You sent him."

"Yes," said Varon. "But that was your fault."

*"What?"*

"You'd failed to answer repeated activation notices. Horoscope alerts. I was concerned."

"I opted out of your fucking bullshit!"

"You never had that choice." Varon shrugged. "It was a mistake to send Hopkins, but my resources these days are meager."

"He was on the old team."

"Like you, but from the Navy. Retired. Took a disability pension—payout contract like you refused."

"Why did you send him?"

"To find you. To make sure you were all right."

"My error," said Varon. "Last few years, Hopkins began requesting clarifications. He'd developed paranoia, his own agenda, whatever. But he was the only asset I had on the West Coast, so . . . If he tried to kill you, he was acting on his own. I didn't dare try to clean up after him, make him seem important."

Fire swirled through Jud's brain. He was dizzy; leaned on the arm of a chair.

"His mission was long-range observation," said Varon. "No contact. If he was close enough for you to kill—"

"I didn't kill him." Jud sank into the chair. "I didn't mean to."

"Getting close to you, I don't know what he wanted."

In the mirror of his soul, Jud realized the truth.

"He couldn't stand it anymore," whispered Jud. "Not knowing who he was and what he'd done, why. You wouldn't give him any answers. Gave him me. Enough data for him to figure out we were both on your string. Like family. He didn't want to kill me. He wanted to talk to me. Wanted me to help him find answers."

"Then he was a liability instead—" Varon stopped short.

"Instead of me?" Jud shook his head. "The poor lost son of a bitch. Another one I . . . Another one."

Jud picked up the glass of Scotch.

"Why all of a sudden did you care about me?" he asked.

Varon watched him take a long drink.

"We need to be sure we're secure," said the ex-general.

"Not we: *you.*" Jud downed all his Scotch. He leaned across the table, took the bottle, and refilled his glass.

"You're in somebody's gunsights," said Jud.

"These fucks don't use guns! If they did, I could—"

"So it's the law." The Scotch warmed Jud's blood. He felt his brain go clear. His heart went calm—and cold.

"You've stepped on your dick, General. Iran-contra."

"They came to me!" shouted Varon. "Nobody better for the job, and they damn well knew it! Forget about that Inspector General's report that squeezed me out of the Pentagon, *they needed me!* I was running covert ops when those White House namby-pambies were in prep school! I knew Iran—even that peanut farmer Jimmy Carter knew enough to tap me for the second rescue mission! Nobody can do it like me: not Dick Secord, not Ollie North, Poindexter—Casey, he knew! He knew I could get the job done!

"So what if I made money? I don't come for a whistle and a song like some cherry schoolgirl!"

"What did you do?"

"The damn job! I raised money! Put together arms deals! Met with some damn Iranians—never trust camel jockeys—I—"

"No," said Jud. "I've been drunk for years, but I can figure that score. You weren't a top man, so you won't take a hard fall. Not just for following orders.

"It was the project I turned down," said Jud.

"Their idea," insisted Varon. "Not mine. I just told them it could be done, that I thought I had a way. An asset."

"Me." Jud shook his head. "You thought I was dumb enough to help frame the Nicaraguan government for coke smuggling?"

"You had that area of expertise," said Varon. "Contacts, the bona fides. If you were half as good as you'd been before . . ."

"You would have burned me," said Jud. "Fronted me out. You would have had to. I'm a drunk: usable, expendable. How would you've worked it? Busted, gunned down in an alley? A car wreck?"

"They wouldn't have gone for that," said Varon.

Jud drank half a glass of Scotch. "I bet that's true. They'd probably started to back away from your horror-show games before I said no."

"Give a guy a big desk, he starts to forget what it takes to get there and do the job."

"Why did Mathew Hopkins have to check me out?"

"The grand jury and special prosecutor are still out there," said Varon. "They still want blood—mine or yours."

"There's a loose end," said Jud. "Something a nickel-dime government gumshoe might find that could lead to me. A loose end of yours—in North's notebooks or computers, somewhere.

"If I talked, you'd be guilty of cocaine conspiracies as well as Iran-contra. Hell, if I really flipped: Laos, Watergate, Chile, Monterastelli . . . Bad on their own and reason enough for the feds to hunt down your *appropriations*. Remember the coke money you had me send? Bought these walls, right? I could help a prosecutor drive a stake right through your medals."

The room was warm around Jud. He felt soft, fluid.

"They must really want you," he said. "And you know it. But you didn't know what kind of shape I was in, so you sent poor, hurting Mathew Hopkins to find out."

Jud laughed. "The lost seeking the lame.

"He wasn't supposed to whack me," said Jud. "But if he'd reported me as anything but a gutter drunk with no credibility . . ."

Varon's hands straightened file folders on the table. An open briefcase waited by his chair. File folders, yellow pads, pens on the table. A tray of glasses and a bottle of Scotch—*three* glasses. Jud blinked.

"You're expecting somebody," he said. "You're killing time, waiting for somebody."

"Some people who can help us."

Jud threw his glass across the room; it shattered above the fireplace.

"Save your dramatics," said Varon. "You had to come here for help. The Agency's on your trail, the L.A. police. Hopkins made you a murderer. Who knows what else they can pin on you from the last few weeks. You need me."

He poured Scotch in another glass, pushed it toward Jud.

"Just like you need this." Varon laughed. "Give me any shit and I'll feed you to the Marines."

"Chandler," muttered Jud. "Wes Chandler."

"How the hell do you know that name!"

Jud scooped the fresh drink into his steady grip. "You got people, I got people."

"You got nobody!"

"Then what are you worried about?"

\*   \*   \*

Nick kept the Porsche's motor running, headlights off as he sat parked in the shadows where the paved public highway met Varon's gravel road. Nick's Jeep waited deeper in the woods. Rain fell through a cone of yellow light from the pole high above the crossroads. Cool, wet air and the chug of the Porsche engine flowed over him through the open windows. He could smell the rain in the trees, the damp earth; he could smell his own sweat.

Time had lost proportion: he'd been there three minutes, he'd been there a heartbeat, he'd been there forever.

*They're all right. I'm fine. I'll be home soon. Safe. Sylvia, Saul: who'll teach Saul that—*

Car lights silently knifed through the rain on the public highway to Nick's right, a narrow beam that widened, brightened . . .

Turned.

Gravel crunched beneath the wheels of a Cadillac as it rolled onto Varon's road. That long, dark car passed through the streetlight's cone in an instant, but time had lost proportion, and in its elasticity Nick saw the Caddy fishtail on the wet gravel, saw its brake lights flash red, its driver countersteer and fix the hood down the tunnel where Jud and Wes had gone.

Where they were unaware.

Nick didn't know how or why the Caddy was there, but he knew it meant danger for the men he'd left down the tunnel, danger rippling out to him, to his family. He knew so in a heartbeat, because in that elastic eternity the streetlight showed him the Caddy's driver:

Jack Berns. Renegade private eye. Who'd touched Nick with cold hands he thought Nick wouldn't feel: shadows, bugs.

Beside Berns in the Caddy: a man whose face was a white-bandaged blur. Nick's recognition was instant, intuitive, and absolute: the ambushed man from Union Station whose revolver was now gripped between Nick's trembling thighs.

There'd be other guns: in the Caddy, in later time.

In the second heartbeat, Nick knew what he had to do.

The Cadillac slid down the tunnel road.

A Porsche pulled out of the woods at the crossroads and accelerated into the Caddy's slipstream.

Nick. Running dark. Red taillights in his eyes.

Perhaps if he'd been a poet, Nick would have been filled with a sense of inevitability, of karma. He would have remembered the abstract manhood dreams of his Michigan cruising nights; the schooling of a hundred drag races down open highways; the razor thrills of teenage games of chicken, hunching over the wheel of his father's '64 white Chevy Impala as he hurtled down a country road toward headlights racing straight at him under the command of an equally crazed teenager. A poet might have appreciated this final link in the chain Nick forged when he'd sought magic in the shadows, a chain that now meant if he did nothing, he doomed his allies and left himself and his family at risk. He could have experienced wondrous transcendence, *the greater truths* of heroes and villains; the purity of ultimate choice; the irony of doing a wrong thing for the right reasons.

But what filled Nick was the great weight of fear.

Fire raged in his mouth, lava surged in his bowels, and electricity shook his whole being. The world existed simultaneously at high speed and in slow motion. A monster roared in his head. His neck and shoulders ached like steel; he could smell and taste fumes and metal from the Porsche. His shirt was soaked. Through the open windows, raindrops hit his face like icy machine gun bullets. His engine whined, gravel crunched beneath his tires. And as the Caddy's blurred red taillights raced closer to his windshield, Nick clung to wordless prayer.

Faster, he drove faster.

The gun: he sucked in his gut, jammed it in his pants. Pulled the shoulder belt across him and locked it in place.

Taillights, like two red eyes staring back at him, a quarter mile ahead; three miles to the house.

Running dark, heavy rain: even if Berns checked his mirrors, he wouldn't see Nick.

An eighth of a mile. Berns and the man from Union Station were silhouetted behind the Caddy's headlights and the glow of their dashboard. The Caddy drove right down the middle of the road.

Maybe they'd hear the growl of Nick's engine; maybe they wouldn't: talking, radio on, windows rolled up.

A hundred yards, one football field.

Seconds later, fifty yards. The Caddy was a solid shape, dead in front of Nick's hurtling ride.

The Porsche drifted right with Nick's touch, a smooth machine. Obedient. Powerful.

The Caddy lined up off center to Nick's left at forty yards. At thirty. Twenty. Two car lengths away.

Nick cut his wheel to the left and floorboarded the gas pedal.

The Porsche surged, a compact mass of rolling metal muscle that slammed at an angle into the left rear bumper of the bigger, heavier Caddy.

Physics ruled.

The Cadillac fishtailed, its crumpled rear end swerving away from the impact, it's headlights swinging to the right until it skidded sideways down the gravel road at forty-four miles per hour and . . .

The Porsche shuddered with the crash, bounced back—tires slipping over wet rock, the rear end sliding to the right, the passenger's side . . .

Slamming into the side of the Cadillac, two steel hands applauding in the night.

A crash of metal.

The night spinning, flying past Nick's eyes, the steering wheel ripped from his hands, the Porsche whipping around, zigzagging backward down the road, hitting the barrow pit, rear axle snapping, high centering—rolling. Windshield exploding, glass shreds showering Nick. *Rolling:* pop up and crash down on all four tires, inertia diving toward China as . . .

The Caddy flipped, rolled, and spun like a top, flew off the road, over the barrow pit, slammed into a wall of trees.

Nausea, spinning, stopped. Still.

*Sticky wet* ran down Nick's forehead. He stared out the jagged hole of the shattered windshield. His arms ached, his shoulders and neck, and his knee throbbed where it had banged the steering column. But he felt the pain and knew that was good. He could move. He climbed out of the Porsche.

Didn't feel the rain.

He was half a football field down the road from where he'd rammed the other car. The Caddy was twenty yards farther, its rear end sliding down the far edge of the barrow pit from a stand of mangled trees. Steam hissed from under its crumpled hood.

*Jesus,* thought Nick. He didn't know whether to be glad or guilty.

The gun was still in his pants. He drew it, aimed at the Caddy, crouched, and shuffled toward it through the storm.

He heard them moan, swear. Jack Berns crying, *"My leg, my leg, my leg!"*

The Caddy's passenger door gaped open. A man tumbled out. In the rain and the dark, Nick couldn't make out all the details, but he saw the whiteness of face bandages, a dangling left arm cradled by the right. The man's feet slid out from under him and he slipped down the wet grass of the barrow pit slope.

*"'elp me!"* moaned Jack Berns from inside the Cadillac. "Help me! My leg, broke my leg!"

From the man collapsed at the bottom of the roadside ditch, Nick heard, "Can'. Can't."

"Shit!" yelled Berns. "Shit!"

"Wha' happened?" cried the man in the ditch. "What happened?"

*They didn't see me!* thought Nick. *They still haven't! They don't know!*

That secret made him feel safer than the gun in his hand. As quietly as he could, he backed across the road, lay prone in the opposite barrow pit, eyes and gun trained on the Caddy, confident that the two men there were done for the night.

And that they couldn't retaliate on Nick because they hadn't seen him.

If they crawled out of the ditch . . .

*Then,* said Nick. *Decide that then.*

But he knew he had the edge; he had the gun, he had secrecy. And even if they made it back on the road, they were now little threat to Jud and Wes.

To Sylvia and Saul.

There was a phone in Wes's attaché case in the Jeep. Help could be summoned for those two men at any time, anonymously. They were only wounded. Nick promised himself that they deserved their pain, that they were guilty—more guilty than him.

Wes and Jud: they'd finish . . . what they had to do in the house a mile down the road. Walk out. Nick was between the house and the men injured in the ditch. He'd link up with Wes and Jud before they reached the wrecked cars, quietly lead them out, away from the eyes of the men in the Caddy. More secrets. More safety.

When they were done with what they had to do.

The rain washed blood off Nick's face as he lay sprawled on his belly. He saw the world over a gunsight. Rocks dug into him, mud sucked at his weight: he could taste the earth, smell it, more real, more solid than he'd ever known. His breath slowed, he felt the chill of the night, the reverberation of what he'd done. He'd wielded the dark magic, and now he realized what he'd wondered about for so long: he was powerful. Dangerous.

That knowledge was hollow and bitter, unforgettable.

Nick ached with the intensity and damnation of the moment. Of all the rivers that flowed within him, the one that sought magic and made him write had always seemed the deepest; now he knew deeper currents; he thought of Sylvia, Saul, the flow of visions of what should be. It occurred to him that this moment where he lay in a ditch, gun in hand, was too overwhelming for him ever to write about; too sacred to sculpt for public presentation. Then he knew that was a lie, and that in that lie was his redemption.

He lay in the rain. Ready. Waiting.

A mile down the road, in the house, Varon sat on the couch and frowned. "Did you hear something?"

"No," lied Jud. He gripped the arm of his chair, silently screamed, *Nick!*

"Doesn't matter what you hear," said Varon. "I'll tell you what you need to know. I'll take care of you. I always have."

"Why?" asked Jud.

"Because that's what you wanted. And you were lucky enough to be born in the right place at the right time."

"That's not right," whispered Jud.

"It's enough."

All the world pressed in on Jud. He shrank into his chair, dizzy, nauseous. The pounding in his head: he couldn't think. He couldn't hear well, couldn't see. He was on a raft floating in Scotch, propelled by the steady words of the old man watching him from the couch.

"I gave myself to you," said Jud.

"For a good cause," argued Varon. "For the country. For what needed to be done and could only be done by men who understood the necessities of a life worth living."

Jud's hands pressed his forehead. His eyes closed.

"Did you ever see your aptitude tests?" Varon licked his lips. Set his glass on the coffee table and kept his hands, his black-haired hands, hovering above the file folders. "We checked back to high school on you, ran you through exams shrinks designed—not that I need them to know a good man like you. They confirmed what I'd been told: brilliant, tough. Driven."

"I think they're here somewhere," said Varon. He shuffled file folders, examined one labeled SWITZERLAND.

Watched the man slumped in the chair not move, not look.

"That's not it," said Varon. He shuffled more files on the table. "Maybe it's in here."

The general dropped his left hand into the open briefcase sitting on the floor.

Pulled out an Army .45 automatic, the pistol sweeping across the table, its bore hunting for . . .

The gun barrel clanged into the Scotch bottle.

Jud, eyes open: *gun.* Thousands of reaction drills—Army, Special Forces, Secret Service academy, intelligence schools, martial arts—no thought, no desire: *reaction.* Twisting in the chair, struggling to get to this feet, move, reaching—

The gun roared.

Left-handed, wrong-handed, Varon scrambling away from the suddenly alert target—*not drunk enough*—trying to stand between the couch and the coffee table, recovering aim after hitting the Scotch bottle, fumbling *wrong-handed:*

The first bullet screamed past Jud's head.

Gun bucking, lining up again, switching grips as Varon made it to his feet . . .

As Jud kicked the coffee table into the old man's shins.

The gun roared, second bullet missing wider than the first as Jud dove toward the old man. Varon slammed the gun down across Jud's neck, scrambled backward on the couch. Jud sprawled across the table reaching, grabbing . . .

Catching: a vise gripped the hand holding the gun.

Climbing backward up the couch, the general kicked the head of the man who was crushing his hand. He jabbed at Jud's eyes with his free hand—missed. Jud pulled and pushed and crawled his way on top of Varon.

The couch overturned and flipped the two men to the floor.

*Never let go.* Jud rolled, held the wrist, trapped the gun that swept madly across the room, searching for the target. The two men tumbled to their feet. Varon kicked toward Jud's groin—hit his thigh.

The general was sixty-four. Two decades out of the jungle. Strong. For a man his age who never exercised. The stress of the last few months had kept him on an adrenaline edge. His body slammed into maximum overdrive. His fingers were being crushed against the gun. A tremor shook him. His heart raced as he smashed his fist into the bloodied madman reaching for him. After graduating from West Point, Varon had trained in commando skills. But he'd never gone beyond the standard program—he knew his most deadly weapon was his brain. He slammed his soft shoulder into the chest of the gorilla he'd once ruled, twisted, and tried for a shoulder throw.

Two massive arms locked around Varon's chest. His wrist bent—snapped. The .45 hit the carpet. The general screamed. His arms were pinned to his side. A fist dug into his breastbone as steel bands tightened across his ribs.

All the right tricks failed: Varon kicked Jud's shins, stomped his feet. The madman's embrace tightened. The general's hands couldn't reach a nerve. His head butted back, thrashed from side to side. He felt Jud's rough face against his cheek, heard his words screaming in his ear:

"You threw me away!"

And Jud jerked the old man off his feet, whirled him around and around like a partner in a crazed dance.

Waves, colors flashing in Varon's eyes, his head throbbing, ribs cracking, and *no air,* walls sliding past as he spun round and round, reeling, stopping, in front of him, the picture windows to the night, the black night, a wall of darkness—

*Exploding.*

A thousand shrapnel diamonds shattered into the house.

Varon flew across the room, hit a wall, the floor.

Jud tripped, sprawled to his face, rolled, and looked to the giant jagged hole in the picture window. The last of the glass fell from the frame.

A dripping-wet, white steel lawn chair lay by the couch.

Outside in the storm stood a man in a black jacket, his gun aimed into the house.

At Jud.

Panting, catching his breath, Jud called out, "Come on, Erasureman! I've been waiting for you! You're late, you're years too fucking late!"

"I'm Wes Chandler!" yelled the man with the gun, stepping through the hole he'd made. His gaze shifted between the two men on the floor. "I'm a friend! Nick Kelley—"

"There's nobody else," said Jud. "Just me. Come on. Come on."

Step by step, his gun forward, Wes moved to where Varon lay: glassy eyes. Slack jaw. A line of blood in the corner of a gaping mouth. Wes touched the old man's chest: the breastbone was squishy, splintered. The flesh over the old man's heart felt like a water balloon.

"He's dead," said Wes.

"Another one," muttered Jud. "Should have been the first. Should have died before I was born, before he made me."

"Come on," ordered Wes.

But Jud laughed: a deep, rumbling bass, choking up octaves to a hysterical pitch, a whine; a sob.

"We don't have much time. Nick is out there, alone."

"Let him go," said Jud.

"That's not my deal," explained Wes.

"What is?"

Wes stood there, gun pointed at the floor; without words.

"They fucked you, didn't they?" said Jud.

"Not so much that—"

"What are you going to do, Marine?" Jud shook his head. "I used to be a soldier."

He pushed himself to a sitting position, stared at the corpse nearby. "His soldier. *My* soldier."

"We'll work something out," said Wes. "I saw through the window. He had a gun, you . . . Self-defense."

Again Jud laughed. "What about all the others?"

"That's not for me to say."

"Sure it is. You've got the gun."

The Sig dangled at the end of Wes's arm.

"The CIA," said Wes. "The Pentagon—Congress, all of them: we'll make *them* work it out."

"Why?"

Again Wes had no answer.

"It's our call, Marine. We're on the line. Besides, they don't want to do that."

"You've got to come in."

"Where? The CIA? What do you think they'll do about this? About Varon and the shit he pulled? What do you think they'll do to me? A drunk farm? Locked up somewhere? They trained me to get out of anywhere, and they know that. Lobotomy? What can they do with me?"

"They need to know—"

"You trust them to do the right thing?"

Wes blinked.

"You can't let me walk," said Jud. "They won't stop until they know I'm accounted for. How many more people am I going to run over with their parade? The booze has got me. The ghosts have got me. You found Lorri. You saw what I did to Nora."

"That was a combat—"

"So what?"

Jud pushed himself to his feet. He reeled, staggered, but faced Wes.

"What do you want?" whispered Wes.

"I don't want those fuckers to win. I want to be free. I don't want to hurt anybody else. I want to beat them. I don't want to hurt anymore."

"If—"

"No ifs, no ands, no buts." Jud smiled. "You know."

"We can buy time to—"

"There's no more time. There's no other place." He pointed his finger at Wes. Like a gun. "They've got you, too."

"No."

"Yes," said Jud. "You think that they'll let you walk free and clear if they make the play?"

The rain blew into the house. Wes retreated a step.

"Clock's running, Major. Nowhere to run, no time to waste."

"Let's go."

"No. You can't either. You leave now, you take me with you, pin me for them . . . they win. They own you then. I know."

"Do what you're supposed to do," said Jud.

"That's not my job."

"Sure it is. It's what has to be done. Do it for me. Do it myself, means I lost. Don't do it, they win. You do—"

"Stop it!"

"You do it," said Jud, "I'm free. Nick's safe—without me, he can't make enough trouble for them to care. If you do it, don't confess, they'll never know what you've got on 'em, so they'll leave you alone. Hell, you do it, they're stuck with their own shit! Let the straight world have all this! Drop a dime when you go, let the local yokels find Varon, me, his files. Shit, call the *Post.* But don't tell 'em who you are. Leave a house full of questions. That won't change the world, but let this shit rise to the top, a bloody mess smeared on the spooks' walls. Them having to scrape it off is the only way anything good'll happen, and we can't control that. Hell, do it for the damn country, it needs exercise."

"You're crazy!"

"So what? They tapped you, sent you out, set you up: who do you owe what?"

"I don't owe you this."

"Then I'll owe you one." Jud laughed. "I'll pay it off. You do this, you'll be free. Me gone, they won't care about you. It's the only way to finish your job. It's the only way you can walk. Forget about me, Nick, what could happen. Do it for yourself.

"You know how I'm going to pay you off? I'm not going to give you an excuse. I'm not going to fight you, force you to take me out of the box. Make it easy. Make you always wonder if you couldn't have beaten me another way. I know what that's like. You start apologizing to your ghosts. You start to owe them. Then they own you, then you're lost. No maybes: that's my payoff to you. Clear choice, no question. I'm going to make you do it *clean.*

"Only one thing."

Jud shuffled across the room.

Wes couldn't move. Couldn't speak. Couldn't feel, yet was so completely *there* that he was gone into a new place, a new time.

Arm's length away, Jud stopped. Bent. Wrapped his fingers around the Sig's barrel and slowly raised it to the end of Wes's straight arm. Raised it until the bore kissed his chest.

"One thing," said Jud, holding the gun to his flesh, "I'm not going to die on my knees."

The hammering of Jud's heart vibrated through the gun into Wes's arm, shaking him with each beat. Each blow was a nail of truth. Wes knew that if he brought Jud *in,* the CIA would pull Jud into the cloak of shadows, unseen forever, never known, never judged. Wes's hands would wrap the cloak shut; his touch would be there and theirs. Varon would become a hidden footnote, an obituary. Wes thought of Noah Hall and Director Denton, of owl-glasses Billy Cochran: one and all, somewhere down the line, they'd betrayed their duty, betrayed him, turned their gunsights on him. He owed them nothing. He owed Nick a bottom-line truth; he owed Beth an honest confession she could understand, a confession whose consequences he had to risk. This man standing before him, this heart beating and shaking Wes's whole being: he owed him what Wes would want for himself. Jud's heart beat against Wes until it felt like they'd merged into one being with two lives: they were one, and the pain and hope that Jud felt became the only hope Wes had for ending the pain, for getting free, for doing what had to be done, and his finger tightened on the trigger.